## *"You ready?"*

Michael's eyes held a challenge as he scooped up a portion of chocolate cake.

Feeling wicked, Polly took a bite and then licked his fingers. When his face flushed and his breathing became irregular, she knew she had hit her target.

"Try that one," she ordered, pointing to another cake. "Wait, let me feed you."

He laughed aloud, but he let her lift a chunk of cake to his lips. She popped it into his mouth and snatched her hand back before he could catch her.

They both reached for the next plate with reckless abandon.

Michael got to it first. "What will you give me if I let you have a bite?"

He brandished the cake under her nose, close enough that she could lick it right off the plate. She flicked her tongue over her top lip just to drive him nuts.

He dropped the plate on the counter and grabbed her. "We need to get out of here."

"Yes, we do." She took his hand and practically dragged him toward the door.

*For more, turn to page 9*

# The Sister Switch

## *"You didn't know about my wedding?" Cassie asked.*

"Your *what?*" That got a charge out of Dylan. "So who are you marrying? And what the hell were you doing here with me?" He glared at her as he hopped into his clothes.

"I was...I wanted some excitement. Trading places with my sister seemed like a good idea at the time. I had no idea it would turn into..." She waved a hand in the air. "All of this."

Dylan's face was a study in shock and outrage. "The guy you're supposed to marry. Who is he?"

"His name is Skipper. He's very nice and his family is very rich, but..."

"But?"

"He's boring!" she shouted. "He's boring and predictable."

"This is obscene," Dylan said angrily. "How can you even consider going through with this wedding? You can't marry someone else, Cassie, because it's very obvious you're in love with *me.*"

She blinked. "I am?"

*For more, turn to page 197*

HARLEQUIN DUETS

ISBN 0-373-44139-8

Copyright in the collection:
Copyright © 2002 by Harlequin Books S.A.

The publisher acknowledges the copyright holder
of the individual works as follows:

STAND-IN BRIDE
Copyright © 2002 by Julie Kistler

THE SISTER SWITCH
Copyright © 2002 by Julie Kistler

# Stand-In Bride

## Julie Kistler

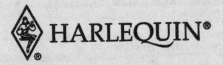

TORONTO • NEW YORK • LONDON
AMSTERDAM • PARIS • SYDNEY • HAMBURG
STOCKHOLM • ATHENS • TOKYO • MILAN • MADRID
PRAGUE • WARSAW • BUDAPEST • AUCKLAND

Dear Reader,

I think there are a fair amount of people fascinated
by the idea of identical twins who pretend to be each
other. Maybe it's just those of us who aren't twins!
But when my editor asked me to write a Double Duets
book, trading twins popped into my head immediately.
As a friend said when I was still in the early stages,
how can you do two books about identical twins and
*not* have them switch places? It certainly provides lots
of opportunity for miscues and misunderstanding,
which makes it perfect for romantic comedy.

With the idea of two very different twins trying out
each other's lives for a little while, I was up and rolling.
The more different I made them, the more difficult it
was for each sister to keep up her charade, and the
more fun it was to write. While Polly talks a mile a
minute, Cassie is quiet and reserved. While Polly left
their small-town home as soon as possible, opting for
a more urban, fast-paced lifestyle, Cassie was content
to stay in tiny Pleasant Falls, planning to marry an
upstanding citizen and start a settled, sedate life. But
now… With a bad case of greener grass staring at
them, they exchange lives. Just days before Cassie's
wedding!

I had a lot of fun with *Stand-In Bride* and *The Sister
Switch*, and I hope you do, too. Enjoy!

*Julie Kistler*

## Books by Julie Kistler

**HARLEQUIN DUETS**
19—CALLING MR. RIGHT
30—IN BED WITH THE WILD ONE*

*Beds & Bachelors

To Birgit, Jennifer, Tanya and Susan,
with many thanks

# 1

*May 17: Fifteen days before the wedding*

POLLY TOMPKINS glanced at her watch. Five minutes. She had five minutes to get to the train station, and she knew she'd never make it.

"I hate to rush you," she said to the chatty woman who was interviewing her for *In Chicago,* a new weekly magazine in town. For the life of her, she could not remember the woman's name. "It's just that there's somewhere I have to be. Maybe we could finish this another time?"

"Just one more question," the reporter said quickly, scribbling away in her notebook. She glanced up when they both heard a high-pitched tone. "Is that your fax again?"

"Oh, just ignore it. It's like that all the time." Or at least when clients like Hiram "Wild Man" Wright, a famous author of macho man books, decided to drive her crazy. One more fax from that man about what kind of limo he needed, what color M&M's candies, what brand of scotch...

Polly smiled, forcefully putting the Wild Man and his annoying demands out of her mind. She did her

best to project warmth and charm as she tried to figure
out how to maneuver this interview skillfully to an end
and get this person out of her office. The last thing
she wanted to do was offend a reporter. When you
worked for Lenora Bridge and Associates, Public Relations, you didn't throw away chances for good publicity.

Especially when your job wasn't all that secure at
Lenora Bridge and Associates. Polly tried not to
wince. The truth was, she just wasn't that good at public relations. She wasn't glib or slick or remotely well
connected. And she knew very well the only reason
Lenora had hired her in the first place was because she
was young and blond and had a nice smile. It was no
surprise when they used her picture three years in a
row for the front of the company brochure.

Polly frowned. When she left college three years
ago, she'd had ideals and goals. So when had Look
Good And Don't Cause Trouble become her career
motto?

"Hmmm… Where was that last question?" her in-
terviewer mumbled, clearly in no hurry as she riffled
the pages of her notes.

*Just get to it, will you?* Polly still had no idea how
Lenora had swung this interview in the first place, especially for a feature called "Chicago's 25 Hottest
Singles." Polly was no one's idea of a "hot single,"
not when she hadn't had a date in over a year. Of
course, *In Chicago* didn't know that.

Polly tried to think "hot." But it was *so* not her.

"Let's see. All I need is three words for the profile

box." The woman looked up expectantly. "Three words that describe you?"

With no time to come up with a good strategy, Polly said the first words that popped into her head. Which was probably the whole point of this exercise. "Cheerful, perky…"

This was terrible. She sounded like a chipmunk. If only she had time to think.

"Third word?" her interrogator prompted. And the clock was ticking.

"Wait, wait. I changed my mind. Smart. Up-tempo. Those are good. And responsible. No, not responsible." How hot was that? Not!

Besides, it didn't fit at the moment, not while she dithered her way through this silly personality profile, leaving her twin sister Cassie, fresh from sweet little Pleasant Falls, cooling her heels at scary Union Station.

"Do you have a third word?"

Impatient, restless, champing at the bit… *Uh, no.*

As she frantically tried to think of one good word to put an end to this interview, Polly's mind filled with pictures of Cassie, panicked and lost, wandering the streets of Chicago. An unlikely scenario—Cassie was the calmest person she knew. But that was in Pleasant Falls. Alone in Chicago was a whole different kettle of fish.

"Why don't you just give me the first word that strikes you?" the reporter said helpfully. "You know, like if I said, 'What's on your mind right this second, Polly Tompkins?' what would you say back?"

*On my mind right this second is my sister, with whom I will always be amazingly connected because she is my…* "Twin." Well, that was as good as any. "That's my third word—twin."

"Really?" The reporter leaned forward, more interested now, which was not what Polly had intended. She wanted to be rid of the woman, not keep the conversation going. "So you're a twin. Identical?"

"Yes. I mean, we look identical." Polly automatically fell into the same explanation she always gave when people asked this question. "But even though we look alike, our personalities have always been pretty opposite. I'm outgoing, she's quiet. I'm impulsive, she's a planner. Like that."

"Well, isn't that fun?" The woman winked at her. "So, tell me the truth—ever switch places?"

"Not in years and years." And she was not going to get into anecdotes about the time she pretended to be her sister during a sixth grade math test to save her from flunking, or the horrible night when she'd sent Cassie in her stead to break up with the cheating rat of a boyfriend Polly didn't want to face.

Michael Kennigan. *Oh, yeah.* Michael. Her heart constricted just thinking about him after all these years. Seven years… Had it been that long?

Of course it had. With Cassie as her proxy, Polly had successfully managed to dump him the day after high school graduation. And she hadn't spoken to him since.

Anxious to be finished—and to get Michael Kennigan out of her head—Polly rose and swung open her office door. "My twin, Cassie, is here for our birthday, which is why I need to get going. I did tell you that tomorrow is our birthday, right? Oh, wait—that was your first question, wasn't it? You know, birthday, zodiac. Right back there at the beginning."

"Birthday, zodiac…" The reporter began flipping pages in her tiny little notebook, making no move toward the door. "Right. Got it."

Given the way she was babbling on, Polly realized she probably should've gone with some variation of "chatty" among her three words. Chatty, talkative, garrulous, motormouth… She'd heard it all before. "Anyway," she tried again, determined to get to the point, "Cassie—my sister—is coming up from our hometown to celebrate with me, and I'm supposed to pick her up…" She checked her watch. "Five minutes ago. So I'm sure you'll understand if I have to cut this a little short." Inclining her head toward the door as a hint, she pasted on a big smile. "But I'd be happy to talk to you again. Just give me a call if you need to tie up any loose ends."

It was feeble, but her best attempt at PR.

"I think I have everything I need." But the reporter lingered, carefully pulling her jumble of notebooks and tote bags together. Finally, blessedly, at the very moment Polly was contemplating grabbing her by the scruff of her neck and dragging her into the hall, the woman shuffled to her feet and took a step in the right direction.

Snatching up her purse from the desk, Polly kept smiling, waiting until the reporter was safely past her before she swung the door shut and made a break for the elevator. She heard someone who sounded like Lenora herself call her name from several offices back, but she ignored it. It might be bad office politics, but she didn't care. She already had her keys out as she made a beeline for the parking lot, determined to rescue Cassie, stuck at the train station.

Clear of the office at last, Polly tried to put its myriad problems behind her. She and Cassie were going to have a great time this weekend. After all, this was the last birthday they would spend together while they were still single and carefree, so they'd better enjoy themselves.

She gulped. Cassie, getting married. Yikes. Things would never be the same, would they?

But for this weekend, while it was still Just Us Girls, she and Cassie would share manicures and mud packs at the spa, popcorn and videos at home, a shopping trip, and then... And then Cassie would go back to Pleasant Falls and get married.

It was awful.

As she squeezed her car through traffic and pedestrians, Polly tried to figure out why she was experiencing these feelings of doom. After all, Cass was a reasonable, competent adult, plenty old enough at almost twenty-five to get married. Right?

But her heart kept saying *wrong* in no uncertain terms.

"Maybe it's just the groom," Polly muttered darkly. "I can't imagine why in the world she wants to marry a *Kennigan*."

She squealed to a stop, putting the upcoming wedding and the blasted Kennigan family out of her mind long enough to take a good look at a very small parking space. "Hmmm... Can I make that?"

Blocking out the taxi honking up a storm behind her, she did the arithmetic, comparing the size of her small convertible to the parking spot. There was at least a chance she could wedge it in there.

But then she remembered that she was a terrible driver and an even worse parker. No way this was going to work.

On the other hand, this handy little space was right outside Union Station, as if Fate had handed it to her on a platter. Besides, she was already late, and she would be even later if she had to circle around a few blocks looking for somewhere else to drop the car.

Once again she got terrible mental images of Cassie waiting inside the station this very minute, wide-eyed and scared to death, dumped and abandoned in the big, bad city by the train from Pleasant Falls...and wondering why the heck there was no one to pick her up in her hour of need, when her beloved twin had promised to be there.

Polly decided quickly. "Back off!" she shouted at the taxi driver and the even more obnoxious truck driver behind him. And then she cranked the wheel like a stunt car driver, closed her eyes and vaulted backward into the space.

She figured the fact that she didn't hear any crunch of metal or feel the jolt of a collision was a good sign.

She raced inside, skidding to a stop long enough to

read the monitor and figure out which track the train was on. She'd only gone a few steps in the right direction when she saw Cassie headed toward her, lugging a large suitcase and looking quite disheveled, for Cassie. All that meant was that her bangs were ruffled and her lipstick was smudged, but for Cassie, that was dire.

"Cass!" Polly cried, offering a hug before she reached for the suitcase. "I'm so sorry I'm late. The office has been insane with this crazy author coming in on a tour—he's been sending me faxes every other second—plus I had to do an interview this afternoon. Would you believe *In Chicago* magazine has decided I'm one of Chicago's 25 hottest singles? Is that bizarre or what?"

"Same old Polly, a mile a minute," her sister said with a smile. But the smile was wobbly, and there was an edge under her words that gave Polly pause. Cassie was never wobbly or edgy. Even if she was angry or upset, she didn't let it show.

"I *am* sorry, Cass," Polly said quickly. The last thing she wanted was to be the cause of Cassie's first-ever anxiety attack. "I wanted to be here on time— really I did. And I tried. But like I said, everything has been crazy and the traffic…"

"I'm fine."

"Of course you are." Polly beamed as she led the way outside to the car. "And we are going to have so much fun. I have videos—Audrey Hepburn as the princess and the Julia Roberts one with all the weddings—and popcorn and Sno-Caps and Raisinets candies to eat while we watch. And then we have all-day appointments tomorrow at the Principessa salon. After mud packs and cucumber facials, you are going be the glowingest bride since—''

Polly stopped. As she turned to hoist the suitcase into the back seat of her snazzy little red convertible, she suddenly noticed the stricken look on her sister's face. "Cassie? Are you okay?"

"Is this… Is this your car?" Cassie choked out. And then she burst into tears, right there on the street, in the middle of a stream of busy commuters and harried tourists.

Okay, a hair out of place was one thing. But crying on the street? Over a car? This was major. Polly guided her twin into the passenger seat as gently as she could. "Cassie, sweetie, I don't know what's wrong. You don't like convertibles? I can put the top down."

"It's not the car. It's, it's…" She broke off, searching in her small, neat handbag for a tissue. "It's nothing. Really."

"Are you sure?" Maybe it was just the general stress of so many people and so much noise. Or maybe Cassie, too, was upset about the idea of one of them getting married and breaking up the special twin bond.

The most obvious choice, of course, was that Cassie was experiencing prewedding jitters, as in, cold feet. And who wouldn't be freaking out, Polly thought cynically, if she were facing a lifetime hitched to Skipper Kennigan? There was nothing wrong with Skipper, not really. Rich, polite, nice-looking, oldest son of Pleasant Falls' most prominent family... According to Cassie's standards, he was pretty much perfect.

According to Polly's standards, however, he was wrong, wrong, wrong. Rich, stuffy, not very bright, son of Pleasant Falls' most awful family, the odious Kennigans, who ran the town with an iron fist. And his younger brother was the even more odious Michael Kennigan, the very person Polly hated most in the world.

Cold feet? With that set of circumstances, Polly knew her own toes would have frostbite by now. But she wasn't Cassie, was she?

"Are you sure you don't want to tell me?" she asked kindly.

"There's nothing to tell." Cassie's jaw was rigid. "Like I said, everything is fine."

Deciding not to push it for now, Polly hauled the heavy bag into the back of the convertible and set off for home, determined to come up with cheery conversation to distract her sister.

It took awhile—traffic was terrible—but Polly eventually managed to get them out of the Loop, off the expressway and into the Wicker Park neighborhood. Once home to middle-class Germans and working-class Poles, with everything from tiny cottages to mansions, Wicker Park had long since been invaded by yuppies and artists bent on gentrifying the area.

"You didn't live here the last time I visited, did you?" Cassie asked, following Polly up to the bright blue door.

"Uh, no. I've only been here a few months." She

left out the part about the actual owner, a stage designer who had gutted and renovated the place before taking off to create scenery in Europe for a year or two. In the meantime, Polly was his house-sitter, courtesy of Lenora Bridge and Associates, Public Relations. Lenora was pals with the owner, and she had decided it was good for the company if Polly had a cool place to live where they could throw small parties.

So Polly got this fabulous house, and the scenic designer got his house photographed and put in all kinds of magazines without having to buy one jar of caviar. Of course, she would have to move out when he came back. In the meantime, she didn't want to confess to her sister that she was just a lowly house-sitter when she had painted a picture of herself as an urban success story.

"Come on in. It's really cute," she said, opening the front door and ushering her sister in.

"Cute?" Cassie stared at the bright-white entryway, bare except for a strip of lavender neon curling up the corner, and then peeked her head around to gaze into the living room, with its similarly odd, ultra-stylish decor, a combination of plush velvet sofas with bare wood floors, exposed brick and huge pieces of art. "This is a lot nicer than where you used to live."

She looked weird again—nothing major, just a little funny around the eyes—but Polly wasn't taking any chances. So she sped up and dragged her sister along on an impromptu tour of the house, hoping to keep her busy enough to cover up any awkwardness.

That seemed to work, Cassie oohing and aahing over the skylights and the private courtyard and the elegant statuary. And then as she unpacked and settled in she seemed fine. They had a glass of wine, chatted about what their parents and little sister were up to and laughed and reminisced about old times over dinner at a funky little restaurant a few blocks away, all without another hint of distress from Cassie.

Still, Polly was worried. Shouldn't Cass be bubbling over with details of the dress and the flowers and the cake? So why was neither of them even mentioning the wedding?

When there was a long pause, Polly ventured, "So, everything okay for the big day?"

"Fine. Perfect. All set," Cassie responded quickly. A little too quickly. "Oh, look. The waiter's coming with the dessert. I haven't had cheesecake in ages."

And that was the end of that, as Cassie prattled on about cheesecake for another five minutes in a way that was very unlike her. Polly eyed her sister suspiciously, but she bided her time. Tomorrow was another day.

And she had no doubt that, eventually, Cassie would break.

*May 18: Two weeks before the wedding*

IT WASN'T UNTIL Cassie's special Principessa chamomile-and-wheatgrass mud pack began to melt under the strain that Polly finally decided to force the issue.

"Are you crying?" she asked, sitting up and clutching the long bath sheet around her. "You are!"

"We're not supposed to talk. You'll crack your mask."

"Oh, and it's okay to cry on it? Green goo is running down your cheeks." Polly scrambled off the padded table, ignoring all the different parts of her that were currently wrapped in honey and paraffin and banana leaves. "Okay, Cassie. You are going to tell me what's going on with you this very minute."

"Nothing."

"Uh-huh. And that's why Miss Serenity bursts into tears over a red convertible, does a twenty-minute monologue on cheesecake and then cries all over her mud pack. That's why you haven't asked me once if my maid of honor dress fits right or waved your engagement ring in my face or even mentioned Skipper." She stood there, hanging on to her towel for dear life, glaring at her sister. "Give, Cassie. Now."

Cassie sat up, too, her face a study in frustration even under the thick layer of green mud. "You are so pushy. You always have been. And sometimes, well, sometimes maybe it just isn't any of your business!"

Polly's mouth dropped open. She could feel the cracks widening in her own facial mask. Not her business? Since when was anything that concerned Cassie not her twin's business? "That is so cold."

"It's just that… I mean, you wouldn't understand." Looking glum, Cassie wrestled herself back down onto the table. "Your life is so perfect. The snazzy car, the gorgeous house, the glamorous job…"

"Oh, jeez, Cass, if you only knew."

Cassie turned her mottled green face into the wall. "I am so boring and pathetic."

"You are not! You're headed for everything you always wanted, you goon!" Polly began to pace on the cool tile floor. "A nice, settled life in Pleasant Falls with a terrific husband, 2.2 beautiful children and a great house. It's perfect."

"Maybe. I guess so." She shook her head, almost dislodging her towel turban. "But compared to the way you live—"

"My life isn't exactly what it seems." With a deep breath, Polly decided to come clean. Okay, so she'd wanted the folks back home to think she was a big success in the city, but this was more important than her pride. "Here's the real scoop, Cass. I am one big fake. The convertible? It's leased to Lenora Bridge and Associates. The house? It's not mine, either. I'm just living there while the real owner is in Europe."

Cassie seemed to perk up, apparently happy to hear her sister was a failure.

"And my job is the worst of all," Polly continued. "I'm basically a handmaiden to any self-absorbed celeb in town for a press junket. Like this Wild Man guy who's coming next week. Do you know how many faxes he's sent me in the past three days?"

"Wild Man?" Cassie propped herself up on one honey-glazed elbow. "Not Wild Man Wright? He's a legend! Even I know about his books. And you get to hang out with him?"

"Hang out with him? Uh, no." This was so humiliating, but Polly pushed on. "No, I'll be too busy throwing out all but the blue M&M's, finding the only kind of whiskey he'll drink that comes from some peat bog and tracking down the special autographing pens flown in from Brazil. God forbid he should use a Bic pen like a normal person."

"So you really don't like it?" Cassie asked softly.

It was difficult to admit, even to herself. "No, I really don't."

"Are you sure you're not just saying this to make me feel better?"

"Heavens, no!" Well, sort of. But that didn't make it any less true. "Look, sweetie, I think you're just having normal doubts about getting married. I don't think this really has anything to do with me. As a matter of fact, I envy you." Okay, so she was straying from the truth, but it seemed to be working. "I mean, think about it, Cass. Your life is stable and steady, you have roots and you're surrounded by people who love you."

"Yeah, maybe." She seemed to consider the idea. "Stable, steady, roots." She sighed. "It is what I always wanted, isn't it?"

Polly nodded vigorously.

"I don't know what's wrong with me," Cassie muttered, reaching for the bell to summon their spa attendant. "You don't suppose they serve margaritas in here, do you?"

Whew. Maybe the storm was past. But glancing at the tear tracks worn into Cassie's ghastly green mask, Polly had her doubts.

CURLED UP on the velvet sofa with popcorn and gooey brownies, they made it through *Roman Holiday* without incident, although Cassie didn't really seem to get into it the way Polly had hoped.

"That is so dopey," she muttered, actually chewing on one of her newly manicured nails. Polly had never seen her sister purposely mar a nail before. "As if a princess would go on the lam from being a princess, and then get lucky enough to run into this really cute guy, and then go back to the princess thing and leave him behind. Ha!"

Polly had also never heard her sister string together quite so many words about a movie. Oh well. Maybe this was how Cassie blew off premarital stress.

Movie #2—*Runaway Bride*—was an even worse choice. Polly had pulled it off the shelf at the video store because it was romantic and fun and fit the wedding theme, without realizing how it might seem to a jittery bride only two weeks before her wedding.

When Julia Roberts ran away from the altar for about the tenth time, Cassie grabbed for the popcorn, missed, and knocked the whole bowl upside down. Buttery little puffs of popcorn flew everywhere—between the couch cushions, under the coffee table, down the front of Cassie's nightgown....

"Damn it all to hell!" she shouted, leaping to her feet and scattering even more popcorn as she stamped around in a blur of bad temper. "Damn it, damn it, damn it!"

"It's not that bad. Better than if you'd dropped the brownies." Polly would've tried to pick up the mess, but she was afraid her newly crazy sister would stomp on her hand or something.

Looking like a tornado on the move, Cassie yelled, "Turn off that damn video!"

Polly hit the eject button so fast it caught Julia and her video groom with their mouths open.

"Like people can just run away from their grooms!" Cassie raged, throwing her arms around. "Like people don't have any responsibility to their parents or the guy or his parents or the whole freakin' town to behave themselves and act like adults and do their duty!"

Polly waited a second, but her sister showed no signs of calming down as she continued her tirade and waved her hands to punctuate it. "Okay," Polly interrupted, "you're scaring me here. Could you at least take a breath before you pass out?"

Cassie blinked. Shaking, she sat down abruptly, crunching popcorn under her bottom as she sank to the floor. "Oh. I'm kind of falling apart, aren't I?"

"Well, yeah."

"I just don't understand why this is happening." She jumped back to her feet, her eyes imploring her sister for help. "I mean, Skipper is everything I ever wanted and I know our life together will be perfect, but..."

"But?"

"But I'm twenty-five years old, damn it, and I've never done anything the least bit exciting or dangerous or even interesting!" She was getting worked up again, and Polly grabbed a nearby lamp before Cassie got too close. "You were the one who went away to school and got out of Pleasant Falls and marked out your own turf. I've always been the good girl, the dull daughter, the homebody, the one who does what other people tell her to do. And I'm sick of it! I feel like I'm going to blow up."

When they were younger, Cassie's placid disposition and even temper had annoyed Polly. She'd tried to convince her sister more than once to let go and break loose. *Be careful what you wish for...*

Cassie whipped around to face her twin. "Did you really mean what you said before?"

"I—I don't know. What?"

"That you envy me. That my life in Pleasant Falls is great and you'd rather have it than the one you have."

Had she said that? Sort of. "Okay, well, yeah, I meant it. I guess."

"Good." Cassie smiled grimly. "Then you can have it."

"Have what?"

"My life."

"Your life?"

"Exactly." Practically humming with nervous energy, Cassie blurted, "I think we should trade places."

# 2

POLLY STARED into her sister's placid blue eyes, sure she must have misheard. "What did you say?"

"I just thought of it. It's so perfect." Obviously pleased with herself, Cassie grinned. "We trade places. You know, go for the ol' switcheroo like we used to."

"When we were ten!"

"And when you wanted to break up with Michael and you knew you'd cave if you did it yourself," Cassie reminded her twin delicately, "I did it for you. And we were eighteen."

"Okay, but still—"

"It would work," Cassie interrupted.

Polly was so stunned all she could do was blink. "Let me get this straight. You want to trade places for your wedding? You want *me* to marry Skipper?"

"Of course not." Her sister waved a hand at her as if Polly were the crazy one. "All I want is for you to go back on the train in my place, dressed in my boring clothes and boring makeup, and then you show up at all the stupid wedding parties and picnics Skipper has planned for me. Meanwhile, I stay here, pretend to be you, and hang out with the Wild Man."

"Oh, is that all?" Polly murmured facetiously.

"And then, when you're scheduled to show up to start your maid of honor duties," her sister continued, "it will be me showing up instead. We'll switch back, and no one will ever know."

A ribbon of panic slithered up Polly's spine. "I wonder who I could call to get you an emergency prescription for Valium."

"I don't need Valium. I need to switch places!" Cassie snapped. But then she smiled again, obviously trying to seem sane. "We just slip into each other's lives for a few days. Is it really such a big deal?"

Dazed, Polly put a hand to her forehead.

"Please think about it, Poll."

"I am thinking about it," Polly argued. "But I don't think you are. If you really don't want to marry Skipper, then call it off. That's a lot cleaner than asking me to sub in for you."

"We both know I can't call the whole thing off this close to the wedding. Call it off? Oh, my God, no!" Her cheeks grew pinker, and she fanned herself with one hand. "I feel like I'm suffocating, like I'm going to honest-to-God die."

"You're not going to die," Polly said quickly.

"But I feel like I am," Cassie confided. "I feel like if I call off the wedding, or run away like Julia in the movie, I will die because Mom will kill me and Skipper will kill me and Skipper's mother will *definitely* kill me."

"Okay, okay, so don't call off the wedding."

"I can't. I just can't. But if I don't get out and experience life while I have this one last chance, I'm just going to explode! You're my sister—my *twin* sister. You should understand better than anyone that I wouldn't ask this unless I was really desperate.'' Her eyes found Polly's. "I'm so lucky to be a twin and have this opportunity. Nobody else could do this. But you and I, we can."

Not sure how to respond, Polly kept her mouth shut.

Meanwhile, Cassie sparkled with excitement as she laid out her plans. "I want to live in the city—just for a little while—and drink latte and martinis. I want to wear a red dress—"

"Red?" Polly sputtered, glancing down at her own red silk robe and pj's. Meanwhile, Cassie was over there in a pale blue nightgown with lace around the collar. "In your entire life, you've never worn anything but pastels. You picked pastels when you were twelve and you said that was it, pastels for the rest of your life. Am I wrong?"

"No, and that's the whole point. Don't you think it's about damn time I branched out? Like, maybe tried a damn red miniskirt or a skimpy black dress?"

Apparently it was also time to say "damn" every other word, which was about as extraordinary coming from Cassie as the idea of her wearing a red miniskirt.

But she was on to new territory, something about eyeliner and high heels. "I want to meet celebrities," she said eagerly, spinning around in a circle like she thought she was Julie Andrews in the Alps. "I want to knock back whiskey from peat bogs and dance on the table with Wild Man Wright. Is that so wrong?"

"Well, yes."

"Oh, it is not!" Crossing to her sister, Cassie clasped her hands as if she were praying. "Please, please, please? Can't I be you for a little while? Maybe a week?"

"I would help if I could, Cass, but there's just no—"

"Sure there is!" she argued. "It's perfect, Poll. We just do it long enough for this book tour with the Wild Man, which you don't want anyway. Here I am, volunteering, *begging,* to take the Wild Man off your hands. All you need to do is go to Pleasant Falls a little earlier than you planned, sit through a few boring parties, smile a lot and keep your mouth shut." She shrugged and said grimly, "That's my life in a nutshell."

"You're making this sound easy, but come on," Polly countered. "Aren't you forgetting your groom? Wouldn't Skipper know the difference in five seconds? And what about, you know, *sleeping* with him?"

"Oh, pooh!" Cassie rolled her eyes. "Skipper wouldn't notice if Britney Spears showed up instead of me. Besides, he joined this 'Moral Imperative' group where you're not allowed to do a darn thing till after you get married. So sex is not an issue. He doesn't even want us to kiss until the ceremony because he wants to make it special."

"I still don't think—"

"Trust me," Cassie said sharply. "Skipper will not be a problem."

Polly noticed she'd said "will," as if this were a done deal. But it wasn't. "Even if I could handle Skipper, there are other major problems. Like... Well, you know."

"Michael," Cassie supplied.

The one and only. She'd told herself a million times that she didn't care if she ran into him again, that she would be cool as a cucumber, but she knew it was a lie. Polly took a deep breath. "I've been trying to get myself pumped to see him at the wedding, but I thought that would be an hour or two, max. On the other hand, if he's in town and I'm in town and we're running into each for days and days until the wedding..." Her mouth was still open, but no sound was coming out.

"I know, I know. You'd have a heart attack and probably end up in bed with him in five minutes. But there's no need to worry on that score, either," Cassie rushed to assure her. "He's still in Paris and Skipper said he's not planning to come home for the wedding. I figure he doesn't want to see you, either."

"Michael's not coming at all?" She'd prayed for just that, but now she felt strangely disappointed.

"That's what Skipper said."

"Okay."

"Okay, you'll do it? Okay, we can trade places?" Cassie asked quickly.

"Okay, Michael isn't coming home. That's all!" Polly ran a hand through her hair. "It would never work, Cass. My hair's too long, I talk too much, Mom and Dad wouldn't be fooled—"

"You get a haircut, you try to be quiet like me, and Mom and Dad have been fooled before."

How could she counter all of the objections so fast? Polly's head was spinning. And, God help her, she was actually starting to consider this. Hadn't she always wanted Cassie to take a walk on the wild side? Wouldn't a good twin help her sister grab for that one last chance to be free, to have fun, before a lifetime with—shudder—Skipper Kennigan?

"I need to think about this," Polly whispered.

Cassie edged closer, taking her sister's hand and squeezing it. "You know, it would be good for you, too. I didn't want to say anything because I wanted you home for my wedding, but you have some fence-mending to do in Pleasant Falls. After that speech you gave at graduation—"

"Oh, sure! Bring that up again."

"Well, you were very harsh toward the Kenni-gans." Cassie's mouth dipped into a frown. "All that stuff about dictators and overlords and how everyone else in town was a serf. It was very rude."

"I thought it was the right thing to say at the time," Polly returned with all the dignity she could muster.

"It didn't go over very well."

"I realize that."

Cassie gave her a pitying gaze. "You know as well as I do that the only reason you haven't been back in seven years and why you always make Mom and Dad and me come here to visit you is because you're em-barrassed about that stupid speech and how mad ev-erybody was after it."

"Same old, same old..." she mumbled, feeling as sulky as she always did when the subject came up.

"Isn't it time to get your buns back to town and get over it?" her sister demanded. "You go back to Pleasant Falls disguised as me—"

"The good sister," Polly interjected cynically.

"The sister no one in town hates. Just think—you can reconnect with people without anyone holding a grudge, I can go on the lam and kick up my heels, and then we'll switch back before anyone even knows we did it." Cassie grinned and put her arm around her sister. "No fuss, no muss. And it will be fun, Polly. A lark. Your favorite kind of goofball trick, where we have one over on the rest of the world."

Fun? Could it be fun?

"You have to be there for the wedding, anyway," Cassie added. "I know you were dreading it because you think they all hate you. So why not go a few days early, no pressure, and ease into it?"

As Polly tried to figure out what to do, the phone interrupted with a persistent ring. She ignored it, happy to let the machine pick up while she sorted out the Cassie crisis.

But then she heard the message.

"Hey there, hi there, ho there!" a very loud male voice called out. "Pretty Polly, pick up that phone. I've got needs, honey, and you're the only one who can fill 'em."

The Wild Man. Her teeth began to grind all by themselves.

"Not gonna pick up, huh? Okeedokee. But you better call me back pronto, Pretty P. I got a whole list of stuff for you. And we both want everything just right, don't we, honey bun?''

He was infuriating. ''I hate that man,'' she muttered. ''It is Saturday and my twenty-fifth birthday and the last thing in the entire world I want to do is call that man back.''

''I could call him,'' Cassie offered. ''You can escape to Pleasant Falls and leave him to me. Wouldn't that be nice?''

No Wild Man. No reporters to woo or clients to impress. Just a small-town parade of picnics and backyard barbecues where everyone was happy to see her, or the person they thought she was, and all they wanted from her was a glance at the three-carat engagement rock. For the first time in her life, Polly could mingle in Pleasant Falls as one of the chosen crowd, wrapped in the bosom of the town, in the bosom of her family. It sounded so warm and inviting, so charming and *nice*.

Polly sunk into the plush couch, wondering when her brain has deserted her. ''Oh, God. I'm actually going to do it.''

Cassie waited for the briefest of seconds. ''You will?'' she asked breathlessly.

''I will.''

With a garbled cry of joy, Cassie leapt into the air. ''We're switching places! We're switching places!''

At least one of them was happy about it.

*May 21: Eleven days before the wedding*

IN A WHIRLWIND of shared insanity, they had spent two days exchanging wardrobes, fooling with makeovers and prepping each other with all the vital details they'd need to know to pull off the masquerade.

Polly checked and rechecked schedules and phone numbers for the Wild Man's tour, finally deciding that she was so rotten at this stuff herself that Cassie couldn't screw it up anymore than she did on a regular basis.

Cassie was less relaxed about the obligations she was trading off, however. "You have to do this right," she kept saying. "My whole life is on the line here. So if you're tempted to tell Skipper the truth or give up on it halfway through, *don't!* Please, Polly, I'm depending on you. Because Skipper and his family will crucify me if they find out."

She should've said, *Good thinking, Cass,* and backed out right there. But she didn't. She was the adventurous sister who thrived on challenges. So when the opportunity came, she lifted her chin and said, "I don't do things halfway. Your identity will be safe with me."

And then, with her hair clipped into a replica of Cassie's sleek bob, a pretty peach outfit to wear on the train, and the odd weight of an engagement ring on her finger, Polly felt strangely excited as she bid goodbye to her teary sister and climbed aboard the train bound for Pleasant Falls.

*Maybe this was just what I needed,* she thought. *Mom and Dad and Ashley, welcoming me…. Maybe I do need to go home and figure out where I came from so I can know where I want to go.*

The sentiment and exhilaration lasted at least until Pontiac. But as the train chugged closer and closer to Pleasant Falls, Polly grew more and more apprehensive.

What had seemed like a game while they were trying on each other's clothes now seemed like a very scary proposition. *Mom and Dad and Ashley, all expecting me to be calm and charming and low maintenance, like Cassie.* Not to mention Skipper. What was she going to do with Skipper? This "Moral Imperative" thing sounded okay, but would he really want to stay away from his bride only a week before they got married? She chewed on her nail, pondering the huge, scary obstacles in her path.

"Pleasant Falls," the conductor called out. "We're pulling into Pleasant Falls."

She couldn't be sure if it was the lurch of the train or her own anxiety that made her stumble as she grabbed her bag and made for the exit. "Okay," she said under her breath. "Cass said Skipper or his dad would be waiting to meet me. They'll ask how it was and I'll say fine, thank you for asking, and then I keep my mouth shut. If they push me or want more from me, I say I'm tired, that it was a long weekend, and I could use a nap. Fine, thank you for asking. A little tired, long weekend, need a nap."

But all her good intentions went sailing out the window the minute she stepped off the train and saw her welcoming committee.

Polly almost climbed right back on. But it was too late. He'd already seen her. He was already heading her way.

Michael. Oh, lord, lord, it couldn't be Michael. He was in Paris. And yet here he was, walking toward her with that easy, sexy walk of his and that deadly sparkle of charm in his beautiful green eyes. Nobody had a hard, perfect jawline like that, or narrow, mocking lips that begged you to kiss him, or sharp, smart features stamped with class and arrogance. Nobody but Michael.

Michael. Oh, lord, lord.

"Hello, Cassie," he greeted her, taking her bag, and she remembered suddenly that she was dressed in peach with a shiny, smooth little pageboy, so of course he thought she was Cassie. Wasn't that the idea? He continued, "Cassie, you look great. I guess the engagement agrees with you."

"M-Michael…" was all she could get out.

"I guess you weren't expecting me. I hope you don't mind I came to pick you up," he said ruefully. "Skip and Dad were tied up, so they sent me."

"Of course they did." Polly tried to remember to swallow, to breathe. "Michael. What a surprise."

"Yeah, I know." He shrugged, and the elegance of that small movement took her breath away. *Get a grip, Polly.* "I didn't think I could make it back for the wedding, but a window of opportunity opened up, so I took it. I'm very happy for you and Skip."

"Great. Great." She felt faint.

As always, Michael was attuned to her mood. He narrowed his eyes. "Are you all right?"

"Just a little tired," she repeated automatically. "It was a long weekend. I could use a nap."

He opened the car door for her, still eyeing her suspiciously. "I had forgotten how much you look like Polly," he noted, letting his gaze linger on her face. "I think you look even more alike than you used to."

"You haven't seen her in a long time," she shot back.

"I don't need to."

What did that mean? Was it, *I don't need to because her image is engraved on my heart?* Or, *I don't need to because I never want to see her again?*

She couldn't ask for clarification, could she? So she remained wordless as she got into the car. He took the driver's seat. And she was trapped.

Trapped.

All she could think of was Michael behind the wheel of a Cadillac like this one, driving his dad's car to Homecoming or a basketball game. Or worse yet, Michael in the back seat, flushed and hot, after they'd steamed up the windows with a makeout session.

It was too much, way too much. She shoved her hands through her hair, lifting it off her neck, ruining the line of the perfect Cassie bob.

"So," he said abruptly, glancing over at her. "Skipper said you were up in Chicago, visiting Polly." His gaze grew thoughtful and his voice softened. "How is she?"

*Polly is fine. Polly is not fine. Polly is driving her-self insane just looking at you!*

She didn't know what to think. Should she be thrilled or depressed that he still hadn't recognized her? After all, he wasn't supposed to recognize her, and she and Cassie both would've been in serious trouble if he had.

*Who cares?* she asked herself with irritation. *If he'd ever really loved me, he would've known it was me immediately. He should've known it was me.*

On the other hand, the first thing he'd asked about was her.

"So? How is Polly?" he asked again. "Everything okay up in Chicago?"

"Just fine," she told him, trying to manufacture a smile and keep it casual when she didn't feel casual at all.

He lifted an eyebrow. "And what's she up to these days?"

Ooh, that was an opening. Polly wound up and let loose, determined to make her life sound fabulous, de-termined to make Michael rue the day he'd let her get away. "Polly works in PR for a terrific firm, so mostly she escorts celebrities around Chicago. She loves it," she added with relish. "She just got a new car—a red convertible—and she has a new house, too. A real showplace." Okay, so she was probably overdoing it. But as long as she got to play Cassie, she told herself that she was only saying what Cassie would've.

"Is she seeing anyone?"

Polly sneaked a look at him. Was he just being ob-

noxious or did he want to know if the field was clear?
The damn man was always so hard to read. "Why do
you want to know?"

"Don't worry," he returned darkly. "I don't have
any designs on your sister. You cured me of that back
at the prom."

"The prom? I did?" But Polly hadn't even gone to
the prom. She was morally opposed at the time, considering it a patriarchal and sexist institution. They'd
had a big fight about it, Michael had asked horrid Lana
Pfeiffer instead, and that was the beginning of the end
of the Polly-and-Michael Show.

"Yeah, right. Play innocent." Michael shook his
dark head. "You only ruined my life."

"I—I did?" Cassie did? At the prom? This was
news. Polly desperately wanted to know what he
meant, but she couldn't come out and ask, because
presumably Cassie already knew.

Yikes. She was already confusing herself and she'd
only been playing Cassie for ten minutes.

But Michael mistook her silence for Cassie's usual
reserve. "I guess I'd forgotten how you always try to
smooth over the rough spots." Shaking his head, he
focused on his window, not looking at her at all.
"Polly would've beat it into the ground, talking about
every little detail. But you... You keep quiet. That's
classic Cassie, isn't it? If it's unpleasant, you should
ignore it, forget it, pretend it never happened."

Actually, he was right about all of that. Polly just
had to remember which role she was playing.

"And how about you?" she asked, using her best

impression of Cassie's light, serene tones to change gears and get them onto less confusing turf. "Have you enjoyed living in Paris? Are you going right back?"

"I really don't know."

She could tell from the look on his face that he considered that subject closed, too. Still, it was intriguing. Instead of taking the opportunity to brag, as she had, Michael had chosen to say something mysterious and noncommittal, something that made it sound as if he were hiding some deep unhappiness and his life wasn't that great at all.

*Okay, so he's a bigger man than I,* Polly thought gloomily.

She was happy to put thoughts of Michael temporarily aside when she caught her first glimpse of the old homestead. "My house," she whispered, drinking in the sight of the cozy Cape Cod where she grew up, with the big maple tree in the front yard and her mom silhouetted in the front door, waiting just for her. Well, for Cassie, anyway.

She was out the door and up the driveway before Michael had a chance to turn off the car.

"Hi, honey," her mother called, sliding open the screen door as she approached. "How was the trip? Did you have a good time with Polly?"

The idea of her very own mother and her very own house swamped her with emotion all of a sudden. "The house looks wonderful," she enthused, wrapping her mother in a big hug. "The tree has gotten so big. And oh, Mom, I missed you!"

"You've only been gone four days," Ruth Tompkins pointed out, her voice muffled by the embrace.

"And what's so wonderful about this dumpy place?" Her little sister Ashley, not quite fifteen, hoisted a backpack onto her shoulder and tried to squeeze around them to get out the door. "It's not like it's changed since you left on Friday."

"I know. It's just..." She tried to think of some way to explain her odd actions. "I'm just feeling sentimental, I guess."

"Bride brain," her mother teased, in a sing-song rhythm that told Polly she'd said the same thing a million times.

"Oh, right. Bride brain." Whatever that was.

"If you ask me, she gets away with murder and you just say 'bride brain,'" Ashley complained. "Can I get out the door, please?"

"No, you may not. We're having supper in twenty minutes and you know very well you can't go to Katie's when it's suppertime."

"Mom!"

"Ashley, don't argue with me. Go up to your room and study until dinner."

As Ashley pouted and fussed but finally gave in, flouncing away upstairs, Polly took it all in with a smile. It sounded so familiar, so homey and sweet.

"Cassie, honey, you left Skipper in the car. Oh, that's not Skipper, is it?" With Ashley out of the way, Mrs. Tompkins had a clear view out the door. "Cassie? Wake up. I asked you a question."

Oops. She had to remember to answer to "Cassie" from now on.

Her mother frowned. "Don't tell me it's Michael."

"It's Michael."

She raised her eyebrows. "That's awkward, isn't it?"

*You don't know the half of it.*

"I didn't know he was even in town," her mom continued. "I thought sure you said he wasn't coming."

"That's what I thought." Polly chewed her lip. "He said he had a window of opportunity and changed his mind."

"Well, whatever you do, don't tell Polly. If she finds out he's around, she'll skip the wedding and you won't have a maid of honor." As she opened the door again, she said under her breath, "Sometimes Polly drives me nuts with that chip on her shoulder."

"What do you mean?" she asked with spirit. So her own mother thought she had a chip on her shoulder. The things you found out when people thought you were someone else!

Her mom didn't answer the question. She was preoccupied calling out to Michael, "Good to see you, hon. It's been awhile. Come on in."

Bringing Cassie's suitcase with him, he walked right into the house as if he owned it, and then gave her mother a big, cheesy smile. "Hi, Mrs. Tompkins."

"Michael, I swear you look just the same as when I took your picture with Polly before you went to... What was it? The prom?"

"We didn't go to the prom. I mean, Polly didn't go to the prom," she said swiftly. "I—I went, but Polly didn't."

"Oh, that's right," Mrs. Tompkins agreed. "Polly made a big stink about the prom, didn't she? That Polly! Always a fight about something. Who else but Polly would find something wrong with the prom, for goodness sake?"

The real Polly noted, "I'm sure she had her reasons."

"Polly always had reasons," Michael said dryly. "It's just that her reasons seemed pretty silly to normal people."

She sent him an evil glance. She'd been home less than an hour and they were ganging up on her already. It wasn't fair. It wasn't right. But she buttoned her lip. If she wanted to maintain this masquerade for more than a minute and a half, she was going to have to resist the impulse to defend herself.

"Why don't you take your suitcase up to your room, honey?" her mother suggested. "Come right back down for dinner, okay? And tell Ash to come, too."

"Sure. Right away." She grabbed her bag and beat a hasty retreat to the stairs. What a relief to get away from That Man.

But behind her, she heard her mom ask, "Can you stay for supper, Michael? We'd love to have you,"

She stopped halfway up. *Say no, say no, say no,* she pleaded.

"I'm sorry, but I can't," he told her mother.

Phew.

"All right. But you come back anytime you want, okay?" Mrs. Tompkins raised her voice to command, "Cassie, say thank you to Michael for picking you up. He's leaving."

"Thank you, Michael," she called down the stairs. In a lower tone, she added, "Thank God you're not staying for dinner and may you stay far, far away."

"What did you say?"

She whirled to find her little sister standing in the doorway to the bedroom. "Ash? Why are you skulking around eavesdropping?"

"I'm not eavesdropping." Ashley cocked her head to one side. "I'm just waiting for you."

Sidestepping the teen, Polly dragged the big suitcase into the room. "What do you need?"

Ashley bounded after her, flopping on the bed. "I want to know why you're pretending to be Cassie," she said placidly. "What's up with the charade, Poll?"

# 3

MICHAEL KENNIGAN aimed his father's Cadillac back toward the large, expansive Kennigan estate on the outskirts of town. But his mind was not on the car, the mansion, or anything else that normally bothered him about his family.

Nope. Today his mind was elsewhere. Because he couldn't stop thinking about Cassie Tompkins.

Cassie Tompkins, of all people. Who would've guessed she'd grow up so well? And so much like her sister, the girl he'd always imagined was the one true love of his life. At seventeen, Cassie had seemed vapid and stupid and not worth ten minutes of his time. But now...

Oh, man. When he saw her get off that train, his heart had actually leapt in his chest.

*Better get over it, bucko,* he told himself bitterly. *She's marrying your brother next week.*

POLLY GAPED at her little sister, unable to believe what she'd just heard. "Wh-what do you mean?"

"Oh, give it up, Polly," Ashley scoffed. "You're not even good at it."

But she busied herself unpacking, laying all the beige and cream and peach clothes out on one of the twin beds, refusing to admit she couldn't even fool a child. "Look, it's probably just being with Polly all weekend. Some of her mannerisms must've rubbed off."

"Uh-huh. None of her rubbed off any other time, but now you're suddenly like this weird Cassie robot with Polly leaking around the edges. Like Cassie would ever say 'mannerisms.'" Giggling, Ashley did a clumsy ballet move, twirling around a bedpost. "I know it's you, Polly. And if you don't spill the whole deal, I'm going to run and tell Michael, too. I bet he's already suspicious, anyway." She heaved a big, dramatic sigh. "He is so awesome. Maybe if I tell him the truth, he'll be, like, smitten by my honesty and brilliance and he'll go for me."

"Ashley!" Polly cried, horrified. "You are not going to tell Michael. And he is not going to be smitten with you, either. You're fourteen!"

She lifted her narrow shoulders in a careless shrug. "I know. But that's how old you were when he liked you."

"Yeah, but he was fourteen, too."

"See? You just admitted you're Polly." Her giggles got louder. "You are so bad at this."

Jeez. How humiliating to realize the kid was right. "Look, you are not going to breathe a word of this to anyone, do you hear me? Not for me, but for Cassie. If anyone knew she was ditching out right before her wedding, well, Skipper and all the Kennigans would have a fit." Polly looked deep into her sister's eyes, summoning up all her persuasive powers. "You have to promise, Ash."

"But why?" Kneeling on one of the beds, Ashley scrambled closer and dropped her voice to a conspiratorial tone. "Why did you guys do this?"

"Cassie really needed a break. She said she was going to blow up and die or something." Polly threw up her hands. "It definitely wasn't my idea. Well, it was supposed to be good for me, too, you know, because I can be home and I haven't been home in a while. But mostly for Cassie to take a breather and get away from all this wedding stuff. I've never seen her so whacked out."

"Okay, forget Cassie. 'Cause now you're here and Michael is here and you can, like, get back together or something. Totally together." Ashley grinned and waggled her hips in an MTV move that left no doubt how she interpreted "totally together." "Woo-woo!" she crowed. "Cool!"

"I'm not getting back together with Michael, even if I wanted to—which I don't," Polly added quickly. "I'm being Cassie, remember? Cassie, who is engaged to Skipper? How would it look if I was 'totally together' with Michael while I was supposed to be engaged to his brother?"

"Bummer."

"No, it's not a bummer. It's good." Determined to get back in stride, Polly began to hang up the dresses she'd laid on the bed, putting them back in the closet with all their beige and cream compatriots. "I haven't seen Michael in seven years, and they've been seven excellent years. I don't need or want Michael. I mean, think about it. He was a lying, cheating dog, and I could never trust him. Why would I want that back?''

*Because he was also sexy and funny and the best company I ever had and I've missed him every minute of those seven years.*

Not going there. So she continued, putting on a brave face. "Knowing that I can't touch him because of this whole Cassie-masquerade thing is great. It's like putting up a wall. A nice, sturdy wall."

"Uh-huh. Well, my class just studied Romeo and Juliet and, you know, they had a wall, too," Ashley noted. "It didn't help much."

"Michael and I aren't Romeo and Juliet."

"Uh-huh."

"Quit being such a know-it-all." Polly snapped the empty suitcase shut and shoved it into the closet with a vengeance. "Are you going to promise not to tell or do I have to lock you in your room for the next week and a half?"

"Are you kidding? I think this is great!" Ashley jumped up and down on the spare bed with enthusiasm, and her words came out bouncy and erratic when she said, "Besides, I'm much better at secrets than you are. No way I'm going to be the one who screws this up."

"Kids!" Their mother's voice floated up the stairs. "Dad's home and dinner's ready. Get down here and quit fooling around, will you?"

Ashley stopped in midbobble, and her eyes met

Polly's. "Vow of silence," she swore solemnly, spitting in her hand and then sticking it out.

The last thing she wanted to do was shake her little sister's spitty hand, but Polly did it, anyway. "Vow of silence," she agreed.

And then she made a few vows of her own—to do a better job being Cassie so that no one else would figure it out, to stay away from Michael so that there was no danger of that particular wall being breached and to enjoy uncomplicated moments of family unity like tonight's dinner while she could.

*Fat chance.*

*May 22: Ten days before the wedding*

THE ALARM went off at 6:30 a.m., which was positively indecent in her opinion, so Polly hit the snooze button and went back to sleep.

"Pssssst." It was Ashley, already washed and brushed and perky in her school clothes. "You better get up. Cassie's always up at the crack of dawn and Mom will know something's wrong."

"I don't wanna," she said crossly, pulling the pillow over her head.

"You have to. Sheesh. It's a good thing you've got me looking after you." With a frown, Ashley grabbed the pillow and smacked her with it. "Now get up!"

"Are you two fighting already?" their mother put in from the hall. "Cassie? This is one for the record books. What are you doing still in bed? Give her a couple of weeks off from work and she starts sleeping around the clock.''

"I'm up, I'm up." Polly sprang from the bed and put on a perky face. "I guess I'm still tired from last night." That much was true. She was worn out from pretending to be Cassie at dinner, smiling and agreeing with anything anyone said, no matter how dopey it was. Plus Ashley kept smiling and winking at her, which made it that much harder.

"You better get going, hon," her mom said. "Skipper's downstairs and rarin' to see you."

"S-Skipper? What's he doing here?"

"Like, duh!" Ashley told her, wagging her eyebrows in a definite warning. "Did you forget he comes every morning to have breakfast with you and drive you to work?"

"But I have the week off. He doesn't need to drive me to work."

"Tell him that. He's still here," Ashley said bluntly.

Polly rubbed her eyes. Cassie hadn't said a thing about Skipper and a morning breakfast routine. Why not?

After scavenging around for a robe, she threw it on over the lacy nightgown she'd worn last night. Really, Cassie's clothes were just horrifying. But as she tied the belt on the robe and ran a hand through her hair, ready to face Skipper, her mother stopped her.

"You're not going down there like that, are you?"

She held back the "What's wrong with it?" hovering on her lips. Of course, Cassie would never venture from the room in a bathrobe, her hair a mess, her teeth unbrushed....

"I don't know where my head is this morning," she said in a revoltingly cheery tone, when she knew exactly where it was. Back in the bed, where normal heads were at this unlivable hour.

"Hurry up. Skipper's on his third cup of coffee and he's dying to see you. It's been days and days, you know. Poor boy!"

And with that comment, Mom was off, presumably to pour another cup for the groom, dragging Ashley with her.

"What is he doing here?" Polly grumbled. "What kind of idiot fiancé shows up at six-thirty in the morning and expects a girl to greet him?"

But she washed her face, brushed her teeth, ran a comb through her hair and found a nice beige outfit, throwing together the best facsimile of her pulled-together sister she could manage. "Voilà!" she told her image in the mirror. Cassie to a *T.*

As she slowly descended the stairs into the kitchen, she realized how reluctant she was to face Skipper. Not freaked out or thrown into turmoil, like meeting up with Michael again—that was akin to jumping off a cliff on a bungee cord. Seeing Skipper was more like going to get your teeth drilled.

"Skipper is the dullest man on earth," she murmured. "I can handle him." And if it didn't seem fair to make a fool of him this way, substituting fiancées on him, she was just going to have to tough it out.

With that no-nonsense attitude in place, Polly marched right into the kitchen.

"Cassie, honey bunny!" he cried, standing up and throwing his arms around her. He was an inch or two taller than Michael, with the same dark hair, but that was all they had in common. Where Michael was slim and sculpted, Skipper seemed gangly. And when you looked into Skipper's eyes, there was no spark, no intensity. "Boy, did I miss you!"

And then he squeezed the stuffing out of her. Shocked and surprised, Polly just sort of stood there, like a plaster statue stuck in his embrace.

"Did you miss me?" he asked.

Good grief, her mother was watching, right there near the sink!

But the embrace went on. *Ugh.* He was no Michael, that was for sure. *Oops. Can't think about that. Especially not now.*

"Of course I missed you," she said awkwardly, wondering how long she had to wait before she could gracefully disengage herself.

"You seem a little strange." He screwed up his face as he regarded her. "Are you mad at me?"

"No, of course not." Could she help it if she didn't want his body wrapped around hers?

"You are!" he decided. "You're mad because I didn't meet you at the train. Oh, honey bunny, I'm sorry. Membership business at the club. Dad and I were tied up all afternoon."

Right. Tied up all afternoon, no doubt blackballing

unworthy people from joining their horrid country club. "Oh, so that's why you didn't meet me. I see."

Really, she didn't see. If he were her fiancé and she'd been away, she'd want him panting to have her back, waiting with bells on for that train to get in. If she'd felt a glimmer of sympathy for Skipper, abandoned and deceived by his fiancée, she lost it now. But she needed to distract him, to stop him from watching her so closely. The best strategy with men like Skipper was to get them to talk about themselves. "So, did you get a lot of business done while I was gone?"

"Not really. Dad and I played a few rounds at the club with Benjy and Mort. Were they here when you left?"

Benjy and Mort. And they would be… "You know, I don't recall whether they were here or not," she said finally.

He didn't seem to notice her hesitation. Smugly, he announced, "Looks like the Pleasant Valley Estates deal is fast-tracked and it's all because Dad and I have been wining and dining Benjy and Mort. Great guys, Benjy and Mort."

"Great," she echoed, hoping she wasn't giving her recommendation to Attila the Hun and his best pal. Meanwhile, what was the Pleasant Valley Estates deal? There hadn't been anything called Pleasant Valley around town when she lived there, and this "estates" thing sounded like a big housing development. Where would they put it? What would they be knocking down or digging up for their fast-track Pleasant Valley Estates?

It sounded like exactly the kind of fat cat bulldozing she had been complaining about in her now-famous valedictory speech at graduation. But Polly knew she had to force herself to chill out.

After all, Cassie wouldn't care about housing developments, so Polly couldn't either, for the time being. It was aggravating, but she had signed on to be Cassie and not tick any more people off in Pleasant Falls. And she was going to do it if it killed her.

"Listen, Skip, good to see you. I really..." She attempted to muster up more enthusiasm. "I really missed you, uh, honey bunny."

"Missed you, too, honey bunny." And then he hugged her again. Ugh.

"Isn't it time you were at work?" she tried, moving her hands to his chest to stop him from getting too close.

"Yeah, gotta go." Reluctantly, he pulled away. "Guess I'll just see you at Harvey and Gigi's."

Who the heck were Harvey and Gigi? How could a rinky-dink town like Pleasant Falls keep adding people she'd never heard of? "Uh, Skipper? Where is it I'm seeing you?"

"Don't tell me you forgot the big barbecue." He tweaked the end of her nose. "Silly. It's in our honor. It's also on your schedule. I didn't print you out a schedule just so you could forget the important stuff."

"Oh. The big barbecue. At Harvey and Gigi's. Of course." She laughed to cover her confusion. "If it's

Wednesday, it must be Harvey and Gigi's barbecue. Now where did I put my schedule?''

''Bride brain,'' her mother said with a shake of her head.

Polly just kept her mouth shut.

Thankfully, Skipper left for his office, her mother left to teach her second period English class at the high school, and Polly could relax. First things first—find a phone and get on the horn to her sister. They had promised not to call each other unless they absolutely had to, but this was important. Cassie had some explaining to do.

But she wasn't answering Polly's cell phone. The automated message said that Polly Tompkins was unable to answer her phone right now, and to call back later. Which she did, but Cass had still not turned the darn thing on. Not at 7:00, not at 8:00, at 9:00 or 10:00 a.m. Polly had expected her to be away from the house, since this was the day the Wild Man arrived, but why wasn't she using the cell phone?

Frustrated, Polly angrily dialed the regular number, leaving a guarded message on the machine. ''It's me,'' she said grimly. ''You have to call me right away. Right away. I'm not kidding.''

That, of course, didn't happen. The hours dragged on, and Cassie didn't call.

''Why am I doing this?'' she asked herself for the hundredth time. Michael the sexual bulldozer, Skipper the groper, Ashley the conspirator... It was all more than she'd bargained for. So she did what she would've done in her own home—found ice cream and bath bubbles and settled into the tub for a long soak.

But it wasn't long before her mother and sister both got back from school. Still soaking, Polly heard the garage door open and voices call out downstairs. She knew she had to get up and don Cassie's persona and the boring beige clothes again, but she wanted just another second of bubble bath.

"Honey?" Her mother tapped on the door to the bathroom. "What are you doing still in the tub? Don't you need to make your potato salad for the barbecue?"

"I guess I forgot."

"Cassie, I'm starting to worry about you. Where did you put that schedule Skipper made for you?"

"I don't know."

"Oh, Cassie, really!" She could hear her mom's footsteps pound down the hall and then, a few minutes later, pound back. "It was right on your bulletin board where it was supposed to be. Five o'clock, Harvey and Gigi's BBQ, bring potato salad. I'll start the potatoes, but you'd better get a move on, Cassie."

Recalling her vows to do a better job, Polly toweled off. "Gee, what boring outfit will I wear tonight?" she muttered to herself.

But she found a pretty, full-skirted pink dress with a matching little sweater, and she actually liked what she saw in the mirror. Shiny blond hair in a sleek, chin-length cut, sincere blue eyes with understated makeup, pink lips, rosy cheeks, small pearl earrings... Yep, it was Cassie.

Now all she had to do was bluff her way through

potato salad and then figure out where Harvey and Gigi lived.

But when she came downstairs, she discovered that her mother had taken care of the potato salad, creating a big tub of it while Polly was fooling with lip liner. "Mom, thanks. That was so sweet." Problem one solved. Now on to problem two.

The Tompkins' house was so backward they actually only had two phones—one in the kitchen, right next to her mother, and one in the family room. Polly quietly slipped into the family room and punched in her own number. "Cassie," she whispered, "if you don't pick up this phone, I may have to kill you."

But the machine picked up. "Damn it, anyway, where are you?" she asked the recorder. "I have to find out who Gigi and Harvey are and where they live. This whole thing is going down the toilet. Call me!"

After hanging up, she tried to think of a new plan. Finally, she ventured back into the kitchen. "Are you and Daddy coming to the barbecue with me?"

"Maybe later." Ruth Tompkins wiped her hands on a dishtowel. "I've got papers to grade, but we may drop by for dessert or something. Just to be polite." Her mouth turned down into a grimace. "I know she's your boss, but I never have liked that Gigi."

Okay, so Gigi was Cassie's boss, presumably at the department store where Cassie was assistant manager in the Ladies' Better Dresses area. Good to know.

But, darn it, anyway. Polly'd been hoping she could solve the riddle of where these people lived by trooping along with her parents.

"Well, I could just walk outside and keep my ears open for a party," she said under her breath. "It's a small town. I'm sure to trip over it sooner or later."

Her mother looked up from the bowl she was sprinkling with paprika. "What did you say?"

"Nothing. Nothing." She could hardly ask her mom for directions. For all she knew, this Gigi person lived next door! "Is Ashley home yet?" she asked quickly, taking a new tack.

"Upstairs," her mother answered. "Why?"

"I need to borrow her, uh, lip gloss."

"What's wrong with what you have on?"

"I like hers better."

She heard "bride brain" muttered behind her, but she was already on the stairs. "Ash? Ash?"

Her sister poked her nose out from behind her door. "What?"

"Have you ever heard of someone named Gigi around here?"

She thought for a moment. "Yeah. Gigi works at Kennigan & Sons with you—I mean, with Cassie." Ashley paused. "I think Gigi is like the manager of the department and Cassie comes under her. And Gigi's husband is some bigwig at the bank. Does that sound right?"

"Sure. You don't happen to know where these people live, do you?"

"Yeah. Their kid—who is a butthead, by the way—is in the class behind me. They live up on the hill. The house with the turret."

That was lucky. Polly actually knew that house.

Whew. Ashley had really saved the day. Polly was coming to have a new appreciation for her teenage sister.

She took a step away from Ashley's room, but then turned back. "Do you want to come to this barbecue with me? I think it's for Skipper and me—actually, Skipper and Cassie—so I'm sure you can come, as a bridesmaid. I mean, if you're old enough. Do you go to parties?"

"Like, *yes!*" She added, "Yeah. Okay. I'll come," in a more nonchalant tone. But she scampered to get ready, ending up in a dress that looked like a smaller version of Polly's.

As the two sisters walked up the hill to the big Queen Anne house on the bluff, their blond heads together, they laughed and joked and had a very good time. Two blondes in pink dresses, toting a big crock of potato salad—it was all so sweet and down-home that Polly felt sure the schmaltz police would jump out from behind a tree and arrest her at any minute for impersonating a member of *The Brady Bunch.*

There were cars parked up and down the street and country music blaring as they neared the house, making it clear a party was underway. Tables and chairs and Japanese lanterns had been set up in the side yard, so Polly and Ashley walked right into the middle of it without any trouble.

"Welcome, welcome! Aren't you two just too cute?" shouted a woman Polly assumed was Gigi, the hostess. In Polly's ear, she whispered, "Good job, Cassie, showing off merchandise from the store. It looks good on both of you. I didn't even remember we had it in junior sizes.''

Well, what do you know? Looked like she had done something right for a change. Completely by accident, of course.

''Belly right up to the grill and get yourself a burger,'' Gigi told them, but Ashley disappeared to dish out the potato salad, leaving Polly on her own at the buffet. ''Harvey's only made about a thousand burgers. I guess we're all going to have to eat hearty.''

''You want plain or with cheese?'' a man who must be Harvey asked, holding out two spatulas loaded down with greasy hunks of beef and cheese. He motioned that she should get a bun and he would pile on the burger.

''Hmmm...'' Okay, so she was willing to lie and cheat and be hugged by a stranger. But not even for Cassie was she willing to eat meat. ''I think I'll skip it and go for the salads tonight.''

''Not up for a hamburger, huh?'' It was Michael. She might've known he'd be here, inserting himself into her business every time she turned around. Unfortunately, he'd pretty much cornered her by the condiment table, and there was no way to escape.

Polly made a show of loading up her plate with pickles and olives, ignoring him. But he was hard to ignore. He knew just what buttons to push.

''Nice outfit,'' he mused, raking her up and down with his insolent gaze. ''Very Donna Reed.''

''It's from the store. I work in Better Dresses, you know.''

"I'll bet you do." He was carrying a long-necked beer, and he took a deep swallow. "Your dress reminds me of how different you and Polly are, after all. She wouldn't be caught dead in a dress like that."

"You might be surprised," she muttered, but her words were lost in the blare of honky-tonk music.

Michael leaned closer, dipping his ear nearer her mouth. Near enough to nibble on if she had the hankering. And damn it, she did. He asked, "What did you say?"

"I said that we always dressed differently because people needed some way to tell us apart," she made up on the fly. She crunched a gherkin, hard, hoping he got the message.

"Huh." He took a long draw on his beer. "I never had any trouble telling you apart."

Polly smiled, a tiny, malicious smile. If he only knew. But then, he never had. She remembered sending Cassie to break up with him, and he'd had no clue. And now, here he was, more clueless than before, accepting her as Cassie without a whimper. *You're not doing so hot, Mr. Smarty Pants!*

"You know, Cassie," he went on, proving her point, "I've thought about you a lot over the years."

"You have?" she sputtered, catching a pickle bit at the back of her throat and choking for a breath or two. She could swear... But he couldn't be, could he? Trying to flirt with Cassie? He wasn't that much of a skunk, was he?

His green eyes seemed moody and restless under

the dim light cast by strings of paper lanterns. "Did you think I'd forgotten?"

"Forgotten what?"

"Us."

What "us" was there between Michael and Cassie? Polly was thunderstruck. Never had she even had a hint that the two of them had anything going. But he seemed not to notice her gaping mouth.

He added, "I remember very well the last time I saw you. Right before Polly broke up with me for good. I always wondered what you'd told her—about us, I mean. And if that was the reason she dumped me."

*What? Michael and Cassie?* No, she simply didn't believe it. Michael, maybe, but Cassie would never have done that to her. "She didn't tell me... I mean, *I* didn't tell *her* anything about you. And I don't know what you mean, anyway, because there was nothing to tell."

"Oh, yes, there was," he said in a sardonic, mocking tone, and she could see that he was enjoying torturing her. She wanted to smack him, right across that handsome face.

But she made the mistake of letting her eyes linger on his narrow, clever lips, right where a bead of beer or sweat darkened his upper lip. As she watched, he flicked out his tongue to catch it.

Polly caught her breath, amending her fantasy. First she wanted to smack him, and then she wanted to kiss him, long and hard, until his brother and her sister were nothing more than bad memories.

Why was it that every time she saw him she remembered how long it had been since she'd had a sex life? And why did it seem so all-fired important all of a sudden to kick-start it?

Past Michael, she could see that Gigi's backyard was full of inviting darkness. All she had to do was grab him by his white collar and drag him under the twisted oak or the spreading elm. It might be insane, but it also might be worth it.

"Michael, are you monopolizing the bride?" It was just the senior Mr. Kennigan, but it may as well have been the cavalry.

Polly took a deep breath of the cool May evening air, trying to return her pulse to normal, hoping her face wasn't flushed.

"Cassie, dear, Skipper said to apologize to you. He felt a need to work the room, but he intended to be by your side before this." He frowned. "And now I'm afraid he's had to run Benjy back to the club for his nine-iron. Skipper is helping Benjy with his swing."

"Isn't that kind of him?" she murmured.

"Michael," his father intoned, glancing around the lawn, "there are some people I'd like you to meet. No time like the present to conduct business. If Cassie doesn't mind lending you to me, that is."

"I don't believe he's mine to lend," she said sweetly, not really fond of the old man's implication.

"Just so. Still, it probably doesn't look quite right for the brother of the groom to burden the bride with his presence all night, does it?"

"Sorry. I wouldn't want to burden the bride." With

a little bow in her direction, Michael angled away at his father's elbow, and Polly was free. For now.

So why did she feel so bereft? Pondering her inability to handle her emotions, she found a folding chair under a tree and pretended to be very interested in the olives rolling on her plate. Shouldn't she be relieved that he was finally gone?

But she wasn't. Aside from a little embarrassment at her lack of control, she was mostly feeling dissatisfied, as if there were plenty of things she and Michael had yet to thrash out.

She popped an olive into her mouth. And she was dying to get to the thrashing part.

# 4

*May 23: Nine days before the wedding*

IT WAS DÉJÀ VU all over again.

Six-thirty, alarm clanging, Ashley and Mom railing at her, Skipper waiting in the kitchen... Polly groaned, unwilling to rouse herself.

"Cassie, get out of that bed this instant," her mother said indignantly. "I wish I knew what was wrong with you, sleeping way too late, being so grumpy in the morning. You've never been like this."

"The barbecue ran late, Mom. I didn't get home till—"

"You were home by ten. You had Ashley with you." She shook her head sadly. "Now you're adding lying to the rest of your sins. I swear, Cassandra, you must be sick or something. You didn't even wash your face before you went to bed. I can still see last night's makeup smudged under your eyes."

Okay, so if she had to pretend to be someone, did it have to be someone perfect, the only person in the world who religiously washed her face before she turned in? What a pain!

Her mom edged closer to the bed, her expression

suddenly pinched and suspicious. "Does this have anything to do with Polly?"

"What?" She almost fell out of bed at that one. "Why would it have anything to do with Polly?"

"Well, look at the timing. You went to visit her, maybe the two of you were out carousing or something, and you came back here forgetful and sassy and grouchy." She shook her head. "She must have had a big influence on you over the weekend."

Oh, sure, blame Polly for everything. These people were so unfair. "Did you ever think about the fact I'm getting married very soon and that's serious business? And maybe it's perfectly normal that I would be a little, well, anxious?"

"Okay, okay. I guess you're right," her mother admitted. "But you'd better get out of that bed and get cleaned up and get downstairs. Skipper is waiting. And he brought pork sausage for you."

Oh, joy. Oh, rapture. She didn't eat pork. And what kind of suitor brought sausage to his beloved? Flowers, maybe. But *pork?* "Why would he do that?"

"So I can make it for breakfast for the two of you," Mrs. Tompkins responded, as if it was the most natural thing in the world. She smiled. "And he brought something else, too."

"Don't tell me. He brought me a big ol' ham, a rash of bacon and a side of beef," she said darkly.

"Nope. He brought Michael."

*Oh, lord.* Could it get any worse?

But her mom didn't notice her distress. She was too busy grinning like a possum. "Oh, that Michael. I al-

ways did like him. I can't imagine why Polly broke
up with him."

"Mother," she shot back with spirit, "I would appreciate it if you would not take Michael's side over
Polly's. He was really awful to her, and she is your
daughter, you know." There. Now hadn't she handled
that nicely?

Her mother was unimpressed. "Oh, pooh. Like I'm
not allowed to have an opinion just because I'm somebody's mom. Get over it, Cassie. And get out of bed."

"Couldn't you just once think that maybe Polly was
right to get rid of him?" she persisted.

"Nope. I like him." And Mrs. Tompkins was gone,
back to the kitchen.

Things went downhill from there. Skipper had not
only brought pork and Michael, but he also wanted to
sit next to her and cuddle as he regaled her with tales
of their life to be. First he squeezed her in another
bear hug and then, after she got him to sit down, he
went on and on about some monster house in Pleasant
Valley Estates marked just for them, about whether
they wanted two children or four, and about what
school might be good enough for these mythical kids
to attend.

He was insufferable. In Polly's considered opinion,
Cassie should stay right where she was and never
come back.

Meanwhile, Michael was over at the stove with her
mother, chuckling about omelets and flipping pancakes. Polly kept sneaking glances over there, trying
to figure out what they were up to.

Skipper was clueless. "Don't you love this stuff?" he asked, chowing down on sausage patties hot off the griddle. "Fresh from Kennigan Farms. It doesn't get any better than this."

If he liked it so much, why wasn't he cooking it himself instead of making her mother and Michael do it? And since when did the Kennigans own a farm? When she was young, they'd had a monopoly on everything else in town, from the bank to the department store to the five-and-dime, but they hadn't ventured into farming.

She frowned, listening to Skipper carry on about how successful the pig operation was as she put the pieces together. It seemed the odious Kennigans had gotten even more odious—they were running a mega-hog farm! *Yechhh.* She only hoped her face didn't reflect the disgust she felt in her heart. All those little piggies! All the pollution! The smell! The horror! It was barbaric.

After the third embrace accompanied by a squeeze on her knee under the table, Polly couldn't take it anymore. It was one thing to endure Skipper's affection while her mother looked on, but unbearable with Michael watching. She swatted Skipper's hand. "Remember the Moral Imperative. This can't be good if you're going to stay morally, uh, impaired."

"Cassie!" her mother exclaimed.

But Polly refused to be deterred. "And don't you think all this public display of affection is a little rude while your brother is here?"

"Sorry, honey bunny," Skipper returned with contrition in his voice. "You're right, of course." And he actually looked like he meant it.

"How thoughtful of you, Cassie." Michael's lips curved into a crooked grin as he walked closer, carrying a plate of pancakes. "Didn't want to rub your happiness in my poor, lonely, single face, hmm?"

"Something like that." Inching her chair farther away from Skipper, Polly concentrated on cutting her sausage into tiny pieces and then hiding it under the toast.

Spatula in hand, Michael hovered behind her. "Can I offer you a blueberry pancake?"

"Yes, thank you." More camouflage for the pork bits. As he neatly slid perfect little pancakes onto her plate, Polly remarked, "When did you get so domestic? I don't remember you as the sweat-over-a-hot-stove type."

She read the expression in his eyes loud and clear. *Better than sharing a table with you two lovebirds.*

But what he actually said was, "I got pretty good at it when I was on my own in Paris. Not as good as your mother, of course. She could be a master chef."

"Oh, you!" chirped the master chef in question, obviously thrilled by the compliment.

No wonder he had Mom wrapped around his little finger. Flattery got him everywhere he wanted to go.

"Michael, I think you need to sit down and stop working so hard," Polly said sweetly. "After all, you're a guest." She patted the chair next to her. "Come on. Join us."

"She's right, Michael. You should sit down and relax," Ruth Tompkins ordered. "I can handle this."

That didn't leave him much choice. So he sat, even though she could tell he was reluctant. Taking the seat next to Polly, Michael ate quietly, keeping a close eye on her while his brother blathered on.

She was planning to bill and coo and convince him she was mad for Skipper. But that resolution lasted no more than three seconds.

"Honey bunny, I'm thinking of getting you a fur as your wedding gift. Mum's got a great furrier in St. Louis she thinks I should try. What do you think—fox or sable?"

She almost choked on a hunk of pancake. "Fur? For me? You've got to be kidding. I would never wear fur. Eeeeuw."

Skipper blinked. "But you told Mum that you admired her chinchilla."

"Well, of course I did. And I'm sure it looks lovely on your mother, too," she added hastily. Even though she knew this was not a hot button issue for Cassie, she still felt obligated to keep her sister safe from the temptations of fur. Cassie would thank her later. "But fur is not for me, Skipper. Ever. Remember that, please."

"Hmmm…" It was Michael, getting his two cents in. "This is strange. Last night it was no beef, today I notice you're not very enthusiastic about the pork, and now no fur. If I didn't know better…"

*You'd think I was Polly.* Stupid, stupid, stupid person that she was, climbing up on her ethical high horse when it was more like a Trojan horse.

"You make it sound so funny, like an agenda or something," she said quickly. "But it's really just that I want to fit into my wedding gown, and beef and pork, you know, can really pack on the weight. Why, I'd look just like one of those megahogs! And, fur, sheesh, it adds twenty pounds. Bulky, you know. So that's why I don't want a fur. Besides, it's only May. I want Skipper to give me something I can use right now. Like…"

"Yes?" Skipper asked eagerly.

"I, uh…" She glanced around the kitchen. "How about a blender?"

Michael chuckled. "That's our Cassie. Always practical."

"Exactly," she said smugly. She'd fooled him one more time.

But then he delivered the bomb. "The funny thing is with all this vegetarian and anti-fur talk, you sound a lot more like Polly than you used to." He rubbed his chin. "I remember Polly getting so exasperated with you. Every time she wanted to picket somebody or boycott something, you'd just ignore her. Not ignoring her anymore, I guess?"

"Well, we are twins," she said stiffly. "I guess the older we get, the more alike we become. And sometimes, the things that Polly gets passionate about are good causes. I guess I understand that better than I used to."

"Uh-huh."

But he was looking at her strangely, and she knew she'd better watch her step.

Fortunately, any tension between the two of them went right over Skipper's head. "Gotta run. Dad and I tee off in ten minutes," he told her, dropping a kiss on the top of her head. "Don't forget, tomorrow night's the big party at the club, and last time we talked about it, you said you didn't have a dress yet. Mort and Benjy and some of the other investors will be there, so you'll want to look extra specially pretty. It wouldn't hurt to knock their socks off."

"Socks-knocking is my specialty," she returned, with only a hint of sarcasm.

What had Cassie gotten herself into, anyway? Skipper set her schedule and picked what she ate and where they'd live.... Maybe for her wedding gift, he could sign her up for Stepford Wives R Us. But in fine Cassie fettle, Polly didn't voice any of her objections. "I guess I'll just tootle down to the store and see what's come in since I was there last. That employee discount will come in handy."

"I'm surprised you didn't buy something while you were in Chicago," Michael remarked, arching an eyebrow.

*Well, I would've, if Cassie had told me I needed to.* Instead, she declared, "I prefer the wares at Joseph Kennigan & Sons."

"You really know how to toe the party line, don't you?" Michael asked dryly.

"Of course she does." Skipper chuckled. "Cassie is marrying me, after all. She knows the importance of family loyalty. Of course she'd want her dress to come from Kennigan & Sons.''

Family loyalty... If he only knew how she really felt about the Kennigans. Those megahog-farming robber barons. "Skipper," she began with some asperity, "is there anything on the schedule between now and then?''

"Where's the itinerary I printed for you?''

"I don't know. Upstairs, I guess. But I was thinking..." She was thinking she would much rather sit home in her jammies and have pizza with her little sister and her mom and dad if she could. And not get woken up at the crack of dawn by her dopey fiancé and his good-looking brother. "I was thinking maybe we should wait to see each other until tomorrow night. No breakfast meeting, no picnics, no barbecues. We can both get rested up and ready to rock and roll at that party. What do you think?''

Again, Skipper blinked. "I don't think there's any rock and roll at this party.''

"It was a figure of speech, Skip," Michael put in.

Of course *he* got it, unlike his dim older brother, who appeared to be living in the Stone Age. Darn Michael, anyway, for always clicking with her and making her feel like they had some sort of connection. It was very annoying. But right now... "Well, Skipper, what do you say? Shall we cut to the chase... I mean, can we just see each other tomorrow night?''

Skipper shrugged. "Well, okay, Cassie. I suppose I could omit tomorrow's breakfast and meet up with you at the party. But don't be late—we're the guests of honor again. And don't forget to check your itinerary. I know there are some other things coming up that you shouldn't miss. You know, the final checks with the florist and the bakery and the caterers and all that. Plus, my grandmother. It's all clearly noted on your master schedule.''

''Oh, don't worry. I will be on top of that itinerary like white on rice.'' Phew. A whole day without Skipper. She felt like jumping up and yelling ''Yahoo!'' at the breakfast table. ''Mom, what do you think? Can you and Dad and Ashley and I order a pizza and watch videos tonight?''

''What a super idea, hon,'' her mother said quickly. ''I just wish Polly was here so the whole family could be together.''

Wow, that was a nice thing to say. Polly felt herself getting a little choked up.

But there was one last hurdle. Turning her head, she gazed at Michael. It would be a major relief not to have to worry about him, either. ''And, Michael, will you be attending this party?''

''Wouldn't miss it for the world.''

That's just what she was afraid of.

POLLY TIPTOED away from the TV and into the kitchen.

''Don't forget the pizza wheel,'' her mother called after her.

''I won't. I'll just be a minute.'' Ever so quietly, she lifted the receiver off the wall and dialed her home number. The machine picked up. Damn it! Where was Cassie?

So she tried the cell phone number. For the tenth time.

''The number you have dialed is not in service at this time. If you think you may have misdialed, please hang up and try again.''

What was this? When she'd called before, she'd gotten forwarded to voice messaging.

So she dialed again, and got that same message again. Not in service? Had Cassie broken her phone? Lost it? What?

''Cassie?'' her dad shouted. ''We got the video on hold and the lion's just about to eat that gladiator. Get back in here, will you?''

''Coming, Daddy.'' Short of driving to Chicago herself, she was going to have to trust that Cassie was okay and put her questions and concerns on the back burner.

Maybe she could sort things out and have Cassie's life tied up into a neat, tidy package before she came home.

At this point that seemed as likely as that gladiator not being the lion's lunch.

*May 24: Eight days before the wedding*

THE PLEASANT FALLS high school prom had been held at this very country club some seven years ago, almost seven years to the day.

Polly, of course, had skipped it. But Michael remembered very well what Cassie had worn. White, of course. Something simple and swirly that made her look pure as the driven snow.

Cassie, the prom queen. Michael, the prom king. Their classmates probably thought it was funny matching up one of the Tompkins twins with her sister's boyfriend, making them put their arms around each other and dance to some slow, sappy song.

He'd had a few too many beers out in the parking lot before they got to that phase of the evening. He'd been trying to drown his sorrows, to forget that he was stuck with Lana Pfeiffer when he'd rather have been with Polly. So when it came time for the big dance between the king and the queen, his vision and judgment were fuzzy enough that he could pretend the slinky blonde in his arms was Polly. After all, she looked a hell of a lot like Polly. Looks 10, personality 0.

It was a wretched evening all around, wasn't it?

Michael sipped scotch on the rocks and watched the entrance to the ballroom. When would she arrive? What would she look like? Would she be as beautiful as he recalled from their last appearance in this place?

"Damn it, anyway," he swore, slapping his drink back onto the bar with such force one of the ice cubes popped out.

Why was he so attracted to *Cassie* all of a sudden? When they were young, she had never held any appeal for him at all. The guys on the football and basketball teams, the movers and shakers at PF High, had gone for her in a big way. All that serene sweetness and uncomplicated charm—not to mention the big baby blues and her bouncy chest in a cheerleader sweater— had captivated most of the school, as she flitted from one to another in her dating pool.

But not him. He'd found her a bit too vacant, a lot too blah. Well, not anymore. Now she seemed as vivacious and feisty as Polly ever had.

How in the hell had it happened? He had the hots for his brother's fiancée, for the sister of the girl who had broken his heart. And he didn't know what to do about it.

POLLY WAS extremely nervous. She was used to posh parties and trying to make a good impression, even with celebrities. But somehow the idea of waltzing in front of a bunch of Pleasant Falls' finest was more intimidating.

It was weird how much significance this evening had begun to assume in her imagination. But she'd wanted to feel like part of her family again, and also part of this town. By settling in at home, striking up a friendship with Ashley, reconnecting with her parents over meals and TV, she'd actually begun to feel like maybe she fit in, like she wasn't the square peg anymore.

Tonight was like filling in the other big piece in that puzzle. If she could make it through an important social event at the Pleasant Falls Country Club without falling down or insulting anyone, she would know that she had grown up and succeeded in putting the past behind her.

She'd even compromised on what to wear, adding a little Polly to the overall sleek and serene Cassie mix. The stock at Cassie's department store had been skimpy, anyway, but she finally found a deep coral halter dress that she liked a lot hidden in the Junior Prom section. It was classy—good for Cassie—but a little daring in its cut and color—good for Polly. It even had a shade of cleavage. And it wasn't beige or pink or even peach. No, it was definitely outside the usual neutrals and pastels, thank goodness.

Once again, she was arriving alone. Ashley would be there later, after her volleyball match, and her presence would be welcome.

Polly had hoped her parents would come for moral support, but they begged off. "I've never been inside that country club," her father, a nice, normal man who worked in a hardware store, had said uncomfortably. "And they said you have to wear a tuxedo. I agreed to wear one to the wedding. Isn't that good enough?"

"Please, hon, don't make us go," her mother had added.

How could she? She couldn't. Although she did think maybe Skipper could've bothered to pick her up. Apparently he only ventured into the Tompkins's household in the wee hours of the morning.

But what was the good of being engaged if she didn't even get an escort? She'd have to take that up with Skipper the next time she saw him, which should be any minute.

*Don't chew your lipstick off,* she commanded herself. And then she lifted her chin, thrust her shoulders back, and entered the country club ballroom. *Take that, Pleasant Falls!*

"Cassie, dear, how lovely to see you." Michael's father, the impossibly proper mayor, president of the bank and owner of the department store all rolled into one, greeted her first. His name, like his father's, was Joseph, but being the second Joseph R. Kennigan, he was called "Deuce" by those who knew him well. Skipper was actually the third Joseph R. Kennigan, but he'd been Skipper since he fell off their sailboat when he was four.

Polly was well acquainted with all the details; Michael had been fond of complaining about his family a lot when they were young. They'd had a habit of ditching school and running off to the orchard outside town where they would hide in the apple trees, eat lots and lots of Granny Smiths, engage in rather desperate make-out sessions and talk endlessly about their future.

Michael was upset that his father wanted him to pick one of the family businesses and stay in Pleasant Falls forever. No, they had vowed, they would escape from Pleasant Falls, they would hitchhike all over Europe, swim in the Mediterranean and the Baltic, see the pyramids, make love under the Eiffel Tower, sail with Greenpeace, save the whales and find their destiny together.

Of course none of it had ever happened. Instead, Polly found out he was cheating and dumped him, ravaged the Kennigans in her graduation speech and left town in a huff. Without him.

He'd left, too, and from what she'd heard—relayed by Cassie and others—he'd slid through a series of colleges and jobs, ending up doing something with a chic magazine and a bevy of supermodels in Paris. It was hardly whale-saving, but then she was working in PR, wasn't she? Hardly the Peace Corps. But at least both of them had escaped.

Meanwhile, back in Pleasant Falls, his family didn't seem to have changed much.

At the moment, Joseph II, aka Deuce, was wearing a tuxedo, and he had his even more proper wife on his arm. They stood there, stiff and uncompromising, looking down their noses at everyone else in the room. Deuce unbent enough to say, "You're looking, uh, vibrant, this evening."

She took that as a compliment and bestowed a brilliant smile on him. He seemed to appreciate it, but not his wife.

"Cassie," she said with enough chill to raise penguins, "what an interesting color and, uh, décolletage. Not your usual style, is it?"

"Skipper asked me to knock people's socks off. This is my best attempt," Polly responded with a chill of her own.

Mrs. Kennigan nodded. "Perhaps we should have a talk with Skipper."

"Where is he?" Polly inquired. Not that she really wanted to hang out with Skipper, but she supposed she should at least stand next to him long enough to smile at the investors he wanted to impress.

Deuce volunteered, "I saw Skipper on the terrace

not too long ago. He and Mort Thorsen were smoking cigars and trying out a new three-wood.''

Polly had no idea what that was, but she knew a terrace from a hole in the ground. Not that she wanted to get caught in cigar smoke. *Bleah.* "Fine, then. I'll just mingle till I find my, um, fiancé."

She hesitated, wanting to ask where Michael was, too, if only so she knew not to go there. But it was just too embarrassing to ask his parents, especially since his mother was already giving her the fish-eye.

Her head held high, she sailed across the ballroom, keeping an eye out for either Skipper or Michael. A waiter with a tray of champagne neared her, and she gratefully took a flute of bubbly. A drink was exactly what she needed to make this evening bearable.

Meanwhile, where was Michael? She didn't know any of these people, and although she felt sure she looked good, her confidence was beginning to wobble. Maybe it was time to retreat to the ladies' room and check on her makeup.

But as she entered, two women standing in front of the mirror abruptly halted what had been an animated conversation. *They were talking about me.* She'd assumed this sort of thing never happened to Cassie, that it was just the awkward sister who caught all the flak. But maybe it wasn't so fun being the perfect sister, either.

Quickly, she pulled a lipstick out of her beaded bag, reapplied it, and then got out of there. She snagged another glass of champagne and moved further away from the center of action, patrolling the fringe, hoping to find Skipper and get her obligations over with, or maybe Ashley, so the two of them could laugh about what a stuffy, unpleasant party it was.

Instead, she saw Michael.

His tux fit perfectly, emphasizing his dark good looks and slim, elegant build. He had that same crooked smile that made her knees weak, and his eyes met hers where she stood beside a pillar. She had to lean against it for support. Her body seemed to fill with relief and joy, as if she knew she were welcome and wanted somewhere. It had always been that way with Michael. He was her safe harbor.

Almost without thinking, she took a step in his direction.

But behind her, not far from the pillar, a female voice whispered, ''Did you see that?''

''What?''

''Cassie Tompkins. She's all tarted up in this red dress cut down to here and up to there, and she's slugging back booze like there's no tomorrow. Mindy said one of her boobs fell out of her dress and she had to run to the bathroom to sling it back in.''

Apparently they didn't realize how far their voices carried. Polly stayed where she was, obscured by the pillar, unwilling to come out in the open and see their faces.

''No!'' the second one whispered back, sounding all agog.

''Oh, yeah. And did you hear that she was all over Michael Kennigan at Harvey and Gigi's barbecue? Lynette saw them, and she said it was disgusting.''

"Michael?"

"Uh-huh. She's just a gold digger. She's marrying Skipper for the money, but carrying on with Michael on the side."

Wow, they didn't pull any punches, did they? Gold digger, huh? And here she'd been sure that word went out of fashion in the 1920s. She tossed back the rest of her champagne.

"Who wouldn't, though, with Michael, I mean?" the other one giggled. "That man is like sex on a stick."

"I'd like to get a hold of his stick."

Oh, please. As if Michael would let either of these vicious twits near his...stick. Or any other part of him.

"Supposedly—and nobody knows for sure whether she'll really do it—Polly is going to come back to be the maid of honor. Can you believe it?"

"She won't really come back, will she? The Kennigans would ride her out of town on a rail."

"Even worse, what's going to happen when Polly finds out Cassie has been going at it with Michael? She always had a really hot temper, you know. Could be fireworks."

"I don't know. But I can't wait to find out."

And the giggling got louder.

Polly had been dealing with jerks like that since she was twelve. For Cassie's sake, she wanted to punch their nasty little lights out and give them an up-close-and-personal look at the truth. She didn't.

Instead, she pasted a smile on her face and circled around the pillar, back the other way, right in front of the gossiping harpies, just a couple of girls she vaguely remembered from high school. They'd been jealous, small-minded bimbos even then.

She forced herself to keep smiling as she passed them, noting with pleasure that they couldn't meet her eyes. But she kept on going, out the French doors and onto the terrace, down the stone steps, across the cultivated lawn and into a gazebo she hadn't even known was there.

Refuge.

The night air was cool and refreshing and she told herself she felt a lot better already. "I guess I forgot what it was I hated so much about living in a small town," she murmured, curling a hand around one of the wooden posts. "So now I know. Big deal."

"Cassie?"

She whirled. Of course Michael had known to follow her. The connection between them had never really been severed, had it?

Except that he'd just called her Cassie.

She wanted to fly into his arms, feel his lips on hers, his arms hard around her. But she held her ground. She tried to speak, but the air had become thick and heavy, and she couldn't seem to get enough of it into her lungs.

"Cassie?" he said again.

Barely breathing, she whispered, "Hello, Michael."

# 5

"WHY DID YOU leave the party?" He took a step closer, close enough to smell her perfume across the small gazebo. The fragrance was something sensual and fiery, perfect for a woman in a flame-colored dress.

What defense could a poor, hapless man muster? He'd already tried sarcasm, teasing and even rudeness, and it hadn't changed his feelings at all. He still wanted her.

"Why did you leave?" he asked again.

After a moment, she came up with a small smile. "It was a bit close in there. I needed some air."

Her voice was cool, but he could see the hurt in her crystal blue eyes. Back inside, their gazes had met, and he'd seen her make a move toward him, but then she'd disappeared behind a pillar. By the time he'd found her, she was sweeping from the ballroom, blistering two women with a contemptuous glare, and making a beeline for the gazebo.

Something had happened in there. Anger had given her cheeks a rosy glow and put a sparkle of indignation in her eyes. He didn't know what had upset her, but whatever it was, it had made Cassie even more desirable.

"How about you? Why did you leave?" she inquired.

"I followed you." But they both already knew that, didn't they?

He shouldn't have followed her. But he did. And now, looking at her, wanting her more than he had wanted anything in years, he knew he was in deep, deep trouble.

She spun away, gazing out over a railing into the dark night, and he could see the pale skin of her slender leg, visible almost to the thigh through the deep slit in her skirt. He wanted to slide his hand into that slit, to feel the heat of her skin there and everywhere, to pull her up against him and never let go. He wanted to touch her so badly his hands were trembling.

Frustrated and upset with himself, Michael jammed his hands into his pants pockets.

"I know something happened in there." He paused. "Did it have anything to do with me?"

When she turned back to face him, her mouth fell open slightly, and she licked her bottom lip, sending even more pain and pleasure to his jagged nerves. "Why would you think that?"

He'd forgotten what he'd asked. "What?"

"That I left the ballroom because of you."

"Oh." He tried to jerk himself back to reality and forget about her pretty pink tongue and her creamy thigh and the way her breasts mounded so beautifully in that halter dress, almost spilling out, but not quite. "I just…" He swallowed. "I know it's been awkward between you and me, and I didn't want to think that

I had done anything to upset you or make you feel you had to leave.''

She shook her head. ''You? Does everything have to do with you?'' she asked, her words softened by the gentleness in her expression.

''Sometimes it seems that way.''

''To me, too,'' she whispered.

He couldn't resist moving nearer, placing his own hand on the same wooden post she was holding, trapping her there in the moonlight. Bending his head, he inhaled her scent, almost brushing his lips against her neck. She was so very near, so vulnerable, so warm and soft. She closed her eyes, curving into him, too, and he knew she wanted him to kiss her. He placed his lips against hers, just for a second, but he heard her swift intake of breath, and he pulled back.

''I'm feeling very confused,'' he admitted in a rough, shaky voice. ''I am so attracted to you, but the thing is… It's *you*.''

She slipped under his outstretched arm, eluding his grasp. Her voice held more than a hint of agitation when she said, ''It's just because I look like Polly. We both know there's a history there. It's no wonder you're confused.''

''I know, but…'' He broke off, trying to start again and rearrange his thoughts into something more reasonable. *Good luck.* He'd lost his reason about the time he saw her in that dress. ''Cassie, you aren't the same person you were in high school. And whatever I did or didn't feel for Polly once upon a time, well,

. it was a long time ago. She's not here, is she? And we are."

"Love the one you're with, huh?"

At that, she gave him such a withering glare he couldn't believe he was still standing. Sisterly loyalty? Or just disgust because he was such a dog? Her sister, his brother... There were so many ways he was beneath contempt.

"I don't want to feel this," he confessed, trailing one finger down her bare arm, watching her shiver in reaction. "But I do. It's like…chemistry. Amazing chemistry."

"Good for you. But I'm not interested." She pushed away from him, the shimmery fabric of her dress rustling as she tried to escape out the other side of the gazebo.

"Cassie, don't." He caught her arm and held her there. "Please."

"We can't do this." But she didn't move.

"We can. Just for now. For tonight. We can."

"But they're already talking about us, and Skipper…" She shook her head. "He will be so hurt."

"I know. But Cassie, I want you."

Pulling her by the hand, he reeled her in, deep into his arms, and then he lowered his head, covering her mouth with his. Sweet, moist, tasting of heat and passion and champagne, she was magnificent. Bracketing her face with his hands, mussing her makeup and tousling her hair, he plunged inside her mouth, taking what he needed, pushing them both into a dark, dangerous place.

Finally, she dragged herself away, gasping for breath. "Oh, Michael," she breathed, and she reached out to press one hand into his tuxedo front, as if to steady herself. But her eyes were heavy-lidded, luminous with desire, and he knew she was no more sated than he was.

He wanted to start again, softer this time. He wanted to sink to the floor of the gazebo and make love to her under the stars.

What was he thinking? This was *Cassie.* He had to keep reminding himself that this lovely, lithe blonde was Cassie, not Polly. Whoever she was, it was much too easy to fall into the old patterns, to reach for her because he had always reached for her, to recreate that sense of rightness and belonging.

She had grown so much like the Polly of his heart it was eerie. But she wasn't Polly, damn it.

"I'm sorry, Cassie. I have no excuse for my behavior. After what happened before, when we were kids, I have to be out of my mind."

"What? You mean with Polly?"

Oh, jeez. She was still denying it? "No, I mean with *you.* You know what happened before."

"I do not! I'm... I'm... I'm not who you think," she finished with an air of desperation, edging away from him.

"Yes, you are. You're Cassie. I know that."

"That's not what I—"

"Don't worry," he interrupted. He knew what she was going to say: *You're confused. I'm not my sister. Polly is who you really want. Blah, blah, blah.* He had already made those same arguments to himself. "I know quite well who you are and I know all the reasons this is such a bad idea, and I don't care." He swore, a particularly brutal curse, and thumped himself in the head. "I want you even more. Now that I know what it's like. Oh, God. I'm an idiot."

"You're not an idiot." As she moved closer, compassion glowed in her features, and that only made it worse. She laid her warm hands on his cheeks, gazing right into his eyes. "Michael, this isn't your fault. You have to trust me. There's something I need to tell you, and—"

"Hey, you up there!"

The tiny, insistent voice came from below them, down on the lawn. Michael moved swiftly to block Cassie from view. "What do you want?"

A small figure in a white slip dress appeared on the steps, peering up into the dim gazebo. "It's me. Ashley. I just… Well, I was looking for, um, Cassie, and I could hear you and I thought maybe I'd better…" She screwed up her mouth and chewed on the inside of her cheek, thinking for a minute. And she glanced back at the ballroom. "There are all kinds of people running around, and I thought maybe I'd better, kind of, rescue you before anybody else saw you. Sorry."

He could hear Cassie's sigh, as if she had landed back in real life with a thud, and he knew he'd lost her.

"Don't be sorry, Ash," she said. She whipped around him and sped down the stairs. "Your timing is incredible. Fabulous. Perfect." With her arm around her younger sister, she hustled away into the darkness. And away from him. Which was exactly what he deserved. Thank goodness one of them was still thinking with some small portion of a brain.

"Damn it, Michael," he muttered. "That was low, even for you."

He had kissed his brother's fiancée outside the club where they were having an engagement party. And it wasn't just any kiss, either. It was one of those once-in-a-lifetime, soul-deep kisses. How could he?

The really rotten part was that he was behaving just as badly as his family had always expected him to. The black sheep had returned, and he was worse than ever.

He swore loudly and bashed his hand against the railing. "Damn it, Michael."

POLLY'S LEGS were longer, so she knew Ashley must have really had to hustle to get in front of her. Scrambling backward, her little sister demanded, "What did you think you were *doing?*"

"Something really stupid," Polly said tersely. "Okay? It was stupid. Is that good enough?" She shook her head, trying to end Michael's spell and regain some control. "The worst part is that I almost told him. I was right there, going to tell him. Thank God you interrupted."

She groaned. Michael was tearing himself apart because he was attracted to her, except it wasn't her, it was her sister. "I can't ever tell him. Not now. I wanted to because I didn't want him to be so hard on himself. But after this... I don't think Michael would take this too kindly. I think he'd stick me in front of a firing squad in about three seconds flat.''

''You almost told him?'' Ashley shrieked. ''What were you thinking?''

''Clearly, I wasn't thinking.''

''Oh, brother!'' Her little sister stopped in her tracks. ''It was bad enough, what you were *doing*. I mean, during a *party?* In a *gazebo?* How smart was that?''

Polly winced. ''Well, you know, we had all our clothes on, so how bad could it be?''

''Like, *bad!*'' Ashley retorted. ''Your hair is all messed up and your mouth is all puffy and you were looking at him and he was looking at you, like, *sheesh*, like, total lust magnets, you know?''

''What do you know about lust magnets?''

''Oh, please,'' her teenage sister scoffed. ''I do get MTV, not to mention HBO.''

''You should stop watching those channels. They're clearly not good for you.''

''Me? I'm not the one going hanky-panky-spanky at the country club with half the town watching!''

Hanky-panky-spanky? She didn't even want to know.

Polly strode on, concentrating on her footing so she didn't take a header or sprain an ankle on the lush lawn. That was all she needed.

They were circling around the outside of the place and heading for the car. She had no intention of going back into the ballroom after steaming up the gazebo with Michael. Her sister's reputation would never be the same if people knew what had transpired out there. Unless of course she let the cat out of the bag and said, *Surprise! It's me, Polly!*

A part of her really wanted to come clean, especially to Michael. But if she was persona non grata in this town after one cranky graduation speech, what would she be if they found out about The Grand Switcheroo? Tarred and feathered, that's what. And it wasn't just herself she had to worry about.

*Cassie, you made a fool of your boss, Gigi, and her husband, the bank guy, and Mr. and Mrs. Mayor Deuce Kennigan, not to mention Skipper Kennigan, so you are banned from town for life.*

*And Polly, since you've been known to badmouth Pleasant Falls and now you are the one who perpetrated the fraud, not to mention played hanky-panky-spanky with Michael Kennigan in the country club gazebo, we will stick you up to your neck in a sand trap on the fifteenth green and leave you there. And Michael, the person you were torturing, gets to tee off on your head.*

"Polly, you forgot to say goodbye to Skipper," Ashley told her in her best Miss Know-It-All tone. "Won't he think it's funny if we just leave without saying goodbye?"

"I never even said hello. I never saw him."

"Why not?"

Polly shrugged, resolute in her mission to skirt around the grounds of the entire building to get to the parking lot. "He was busy, okay?"

"But don't you think he'll be mad you ditched him tonight?" Ashley persisted.

"I really doubt he'll even notice."

"He'll notice if someone tells him you were making out in the gazebo with his brother."

Too wise for her years, that child. "No one saw us," Polly maintained.

"I did."

"No one but you."

"You hope."

"Ashley, give it a rest! I already said it was stupid. I just…" She sighed. "I overheard some people talking, and they were saying really mean things, about Cassie and about me and about really dumb stuff that doesn't matter, anyway. But at the time it kind of upset me and I went out to the gazebo to be alone. And Michael followed me. I needed a friend."

"Didn't look like friends to me," she said with major teenage attitude.

"There are friends and then there are friends." Polly moved quickly to something else. "I know I have a problem. I shouldn't have been there with him, and I never should've let it get that far."

*Because now I am going to be haunted by the taste of that kiss for the rest of my life.* She shook herself out of it as best she could.

"You're a mess, Poll. And you make a terrible Cassie."

"I know. I seem to have this weakness for Michael. It's always been that way. He touches me and I sort of melt into a puddle."

"Gross."

"Exactly." Polly hesitated, peeking around the corner of the clubhouse to see if there was a clear path to the car. "I have no willpower when it comes to Michael. It *is* gross."

"This is so bad, Polly." Ashley's eyes were round and earnest. "If you keep melting into puddles with Michael, Skipper will have to find out. And he'll get really ticked at Cassie, don't you think? And then what?"

Polly signaled that the coast was clear, and she and Ashley made a break across the parking lot. "I'm not sure Skipper really cares." She wrinkled her forehead, adding up what had happened so far. "He didn't pick me up at the train because he was at the club with his daddy, he left the barbecue without me because he was trying to schmooze this Benjy guy and when I got here tonight, he was out smoking and playing with his wood."

Ashley burst out laughing at that one.

"Excuse me," Polly said delicately. "I believe it was his two- or possibly three-wood, which is some sort of golf club."

"It still sounds funny."

"I don't care. The basic idea here is that Skipper pays no attention to me and, by extension, to Cassie. He is caught up in his horrible development deals and pork bellies, and he doesn't even know Cassie." Polly set her mouth in a firm line. "Cassie deserves better. I can't believe that you and Mom and Dad let her get engaged to that fathead."

"Mom likes him because he's polite and he brings pork sausage for breakfast all the time," Ashley noted. "She says he's a good eater and will be a good provider."

"That's archaic!"

"Uh-huh. Dad likes him because he comes by the hardware store and talks nails and screws. And me, well, I never did like him."

Polly opened the passenger door for her sister. "So why does Cassie like him?"

"Maybe she doesn't." Ashley lumped herself into the car, musing, "Maybe that's why she's not here and you are. Because she doesn't really like him, and when it came down to it, she had to leave or else she'd have to marry him and she didn't want to marry him, so she left."

Polly buckled herself into the driver's seat and started the car. Thank goodness the engine on her parents' old Dodge roared to life immediately. She was so looking forward to being away from the country club and its seductive gazebo.

"You think I'm right, don't you?" Ashley blurted. "Cassie isn't coming back, is she? And we have to tell Skipper. And we have to tell Mom and Dad! Oh, no! They are going to be super mad. At us! Because we fooled them. They'll think it's all our fault!"

"Ash, don't do this."

"No, I'm totally serious," Ashley wailed. "It's all *your* fault, Polly, because if you hadn't said you'd trade places, then she never would've started all this. And now she's never coming back!"

"Cassie will be here on schedule, and she will get married, and everything will be fine," she said soothingly. "She promised. And we both know that Cassie is the most responsible person we've ever met."

But suddenly Polly had the strangest feeling Ashley might have hit on something. After all, she herself had left tons of messages for Cassie and still hadn't managed to track her down or talk to her.

The last time she'd tried the cell phone, it had been completely out of service, as if Cassie had dropped it in the bathtub or thrown it under a taxi or something. She'd done her best not to think about it, but it was hard to ignore. Maybe Cassie was never coming back. Maybe Cassie had run away from all of them, and had left it up to Polly to pick up the pieces.

"Okay," she said out loud. "I am not going to panic. She may very well be busy with the Wild Man and not even realize that I called so many times. For all I know, the he threw the phone under a taxi. That's possible. That's even plausible."

"Who's the Wild Man? And why does he throw phones under taxis?" Ashley asked in confusion.

"It's a long story. Let's just say that Cassie is pretending to be me, and I was supposed to take this nutty guy who calls himself the Wild Man around Chicago, so Cassie is doing it instead."

Everything was so muddled. How had she let it get this way? How had she let her sweet, naïve sister take on Hiram "Wild Man" Wright when he was certifiable?

"He really is nutty," she went on, feeling more

uneasy by the minute, "and he likes to, you know, fight bulls and wrestle alligators and live by his wits in the jungle. So it's possible he threw my cell phone under a taxi, or even a rhino."

"I don't get it."

"I don't, either. I'm just thinking of reasons why Cassie hasn't called me." She was seized by the sudden, horrifying idea that maybe Cassie was hurt, that she was lying in a hospital somewhere and that was why she was incommunicado. But no. With Cassie carrying loads of Polly's ID, any injury would've been reported back to Pleasant Falls immediately.

And there was the other part—the twin thing. If anything was really wrong with Cassie, Polly knew in her heart she would be aware.

Phew. That was a relief. But she wished she hadn't raised such scary images in the first place.

Her little sister reached over to pat Polly's arm gently. "I'm sure Cassie will come home. You're right, Poll. She's the most responsible person we know."

"That's right, Ash. That's right." Although there was the other side of the coin. The side that said maybe it was good for Cassie to be on the lam. "But what if…?"

"What if what?"

Polly pulled the car into the garage, killed the motor and glanced at her little sister. "If we love Cassie, shouldn't we save her from Skipper?"

"Huh?"

"Maybe it's our duty to save Cassie from pork sausage and fur coats and a house at Pleasant Valley Estates.''

Emboldened by this new idea, Polly was starting to feel more like herself already. Throw off the indecisive, careful persona, and go back to impetuous, bold Polly! The more she thought about it, the more reasonable it seemed. And she was filled with a curious kind of joy and energy all of a sudden.

"Cassie deserves better," she said with conviction. "So maybe we owe it to her to mess things up with Skipper so royally that the wedding will be off and she can leave town and never have to worry about that miserable guy again."

She smiled, waiting for validation from Ashley. But her sister shook her head. "Oh, no, you don't."

"Why not?"

"That would be convenient, wouldn't it?" Ashley pursed her lips. "I see right through you. What you're doing is giving yourself a free ticket to fool around with Michael while you tell yourself you're just doing it for Cassie, so Skipper will dump her and she will be saved from being married to him. Pretty slick, Poll."

"That's not what I meant. I never said I was going anywhere near Michael," she protested.

"That is so what you meant." Ashley jumped out of the car and slammed the door. "First you said you were going to stay away from him and there was a wall between you and all that, and then all you do is hang around him. You're trying to screw it up for Cassie."

Polly exited the car more slowly, carefully closing her door. She was trying to act mature, but it wasn't working. Over the top of the car, she explained the situation to her sister. "I swear, he keeps hanging around with me, not vice versa. I tried to stay away from him. But I woke up and there he was at the breakfast table. Mom let him in, not me! And at the barbecue, he cornered me by the pickle table. And tonight, I told you *he* followed *me*. It's really annoying, Ash, because he has the hots for me, only he thinks I'm Cassie!"

Ashley crossed her arms over her narrow chest. "That's just an excuse." Mockingly, she chanted, "It's not my fault if he follows me. I'm too dumb to say no."

Polly didn't want to give in on this, but she was running out of arguments. Oh, hell. If only Ashley would make less sense. "I tried to stay away from him," she mumbled. It wasn't convincing, even to her own ears.

"But what if Cassie never comes back because you make such a mess with Skipper that she can't?" her sister argued. "That's not fair. And it's not fair to decide for her. If Skipper is what she wants—I mean, after she chills out or whatever—then we shouldn't be deciding she can't have him."

"No," Polly admitted. "We shouldn't."

"Look, Poll, I know Michael is really cute and hot. But while everyone thinks you're Cassie, it's wrong to be kissing him in the gazebo when Skipper could see,'' Ashley said sternly. ''Even I know that's wrong.''

''On so many levels...'' Polly put her head down on her arms, balancing on the roof of the car, giving in completely. How humiliating to know that her four-teen-year-old sister knew more about relationships than she did. ''Ash, honey, you are so right and I am so wrong. I've been focusing on Skipper and what's wrong with him, when I should be looking at myself.''

''Is there something wrong with you?''

''Lots and lots of things,'' Polly said hopelessly. ''For one thing, I keep telling myself I am not going to make the same mistake I made before, and then I do it. I'm a smart person. So why is it that he winks at me, he crooks a finger, and I melt? I mean, I'm a puddle, just like that, when Michael has proved he can't be trusted.''

Ashley kept nodding as Polly got warmed up.

''I am not falling for Michael Kennigan again,'' she vowed. ''I'm furious—do you hear?—*furious,* that he would kiss Cassie. Because that's what he thought he was doing tonight. Sure, it was me. But he doesn't know that! He thought he was cheating on me with my twin sister and he did it anyway!''

''Um, Poll?'' Ashley interjected. ''Like, I don't want to get you off track or anything, but that isn't exactly true. I mean, you did break up with him half a lifetime ago, and he can't be expected to still be true. D'ya think?''

''Half your lifetime, Ash. But not that long ago in mine.'' She heaved a big sigh, unwilling to relent now that she had summoned up this righteous anger. "Okay, okay, so it was long enough ago that he isn't really betraying me. But he sure as heck is betraying his brother. Cassie is engaged to Skipper, and Michael put the moves on anyway. Wrong, wrong, wrong."

"Good one, Poll!"

"Plus there's this secret between him and Cassie that he keeps hinting at." Polly narrowed her eyes. "I keep trying to get ahold of Cassie to find out what that's all about but, of course, there's the phone problem. But he's making it sound as if he cheated on me with Cassie when we were still in high school, and he thinks that I know too, and that's why I broke up with him."

"You lost me," Ashley put in, shaking her head.

"I lost myself, too. I still don't get it." She walked around to the other side of the car, joining her sister near the door to the house. "But I know Cassie would never have betrayed me with Michael. Never."

"So what are you going to do?"

"Stay away from him. For real. I've started enough gossip going in this town, and it's time to stop it, to be the most dutiful and all-around best bride-to-be that Pleasant Falls has ever seen," she promised.

"I don't know," Ashley said doubtfully. "That doesn't sound like you."

"All I can do is try. I'm a very competent person, Ash. Well, not *that* competent. But I think I can—"

She broke off when the door into the house creaked open, silhouetting their father. "Hey, ladies, what are you doing out in the garage all this time? Mom's got cookies and milk for you before you go to bed, so come on in, will you?''

Cookies and milk. It was so cute!

As his daughters filed in through the door he held open, he took a good look at Polly. "Hon, you're a mess. What'd you do tonight, take a roll in the park? You've got grass all over your hem and your hair looks like you've been in a tornado.''

"Don't even ask, Dad." The most dutiful and best bride-to-be that Pleasant Falls had ever seen, she reminded herself. "Don't even ask.''

# 6

*May 25: One week before the wedding*

Déjà vu all over again.

Alarm clanging at 6:30 a.m., Ashley and Mom railing at her, Skipper waiting in the kitchen... Polly groaned and hid her head under the pillow.

"Don't I even get a break on Saturday?" she asked no one in particular. So much for her new resolution to be the best bride-to-be ever.

But at least this time she got up and got dressed without a whole lot of argument, and she found a nice beige outfit to wear without even griping about the color. Last night's vibrant coral halter dress was hanging in the closet, but she ripped it off the hanger and tossed it into the back somewhere. It was way too Polly and way too flashy to find a place in this wardrobe.

But then she retrieved it and hung it off to the side. She could always take it back to her own closet after the masquerade was over. Waste not, want not.

Plastering a smile on her face, breathing deeply and reciting Zen affirmations, she did her best to project calm and serenity as she entered the kitchen.

No Michael. Thank heaven for small blessings. Now she could breathe normally again.

Skipper leapt to his feet and hugged her, just as before, with no indication that he was miffed about missing her at the party last night, or that he had heard even a hint of gossip about her and Gazebo Boy. He rattled on about Benjy and Mort and the land deal and how he had really leaned on the two of them to sign on the dotted line, and everything was just ducky....

Polly lost track. Mom was making waffles this morning—heart-shaped waffles—and Polly breathed in the delicious smells, pouring on the syrup, enjoying her food a lot more than she was enjoying Skipper.

But she was jolted back to reality when he asked, "Did you have a good time last night?"

"When?"

"Last night. The party." He paused. "Dad and Mum said they saw you and you looked amazing. I'm sorry I missed you." He filled his mouth with waffle, so his voice was muffled by the food when he said, "Couldn't be helped."

"You didn't see her last night?" her mother gasped in outrage. "But she was gorgeous. Like a movie star!"

It was extremely unusual for Mom to interrupt or take issue with someone, especially a male someone. And she looked positively livid.

"I can't believe you didn't even see her. The dress! The hair!" Ruth Tompkins slammed a platter with more waffles smack in front of Skipper. "I can't believe you didn't see her."

"I was busy," he said in a rather whiny voice.

''And it will be for the best in the end because this deal with Mort and Benjy is important to both of us and our future, isn't it, Cassie, honey?''

''I—I don't know.'' *Best bride-to-be ever.* ''I suppose.''

But her mother wasn't cowed. She stood behind Polly, placing her hands on her daughter's shoulders as if she were her avenging angel. ''If my daughter dresses like a princess to be with you at an engagement party, then you darn well better escort her and ogle her and make a fuss over her because she deserves it. Hrmph.''

And with that, completely out of character, Mrs. Tompkins stalked out of the kitchen, leaving the two of them to get their own coffee and clear their own plates and all sorts of unusual things.

''That was odd,'' Skipper decided. ''You and your mother are both acting a little strange these days. Must be the stress of the wedding. Because I would hate to think it was the way things were going to be.'' He drew his eyebrows together. ''You know, this could be in your genes. Because, you *are* a twin and your twin has always been…''

''Herself?''

''Well, yes, but… I meant that she isn't like you, the way you're solicitous and considerate and sweet,'' he said hastily. ''And she is…''

''And she is…?''

''Always running off at the mouth and causing trouble.''

''That's our Polly.'' She wanted to smash his head right into his plate, but she held herself back. *Best bride-to-be ever*. She manufactured a big, evil grin. "We're very different, but I suppose Polly and I are also alike in some ways. And you're right—everyone has always thought that I took after Mom while no one really knew where Polly came from. Not the milkman or anything. That would be tough for an identical twin."

He didn't even realize she was being sarcastic, did he? Whoosh, right over his head.

"But now," she went on, "I'm coming to the conclusion that Polly takes after Mom, too. The feisty part of Mom. So maybe I have a feisty part, too." She smiled. "Better watch out, Skip."

He blinked his watery eyes. "I hope not. You're joking, right?"

"Yeah, I'm joking." She rose from the table and began to stack the plates and cups to take to the dishwasher. *Cassie, Cassie, what have you signed on for?* Polly understood even better her twin's need to escape. And she began to hope and pray that Cassie had changed her mind about going through with the wedding while on parole. *Just come back, Cass. We can sort it out*. She would tell her sister that if she could.

Skipper cleared his throat. "Speaking of Polly, I forgot to tell you…"

She glanced over at him. "Hmm?" she asked vaguely.

"Polly. She called yesterday."

Polly almost dropped three plates and a pile of silverware. "She did what?"

"She called."

"My sister called?"

"Yes, that's what I said. Yesterday was the day I wasn't supposed to come by for breakfast but I forgot and came by anyway, and when I walked in, no one was here but the phone was ringing, so I answered it. It was Polly." He paused, tipping his head to one side. "Boy, do you two sound alike. I thought it was you for a minute."

"Really? You did? Isn't that funny." Polly sat back down in a rush. "Did she say anything else?"

"Let me think," he said with a puzzled frown. "She said she was pretty frazzled with work, but everything was going fine and she didn't want you to worry. She said you shouldn't try to get her on her cell phone, because... Well, it was odd. She said a wild man had thrown the phone off a balcony in Cleveland. Does that make any sense to you?"

Polly jumped to her feet. "Cleveland? What were they doing in Cleveland?"

"You know Polly, always in some kind of trouble," he said smugly.

Aside from the fact that that was completely untrue, if Polly had been with the Wild Man, they wouldn't have been in Cleveland, they would've stayed in Chicago like they were supposed to. Polly was very happy to hear that her sister was okay, but *still*... She paced back and forth on her mother's linoleum. How did Cassie get to Cleveland? And why did she let the Wild Man throw Polly's cell phone off a balcony?

"That doesn't sound good." On the other hand, maybe Skipper had mixed up some of the message.

But Skipper wasn't listening. "She also asked about

me, which was kind of surprising, since I always got the impression she didn't care much for me.''

''I'm sure you're wrong.''

''Probably.'' He added, ''Anyway, I told her I was fine and you were fine and I didn't say anything about Michael being here because I didn't want to upset her. She said to tell you that she loved you and she would see you soon.''

''Good,'' she said fervently.

But Polly's head was spinning. Cassie had actually called and had the bad luck to get Skipper. My, my. Fate kept playing tricks on them, didn't it?

But at least now she knew her sister was still alive and kicking and the Wild Man hadn't fed her to lions or anything. And it even sounded as if she still planned to be back soon. Bless her heart.

''So, honey bunny, I have to get going.'' Brisk and hearty, Skipper pushed himself away from the table. ''I know you have a full day.''

''I do?''

''Honey bunny, where is your head?''

A lot of people had been asking her that lately, without the ''honey bunny.''

Skipper continued, ''Did you even look at your list for today?''

''I did. But there wasn't anything on it,'' she swore.

''What about the florist and the bakery and the harpist and the final fitting for your wedding gown?'' he asked, ticking items off on his fingers. ''And you're supposed to stop by the church too, because Reverend Vance wanted to talk to you about verses and vows and things. I know those are all on the list and you haven't done them yet, have you?''

"Those weren't on today's schedule," she protested. "Those were on..." Oops. "Yesterday's. I guess in my quest for the perfect dress for the country club party, I forgot."

"My little noodlehead," he said fondly, giving her that same repulsive squeeze that he gave her every morning. "But you'd better get them done today, do you hear me? One week till the wedding!"

"I know, I know." She wanted to know why all these silly wedding details were her job instead of *their* job. It wasn't as if any of the things he wanted were that tough. If Cassie were here and wanted Polly's company to go to the florist or the bakery, she would've been happy as a clam to ride along. But by herself, pawing through all of the things Skipper and Cassie had picked out... Yuck.

Still, she was trying to be as solicitous and considerate and sweet as her sister. No running off at the mouth or causing trouble.

Glancing around the kitchen, Polly realized she needed to apply herself to something, fast, before she lost her temper. So she dumped the last utensils into the dishwasher and started to scrub the waffle iron. Maybe this would assuage her guilt at always leaving messes behind for her mother. Not that Skipper seemed to have any such scruples.

"I'm off," he called out, pushing his way out the screen door. "Tee time!"

"See ya." Her mood was dark, but she actually felt better after she straightened up the kitchen and started a load in the dishwasher. She wasn't the most domestic person in the world, but she did like a clean kitchen.

With Skipper safely gone, her mother returned. "I didn't mean to snap at Skipper, hon. Sometimes he makes me so mad, though." She set her hands on her hips. "I wonder if he appreciates you the way he should."

"I know, Mom. I wonder the same thing."

"Well, you think about it, okay?" Her mother, who was a good four inches shorter than her twins, stretched up to kiss Polly on the cheek. "You don't be afraid to cut him down to size, you hear me?"

If only Cassie were here to hear it. "Sure, Mom."

For the first time, Mrs. Tompkins noticed that the kitchen had been cleaned. "Oh, honey, you didn't have to do that."

"I kind of enjoyed it."

Her mom made a show of taking her temperature, laying a hand on her forehead. "Are you all right?"

"Very funny." Polly surveyed her handiwork with the sparkling counters and spotless appliances. "I think maybe I have some energy to burn from being away from work all week. I'm so used to being busy that it's weird not having a million details on my mind."

"You don't normally seem that busy in Better Dresses," her mother remarked with a raised brow.

"You're right, but…" But what? But she had been thinking about her own job, not Cassie's. "There's a lot of sorting and shelving," she improvised. "And, uh, inventory and tagging—it's busier than you think.''

"I suppose.''

Her mother's gaze was more suspicious than Polly really needed at this moment. Carefully, she wiped the counter one more time and then rinsed the dish cloth, ready to get out from under the scrutiny. "I guess I'd better get a move on. Skipper has a whole list of things for me to do today.'' She started to leave, but then turned back. "Oh, Mom, can I have the car keys? I have to go to the florist and the bakery and the church and I don't know where all.''

"Skipper asked me the same thing. Isn't that odd?''

Polly was confused. "Skipper wanted to borrow your car?''

"No, Skipper wanted to know if *you* could borrow my car, because he saw that Dad was already gone with the Dodge—he went to Peoria for the day for a hardware show—and there I was, packing up my car because I'm on meals-on-wheels duty all day today, like every Saturday.'' She shook her head. "Sorry, hon, but I told Skipper and now I'll have to tell you that I don't have a car to give you.''

"So you told Skipper I was stuck here with no car and he just went on his merry way without offering to drive me on these errands or anything?'' she asked with a certain edge of irritation. "And he also didn't bother to come back and tell me that he would take the errands for me, or that I was off the hook because I didn't have a car. Isn't that just like Skipper?''

"Maybe you should ask him for a car for a wedding gift instead of a blender.''

"Good idea." But, in the meantime, what was she supposed to do with Skipper's almighty schedule? "I know what I'd like to do with it," she muttered, as there was a chime from the area of the front door.

"Hon, there's the doorbell. It's probably Joni who does meals-on-wheels with me." And she hustled off to get the door.

At the same time, Ashley came flying down the stairs, dressed in a leotard. "Mom," she shouted at the top of her lungs. "Was that the doorbell? Is it Genevieve? Is it my ride for gymnastics?"

Their mother came waltzing back into the kitchen, her eyes merry as she held open the door to the living room. "Not for me or you, Ashley. It's for Cassie."

It took Polly a second. "For me?"

"That's right. Your ride is here." Ruth Tompkins hazarded a glance behind her. "Come on in, Michael."

"Is this a joke?"

"'Fraid not," Michael replied as he strolled into the room, his hands in his pockets. He was wearing jeans and a T-shirt with a leather jacket, and his eyes were hidden behind dark sunglasses. He looked so good Polly immediately started to salivate, and she had to clamp her mouth shut for fear of drooling.

How dare he?

But he went on with his story in a sheepish tone. "Skipper stopped back by the house. He says it's an emergency and since I'm on vacation, he thinks I'm the only one with plenty of time to drive you around." He broke a smile, but it wasn't much of one. "So, where to?"

Polly was rooted where she stood. "Skipper wants you to drive me?"

"Is he stupid or what?" Ashley demanded.

Swiftly, Polly stuck a hand over her sister's mouth. "Do you think this is a good idea?"

He shrugged. "I'm okay with it. I mean, we're both grown-ups, aren't we?"

Mrs. Tompkins glanced back and forth between them. "What's going on with you two?"

"Nothing," they said in unison, as Ashley squirmed under Polly's hand.

"Think of me as the hired help," Michael said, acting all nonchalant and casual. "I'll wear a chauffeur's hat if it helps."

"Right." But Polly wasn't fooled by the submissive act. There was no way in hell that Michael should've agreed to drive her around all day after what had happened between the two of them in that gazebo. They'd clung, they'd perspired, they'd *melted,* for goodness sake!

Michael was no pushover. If he'd let Skipper maneuver him into this, there was a reason. And she meant to find out what it was. Smartly, she told him, "Just let me run and get my list. I wouldn't want to miss anything."

"No need." Michael reached into the pocket of his jeans. He pulled out a sheet of folded paper, which he held aloft.

"He gave you a copy, too?" Polly asked. "Why?"

Now his expression was smug. "To supervise? I guess he wanted to make sure it all got done."

He *what?* What did he think, that she was going to

go play hooky and abandon the minister or the florist willy-nilly? Who did he think she was? Well, best not to go there. But *still*... "You're kidding, right?"

"Nope."

Removing her hand from her sister's mouth, Polly stomped past Michael, ripped the list out of his hand and snarled, "Come on. Let's drive."

Ashley called out, "Don't go!" but it was too late. Polly was good and mad and no vows, no promises, no common sense was going to stop her.

HE SENT A quick look in her direction. "Where to first, ma'am?"

"Don't you dare 'ma'am' me." She crossed her arms over her chest and scrunched down into the leather seat of the small sports car. "Why did you agree to this? Are you insane?"

Michael was rapidly losing his patience. "Do you think I want to be here any more than you do?"

"So why are you?"

"Because Skipper came sauntering in and he says, 'Mike, you're the only one who can drive my beloved.' That's what he said, 'my beloved.' Christ." Michael shifted into fourth gear, accelerating much more quickly than he really should have. "So there's Skipper, big as life, leaning on me, going on and on about how there's nobody else because he and Dad have to close this damn subdivision deal on the golf course today and Mom is at the garden club and that just leaves me and, besides, he's sure I won't mind carting my future sister-in-law around all day."

"Did you think of saying no?" she inquired with a nasty sort of sweetness.

"I did say no." He whipped around the corner so fast the tires on the Porsche convertible squealed like a baby. "So he asks why not. And I say I can't and he says why not and I say I can't and he says why not, and I am this close to saying, 'Because we had our lips locked for half an hour last night and it just doesn't seem right!'"

She dropped her face into her hands. "Oh, my God."

"Exactly." Michael took one hand off the wheel, using it to rake through the short strands of his hair. "What could I do? I couldn't tell him the truth. And because I didn't, there was no reason for me not to chauffeur you around town. So the smartest thing seemed to be to just go along and pick you up, and then you and I agree that we will just drive and not talk, and definitely not kiss, not do anything, but just drive."

She seemed to have gotten awfully small over there. "Okay," she said finally.

"Okay?"

"Okay."

"That's it?"

"It's the best I can offer at the moment."

"I understand. Listen, don't worry. We'll be very good, very casual, nothing we can't handle." Safely hidden behind his sunglasses, Michael focused on the view out the front window. "So where to, ma'am?"

There was a long pause as she pulled out Skipper's schedule and examined it for several seconds. "Um, the, uh, list says the wedding gown should be first. Do you know where Lana's Bridal Emporium is?''

"Yeah." He ground to a stop, reversed the car, and spun around in the opposite direction. "You might remember Lana. She was my prom date."

Lana hadn't been there for much of it. She and some friends had smuggled booze in their cars, and they all got drunk in the parking lot. When he'd asked Lana if she wanted to come back inside, she'd barfed on his shoes. So he took her home, he changed his shoes and that was the end of his prom date with Lana Pfeiffer. Not that Cassie necessarily knew any of those gory details.

Her face had gone completely white though. Michael smiled. That meant she *did* remember what happened between them at the prom. His date had disappeared and he'd been on his own. The same thing had happened to her. So they were all alone, just the two of them, the king and queen. They'd shared a dance, he couldn't restrain himself, and the rest was history. Even if she wouldn't admit it.

He glanced over her way again. "We're here. Lana's Bridal Emporium."

Cassie just sat there, looking frozen in her seat.

"You're going to have to get out if you plan to try the dress on," he told her. "You can hardly do it out here in the parking lot."

Lifting her chin, she calmly got herself out of the car and marched in the front door of the small bridal shop as if she were going to her own execution. With his sunglasses in his hand, Michael ambled after.

"Cassie!" Lana cried, coming out from behind the

counter. Lana still had the big '80s hair she'd worn to prom, but her smile was sincere. "I know what you're here for. I expected you yesterday, but that's okay. If we need her, we can call Kayla to come in for alterations."

She didn't seem to notice that Cassie looked like she was in shock. Maybe all the women who came for fittings were in shock.

So Lana turned to him. "Hey, Michael! Haven't seen you in awhile. How you been, babe? Running around with Skipper's bride, huh? Aren't you nice?"

"He's very nice," Cassie answered for him. "Is my gown here somewhere?"

"Oh, sure, sure." Lana led the way to the back of the store, to the dressing rooms. "I'll hang it up for you and then you strip and I'll help you get it on. I guess you'll want to show Michael, huh?"

"Why?" she asked.

"To see if it fits." Lana poked her in the shoulder. "You need a guy's opinion. And he's perfect. You can't show the groom, but you can show the groom's brother without a hitch."

Cassie just shook her head. Michael understood the feeling. He didn't want to see her in this wedding gown any more than she wanted to model it. After all, it was the wedding gown she'd wear to marry his brother.

The word "torture" occurred to him.

But Cassie seemed meek enough as she let Lana guide her into the room, and then there were a few giggles and whoops and the rustle of fabric as they did whatever women do in dressing rooms. Every tiny noise made him think about bared skin, about zippers and straps, about lingerie and lace. He couldn't stand it.

And, finally, when he was about ready to fidget himself into insanity, Cassie finally emerged.

"It fits perfect," Lana announced, following behind her and fooling with the folds of the skirt.

Cassie's gaze was lowered, directed at Lana. But then she stepped forward, looked up, and their eyes met.

Click. Electricity. Connection.

Michael couldn't tear his gaze away. *Oh, man.* Talk about drop-dead gorgeous. There was no question that white brought out the purity and sweetness of Cassie Tompkins. She looked more like some fantasy princess than a real woman. Just like she had at their prom.

But there was something else there, too. She carried herself with such spirit and pride that his heart swelled. She was so much more than he'd ever thought Cassie could be. It was as if every wedding dress in the world begged to be worn like this one.

Last night's gown had been a whole different kettle of fish. Now that was a living, breathing woman, all sex and sin and things he would never expect to find in Cassie.

But with this one, she seemed almost untouchable. The secret was that she was very, very touchable, but only by one man. And he was the man.

He didn't know much about dresses, but he knew this one was simple, cut fairly straight in the front, poofing out more at the skirt.

It didn't matter. She looked like the quintessential

bride, so virginal and romantic, and it was really more than his heart could take. He was smitten by Cassie, there was no other word for it, and this outfit brought home the reality that, one week from today, she would be his brother's wife. His ungrateful, unpleasant, unworthy brother.

Life just wasn't fair.

"Do you like it?" she asked.

"It's amazing. You're amazing."

She smiled. Would anyone notice that his heart was bleeding?

From behind Cassie, Lana Pfeiffer joked, "Better watch it, Michael. Girls in wedding gowns are irresistible. But this one's taken."

Yeah, he knew.

Abruptly, he turned away. "Hey, Lana, can you get her out of that? You said it didn't need alterations, right? We have a lot of other stops to make."

He just couldn't look at her in that dress for one more second.

# 7

SITTING IN HIS CAR AGAIN, en route to the florist, Polly
pondered what had just happened.

How very strange. When they were alone in the
dressing room, Lana Pfeiffer had told her the most
interesting story about that fateful prom night. She'd
leaned in close to Polly and whispered, "You know,
I went to prom with Michael Kennigan."

"Yes, I know," Polly returned coolly, remembering
a lot more than that.

"It was too funny. We really didn't have a good
time at all. I was kind of wilder than him, and I got
loaded in the parking lot and he came out to get me
and I ralphed all over his shoes." Lana put a hand
over her mouth to stop the giggles. "One of those
dates you never forget."

"You mean you threw up on his shoes?"

"All over his shoes. It was totally gross. But you
know how it is when you're that tanked—you don't
know where you're going to unload."

"Lovely."

"Tell me about it." Lana lifted the wedding gown
high above her. "Arms up." As the dress settled over
her head, Polly heard Lana add, "But he was a perfect
gentleman."

*That's not what I heard.*

"Yeah, he took me home and he didn't even get mad about his shoes. I think he went back to the dance because he was the prom king, you know." She laughed. "Of course you know. You were the queen."

"Right." He was a perfect gentleman and took Lana home? But she thought… She thought he'd had sex with Lana, right there at the prom. Cassie had come running home and said, *Polly, you have to break up with him. He cheated on you at the prom. I saw it.*

So who did he have sex with? And why did Cassie let her think it was Lana all those years?

Yes, it was very mysterious. But at least she didn't have to hold onto her hatred for Lana Pfeiffer anymore. All she'd done was toss her cookies on his shoes.

While she was still mulling it over in her mind, they hit the flower shop. Although she wanted to double-check the order lickety-split and get on her way, Lucille the florist spent a lot of time gushing and fawning and assuring her that they were doing their utmost to make sure the "Kennigan wedding" went smoothly. Plus she went on and on about how much she adored Skipper and had ever since he was a tot and how lucky Cassie was to be snaring such a fine husband.

Polly was uncomfortable with all of it, especially the Skipper part, and she felt sure Michael was, too. Every time they turned around, he was reminded that she was supposedly promised to his brother. Plus this lady and her bowing and scraping underlined the family position and prominence that had always given both of them hives.

Finally, just when she thought she might have to kill someone, they got away from the clingy florist. Polly had no idea what Cassie had ordered or whether it was accounted for, and it really didn't matter. Flowers were beyond her at this point.

All she could think of was the light and heat in Michael's eyes when he'd looked at her in that wedding gown. She'd felt beautiful and adored and desirable, all at the same time.

"What's next?" he asked, bringing her out of her reverie temporarily.

"Um, bakery. Check on cake."

"Where is the bakery?"

"I don't know." Her admission should've struck Michael as suspicious if he were paying attention, but he clearly wasn't.

Polly smiled to herself. He seemed positively smitten, and she loved it.

"Could it be the Happy Times bakery or Valerie's?" he asked, squinting at signs on Main Street.

Neither of them had been there when Polly was young. She just hoped that Cassie hadn't commissioned her cake out of town or something.

Polly glanced at her Main Street choices. Since the Happy Times bakery had a few pathetic doughnuts lying abandoned in the front window and Valerie's display was a huge wedding cake surrounded by white tulle and orchids, she knew her sister would go for

Valerie. "That one," she said, pointing to the white tulle.

Michael had been treating her like fine porcelain ever since the wedding dress incident, and he carefully guided her up to the small shop. She could get used to treatment like this.

As they entered, the bell on the door dinged to announce them, but there was no one behind the counter.

So maybe they should've tried Happy Times after all. "Hello?" Polly called. "Anyone here?"

A pretty young woman with a deeply furrowed brow came running out from the back room. "Sorry. I was just... Never mind." She took a breath and tried to assume a more professional stance. "May I help you?"

Polly was used to everyone in this town taking one look at her, recognizing her as Cassie, and making a big fuss over her and the upcoming nuptials. After all, Cassie was marrying Skipper Kennigan, heir to the local dynasty. Even in this day and age, that carried a lot of weight.

But this girl acted as if she'd never seen either of them. Polly relaxed. How refreshing not to be recognized or expected to behave in a certain way.

"I'm here to check on a wedding cake," she informed the girl.

"Oh." She pulled a big book out from under the counter. "Are you wanting to order today? Or did you already order and you just want to confirm that it's all okay?"

"Just confirming."

"Okay." She began to flip pages in the book, looking confused and harried, and not coming up with anything.

"Is this your first day?" Polly asked kindly.

"No. Yesterday was. I'm Vonda." She pointed to herself just to make sure they knew who she was referring to. "You probably talked to my sister, Val, when you were here before. Val owns this place and she's really good at this. I mean, the store is pretty new, but Val just does great. Her cakes are so yummy, and pretty, too." Her tense face now beamed at them from behind the counter.

"Yeah, I kind of guessed that." Polly waited, but there still didn't seem to be anything happening back there. "Is Val around?"

"No, she had her baby yesterday. Last night." She nodded. "Three weeks early, but they're doing great."

"Oh, I see. You're filling in for your sister and you didn't really get a chance to learn the ropes before she left." Now *that* was a situation she could relate to.

"Yeah. I'm really sorry. I'm sure Val would know right where to look to find your order."

"That's okay," Michael offered. "I mean, come on. Your sister's baby is more important than a wedding cake."

"That is so nice of you! The only other person who's come in since Val's been gone wasn't nearly as nice." Vonda screwed up her face. "She was so mean I was practically crying before she left. But you're real nice."

"Aren't you a sweetheart?" Polly whispered into his ear.

"I try."

"Would you like to taste some cake?" the girl asked hopefully. "I know where the samples are. I mean, I made today's cakes, but Val taught me, so they're real good and everything."

"Yes, by all means, let's taste cake." Michael put his arm around Polly. "I love that part where the groom smashes cake into the bride's mouth, don't you?"

"No, it's awful," she told him with a stern look.

But when Vonda came back with three different plates, Michael picked up the first one with a definite air of mischief. After spearing a fat, sticky wedge of cake and frosting, he held up the fork, letting the cake shimmy ever so slightly in front of her eyes. "Are you sure you don't want to practice your cake-in-face act?"

"I'm sure." She held up a hand to ward him off.

"That one there is what we call the Royal Wedding," Vonda recited with painstaking care. "It's a sour cream white cake with buttercream frosting. And we can do the color any way you want it. You know, with flowers or squigglies or whatever."

Polly didn't have the heart to tell her that they didn't really need a full audition. "Sounds yummy," she said in her most encouraging voice.

Michael wiggled the fork. "Come on, try it. You know you want to."

The hunk of cake hovered there. "Can you be

trusted?'' she asked softly. She couldn't believe she was asking Michael that. The answer was no, of course. ''Be nice, Michael.''

But she tamped down her distrust, closed her eyes and opened her mouth.

And he neatly placed the sweet, heavy dessert inside, as gentle and polite as you please. He cupped her chin with his other hand, as if to keep her steady, but he left the hand there longer than he needed to. She didn't tell him to take it away, even when she pressed her lips down to take all the frosting from the fork.

''Mmmm, that is good.'' Closing her eyes so that she could savor the scrumptious cake as well as the feel of Michael's strong, warm hand on her chin, Polly let the dessert slide around in her mouth. Delicious. Michael brushed a crumb from the corner of her mouth, and she smiled at him. ''If I ever get married, I am definitely getting my cake from you, Vonda.''

Meanwhile, the girl behind the counter seemed transfixed by their antics. ''If you get married?'' she asked in confusion. ''But I thought you were.''

''She's just teasing you,'' Michael remarked. His expression changed slightly, taking on a grim undertone when he added, ''The wedding is a week from today. June first.''

''Oh, cool! A June wedding. Those are my favorite.'' Vonda giggled. ''I'd say you two need to get married and quick. You already act like you're on your honeymoon.''

*The wedding is a week from today.* Polly couldn't stand the look on Michael's face. Rather than face it directly, she changed the subject. They needed to talk, and yet that was the last thing she wanted to do. So she took the easy way out, and continued to tease him instead. *Coward.*

``I want to try that chocolate one,'' she teased, making her voice low and husky. ``Bring it on.''

His eyes held a challenge when he scooped up a really big portion of the second dessert. But this time he held it in his fingers, not on a fork. ``You ready?''

They were playing a very, very dangerous game. Too bad. She opened her mouth as wide as she could and waited for a long moment as he tantalized her with it. Just when she was about to give up and close her mouth, he tipped closer and brought the cake home.

Feeling wicked, she licked and even bit him, practically vacuuming frosting and crumbs off his fingers. His face was flushed, his breathing sounded irregular, and she knew she had hit her target.

``Oh, my God,'' she mumbled with her mouth full. ``This is fabulous, Vonda.'' But she was staring at Michael when she said it.

And Vonda was staring at both of them. ``Chocolate Decadence,'' she whispered. She cleared her throat. ``Wow. I never saw anybody eat it like that before.''

Polly ordered, ``Michael, try that one. Try that one! Wait, let me feed you.''

He laughed aloud, but he let her lift a chunk of cake to his lips. She was no fool. She popped it into his mouth and snatched her hand back before he could catch her. His gaze was mocking, as if he knew very well what she was doing. But he tasted. He considered.

He shrugged. "It's okay. I don't know. I liked the other one better."

Polly smacked him on the shoulder. And then they both reached for the third plate with reckless abandon.

Vonda read off a card for this one. "That's the Princess of Wales cake," she rushed to tell them, her words tumbling on top of each other. "Delicate lemon chiffon cake with raspberry filling between the layers."

Behind the counter, Vonda watched and waited breathlessly, fanning herself, and Polly smiled. It was kind of fun in an exhibitionist sort of way.

Michael held the plate just out of her reach, taunting her, not quite letting her get her fork in. "What will you give me if I let you have a bite?"

"I'll let you have a bite," she said with her naughtiest inflection.

"You don't play fair, do you?"

But he brandished the cake under her nose, close enough that she could lick it right off the plate without bothering to use her fork. "No," she whispered, flicking her tongue over her top lip just to drive him nuts. "I don't play fair."

Michael dropped the plate on the counter and grabbed her.

"Whoa. You guys should come in here and eat the cake all the time," Vonda said shakily. "I think people would pay to see this."

"We need to get out of here," Michael murmured into her ear.

They were practically making out, with only a plate-glass window separating them from Main Street. What a terrible idea. ``Yes, we do.'' She took his hand and made a move towards the door.

``Cake,'' he reminded her.

``You want to take more cake with us?''

``No. We still need to check on the wedding cake.''

As if either of them cared one bit about Cassie and Skipper's stupid wedding cake at this point. Polly gritted her teeth. He might as well have dumped cold water on her head.

Michael kept his hand around hers, but he leaned over the counter, closer to Vonda. ``I don't mean to be pushy, but I have a suggestion. I'm going to guess that your orders are filed under either the date of the wedding or the bride's name. It's June 1 and her name is Cassie Tompkins.''

``Oh.'' She jumped back from the counter and found another set of books. ``Wow. You're right. There it is. And you must be Mr. Kennigan.''

``Right.'' His eyes clouded to a stormier green.

Polly bit her lip. The wrong Mr. Kennigan. Of course, she was the wrong Ms. Tompkins, too, but he didn't know that. She knew she should tell him. She should tell him *now*. But she could only imagine what he would do. He'd probably throw her out into Main Street and let oncoming traffic have her.

He certainly seemed to be happy with his fantasy image of Cassie. It would probably kill the whole thing to stick the real Polly into the mix.

As he checked over the order, Polly stewed. Sending the two of them on a wedding check had been such a bad idea, but for all the wrong reasons. Not because she was tempted to jump his bones—well, she was always tempted to jump his bones—but because she couldn't help thinking that it should have been *them*. Even though they had never been the type for traditional wedding trappings—the flowers and the cake and the dress—it should have been *them* getting married, not Cassie and Skipper.

*Oh, no. I'm starting to get swoony over Michael again.*

"Okay. Looks fine to me." He took her arm and steered her toward the door, but she spun back at the last minute.

"Thanks again, Vonda. What happens if Val isn't back before next Saturday? I mean, will someone still know to make and deliver the cake?"

"Yeah. I think so." The poor girl wrung her hands with dismay. Or maybe she was just exhausted after watching them play erotic cake games. "But don't worry. If she's not going to be back by then, Val will think of something. She's the most reliable person I ever knew."

Funny, Polly had said the same thing about her sister. And look where that got her.

Back in the car, she tried not to think about what had just happened. It was a game, that was all. They were playing with their food, and both enjoying the idea that poor, deluded Vonda thought they were a couple. But the game was over. And now, unless she wanted to spill her guts, they had to go back to Plan A and "not do anything, but just drive."

Relentlessly cheerful, refusing to think about the fact that she was behaving like pond scum, Polly zeroed in on the damn list. At least it was safe. "Well, the good news is that we have checked off the dress, the flowers and the cake. This is kind of like a scavenger hunt, isn't it?"

"So what do we have left?"

"The minister." She sent him a concerned glance. "Maybe we should skip the minister. I don't feel much like standing in front of a man of God at the moment. He'll take one look at me and put a scarlet A on my forehead."

"I don't think ministers do that."

She had no desire to talk about ministers. She wanted to know what Michael was thinking. After all of this, could he possibly still think she was Cassie? It wasn't like she was even being careful anymore.

*Michael, how dense are you?*

"Are we still heading for church?" she asked doubtfully, trying to get her bearings from the landmarks around them. As pillars of the community, the Kennigans had always belonged to the town's biggest, fanciest church, built a few miles out in the country in a wooded area.

"Yep. God forbid I should get Skipper on my case because I didn't complete the required tasks."

Michael hit the gas, sending them roaring down Main Street, around a corner, past Dairy Queen and the bank, past Joseph Kennigan & Sons department store, and toward the edge of town.

Polly sat up. "I haven't been this way in a long time."

"Why not? I mean, how could you have avoided it?"

"I don't know. I guess I go between my house and the store and that's it." She stared out the window. "Wow! That was my old grade school. You went to the other one, didn't you, Michael? They consolidated and now everyone goes to that one. This one became a..." She read the sign. "Sports club. And look, the Dog 'n' Suds!"

She and Cassie had worked there one summer and eaten themselves sick with chili dogs and root beer. But it seemed to have fallen into disuse. Too bad. What kind of world was it where no one needed a perfectly good Dog 'n' Suds?

"Cassie, I'm the one who hasn't been back in years," Michael observed. "You live here. Why are you so jazzed by stuff you could see every day if you wanted to?"

"I, uh...I don't know." She edged herself back into her seat and away from the window. "I guess I just don't look. I must be feeling nostalgic today or something."

"Or something." He took the turnoff that led even further out of town, but slowed down as they drove past an athletic field, complete with goalposts, and the brick building sprawled behind it.

"The old high school," Polly murmured. The very place where she and Michael had passed notes and shared lunches and kissed next to their lockers like children in love are desperate enough to do. Of course, it was also the place where Michael took the wrong girl to the prom and Polly delivered her infamous valedictory speech. So the memories were not all charming.

"Yeah, I felt the need to walk down memory lane as long as we were going this way." He turned off the car. "Do you mind?"

"No, I don't mind. I haven't been back here in ages. So it'll be memory lane for me, too." She tried to find a serene smile appropriate for Cassie, but it was a bit wobbly. There was just so much wound up with Michael and her and this place. She had to remember to breathe and concentrate. Otherwise she would be whimpering into Michael's shirt before they took two steps.

"Not that our memories are the same. We didn't hang out much then." Michael had his sunglasses back on as he made a big deal out of opening Polly's door with a flourish. "Since they built that new school on the other side of town, this one has been closed. I think it will eventually be renovated into a junior high. But I'm sure you know that. It's all part of my dad's master plan."

They had closed her high school. Wow. Nothing stayed the same, did it?

"We can still walk around back, though. Polly and I used to do that a lot."

*Yes, I know.* For excellent students, they had been very bad about skipping classes and running off behind the football bleachers or way back, beyond the softball field, over the little stone bridge and into the orchard across the creek from the school property. It had been their refuge, their private place. They had talked for hours, about everything and nothing, and shared all their secrets.

It felt so wrong to come back to the orchard under false pretenses. But Michael's position was even worse. For all he knew, he was bringing Cassie here.

She felt wounded. *This was* our *special place, Michael,* she wanted to cry.

"This way," he said, catching her hand and leading her across the softball diamond. She didn't need directions. This route was etched into her brain permanently.

They were almost to the bridge—good grief, the bridge where he'd kissed her for the very first time!—when she just couldn't stand it anymore. "Michael, I don't think…" She dragged back on his hand. "This isn't right."

"What do you mean?"

She tried hard to think of a way to express this without giving it all away. "Listen, Michael, Polly told me all about the things that happened here between the two of you." She wavered. "It feels very disloyal to Polly to be here with you."

Disloyal to Polly. That was rich. Her lies were piling on top of each other so fast she couldn't tell them apart anymore.

But Michael took her objection seriously. "I understand. And I'm not going to kid you. I always thought that Polly was the love of my life," he said simply.

Polly had always thought so, too. *The love of my life.* Hearing those words in Michael's voice, from Michael's lips, was almost more than she could take.

He backed up onto the stone bridge, drawing her with him. "But now I'm not so sure. I'm not at all sure that what I am feeling for you isn't even stronger and better than what I felt for Polly back then. We were just kids. Now…"

His face, his striking, handsome face, was cast partially in shadow, softening the hard angles of his cheek and jaw. He was an incredibly beautiful man, and she had the most difficult time not believing every word he said and running right into his arms.

Last night's lust was not the same. That was simple passion and she knew it.

But today, with the dresses and the cake and now this, it was more. Her heart filled with love for Michael, for the boy she had known, and the man he had become.

And that made it impossible to hold back.

"I think I'm in love with you," he whispered, and he pulled her close and lowered his mouth to hers.

It was as wonderful as it had always been, with all the intensity and electricity that had made her so sure he was her one true love. Eagerly, trustingly, she pressed herself into his embrace and his kiss.

"Cassie," he murmured, trailing his lips over her cheek and her hair. "Oh, Cassie."

And Polly stiffened. She and Michael had shared

their first kiss on this bridge. And now he was making out with her sister in that very same place.

She pushed him away so hard he almost fell over the side of the bridge into the creek.

"What's wrong?" he asked, dragging himself upright by hanging onto the railing.

*You called me Cassie. You idiot! How could you kiss me like that—twice—and not know it was me?*

And it wasn't just that. She was as angry with herself as she was with him. It was the lack of control, the utter inability to stop herself from acting like a total dope.

She spun away, determined to leave, and then wheeled back so abruptly that Michael piled into her from behind. "We can't be this stupid. Anybody could come by and see us. Half the town probably already did!" Polly dashed a hand through her bangs. The more she thought about this, the worse it got. "Do you realize that we were licking cake off each other's fingers with nothing but a plate-glass window separating us from Main Street? On Saturday morning?"

Polly changed direction again, not even sure where she was going. "Cassie, stop!" Michael commanded. "I'm sorry! But you can't deny what's happening here. You can't marry Skipper. You can't. I won't let you."

Oh, man. What a muddle. Surely he deserved to know that she had no intention of marrying Skipper. But how could she tell him that without spilling it all? And what would he do if he knew?

All she really wanted was to run away into the orchard like they used to. Was it still possible to find a handy tree for refuge?

"I don't know what to do," she mumbled. "Everything is so mixed up."

"I know, I know it is, sweetheart." He tugged her into his strong, comforting embrace. "But we'll figure it out."

"How?"

Michael held her like that, soft and sweet and uncomplicated, on the bridge where they'd shared their first kiss, for a long time. It felt so right. How it could be such a mess?

"I think you'd better take me home, Michael." She detached herself, putting on a brave face.

"What about the minister?"

She almost laughed. Here he was begging her to cancel the wedding, and he still wanted to complete their appointed rounds? "I think I'd better see the minister by myself." And throw herself at his mercy and ask for forgiveness for all of her sins and maybe even ask him how a basically good person who had made some serious mistakes went about divulging secrets and righting wrongs.

Michael drove her home without a word, bless his heart. But when he pulled up to the curb in front of the Tompkins's house, he reached across the gearshift and took her hand. "You can't marry Skipper, Cassie. You and I both know that."

*I don't know what Cassie can do.* "I have to talk to my sister," she whispered.

He looked surprised, but he leaned over to open the

door for her, and Polly beat a hasty retreat up the driveway.

"Hello, Cassie," the Tompkins's neighbor, Mrs. Withers, called. Out with her dog, the woman eyed Polly and the snazzy Porsche with evident interest.

Polly glanced around. Mrs. Benson across the street was watching from behind her curtains, and Mr. Terrazzo on the other side was leaning on his rake and trying to peer into Michael's car.

"Great. Every busybody around thinks something is going on." Just what she needed.

INSIDE, things weren't much better.

"What were you thinking?" Ashley demanded.

Polly looked to her mother for support, but the eldest Tompkins woman in the household sided with the youngest. "I'm with Ashley," she avowed, crossing her arms over her chest. "It's pretty ugly to be fooling around with the groom's brother a week before the wedding."

"Who says we were fooling around?"

"Lana at the bridal shop, Lucille at the florist and Tom Atkins," her mother continued, "who happened to be walking down Main Street outside Valerie's Bakery and says you two were giggling like a couple of kids on your way out the door."

Thank God he'd only seen them coming out the door and not what they were doing inside the door.

"What a bunch of gossips and snoops. Is there even one person in this town who minds his own business?" Polly asked angrily.

"Not when a Kennigan wedding is involved."

"It's gross," she declared.

"And you've lived in this town your entire life and you ought to be familiar with it." Mrs. Tompkins shook her head. "And whether or not they're a bunch of Nosy Parkers does not change the fact that you have no business with Michael and you know it."

"I didn't do anything wrong!"

"Ha!" Ashley spit out. "Ha, ha, ha!"

Mom sent her a curious glance. "What do you know that I don't know?"

But she didn't get an answer. The kitchen door shot open, and Skipper stalked in. One look at his choked, purple face, and Polly knew people had been talking to him, too.

Could things get any worse?

# 8

MOM AND ASHLEY scattered as soon as they saw the look on Skipper's face.

"I guess you've heard the same gossip as everyone else," Polly ventured. She stayed where she was, perched on a kitchen chair. Now all they needed were some rubber hoses and a very bright light.

But Skipper just paced back and forth in front of the refrigerator, muttering beneath his breath. Finally, he managed to make himself look at her. "Of all the women in the world, I never thought you would do this to me, Cassie." He shook his head sadly. "I thought you were pure and moral and good."

Oh, please. Where did pure and moral and good get a person? It made you run away to Cleveland with wild men.

"I haven't done anything!" she swore. She wished she had. Maybe she wouldn't be so frustrated and cranky right now. A good roll in the hay with Michael would definitely cure what ailed her.

But Skipper brought her back to his sordid reality. "There is so much talk!" he sputtered.

"Yes, I know. But it really isn't—"

"When you're a Kennigan, you have to avoid this kind of scandal. All it takes is talk. Talk can be so damaging," he maintained, wiping sweat from his brow. He looked like he was the one being interrogated.

Poor Skipper. She supposed a person in his position—trying to be Mr. Big Shot all the time, with his deals and his golf and his cronies—really did suffer if everyone in town was giggling behind his back. Of course, it wasn't fun for anyone to be called a wimp or a cuckold.

"I'm sorry. It won't happen again." She looked down at her hands. "I swear."

A long pause hung between them.

Finally, Skipper fumed, "So, is it true? Are you having an affair with my brother?"

"Of course not!"

"Sometimes I really hate Michael," he gritted. "Thinks he's so smart and such a chick magnet. What I said about you—about being pure and good—is the opposite of Michael. He's just a...a...*despoiler.*"

How unkind. Polly sat up straighter, refusing to be intimidated. "Look, it's true that Michael has grown somewhat fond of me. But I think it's just that he looks at me and sees Polly." Wishful thinking. But it was a good way to dodge the problem, wasn't it? She smiled brightly. "I truly believe that Michael's heart still belongs to Polly."

Skipper ground one toe into the linoleum. "Maybe this is because... Do you think it might be because, you know, we haven't consummated our relationship? Do you think maybe you have needs that are pushing you to Michael? He has that animal magnetism."

``Oh, heavens, no!'' she lied through her teeth. Did she have needs pushing her to Michael? Was she breathing?

``Because if that's it, well, I can set aside the Moral Imperatives and, you know, do my part to consum—''

``No, no, not necessary.'' *Think fast, Polly,* she told herself. ``One of the things I love most about you is your moral fiber, Skipper. I would not want you to abandon what you believe in.''

He nodded. ``But if you change your mind—''

``No, no, I don't think so.'' She rose from her chair, patting Skipper absently on the shoulder. ``I think the best thing I can do right now is just rest and relax here at home. I think it's very hard for both of us to maintain our standards of, um, moral excellence, if you keep coming over for breakfast, for example. It's just sort of intimate, isn't it? Kind of jumping the gun on intimacy. And I think staying away from you is my best shot at staying, uh, pure, till the wedding, I mean.''

If that wasn't a nonsensical piece of logic, she'd never heard one.

But bless his addled brain, he actually seemed to be buying it. *Good job, Poll. Abuse him, confuse him, excuse him!*

Looking all woebegone, Skipper trundled over and framed her head with his hands. ``Please don't go near Michael, okay?''

``Girl Scouts honor,'' she replied, holding up a few fingers.

He gave her that customary bear hug, and then, thankfully, Skipper ducked out the back door.

``I thought he would never leave.''

She sank back into the same old chair, the one with a good view of the clock. Ticktock, ticktock. Lord, lord, that thing took its time.

Could she possibly make it until tomorrow? If things went according to plan, and they hadn't so far, Cassie would be arriving on the three o'clock train.

*Please, Cassie, get home quick. I hate your life and I hate your fiancé and I hate myself and I don't know how much longer I can do this.*

## May 26: 6 days before the wedding

ASHLEY CAME bounding into the living room, where Polly was pretending to watch *Meet the Press.* ``Was that the phone?'' she asked quickly. ``I thought I heard the phone.''

``It wasn't the phone.''

``I thought I heard the phone.''

``Well, you didn't!'' Polly laid her head on one hand. ``It's better if she doesn't call, Ash. If she calls, then she won't be on the train, will she?''

``I guess not.''

``So go do cartwheels on the lawn or play with your makeup or something. Just calm down.'' Good advice. Now if she would only follow it. ``You can ride with me to pick her up, okay?''

``All right. But if you hear from her, let me know.'' Then she was gone.

Polly ate a pretzel, spit it out, chewed her nail, critiqued the performances, hairstyles and wardrobe of every person on *Meet the Press* and generally went insane.

As soon as Cassie came back, the nightmare would be over. And it had better be soon. Then Cassie could deal with Skipper herself—and Polly planned to be very apologetic about the scandal she had created in her sister's absence—while Polly messed up her hair, put on some primary colors, latched on to Michael, greeted him as if she had been away for seven years, and let the chips fall where they may.

All fixed. If only Cassie would come home.

Swearing, Polly leapt to her feet and hit the off button on the remote. "I'm taking a walk!" she shouted to anyone who cared. She pounded out of the house, waving to Mrs. Withers, Mr. Terrazzo and Mrs. Benson, who were all tracking her every move, and then went further down the block. Fresh air, sunshine, lovely May breeze... Yes, it was just what she needed.

By the time she got back to the Tompkins's house, she hoped at least an hour had passed. That would make it one hour closer to Cassie's return.

But the minute she stepped in the front door, she knew the news was not good.

Ashley was waiting, chewing the side of her cheek, bouncing from one foot to the other, holding on tight to a piece of notebook paper. "I, uh, have a message from, um, our other sister," she announced, darting glances over her shoulder as if she were on the lookout for eavesdroppers. "She called while you were gone."

``And what did she say?''

Ashley waved the sheet of paper. ``I wrote it all down, exactly what she said. And I want you to know, I did not tell her how bad you've screwed things up. I wanted to tell her, you know, that I knew, you know, the *whole thing,* but Mom was right there and I couldn't. I did say, like in code, that you were really hot for her to get back.''

``Okay, okay.'' Another second and she would grab the paper from Ashley's hands. ``So where is she? When is she coming?''

``She didn't say,'' Ashley said woefully.

``She didn't say?'' Polly went for the paper and read Ashley's round, careful handwriting.

Sorry not there yet. Things not going well. Must clear up a problem before can leave. Hang on. I will be there soon.

Polly glanced up at Ashley. ``That's it? That's all?''

``It was really noisy where she was and she said she had to go.''

``And you let her do that?'' Polly demanded.

``What could I do? I'm just a kid! And Mom was right there.'' Ashley dipped her voice. ``She would've heard every word. I was concentrating so hard to not call her, you know—'' she dropped to a whisper. ``—Cassie. And I wanted to know what was going on and if she wanted us to break up with Skipper or what, but I couldn't ask.''

``It's not your fault.'' Polly slumped into the easy

chair and then hopped back up again in the same motion. She needed to move. She needed to think.

"It's not so bad, is it?" Ashley tried. "I mean, she says she'll be here soon. Maybe it'll be tomorrow. And Skipper isn't here today. Or Michael. So you can keep hiding out, away from both of them, you know, until she gets here. I mean, I have school tomorrow, but maybe Mom will let me stay home sick. And then we could watch soaps and eat ice cream and it won't be so bad."

"Sure. It won't be so bad."

Polly found a smile for her little sister, who was trying so hard. Inside, she wanted to scream and tear her hair out. She wanted to steal the Dodge and drive to Chicago. Except maybe Cassie was in Cleveland.

One thing she refused to do was wait there like a sitting duck while the days ticked off, one after the other, propelling her toward a wedding with a man she didn't even like.

"I love you, Cass," she whispered under her breath, "but I will not marry him, not even for you."

Besides, she had divided loyalties. Somewhere out there, Michael still thought that the woman he loved was beholden to his brother. And she couldn't leave him like that, could she?

"I have to tell him the truth," she decided. "But how? And when?"

*May 27: Five days before the wedding*

SHE HAD THOUGHT and rethought, puzzled and agonized, but she still didn't have a plan. It was getting to the point where she thought her best bet might be a psychiatrist. But she didn't have one.

The phone rang, making her jump about a foot. "If that's you, Cassie, and you're not coming again today, I am going to throttle you."

But it wasn't Cassie.

"Honey bunny?" a grating voice inquired. "How are you doing? Everything okay?"

"Just ducky," she said breezily.

"Ducky? You know, you're starting to sound like a different person." He didn't give her time to answer, just ground on in that peevish tone. "I hope you're resting and recuperating, because I really want you to be your old self again for the wedding."

"Well, I—"

"I mean," he went on, overriding her, "that there will be a lot of important people there. I would hate for you to be moody and eccentric when it's critical to make a good impression."

*Oh, pooh!* Moody and eccentric? Most people called it having a personality. "I shall do my best," she said flatly.

"Great, great." Skipper seemed to be distracted by something. "Listen, honey bunny, I called because I just heard from Reverend Vance and he said you still haven't made it to talk to him about the vows. Now can you do that today? It really needs to be settled ASAP."

Like she cared about vows. Like she wanted to cower in front of a minister and lie to him, too.

But on the other hand... Men of the cloth were bound by confidentiality rules, right? Just like psychiatrists. If she went to talk to Reverend Vance, maybe she could unload some of her problems and let him figure it out. After all, sage counsel was his business. He knew all about lying and cheating and sinning and forgiveness. The perfect guy to talk to.

"Okay, when Mom comes for lunch, I'll drive her back to school and then borrow the car. I'll do it this afternoon," she promised.

"Don't forget."

"I'm unlikely to forget in the next three hours," she responded, trying to keep the acid out of her voice. "'Bye, Skip." And she hung up on him before he made her scream with frustration.

Her mother agreed without a fuss, saying, "Maybe it would be good for you to talk to Reverend Vance, dear." Polly set off for the church like a woman on a mission.

"Hello," she called out, walking into the chapel. "Reverend?"

"Yes?" He popped up behind her and scared the life out of her.

She didn't recall ever meeting Reverend Vance before, but he was very tall, with a beard, bushy eyebrows and an imposing manner. She had pictured someone wee and twinkly, someone more like the guy who played Santa Claus in *Miracle on 34th Street*. This wasn't going to be easy.

"Cassie, nice to see you." He took her hands in both of his. "I was getting a little worried you weren't going to come in. Maybe cold feet, hmm?'' He chuckled then, scaring her even more. He wasn't a good chuckler.

She searched for something to say, but nothing came.

"So, Cassie," he said in a solemn tone, "did you want to talk about which verses you wanted to use in your service?"

"Not exactly."

While she dithered, he scrutinized her. "I get the sense that you are troubled." He took a deep breath, drawing those massive brows together, steepling his hands. "Would you like to come into my office and talk about it?"

"Yes, Reverend, I would."

But then there she was, ensconced in a plastic chair, across the desk from him, and it wasn't any easier to come out with it. "Tell me, Reverend Vance, are you bound by any rules of confidentiality?"

"Certainly." Now he was very grave indeed. "What you tell me in the sanctity of my office is just between us."

"So you wouldn't tell Skipper or his father or mother or my mother or—"

"None of them."

"Okay." Polly hesitated. "And confession is good for the soul, right?"

The Reverend narrowed his eyes. "Why don't you just tell me what it is?"

"I'm not Cassie," she blurted.

He sat back in his chair. He repeated, "Not Cassie?"

"Had you heard that Cassie had a twin? I'm her twin," she said helpfully. "Polly. Had she ever spoken of her sister, Polly?"

"I don't know." He tapped a finger on his desk. "I assume you've come to town for the wedding. Are you and your sister estranged, is that it?"

"No, not at all. The problem is that I've been pretending to be her."

"Excuse me?"

"We traded places, Reverend." Eager to get it out, Polly elaborated. "Cassie wanted to get away and experience city life before she got married, but she couldn't do that because Skipper is kind of controlling, as you may or may not know. I live in the city, and she wanted my life, so we switched. It's caused all sorts of problems, um, sir, as you might imagine."

It took a long time for him to speak. "Well, that is a shocker."

"I know."

"You traded places? You took on each other's lives? And no one noticed?"

"Just my little sister. I mean, as far as I know. I'm assuming that Cassie hasn't told anyone, wherever she is, but I really don't know." She smiled apologetically. "So what do you think?"

He ran a large hand over his forehead. "What do I think about what?"

"About my situation."

"I'm not sure what it is about it that is bothering

you." Leaning back in his chair, the Reverend stared at the ceiling. "Lying, certainly. That's not good."

"No, it isn't. And..." She gulped, ready to plunge. "The thing is, while I've been back in town, I have become very attracted to my old boyfriend, who is unfortunately Skipper's brother. And he's attracted to me, too. We used to be involved, way back when. As our real selves, I mean. But now he thinks I'm Cassie."

"So one brother is cheating on the other one, or he thinks he is, because one sister is pretending to be the other. Is that about it?" he asked in confusion.

"Basically. Plus Cassie didn't come back when she was supposed to. So what do I do?" she pleaded. "Do I keep pretending to be Cassie so that she still has a wedding to come back to? Or do I tell Michael the truth so that neither of us is tortured any longer by the lie?"

His eyebrows shot up as she hurried through the rest of her summation. "And meanwhile, even if I don't tell Michael the truth, everyone in town is gossiping about us and it may screw up the wedding, anyway, because they all think I'm being unfaithful to Skipper!"

After that torrent of words, there was complete silence in the Reverend Vance's office.

"My dear, you are in a pickle," he said at last.

"I already know that. I was hoping for something more in the nature of advice or counsel." She gave her most charming and sincere smile. "I was hoping you could tell me what to do."

"Only you can decide what to do," he offered kindly. "But it seems to me, in general, it's always better to err on the side of the truth."

In other words, tell Michael, tell Skipper and let the shouting and recriminations begin. "That's pretty much the way I was leaning," she murmured. "But..."

"Yes?"

"But will he ever forgive me, Reverend?" she asked urgently.

"Skipper?"

"No, Michael."

"Well, I suppose..." His gaze was direct under those beetled brows. "Do you love him?"

"Yes." What a relief to say it. "I've been denying it for so long, but I really do." Oh, Michael. How could she have ever thought for one second that she didn't love him? It was just who she was, who she had always been. "I guess I thought, when I left Pleasant Falls, that he would come and find me and apologize for sleeping with whoever it was he slept with on prom night."

"Oh, my."

"Water under the bridge, Reverend, really." She waved a hand to indicate that she had moved on. "So I thought we would, you know, hash it out and that I would eventually forgive him and we would be together again. But he never came."

"But you have a chance now—"

"I don't know. That's the thing." Polly hitched her chair closer and bent forward, leaning on his desk.

"You see, now he thinks he's in love with my sister. He isn't, of course, but he thinks he is. And I think he has this idealized image of who she is, combined with me, I mean. So I think he's sort of mixed up about who's who."

Wearily, Reverend Vance shook his large head from side to side. "I'm afraid you have more issues than I can really comprehend in so little time. But I can tell you that if you love this man, the only way to know what he feels is to tell him the truth and let him make his own decision."

Polly nodded. "Thank you, Reverend." She stood up, offering her hand. "You are a very wise man, sir. And if my sister does come back, and if there is a wedding, she will be very lucky to have you presiding."

"You know, you really aren't very much like your sister." He took her hand in both of his again, shaking it heartily. "I've met Cassie and I thought she was a lovely girl. But she's rather contained and calm, not given to excess verbiage. Whereas you are irrepressible, aren't you? I don't understand why anyone is fooled."

"I think they see what they want to see, you know?" she said softly.

"I suppose." He squeezed her hand. "Come back and see me again if you feel the need. You do have the most unique problems."

Polly returned to her mother's car feeling much better. Scared, but better.

She had driven out to the church on the fastest highway, but she went back a different route, the one that wound around by the high school. It wasn't on purpose, but it may as well have been. Because when she came up on the school, she saw a distinctive black Porsche sportscar parked in the lot.

She knew that car, and she knew exactly who was parked at the high school. Michael.

"Be brave," she told herself, trying to get her feet to move all the way across the old softball field and out to the small stone bridge.

She saw him first. He was standing on the bridge, exactly where she'd known he would be, his elbows balanced on the railing and his hands clasped in front of him. He seemed to be staring down at the trickle of water in the creek below.

She called out, "Michael!" but he couldn't hear her. There was the loud, monotonous drone of machinery or helicopters or something, drowning out most everything around them.

Coming up closer behind him, she tried again. "Michael?" She braced herself. "I need to talk to you."

He started and spun around. "What?" he said, a hand to his ear.

But she could hardly hear herself think. "I need to talk to you!" she shouted. "Can we go somewhere else? Somewhere quieter?"

"What? I can't hear you."

"What is that noise?"

If it was an airplane, it should've flown over by now. But what lawn mowers or tractors were that loud? And what would they be doing out here?

Polly shifted around, scanning the schoolyard or the orchard beyond them for the source of the noise, which ebbed down to a lesser nuisance as she waited. "What was that?"

"Earth-moving equipment on the far side of the orchard, making way for Pleasant Valley Estates," he returned coldly. "It's where you and Skipper are supposed to live your perfect life, I think. I'm surprised Skipper didn't have you out here picking out a lot."

"Pleasant Valley Estates? Here?" She was aghast, and she sped to the far side of the bridge where she could see. "They're knocking down the orchard to build Pleasant Valley Estates?"

"Of course." His eyes were hooded. "How could you not know that? It's all Skipper and my father have been talking about for months. That's why they wanted me back here. They want me to head up this new development division of Kennigan Inc."

"You?" Not only were they ruining the town, but they were going to suck Michael into their evil schemes as well? "You can't!"

He shrugged, turning back to his lazy inspection of the creek. "Why not? I don't have anything in Paris to go back to. Dad and Skip think this is just the ticket for me."

She grabbed at his leather jacket, trying to pull him closer so she could shake him. "Don't you dare even consider this, Michael. You're better than this. You have a life in Paris and maybe it isn't everything you ever wanted, but it isn't being a corporate shill for your horrible family either."

``A corporate shill?'' he quirked an eyebrow. ``Sometimes you sound so much like Polly it's amazing.''

``A shill, a snake, a sell-out. That's what you would be.'' She covered her ears with her hands, trying to block out even the smallest whimper of bulldozers. ``I can't believe they're tearing down the orchard. It's obscene.''

Her orchard. Hers and Michael's.

He wasn't talking, so she did. ``If you had any guts, you would fight your family on this,'' she argued. ``You would throw yourself in front of that earth-mover or dump truck or whatever it is. Michael, you can't work for them. You can't be a part of this obscenity.'' Her voice trailed off. ``You just can't.''

``Don't worry about me. If you go through with the wedding, I'm hardly going to stick around and work for my family.'' He laughed bitterly. ``Yeah, that would be wonderful, tripping over to your place for Sunday dinner with you and Skip and the kids.'' Michael stood up, abandoning his railing. His voice was ferocious when he spit out, ``I'd rather die.''

``But, Michael…''

``Unless you came out here to tell me you're not going through with the wedding, this conversation is over.''

*Now is your chance, Polly! Tell him.* But the words stuck in her throat.

``You know, Skipper told me to stay away from you,'' he said angrily. ``He said you just feel sorry for me because you think my heart will always belong to Polly and she doesn't want it.''

"He had no right to say that. I never said anything like that," she protested.

"Well, just in case," he returned, his beautiful eyes so chilly it was painful to look into them. "Just in case that's what you think, I want you to know that I did love her. I loved her fire and her spirit.''

*My fire and my spirit?* He still felt the same way. She knew it. "Michael, there's something I have to tell you—"

"But you have the same fire and spirit, Cassie. And you have a serenity, a grace and a purity that she never did.''

Polly stepped back. Serenity, grace, purity. He sounded just like Skipper. People always said those things about Cassie, when what they really meant was that she kept her mouth shut. So she was quiet. Big deal. What was so great about being quiet?

"What a bunch of baloney," she muttered.

But Michael was on a roll now, and if he heard her, he didn't show it. "See, that's the difference. You have depth. Polly pretended to have depth, spouting nonsense about her causes and the issue of the week, but underneath, she was immature and judgmental and unfair.''

That stung. Immature, sure. She was seventeen at the time. "Judgmental? Unfair?''

"Think about the way she broke up with me and flounced out of town. I thought we meant more than that to each other." He jammed his hands into the pockets of his jacket. ``But where's Polly? She's been off sulking for the past seven years.''

``And you haven't?''

``No.'' If looks could kill, that one would have. ``I've been trying to get on with my life without her in it. The joke is that I am finally at a place where I can do that, where I really don't miss her anymore, and what happens? I fall in love with her sister.''

Polly stilled. Carefully, slowly, she asked, ``So you really don't have any feelings for Polly anymore? And if she walked right up to us here on this bridge, you would tell her to get lost?''

``Absolutely.''

Quickly, as quickly as she could go, Polly backed away. ``I, uh, have to go.'' And she raced off the bridge, across the outfield, over home plate and around to the parking lot in record time. She sat for a second in the car, panting, attempting to catch her breath, before she turned the key. And then she was out of there.

``DAMN IT, CASSIE.''

He watched her running away, just like her sister. How many times were these Tompkins women going to stomp on his heart and then run away?

Well, it was all for the best. She acted, sounded just as judgmental and unfair as Polly, with all that crap about corporate shills and snakes and obscenities.

``What a crock,'' he said out loud. And how exactly like Polly, like all the things that had driven him nuts, even when he'd thought he loved her. If Cassie was going to turn into a carbon copy of Polly, then he didn't want her, anyway.

He froze.

A carbon copy.

It couldn't be.

She couldn't be.

``But she *is*...'' And she had been all along. ``Polly.''

Michael sat down on the bridge, feeling like the world's biggest stooge. Of course. How could he have missed it?

The surprising chemistry between them; her getting suddenly fussy about beef and pork and fur; the sexy, sizzling red dress; the soul-deep kiss in the gazebo; the cake seduction; the scenes on this bridge... Images toppled over each other in his brain.

Had they been changing off and on? Had it been Cassie some of the time, and Polly others?

No. That was definitely Polly. Ever since she'd stepped off the damn train. And on some level, he'd known it all along.

MICHAEL DROVE around for a good hour, deciding how best to bring the little liar to her knees. He still didn't have much of a plan, but it didn't matter.

The key was to make her sweat for awhile, to let it get closer and closer to the wedding, just to make her crazy, and then, then...

``Then I'll make her confess.''

He was going to enjoy every minute of this.

# 9

*May 29: Three days before the wedding*

POLLY WAS BESIDE HERSELF. She had chewed off every nail she had, snapped at every person she knew and was reduced to spending all of her time in her bedroom with the door shut and her little sister's earphones on. She'd never liked hip-hop much but, hey, it got you through the day.

She was no longer making any pretense of behaving like Cassie. Everyone thought she was insane anyway, so what was the point?

It was late Wednesday afternoon, the wedding was on Saturday, and still no Cassie. She wasn't answering the phone at the house. The cell phone was still out of order. And Polly didn't know what else to try, short of the police.

Where was Cassie?

"I have to try the office," she decided. She didn't know how risky it might be, calling her own secretary and asking for herself, but then she didn't know how good or bad a job Cassie had done, either, so they might not even care if there were two of her.

She wasn't scheduled to be in the office, anyway, since she had expected to be off and back in Pleasant

Falls for the wedding. Cassie should've been done with the Wild Man last weekend, so there was no reason for her to be there. But where else could she try?

Determined to find Cassie and be done with it, Polly dialed the number for her office.

``Hello, Lenora Bridge and Associates,'' a cool female voice answered.

``Polly Tompkins, please,'' she mumbled in a husky voice.

``Excuse me?''

``Polly Tompkins,'' she said more clearly.

``Oh, I'm sorry, but she's no longer with Lenora Bridge and Associates.''

``Excuse me?''

``I said she's no longer with Lenora Bridge and Associates.'' Dropping her voice, the secretary said. ``She was terminated, if you want to know the truth.''

``Terminated?''

``Yeah. She had that guy they call the Wild Man as a client, and, well, things got pret-ty wild, and Lenora had a fit and fired her.'' She broke off. ``Oh, I shouldn't have said that, should I? Anyway, she's not here. So if you were one of her clients, I can forward you to someone else in the company.''

``No, just a friend,'' Polly whispered. She hung up the receiver with a limp hand, almost missing the cradle. She was numb. Fired? Her sister got her fired? ``How the hell did she do that?''

She hadn't yet begun to recover from the shock of knowing she no longer had a job when Skipper came ambling in, once again entering through the kitchen without even knocking.

"This isn't your house, you know," she snapped. If Cassie could lose Polly's job, then Polly could return the favor and lose Cassie's fiancé. "At least I kind of liked my job," she mumbled.

"Hi, hon," he said tentatively. He gave her a hug at arm's length.

Polly had decided that Skipper was in lion tamer mode when it came to dealing with this bizarre version of his bride. He kept his distance, he made sure there were chairs and other furniture in between them, and he frequently told her how fervently he was hoping she would get over it.

"Skipper, what do you want?" she asked vaguely. She was still back on "terminated" and "no job."

"Just one thing, honey bunny," he said sweetly. "One last item on the list. You have to go down to Teutopolis to visit my grandmother. It's a tradition. If you want to marry a Kennigan, you have to get Grandmother's permission."

"Okay." She smiled. "Then the wedding is off."

"Cassie, what is wrong with you? I think you've lost your mind." He backed off even further, his mouth agape. "Do you really want to cancel the wedding over a simple visit to my grandmother?"

*Don't mess with me,* she felt like shouting at him. *The man I love doesn't love me, my sister has deserted me and I don't even have a job to go back to.*

Out loud, she told him, "No, I want to cancel the wedding because I don't want to get married. Surely you've noticed that I'm falling apart. Do you really want to marry a crazy person?"

"Cassie, sweetheart," he said in a soothing tone, "I really do think maybe you need professional help."

"That won't change the fact that the wedding is off. Finito. Done with. Over." She took a seat on the couch and crossed her arms over her chest, signifying that she wasn't going to change her mind.

"Do you know what a scandal that would be? Do you seriously want to ruin your life in this town forever?" Skipper's face was flushed and his eyes were scrunched so tight she wondered how he could see.

"Okay," he continued, in a small, mean voice, "so you've decided to get hormonal or psychotic or whatever for a few days. But you belong here, Cassie. You grew up here, you've always said that you wanted to stay here for the rest of your life. Think about that. Think about whether you will be welcome in Pleasant Falls if you cancel your wedding to a Kennigan."

"Do you really want to blackmail me into marrying you?" she asked, aghast.

"It's not blackmail. It's common sense. And I love you." He seethed for a minute, trying to get himself under control. "I know you love me, too. It's just fear. But once we get past it and get married, you will be the Cassie I know and love."

"And if that doesn't happen?"

"Then you'd better find somewhere else to live. And warn your dad that the lease on his hardware store is up and your mother that the school won't be renewing her contract."

Just when she was ready to pull the plug, he had to get ugly on her. And she had no doubt he could do exactly what he said. Okay, so Cassie had gotten her fired. But was Polly ready to ruin her entire family's life in Pleasant Falls forever?

Yeah, maybe she was. It was all going to blow up on the wedding day, anyway, whether Polly lit the fuse this minute or not. Unless, of course, Cassie miraculously reappeared between then and now. Right. And the Easter Bunny would be carrying her luggage.

Was she ready to have her family's life here shredded to tatters? Maybe. Maybe not.

"I'm not thinking very clearly right now, Skipper. Give me a few hours."

"You do that, Cassie. You think about the consequences. To you, to your parents and to your sister. Because no one humiliates a Kennigan in this town and gets away with it."

*It's not me who's humiliating you, Skipper. It's Cassie. And maybe she deserves what she gets.*

On the bright side, things couldn't get any worse than this, could they? Everything ought to be roses from here.

POLLY WAS SETTLED into bed with Shaggy singing in her ears. The song was all about infidelity, which was kind of amusing under the circumstances, and Polly was enjoying it, humming along.

Maybe that was why she didn't hear her bedroom window scrape open, but she definitely saw the dark silhouette of a man creeping over the sill and into her room. He was wearing a bright white T-shirt that glowed in the dim room, and beat-up blue jeans that fit him like a glove. Yum.

Polly sat up in bed, pulling the covers up to her chin. As always, all she had to do was look at him and her pulse skyrocketed. Her whole body jumped to life, with little tremors there and tingles here. Michael. In her bedroom. Yum.

"What are you doing?" she asked, trying to keep the tremors and tingles out of her voice.

He signaled that she should take off her headphones. "Hi," he said casually, as if second-story work were quite normal for him. "How are you?"

"Losing my mind. And you?"

"I'm okay." He sauntered over closer and made a place for himself on the edge of her bed.

She could feel the heat of his thigh through the quilt, searing her bare leg. "Well, gee, make yourself at home."

"Thanks, I will."

They stayed in that position for a few beats, staring at each other, with Polly nonplussed and Michael as happy as a clam.

Finally, Polly broke in. "Are you going to tell me what you're doing here? Or did you just scale my wall and break into my bedroom to sit on the bed for a while?"

"No, actually, I have a reason."

"I thought you might." She waited. "And that reason would be…?"

"A trip to grandmother's house," he supplied cheerfully, looking every bit the Big, Bad Wolf.

"A trip to…?" That was out of left field. "And why, exactly?"

"Well, I wanted to let you know that I'm completely reconciled to the wedding and everything is A-okay with you and me." He winked at her. She couldn't believe it, but he actually winked at her. "Skipper is bound and determined that you need to visit my grandmother, the old bird, and get her permission to marry our boy Skip. So I'm doing Skipper a favor by taking you. Don't worry—he knows all about it."

"And why did you sneak in my bedroom window under cover of darkness to proffer this marvelous trip?" she inquired, trying her best to maintain a chill. But with Michael and moonlight and her own frayed nerves…she was ripe for seduction.

He shrugged. "No one else is supposed to know. Skipper doesn't want the two of us seen together."

A trip to the country with Michael… She shrugged back. "Okay, I'll go."

"That's it?" he asked.

Finally, she had surprised him. He narrowed his eyes, taking her measure, and she smiled. "Yeah." She settled back under her covers and reached for the headphones. "Close the window on your way out, will you?"

He lifted his hands in surrender, moving effortlessly to the window. He had one leg over the sill when she said, "Oh, one more thing, Michael. If you asked me right now to come out that window with you, to run away from this terrible town forever, even knowing that you don't love me, I would go. Just in case you wanted to ask.''

''Why don't you just meet me at noon at the old Dog 'n' Suds?''

''Not asking, huh?''

''Not asking.''

Pity. Polly posed one last question. ''So where should I tell people I'm going?''

''Live dangerously,'' he whispered across the room. ''Don't tell them.''

Live dangerously. That she knew all about.

And then Michael slipped out the window, gone as swiftly as he'd arrived.

Polly snuggled down into the bedclothes. She had no illusions. Michael didn't love her, not as Polly, who was—in his eyes, at least—judgmental and unfair but not as the virgin goddess Cassie, either, since he now purported to be thrilled with the idea of marrying her off to Skipper. Nope. No illusions left.

But she didn't care. It was still a heck of a lot more fun riding off into the country with Michael than it was sitting around waiting for Cassie.

And maybe this was her ticket out of trouble. Maybe on the way to grandmother's house she would tell him the truth and see if he had any theories.

It would feel good to tell Michael the truth. Not because she thought he would rescue her or carry her off into the sunset. Fat chance. No, it would feel good because it was Michael. And she owed him the truth.

Dog 'n' Suds. Noon. Best invitation she'd had in years.

*May 30: Two days before the wedding*

SHE WAS HUMMING the song about the big, bad wolf even before she got to the Dog 'n' Suds.

It was kind of fun, sneaking over to the faded ice-cream stand at high noon, disguised in jean shorts and a T-shirt that belonged to Ashley, with a baseball cap pulled over her head. No one would ever think this was Cassie Tompkins. Polly felt as if she were on a spy mission. And in a way, she was.

It only heightened that impression when Michael met her in one of his father's Cadillacs, a big monster of a car with tinted windows. Not even Mrs. Withers would see in those windows or figure out who was riding around with whom.

Safely in the passenger seat, belted down for the duration, Polly turned on the radio, figuring that was safer than trying to think up casual conversation with Michael. He'd been a mocking old boyfriend-once-removed, a passionate suitor and, last night, an intruder, but she couldn't really envision casual chitchat with any of them. And she wasn't quite ready to get into a deep discussion about her deception yet.

Michael had other ideas. "So, Cassie," he began, sliding a hand over to pat her on the knee, "I know you and Skipper have plans for a family and a house, but I'm sensing some conflict on the horizon, since you weren't too happy about Pleasant Valley Estates. How are you going to handle that?"

"At this point, I'm not really planning anything," she murmured, distracted by his hand on her knee.

"Yes, but, Cassie..." His fingers moved to her cheek, and he stroked it, tracing a path from her ear to the corner of her mouth. She had the urge to bite. He whispered, "I find myself very interested in what you see in your future."

What in the world was this all about? He was only supposed to be taking her to Granny's house because he was determined to see her married. So what was with the hanky-panky?

Polly removed his hand from her face. "I see a car wreck if you don't keep your hands on the wheel and your eyes on the road."

"I don't think we're in any danger, Cassie," he said sweetly. And then he winked. Again!

"Michael," she protested, "you said you were reconciled to the idea of the wedding."

"I am," he swore. He grinned and blew her a kiss. "But I thought you might like to have some fun first."

"I'm not that sort of person," she said stiffly.

"Sure you are, Cassie."

"No, I'm not," she insisted.

"Cassie, Cassie, Cassie..." But his hand was back on her knee.

He also seemed to have a real fascination for her name today. Since it wasn't actually her name, that was kind of a problem.

It took two long hours to get to his grandmother's house, which meant two hours of playing "keep away" and trying to figure out what he was up to. He kept pushing her on what she wanted out of life and where she saw herself in ten years and all these other strange things, plus he made lots of sly comments about her willingness to cheat and lie—nothing really straightforward or objectionable, just references to what kind of games she might play or secrets she might keep or what might be simmering below her surface.

Was he offering openings for her to confess? Was this a sexy variation on good cop-bad cop? Or was she reading too much into it?

In the meantime, while she tried to get a handle on the mystery that was Michael, he was driving her bananas. It was all she could manage to keep her body parts to herself, let alone play verbal volleyball.

She was actually thankful to arrive at Granny's, which turned out to be a pleasant farmhouse way outside the small town of Teutopolis, or T-Town, as it was called. His grandmother, a very tiny woman with a bun wound on top of her head and a severe expression, stood on the porch waiting for them.

But when Michael came around to open Polly's door, he breathed on her neck and nibbled her ear. It only took a second, and he was blocked from his grandmother's view by the car, but Polly made a squeak and almost hit her head on the car door.

"Stop that!" she whispered.

He held out his hands, palms up, with an innocent "Who, me?" expression, but she wasn't fooled. This was apparently Tease Polly Day at Granny's house.

Meanwhile, Granny was no picnic, either. "Come on, come on," she prompted, holding open the door. "I made supper and I'm hungry."

It was only two-thirty and Polly had had lunch, but she tried to be polite about the overcooked fish sticks and limp green beans. Apparently Granny was a thrifty sort, and she seemed to delight in reciting a complete tally of what she'd paid for every item on the table.

"Who are you again?" Grandmother Kennigan demanded. "Are you Ann?"

"No, she's Cassie," Michael answered for her. "She's going to marry Skipper."

While under the table, he had his hand on her knee again. And she could hardly slap him in front of his grandmother. But she just might.

"Skipper? If she's hitched to Skipper, then what's she doing with you?"

"I drove Cassie here so that she could get your blessing to marry Skipper, Grandma," Michael went on. "Don't you want to give her your blessing?"

"Can't she talk for herself?"

"She might if Michael would let her," Polly said tersely.

"Hmph. No. I don't like her," the old woman snapped. "Dressed like a chippy. I don't think Raymond should marry a chippy."

She went on with her objections to this Ann person marrying Raymond, whoever that was, and Michael moved his foot over on top of Polly's. She closed her eyes and tried to pretend she was somewhere else.

But now his bare foot was rubbing the back of her calf and it felt awfully good. Not to mention his fingers tickling the fringed hem of her shorts, sliding in under the edge, making her think of lots of things that had nothing to do with grandmothers.

He pressed a little higher, and she almost choked on a green bean, letting out a small moan before she could stop it.

``Hussy!'' Granny hissed.

``I didn't do anything!'' How many times had she said that lately?

His grandmother toddled off to take a nap while the two of them cleaned up the remains of the meal, but that only opened up the field for Michael and his little kisses and caresses even more.

``This is gross, Michael. Stop it!''

``Ssshh. You'll wake up my grandmother.'' But his lips were nuzzling the nape of her neck and she couldn't think.

``Can we leave while she's napping?'' she begged. ``She's not a very pleasant person, is she?''

``No, we can't leave. She'll want us to eat pudding and play Parcheesi when she wakes up. Believe me, I've done this a million times and I know the routine.''

``You knew this routine and you came, anyway?'' Polly leaned back into him, giving him more room to nuzzle.

``I kind of like her,'' he admitted. ``Don't move. I think I hear her getting up.''

What with pudding and Parcheesi and more haggling with Granny over whether Polly was a hussy or not, they didn't get out of there for hours. While they'd been inside, the sky had grown very dark and ominous, and big, fat raindrops were starting to fall as they ran to the car.

"I didn't see anything about bad weather coming in," Michael said, gazing out the windshield at the gathering storm. "Better turn on the radio. It looks nasty."

The rain grew harder, beating against the car, and visibility was not good on the poorly lit, winding road. There were flashes of lightning and deep, sonorous booms of thunder that all seemed very close. Even in the big Cadillac, Polly felt buffeted by the wind and rain, and she kept darting glances at Michael to see whether he was scared. He didn't seem to be, but his hands were white on the wheel.

Polly swallowed. While she was happy to be out from under Michael's seductive assault, distracted as he was by the weather, she was awfully worried.

She didn't know how long they had been driving, but she would've thought they should be home by now. Still, she didn't recognize anything. "How far are we?" she asked.

"Not far."

"I didn't say where I was going, and my parents will be worried." Glancing at the clock on the dashboard, she whispered, "It's getting late, too. We will be home soon, won't we?"

But as they crested a hill, they heard a really huge boom and crack right behind them, and a streak of lighting sizzled in the air. "That was too close."

Polly hunched down in her seat, fully aware that hunching was not going to provide much protection.

But she flinched when another lightning bolt split the sky.

Michael skidded to a stop. ``The bridge is out,'' he muttered. ``Completely washed out.''

Polly peered out her window, but she couldn't see anything. It was too dark and the rain and the wind were just incredible. ``Can we turn around and go back?''

``We can try.'' It took a few minutes, but he maneuvered the big, bulky car around and set out in the other direction. They didn't get far. A whole tree was now blocking the road they'd just driven on. ``Must have been lightning. It sounded really close. I guess it was.''

``So what do we do?''

``The best thing to do is just wait it out. Want to hike for the nearest farmhouse? Maybe look for a barn?'' he suggested.

``In this storm?'' Polly wasn't touching that with a ten-foot pitchfork. ``I'm staying here.''

``Okay.'' He switched off the ignition. ``Climb over,'' he ordered.

``Climb over where?''

``The back seat. Come on. It'll be like old times.'' He vaulted into the back and held out his arms. ``Don't worry, I'll catch you.''

Polly wiggled her way back there, not nearly as elegantly as he had. It *was* like old times. They'd never ridden out a storm or stayed a whole night in the back seat, but they'd spent some very steamy hours there.

With his back against one door, Michael stretched

out his legs on the seat, pulling Polly up on top of him, secure in his lap. He fastened his arms around her and tipped his head down next to hers.

``Does this remind you of anything?'' he asked with what she could've sworn was a leer. With him behind her like this, she couldn't really see his face, but that had certainly felt like a leer. ``Remember?'' he whispered, biting down gently on her ear. ``The first time we made love it was in the back of a car.''

``It was not. We did no such thing.'' She had vivid recollections of every single time she and Michael had made love and not one of them was in a car, especially not the first time, which was very definitely in the apple orchard. So what was he talking about?

But he didn't know he was talking to Polly, the person in the orchard. He thought he was talking to...

``Cassie?'' she shrieked, tumbling away from him into the trough of leg room below. Scrunched into a heap, she managed to get herself turned around and onto her knees so she could accuse him to his face. ``You slept with *Cassie* in the back seat of a car?''

``What do you mean, I slept with Cassie?'' His words were sing-song and insincere, dripping with fake surprise. ``Why, I thought *you* were Cassie.''

Polly's mouth fell open.

``Gotcha,'' Michael said with glee. ``So, tell me, how've you been, Polly?''

# 10

---

DID HE SAY *Polly?* So he knew. He knew.

But Polly was too furious to care. The storm outside had nothing on her. "You slept with Cassie!" she said again, still crackling with outrage. "So that's the big secret that the two of you share, huh? When you thought I was Cassie, you kept telling me about what *we* had done, and I wondered what you meant but I never thought... Oh, my God!"

Michael was actually laughing, damn his hide. Trying to balance on her knees and outstretched arms, she had no choice but to crawl all over him in the intimate, clumsy confines of the back seat. She wanted to slap that snarky smile right off his handsome, cheating face.

And then her brain rearranged the pieces. "Prom night," she spit out. "Cassie told me that you cheated on me with someone at the prom. But I never thought it was Cassie!"

He made a grab for her, probably hoping to force her to sit still, but he missed. "Polly, calm down."

"Calm down?" As her mind whirled with these new revelations, she scuttled as far away as she could go, hugging the other door. The rain was still slashing against the windows, punctuated by intermittent bursts of thunder and lightning, but it couldn't compare to the noise in her head. How could she not have known that Michael had slept with her sister? ``All these years I thought it was Lana. But after I saw her at the bridal shop and she told me about barfing on your shoes, I knew it wasn't her.''

``Lana? You thought I slept with Lana?'' he demanded, showing some outrage of his own.

Polly narrowed her eyes, staring daggers at him in the darkness. ``Cassie came home from the prom very upset. She said she'd had a rotten time and I hadn't missed anything by not going. And then she told me, for my own good, that she saw you fooling around with someone else and she thought I should know. But she never let out even a peep that it was *her*.''

``Oh, get over it,'' Michael snapped. He caught her by the wrists and hauled her across the seat until they met in the middle, both of them on their knees. Right into her face, he proclaimed, ``I never slept with your sister. I just said that to get you to admit that you were really you. And it worked, didn't it?''

Struggling to free herself, Polly kind of snarled at him but didn't answer.

``The only thing that happened between Cassie and me,'' he said slowly and deliberately, ``was a couple of lousy dances and one very drunk kiss. She slapped me silly, told me I didn't deserve you and then ran home, apparently hell-bent to convince you to dump me. Which you did.''

Polly glanced up, not sure what to believe. Was he

sincere? He certainly looked sincere. "A kiss? Are you saying it was just a kiss?"

"Yes, that's what I'm saying." Michael's eyes blazed with old, deep pain. "But you dumped me, anyway. Given the timing, I thought it was probably because of Cassie. That's why I said that she had ruined my life, because she ran home and tattled about one stupid kiss and that was enough to send you packing. I mean, I admit it was stupid, but it was hardly worth losing you forever."

Polly sat back on her heels. "Well, I didn't know it was just a kiss," she mumbled.

"You didn't ask," he said darkly.

"With or without tongue?"

He punched his fist into the leather headrest in front of him. "Polly, what is wrong with you? Does it really matter?"

"No. I suppose not. You just have to put yourself in my place—"

"Don't you think there's too much of that going on already?" he sniped.

"Michael, I loved you," she tried to explain. "I loved you so much. You were the only person in the whole town who understood me and loved me, anyway. I told you that the prom was stupid and archaic and sexist, but did you trust me or support me? No! You rented a tux and took Lana Pfeiffer and got yourself crowned king, for goodness sake. When my sister came home and told me you'd betrayed me, what was I supposed to think? I already felt betrayed. And then, when I sent Cassie to break up with you—"

"You did *what?*"

Polly sighed. "Yeah, Mr. I-Can-Tell-The-Difference. I sent Cassie. She pretended to be me and she broke up with you so I didn't have to."

He slumped back against the door. "Why? Too chicken to do it yourself?"

"Well, yes, if you must know." From the beginning, all he'd had to do was smile, and she'd end up a puddle at his feet. "I couldn't risk you kissing me or touching me and making me change my mind."

Michael shook his head. "You should never have broken up with me at all. If you'd really loved me, you would've given me the benefit of the doubt."

"I did love you," Polly whispered.

"Yeah, right," he said savagely. "And that's why you've been playing me for a fool again, pretending to be Cassie this whole time, making me think I was going crazy, falling in love with someone I'd never even liked that much."

"Look, it was a ridiculous idea. I didn't want to!" she protested. "But she needed me. I promised her that I would take her place just long enough for her to get her head together before she married Skipper. I had no idea you would be here. If I'd known, I'd never have agreed to it. But once it was started…" She knew it was lame, but she said it, anyway. "Well, it was hard to stop."

"Uh-huh." Michael pulled up his knees, dangling a wrist over one of them. His voice was beyond cynical when he inquired, "So where is she? Were you going to keep doing this indefinitely? Were you prepared to marry the stiff, too?''

''No, I wasn't going to marry the stiff. And I don't know where Cassie is,'' she admitted. ''She was supposed to be back days ago, but she didn't show. There've been two phone messages, so I'm pretty sure she's alive.'' Her jaw tightened. ''Of course, she may not be after I get my hands on her.''

''Unless I get there first.''

Polly ran her hands through her Cassie-inspired hair, ruffling it but good. ''What a mess.''

''So what about Skipper?''

''He doesn't know. Yet.'' She sent a surreptitious glance Michael's way, weighing his mood. Was he still mad? Was she? She wanted so badly to leap over the chasm between them and get back into the safe harbor of his arms. Yes, the storm was scary and a major chill had permeated the window, but it wasn't just safety or warmth she wanted. She longed for Michael, to hold him and love him. It was the way life should have been for the two of them, and she wanted it back.

''So when were you planning to tell Skipper?'' he asked dryly, breaking into her thoughts.

''I told him yesterday that the wedding was off. I mean, I tried.'' She shivered, hugging herself and rubbing her arms.

''You're cold,'' he murmured, moving closer. ''Come here.''

And then he bracketed her shoulders with his hands, casually nudging her until she relaxed. She was hard up against the length of his body, her head tilted into his warm, strong chest, as he spread his leather jacket over both of them. Polly closed her eyes, settling in just the way she'd wanted to, with his arms holding her tight.

"Michael, it was horrible," she told him. "Skipper said that Cassie would never be able to hold her head up in this town again and my dad would lose his lease and my mom would lose her job, all that would happen if she—I mean, I—called off the wedding."

"Like he gets to decide that," he said derisively.

"I don't know." She pushed herself up an inch or two, tipping her head back to find his eyes. "I was so confused. I love you so much and I wanted to tell you the truth. But how could I just wreck my sister's life for my own selfish reasons?"

"First of all, your reasons are not selfish. Cassie made this mess, and it's past time for her to get herself out of it." Michael frowned. "And second, it's not like you can marry Skipper, no matter what."

"I know that!"

"Because," he said, dropping hungry little kisses on her nose and the corners of her mouth, "you're going to marry me."

"I am not."

"Yes, you are." Michael's kisses started to get longer and more ardent, as he slid his lips over her cheek and ear and skated one hand under the edge of her shirt to find bare skin.

She couldn't hold back a small groan of pleasure. It had been so long since anyone touched her or held her this way. As his fingers crept farther under the soft fabric of her T-shirt, inching upward, Polly smiled and pressed into the caress, giving in to the pure pleasure of anticipation.

Right next to her ear, he whispered, "You're going to marry me, because if you don't, I'm going to become a corporate shill for my family and commit obscenities all over Pleasant Falls."

"Michael, please, I don't want to talk about this," she begged as his hands slipped onto even more sensitive turf, one teasing the lacy underside of her bra while the other fiddled with the button at the top of her shorts. "We are in the back seat of a very comfortable car. Ohhhh."

"Marry me," he murmured.

The button slipped through the hole. The zipper scraped down.

"Marry me."

Her words were unsteady. "We're miles from nowhere. It's dark. There's thunder and lightning and I'm cold."

Her whole body trembled as she said that, but it wasn't from cold.

"Marry me," he persisted.

"I have missed you so much for so long," she murmured, pushing up so that he could ease her shorts down over her hips. "Ohhhh. I want your clothes off. I want to get my hands on all of you. So, can we talk about marriage some other time?"

With a fierce, possessive kiss, he pinned her to the seat, covering her body with his, rocking his hips into her to telegraph his intent. "You talk too much," he growled.

"Thank you," she moaned, tangling her bare leg around his jeans, reaching for his belt.

In their haste to get naked and get together, his jacket flew into the front seat, her bra ended up draped on the dashboard, his jeans were still around his ankles, and she had no idea what happened to her underpants.

As they tangled together, slipping and sliding down sweat-soaked skin, Polly throbbed with desire, needing him with every moment of pent-up frustration of the past seven years. She was hasty, eager, wanton, but she couldn't stop, didn't want to stop.

And Michael was every bit as greedy and reckless as she was. He was with her and inside her, every stroke bringing her closer to paradise, and she gasped with the heat, the joy and the amazing *rightness* of it. They belonged together. They had always belonged together.

Making love to Michael was like recapturing the other half of her heart. His left hand lay splayed on top of her right, finger to finger, as together they reached for absolute bliss.

*May 31: One day before the wedding*

POLLY AWOKE to a major pounding in her head. Or maybe not in her head. Pounding coming from somewhere, though. Were those voices she heard?

Still half-asleep, she opened her eyes, but all she

could see was some kind of plush maroon fabric, as if she had been sleeping with her nose pressed to a soft cushiony wall. She tried to turn over, but her body was scrunched between the wall and something warm and hard. Make that *someone* warm and hard. Someone *naked* and warm and hard. She smiled dreamily.

"Michael?" she mumbled. The front of him was pressed to the back of her, and he felt delicious. Memories of last night began to filter back into her sleepy brain, and she slid back and forth against him just enough to create the desired effect.

"Mmmm..." he managed, tossing an arm over hers, finding her breast with unerring aim, teasing and tantalizing her all over again. Even half-asleep, he was very good at this.

She shifted around to face him, rubbing her breasts against his chest. "This is a marvelous way to wake up," she whispered, feeling very naughty for so early in the day.

Bam. Bam. Bam.

"What is that pounding?" she asked, lifting her head.

"Whoever's in there, you better come out!" a loud voice blared from what sounded like a bullhorn. "Naah, I can't see. Damn windows are all steamed over."

That got her attention. Polly sat up, almost clonking Michael in the head. "Michael, someone's out there, someone looking for us!"

"Looks like they found us," he said lazily, stretching his arms as he fastened them around her.

"Michael! They may break in here. And we're naked! They may think we stole the car or carjacked it or something!"

"I doubt it." His jeans were pooled near the far door, and he made a casual effort to shrug back into them. "Probably just a posse sent out by Skipper to look for you. Or Cassie, I mean."

"Oh, hell. He still thinks I'm Cassie!" Meanwhile, where were her clothes?

Someone pounded on the back window with a stick or pole or something, making a very loud noise and freaking Polly out. "I can't find my clothes!" she cried.

"I can wrap myself around you," he offered, smiling sleepily. And she lost her heart all over again.

"Michael, I love you," she laughed. "We are hip-deep in doo-doo and I still love you."

He reached around her, produced his T-shirt, and handed it to her without comment. She barely managed to get it over her head and around the important bits before the crashing and bashing became louder.

"Come out of there!" the loud voice roared again.

Still on his stomach, Michael unlocked the door and pressed down on the lever, half-crawling and half-falling out the door. But he bounded to his feet neatly enough, holding out a hand to help Polly make a more circumspect exit from the back seat of the car.

"It's them!" someone yelled. That voice and that irritating, self-righteous tone could only be Skipper.

His face was practically gray as his eyes raked up and down the two of them where they stood there, barely wearing one outfit put together, all tousled and flushed. They might as well have carried a neon sign that flashed We Just Had Great Sex!

Poor Skipper.

"It's not what you think," Polly put in quickly, searching the crowd of men for a friendly face. But with Skipper and Deuce Kennigan backed up by a pack of relatives and lackeys, there wasn't much to find. They weren't carrying shotguns or ropes, but they might as well have been. "Just give us a chance to explain," she tried.

Voices tumbled on top of each other. "Cassie, how could you?" "Michael, how could you?" "She the Tompkins girl that was supposed to marry Skipper tomorrow?"

Michael reached over and took her hand. He brought it up to his lips and kissed it, which she thought was very sweet, if not exactly the smart thing to do at this moment.

"Everyone calm down," he ordered. "She's right. It's not what you think."

Making a fist, Skipper skidded closer. "Not what I think? We find *my* fiancée and *my* brother wrapped up in the back seat of a car after an entire night of debauchery, and it's not what I think?"

"Um, I'm not your fiancée," Polly offered helpfully.

"Not anymore, you're not," one of the other men quipped, as several others snickered.

"I'm not Cassie!" she exclaimed. "Is that plain enough for you? I'm Polly. The twin. The bad one."

"And you expect me to believe that?" Skipper demanded. "How stupid do you think I am?"

"Stupid enough not to know I've been Polly for the better part of the past two weeks and you didn't even notice." She tugged at the hem of her T-shirt, not really enjoying all the staring and the gaping. "Well, actually, I've been Polly my whole life. But I've been here, in Pleasant Falls, sort of pretending to be Cassie for a week and a half."

"Sort of?" Michael's father inquired. "What does that mean?"

"Okay, I was pretending to be Cassie." As Skipper began to protest, she held up a hand. "She had cold feet, okay? Really frigid cold feet. She fell apart when she came to see me in Chicago for our birthday. And she was the one who convinced *me* that we should exchange places, just for a few days, just to give her time to catch her breath. At that point, as far as I know, she had every intention of coming back and marrying you, or she wouldn't have asked me to take her place, because what sense does that make if she's not coming back?"

"I don't get that, do you?" someone asked. Another one complained, "She sure does talk a lot."

If nothing else, that proved she was Polly.

"Where is Cassie?" Skipper gritted out, one word at a time. He was so angry he was shaking, and she didn't blame him.

"I don't know. She should've been home days ago. But she didn't come." She exhaled a long, heavy sigh. "I really thought she would come before now, Skipper, and at least tell you herself that she didn't want to marry you—instead of making me do it, I mean. But since she hasn't shown, all I can say is that the wedding is off.''

``Once again, these Tompkins women have embarrassed us,'' the senior Mr. Kennigan puffed. His color was a lot higher than his son's as he wrenched open one of the front doors of the Cadillac, presumably to let the Tompkins stench out. But when he—and everyone else—caught sight of her bra on the dashboard, he slammed the door shut again. ``Don't think I've forgotten who you are, Polly Tompkins, or what you've done.''

``It's been seven years,'' she said wearily.

``I haven't forgotten!'' he shouted. ``I haven't forgotten a word of it. And now this is just par for the course. I told Skipper to stay away from the other one, that the Tompkins were fruit of a poisonous tree. But he was in love. Well, the hell with love! No more Tompkins!''

``Excuse me.'' Michael's dark brows slashed together. ``If you keep that up, I'm going to have to disown you, both of you. I might even sue you. Is that what you want? I love this woman, and I want her to marry me as soon as possible because I don't want to lose her or be without her for one more minute. If you have a problem with that, I'd much rather lose you.''

``Michael, are you really asking me to marry you?'' she asked quietly. ``I know you said it before, but there were, um, extenuating circumstances. You had just found out that I was me and I had just found out that you didn't cheat on me at the prom and we were both hot to make up. That kind of emotional turbulence colors things, so if you don't want to get married but you feel like you should take a stand or get behind me or whatever, well, I will understand.''

''She sure talks a lot,'' somebody griped again.

''Polly, do you have an answer for me?'' Michael prompted. ''Will you marry me?

''Yes! Yes, I will.'' Leaning closer, she whispered, ''I would throw my arms around you but I'm afraid my shirt would ride up and I would be, you know, exposing my backside to this whole pack of Kennigans.''

''Oh, Polly,'' he said with a sigh of resignation, ''you really do talk too much.'' So he bent down and kissed her instead, saving her from exposing anything she didn't want to. And then, with Polly tucked into the curve of his arm, he faced down his family one more time. ''Dad, Skip, I'm very sorry about the wedding. But you know, you will get over it. And in the meantime, you will not ruin or attempt to ruin or even upset any of the Tompkins family. Because I like this one, and I'll do everything I can to see she stays happy, even if it means living far, far away from Pleasant Falls.''

''That is so sweet,'' she murmured. ''But you know, Michael, I'm not afraid of a few Kennigans. Who knows? Maybe you and I should stay here. Well, not this exact spot on the road, but you know what I mean. We could stay here and start a new Kennigan dynasty.'' She closed her eyes and savored the moment as he kissed her again.

``You aren't serious, are you?'' he asked, with a mischievous glint in his beautiful green eyes. ``Kids, family, all within spitting distance of Pleasant Falls? A Kennigan dynasty?''

``Well, it would be a more free-spirited branch of the family.''

Polly smiled, beaming with happiness as she contemplated their future. ``And I should probably warn you that I plan to fight, tooth and nail, to stop Pleasant Valley Estates and every other atrocity the Kennigans think up. In fact, I'm looking forward to it.''

Michael shook his head, laughing out loud. ``God, Polly, I've missed you. How did I ever not recognize *you*?''

## he Harlequin Reader Service® — Here's how it works:

cepting your 2 free books and gift places you under no obligation to buy anything. You may keep the books and gift d return the shipping statement marked "cancel." If you do not cancel, about a month later we'll send you 2 additional oks and bill you just $5.14 each in the U.S., or $6.14 each in Canada, plus 50¢ shipping & handling per book and plicable taxes if any.* That's the complete price and — compared to cover prices of $5.99 each in the U.S. and $6.99 ch in Canada — it's quite a bargain! You may cancel at any time, but if you choose to continue, every month we'll send u 2 more books, which you may either purchase at the discount price or return to us and cancel your subscription.

'erms and prices subject to change without notice. Sales tax applicable in N.Y. Canadian residents will be charged plicable provincial taxes and GST.

NO POSTAGE
NECESSARY
IF MAILED
IN THE
UNITED STATES

## BUSINESS REPLY MAIL

FIRST-CLASS MAIL    PERMIT NO. 717-003    BUFFALO, NY

POSTAGE WILL BE PAID BY ADDRESSEE

HARLEQUIN READER SERVICE
3010 WALDEN AVE
PO BOX 1867
BUFFALO NY 14240-9952

If offer card is missing write to: Harlequin Reader Service, 3010 Walden Ave., P.O. Box 1867, Buffalo NY 14240-1867

# Play The Lucky Hearts Game

### and get...
## FREE BOOKS & a FREE GIFT...
## YOURS to KEEP!

**Yes!** I have scratched off the silver card. Please send me my **2 FREE BOOKS** and **FREE GIFT**. I understand that I am under no obligation to purchase any books as explained on the back of this card.

*Scratch Here!*
then look below to see
what your cards get you...

**311 HDL DH37**                                    **111 HDL DH36**

NAME                              (PLEASE PRINT CLEARLY)

ADDRESS

APT.#                    CITY

STATE/PROV.                              ZIP/POSTAL CODE

Twenty-one gets you
**2 FREE BOOKS** and
a **FREE GIFT!**

Twenty gets you
**2 FREE BOOKS!**

Nineteen gets you
**1 FREE BOOK!**

**TRY AGAIN!**

Visit us online at
**www.eHarlequin.com**

DETACH AND MAIL CARD TODAY! (H-D-04/02)

© 1998 HARLEQUIN ENTERPRISES LTD. ® and TM are trademarks owned by Harlequin Enterprises Limited.

# The Sister Switch

## Julie Kistler

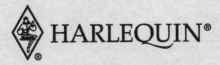

TORONTO • NEW YORK • LONDON
AMSTERDAM • PARIS • SYDNEY • HAMBURG
STOCKHOLM • ATHENS • TOKYO • MILAN • MADRID
PRAGUE • WARSAW • BUDAPEST • AUCKLAND

# 1

---

*May 21: Eleven days before the wedding*

CASSIE TOMPKINS, bride-to-be, couldn't hold back any longer.

"I'm free!" she called out. "Thank you, Polly!"

She was fully aware that her words would never reach her twin sister, hidden somewhere inside the departing train. It didn't matter—Cassie was too happy to stop the words from bubbling over. This was all so exciting!

For once in her life, she had a chance to be reckless and wild and irresponsible—a chance her wonderful twin had just handed her on a silver platter. By getting on the train to Pleasant Falls, Polly was giving Cassie the time she needed to *not* be the bride-to-be. Instead, she would be kicking up her heels, acting like a glamorous city girl, escorting a famous author around Chicago.

And not just any old author. No, it was Hiram "Wild Man" Wright, well-known wacko and storyteller extraordinaire. Cassie had never read any of his books, but she'd certainly seen him on TV, and she knew he was very entertaining and interesting.

Okay, so some people, especially people in their hometown of Pleasant Falls, might think it was low-down and dirty that the twins had decided to switch places, especially so close to the wedding. But to Cassie, it was a godsend.

So while Polly pretended to be the dutiful fiancée in boring Pleasant Falls, all pastel lip gloss and pearls, the real bride-to-be was going to strut her stuff in high heels and chic little suits on the streets of Chicago. She'd never done anything like this before, but everyone deserved one opportunity to go a little crazy, didn't they? Especially if they were supposed to marry Skipper Kennigan, Pleasant Falls' most stuffy citizen, in eleven short days.

But she wasn't going to think about Skipper right now. Not him or his domineering family or the 2.2 children they were scheduled to have within the next five years or the perfect life he had planned for them, stretching out ahead of them "'til death do us part." She would think about all that later.

Cassie would have a week in Chicago, and then she would be back in Pleasant Falls, back in her regular rut, back playing the perfect fiancée to Skipper. Until then, she was not going to think about Skipper or their future. With determination, she banished it all from her mind and focused on today instead.

"Woo-hoo!" she shouted. "It's my last chance to have some fun, and I'm going to enjoy it. With the Wild Man! Woo-hoo!"

It was all so exhilarating she could barely stand it. Hiram "Wild Man" Wright was arriving, and she would be meeting him at the airport. Plain old Cassie Tompkins, running around with the famous Wild Man. Who would ever have guessed?

But her last exuberant "woo-hoo" had earned her a few odd looks from busy commuters, and Cassie ducked her head to avoid attention. She'd spent her whole life being the quiet, well-behaved sister, so it was hard to break the habit, even if she was already wearing Polly's clothes and makeup, even if she was already assuming the identity of her more assertive sister.

Still, as she watched the tail end of her sister's train disappear down the track, bound for monotonous Pleasant Falls, Cassie couldn't help feeling free, free, free! She wanted to dance out of Union Station, singing all the way.

All this fooling around and recklessness was really very unlike her. But was it like Polly? Cassie frowned. While she was pretending to be Polly, she was going to have to be believable as a hip and trendy publicist, the sort of person who could be named one of "Chicago's 25 Hottest Singles" by *In Chicago* magazine. On the whole, Cassie decided that hot singles were probably not tap dancing in Union Station just to celebrate a little independence. So she contained her enthusiasm, lifted her chin, maintained a cool expression and did her level best to look like any other urban sophisticate on a routine day.

But she also felt a tiny tremor of fear as she tripped out into the sunshine, clicking the heels of her sister's fabulous Manolo Blahnik shoes onto the pavement.

The fashionable footwear was like a symbol of the life she had borrowed. Now that she was walking in Polly's fire engine-red high heels, there was no turning back.

*What have we done?* she wondered, making her way back to the place on the street where they had left Polly's snazzy convertible. Trading lives so close to the wedding... *What have we done?*

She took a deep breath. "It's going to be fine," she said firmly.

Revving up the engine of her sister's car, she va-roomed out into traffic, narrowly missing the bumper of a taxi and earning herself a long blast on a horn and some choice words from the cabbie. She ignored it. Now *this* was life in the city. Noisy, boisterous, energizing—all the things she wanted to experience.

As she tried to read her directions and drive at the same time, she came perilously close to several accidents. But driving a fast car on a beautiful spring day, passing trucks and squeezing around taxis... What more could she want? "Thank you, Polly!" she shouted again, letting her words blow past her in a rush of air.

A good-looking man in a silver Mercedes pulled up next to her, stared right at her and then winked. A long, sexy wink. Wow! Cassie was stunned for a minute, but then she blew him a kiss, hit the accelerator and sped off.

"I can't believe I just did that," she said under her breath, giggling at the very idea of Cassie Tompkins blowing kisses to unknown men. What a wonderful day! She had never driven a convertible, never flirted with an absolute stranger, never let the wind whip her hair into a big, gonzo mess. And it felt great.

*May 22: Ten days before the wedding*

Cassie awoke at 6:15 a.m., as she always did, raring to go on her first full day as Polly. First she made breakfast, which was very *not* Polly, but a person had to ease into these things.

She lounged around for a little while, enjoying having the run of Polly's charming little house in the Wicker Park area. It was an adorable house, chock full of art objects and trendy furniture, very urban and hip and cool. Cassie could feel herself acclimating to this new world.

She couldn't acclimate too long, however, because she had work to do. Charging back into the kitchen, she went right to the list Polly had left her, the one that detailed the things she was supposed to keep together to officially take over her twin's life.

Polly had left extensive lists, Post-It notes, and enough info to make sure even a three-year-old could stay on track. First up was supposed to be preparation for meeting the Wild Man at the airport early this evening, but Cassie spared a moment to scan the agenda one more time, since it was her favorite part. In fact, she had it mostly memorized, with all its radio interviews and signings and a few special appearances at the zoo and even a luncheon at something called the Explorers' Club, where Hiram Wright would have lunch with the person who'd won a contest sponsored by his publisher. It was too exciting.

"'Wild Man' Wright," Cassie said with glee. "I am so lucky."

Polly had been dreading this assignment, and Cassie still wasn't sure why. Who wouldn't want to hang out with Wild Man Wright? He was majorly cool, whether he was cooking bugs with Rosie or teaching David Letterman the best way to wiggle out of quicksand. He preached living by your wits, surviving anywhere from Brooklyn to Borneo, and having a great time along the way.

Yes, he was a crazy old guy, very eccentric, but he certainly knew how to create excitement wherever he went. Which was exactly what Cassie was looking for. So how could escorting him around Chicago while he promoted his new book *Life On the Edge* be anything but a hoot and a half?

But she reminded herself that this wouldn't have been a joyride for Polly. This was her job. And Cassie wanted to make sure she dotted every *t* and crossed every *i*. Or something like that.

"Hmmm…" she mused, moving on to the sticky notes that dealt with Things To Do before the Wild Man Gets Here. "Five pounds of Blue M&M's peanuts. Wonder why only blue? Oh well. If it's what the Wild Man wants, it's what the Wild Man gets." Aloud, she read her instructions from her sister. "'There are about 20 one-pound packages in the cupboard above the sink. You'll have to pour them all out and then sift out the blue ones.'"

Cassie frowned, trying not to feel insulted. "Well, duh. Does she really think I don't know how to pick out the blue M&M's ones?"

But the next instruction was even more annoying. "'Put them in baskets—he will only eat out of natural materials.' Natural materials? Ha!"

She had no intention of dragging candy to the airport in baskets when plastic bags with handy zipped tops would do. So after she chased wayward M&M's under the cabinets and behind the coffeemaker, she loaded all the blue candy into plastic bags and weighed them to make sure there were a full five pounds. "Phew," she said, glad to zip the top on the last bag. She loaded the bags and the required baskets into a large shopping bag, ready to take to the airport.

Then she had to call Mickey's Rare Wines and Spirits to check on the delivery of special whiskey from a Scottish peat bog. The store's incompetence forced her to be pushier than she really wanted to, but after a bunch of squabbling, they finally promised the scotch would be delivered within the hour.

"Just see that you get it over here on the double," she commanded, feeling like a character in a movie. "Oh, and put it on my account."

See? She could be assertive and up-tempo and efficient. She could out-Polly Polly!

Next up was pens. She located and sorted the box of special Brazilian fountain pens the Wild Man required for autographing books, and then filled them all with some sort of fancy ink that came in little glass bottles. Sloppy work. She hoped Polly wasn't too fond of that butcher block table, the one that now had ink splotches all over it.

The sum of her tasks hadn't seemed like much on paper, but she was starting to feel a little wilted.

Meanwhile, the clock kept ticking, and according to the schedule Polly had left her, she had to leave in half an hour to go to the airport. But she hadn't finished! And where was that delivery boy with the peat bog scotch?

Quickly, she scanned the last few memos. "Oh, no! I was supposed to read his book before I picked him up."

But there was no time to make it through all of *Life On the Edge* now. Distracted, Cassie chewed the ragged end of her fingernail. She was pretty miffed she'd broken a nail trying to get the lid off an ink pot, and she certainly hoped she could file it before anyone saw it like that. As soon as she figured out this book thing, she would look for a nail file. Trying to be positive, she murmured, "Well, maybe I'll have time to read the book while I'm waiting at the airport."

First she had to find it, of course. She tried the living room and the kitchen, where most of the things Polly had set out for her were located. No luck. She finally found *Life On the Edge* on Polly's bedside table. As she reached for it, she caught a glimpse of herself in the mirror over her sister's dresser.

"Good grief!" And she was worried about a chipped nail? Not only was there ink all over her hands and a big smudge on her cheek, but there was a small splotch just above her left breast, too. She'd gotten ink on Polly's adorable red linen dress! What was she going to do?

Plus, her hair looked like she had styled it in a tornado, her face was flushed and blotchy and her eye makeup had smeared, making her resemble a raccoon. This would never do for her first day on the job. Or any other day, for that matter.

Everyone in Pleasant Falls knew that Cassie Tompkins prided herself on being immaculate, well-dressed and incredibly together. As the assistant manager of Ladies' Better Dresses at Joseph Kennigan & Sons department store, she was very careful about what she wore and how she looked. So how had *this* happened?

She was willing to let her standards slide a little, now that she was supposed to be Polly, who had never been as careful about appearances. But not this far. She shuddered. Not anywhere near this far.

Trying not to panic, Cassie ran to the bathroom and carefully scoured the stain on her dress. With a big wet spot on her chest, she grabbed her cosmetics bag next, hoping she'd brought some kind of heavy duty scrub to grind off the ink on her face. But her favorite strawberry complexion foam did absolutely nothing. And the doorbell rang just as she applied a gritty mixture of You Glow Girl hazelnut-and-elderberry exfoliant to her cheek. Not bothering to remove the heavy gunk, she raced to the front door, wrenched it open and snatched the heavy, bolted box with the bottles of scotch right out of the delivery boy's arms.

''But, wh—'' was all she heard before she used her

bottom to slam the door on him. She had no time to waste on late delivery boys.

Meanwhile, who knew peat bog scotch came in its own little vault? Doubtful she could even open the padlock, she glanced at the case. Oh well. She could worry about that later, she decided, setting the wooden box near the door, next to the other items she had to remember.

``Okay, pens, M&M's, scotch... Check.'' She frowned. ``And here's the book, which I am either going to have to read in the car or after I get there.''

That made no sense and she knew it, but she had worse problems at the moment. Like what she looked like with a large wet spot over one breast, facial scrub still stuck to half her face, hair like a circus clown and a terrible need for a manicure.

She got most of the ink and the dried bits of elderberry scrub off her cheek, thank goodness, but trying to turn her hair into her trademark straight, shiny bob was a lost cause at this point.

``I look like I'm doing Madonna,'' she said in horror, trying to pat down her wild and crazy ``do.'' Which was worse? That her celebrity client thought she was just sloppy and unkempt, or that he thought she was so lame she was stuck in a time warp, sporting big '80s hair? It was too late to do anything about it at this point, even if it was distressing.

She used a blow dryer on her dress, but the small dark ink stain was still visible when it dried, plus the linen was now wrinkled in that spot. Change? Or not change? She spied a large orange silk flower, something like a mum, that just happened to be sitting on Polly's dresser, so she grabbed it up and pinned it over the ink blot. Very *Sex and the City,* even if it was a season out of date. Good enough.

Then she found a can opener, wrestled the latch on the crate of scotch, broke another fingernail, finally got the darn thing open, pulled out two bottles—surely that would be enough to carry the Wild Man for one night?—and juggled all the junk she had accumulated into Polly's small car.

"Phew." Finally, after all that, she was on her way to the airport, no more than five minutes behind schedule.

Success! She was very pleased with herself for all she had accomplished so far, given the hoops she'd had to jump through. And now she had Wild Man Wright on the horizon. She could hardly wait!

EVERYONE IN Chicagoland seemed to want to go to O'Hare airport at the very same time she was driving, and road repair slowed her down even further. All the extra time Polly had built into the schedule melted away, and Cassie began to worry more seriously. She had visions of Hiram Wright cooling his heels waiting for her, growing angrier by the minute. It didn't seem like a good idea to keep someone nicknamed "Wild Man" waiting.

At least the stop-and-go traffic gave her an opportunity to flip through a few pages of *Life On the Edge.* From chapters one, "Traveling Light," and two, "Wrestling with Adventure," Cassie got the basic idea. When she'd seen him on TV, he seemed fun and outrageous. But skimming his book, she got a somewhat different picture.

His advice was ridiculous, for starters. No woman in her right mind would wash her hair in a rain puddle or hop a boxcar to see the country. *Eeew.*

Not that she thought any less of him. She felt sure that Mr. Wright was a lovely person, even if he did think Dumpster diving for almost-new doughnuts was an acceptable way to acquire food. When everyone knew that well-bred ladies did not eat *used* food.

Too bad there was nothing in *Life On the Edge* about surviving a large metropolitan airport. Cassie was beyond confused and anxious as she parked the car, navigated the endless ramps and elevators and escalators, and wound her way to the main terminal, her darling Gucci purse strapped over her shoulder, two bottles of Scotch and a copy of *Life On the Edge* in one arm, and a shopping bag stuffed full of M&M's, baskets and pens in the other.

All this mega-airport stuff was new to her, and she hadn't realized it would be so busy, so complicated and so intimidating. All she needed was to screw up her first assignment and have the Wild Man on the rampage somewhere in O'Hare while she dithered in the parking garage. She almost shouted ``Hallelujah!'' when she spotted the long counters that meant she was finally at the terminal.

Finally. She ran up to the nearest bank of monitors to look for the right gate.

``Flight 473, New York, Gate K-26, arriving at…

Thank goodness. His plane is late.'' She sighed with relief.

She took what seemed like an endless string of people movers and concourses, ending up at K-26 at precisely the moment the plane was due. But the gate was deserted. This couldn't be right.

``Excuse me,'' she tried at the counter. ``When is the plane from New York coming in?''

``That gate's been changed. You'll need to go to G-14,'' the gate attendant said in a bored tone.

``G-14? But that's all the way back—''

``You'll have to go to G-14.''

Cassie almost swore, which was not like her at all. But she managed to hold it in, took a deep breath, and set off for G-14. Which was, of course, on the other side of the universe from where she was now. And when she got there, still lugging whiskey, chocolate, pens and the book, that gate, too, was deserted.

``That flight's been in for a few minutes,'' the gate agent—who looked like a carbon copy of the last one—announced. ``If your party isn't waiting here, you can try Lower Level Baggage Pickup, or you can page within the airport.''

Hmmm… Baggage Pickup. If memory served her, the first chapter of the Wild Man's book was subtitled ``Never, Ever Check Luggage.'' It spelled out his no-frills philosophy, where you were never supposed to pack more than a Swiss army knife and a foldable poncho. Unless he really didn't practice what he preached, she found it unlikely that Mr. Wright would be down picking up baggage. Which meant he should be here, right?

"Okay, Wild Man, where are you?" Cassie squinted, peering around the waiting area. She saw a sleeping woman, a middle-aged man reading a newspaper, and a few other folks gazing at the overhead TV sets, none of whom matched her mental picture of Hiram Wright.

Just to be sure, Cassie dumped her parcels into a nearby chair, plucked out *Life On the Edge* and flipped it over to the back of the book jacket to refresh her impression of what he looked like. He was a regular old guy, in his sixties or even seventies, with a thick gray beard, bushy eyebrows and an ornery look in his eye. But there was no one like that within a mile of Gate G-14.

So where was he? He'd been faxing back and forth with Polly for some time, finalizing arrangements, so he knew she was supposed to meet him. Wouldn't he have waited?

But given what she knew of the Wild Man, he might also be canvassing the bars, looking for someone to regale with tales of the Amazon, or even in the control tower, wired up to tell someone how to jump out of a plane without a parachute.

"Excuse me," Cassie said sweetly to the woman at the counter. "Could you possibly page someone for me?"

"Phone's over there." Without even looking up, the gate agent waved a hand in the vague direction of the far wall.

With a sigh, Cassie hauled herself and her unwieldy bundles over to the red phone that she now saw said Paging Phone above it. It took a minute to tuck all her items safely around her feet, and then she picked up the phone.

``Hello? If you don't mind, I need you to page...'' She was going to ask for the Wild Man, but that seemed silly. And she didn't want to say the whole ``Hiram Wright'' since he was, after all, a celebrity, and it might call attention to the fact that he was in the airport and vulnerable to autograph-seekers and fans. Polly had been very specific about not divulging his whereabouts to just anyone.

With that in mind, Cassie said, ``I'm looking for Mr. Wright. Could you page him for me, please?''

``Mr. Right?'' the female voice on the end echoed. ``Is this a joke?''

``No. Why?''

``You're looking for Mr. Right?'' the operator scoffed. ``Honey, aren't we all?''

If she were a different person, Cassie would've given this annoying person a piece of her mind. But even disguised as Polly, she couldn't help trying to be polite. Delicately, she said, ``Not Mr. Right like that. *W-r-i-g-h-t.* He was supposed to be on the American Airlines flight that just got in from LaGuardia at Gate K-26 but came in at G-14 instead.''

``Got a first name?''

``No. You can use my name, though. You can say that Cass, um, I mean *Polly* Tompkins is trying to find him.''

"So you want to be Cass or you want to be Polly?"

She wasn't doing so well trying to be Polly, was she? And the sister switch was still young.

"I'm Polly," she said quickly.

"I got one Polly Thompson, desperate to find Mr. Right." The operator's voice dripped with sarcasm. "Whatever you say."

"Polly *Tompkins,*" Cassie corrected. But the paging lady had already hung up.

"How rude!" Cassie exclaimed. People in Pleasant Falls did not behave like this. Well, there was her future mother-in-law, who had a pretty sour disposition but, otherwise, everyone in town was nice and warm. They never made fun of you or hung up on you. Of course, they didn't have an airport or any Wild Men, either.

Cassie stayed there next to her packages, hoping she didn't have to call the paging lady back anytime soon. Meanwhile, she was exhausted. A hundred days in Ladies' Better Dresses didn't hold a candle to one afternoon at O'Hare Airport.

She was beginning to wonder whether the operator who had hung up on her planned to do the page at all, when the PA system suddenly let out a stream of static, startling her. "Will Mr. Wright please meet your party at Gate G-14?" it blasted through the static. "Arriving American Airlines passenger Wright from New York. Polly Thomas is waiting for you at G-14."

Her name wasn't Thomas, but close enough that she figured he ought to get it. The announcement was plenty loud, anyway. Cassie kept an eye out for any old men ambling up to the gate. Nope. All she saw was...

"Whoa. Who is that?"

Whoever this guy was who was casually chatting up the gate attendant, he was definitely not an old man. Tall and slim, he was wearing soft, slouchy khaki pants that cupped his bottom in a very intriguing way as he leaned into the counter. A *very* intriguing way.

She let her eyes linger longer on his adorable backside than she should've, but then he straightened and turned, and she got a better look at his face. Oh, my. It was every bit as nice. Maybe nicer. Although his expression was a little cranky, he also looked like he'd just walked out of a J. Crew catalog. Or maybe an Abercrombie & Fitch boutique. He had the drop-dead good looks, along with the *hot-cha* body and moody attitude, that all the guys in the ads had. And when it came to catalogs, Cassie knew her men.

He also had those little crinkles in the corners of his eyes, the kind that spoke of too much sun or too many smiles. She loved those crinkles. Always had.

With a sigh of regret, she tore herself away. As nice as it was to enjoy the eye candy, Cassie had other things to think about. Like where Mr. Wright might've wandered off to.

But the woman at the desk, now simpering and smiling for the handsome man, raised a hand and pointed right at her, and then he turned around, raked her up and down with a rather insolent gaze, and began to amble her way. Cassie stood up straighter. Why would the gate agent be sending Mr. Catalog Model over to Cassie? And why did he look even grumpier than he had a second ago?

Maybe he needed the paging phone. She edged away from the phones, assuming that they were his target. But she had to scoot over the scotch and the bulky bag with the pens and the M&M's, and then gather them up so he wouldn't trip over them if he needed to use the phone. She ended up bent over and in a rather undignified position when he got there, which was exactly what she didn't want when it came to a chance encounter with the Hunk of the Month.

"Polly?" he asked impatiently.

She blinked, clutching a bottle of whiskey to her chest, ruffling the huge flower pinned there. It took her a second to get around the fact that he was absolutely gorgeous. The proximity of someone *that* good-looking seemed to make her forget that she had a mouth and the ability to speak. And then she didn't process the idea that she was supposed to be answering to the name "Polly" at the moment.

So she just sort of stood there, gaping at him like a fish waiting for a hook.

"Polly?" he said again, and she kind of gulped.

Who was this amazing man? And what did he want with her sister?

# 2

"POLLY TOMPKINS?" he repeated, louder this time. "Are you Polly Tompkins or not?"

"No, I'm... Oh, *Polly.*" Cassie steadied herself, trying not to drop the whiskey or knock the flower off her dress. "But you're not...I mean, you can't possibly be..."

"He described you as a perky blonde," Mr. Catalog Model scoffed, "but he left out the part about you being a few egg rolls short of a PuPu platter."

"I am not!" She wasn't sure exactly what that meant, but she knew it was an insult. "I mean, I *am* Polly. Polly Tompkins, PR representative with Lenora Bridge and Associates. I am totally and definitely Polly Tompkins. At your service." She paused, tipping her head to one side, confused. "If I'm supposed to be—at your service, I mean. Am I?"

He blinked, as if he didn't have a clue what she was asking. If only she really *were* Polly, who always seemed to know what to say. Usually Polly said a little too much, actually, but she was never at a loss for words.

"Are you here for me?" Cassie asked, attempting to be clearer. "Am I supposed to be here for you?"

"You were, fifteen minutes ago. You're late."

His eyebrows, a shade darker than his sun-dappled hair, drew together over the most perfect pair of eyes she'd ever seen. Were they green? Or blue? Some kind of dazzling bluey-green, she decided, not turquoise or aqua but sort of teal. And man, were they potent, the way they seemed to shoot sizzling little arrows her way. How did he do that?

"So are you going to bother to explain why you were late?" he continued in the same maddening tone. "Or are you going to stand there with your mouth open?"

Ouch! He might be cute, but he was also surly. "Excuse me, but I still don't know who you are," she told him with chilly courtesy. "I thought I was meeting Mr. Hiram Wright, the author. And as far as I know, you are not him."

"Of course I'm not him!"

Thank goodness. That was all she needed, for Hiram the ancient guy to have mainlined from the Fountain of Youth and turned into *this*. "So who are you?" she prompted, trying to sound professional and unaffected by his good looks and his eye crinkles and his bad attitude.

"I'm Dylan Wright. His nephew. I travel with him. Believe me, he needs a keeper." His tone was full of repressed fury, and Cassie sensed there was more to this than she knew yet.

It wasn't her way to ask all sorts of probing questions, but the nephew, if he really was Mr. Wright's nephew, wasn't volunteering anything, either. "If you

travel with him, where is he?'' She thought that was
a pretty good place to start.

"He ditched me," he returned darkly.

"Ditched you?" Cassie gulped. What in the world
did that mean?

"Yes," he repeated, "he ditched me. We got on the
plane at LaGuardia right on schedule, and I should've
known there was something funny about that, because
things never go according to schedule with my uncle."

Polly had said something about that, too, that Cassie
should be prepared, because the Wild Man was noto-
rious for throwing wrenches into the works. She felt
a flicker of unease. How bad was this going to be?

"So we sat down," Dylan went on in the same
disgusted tone, "we buckled in, and all of a sudden
he said he needed to use the rest room. He climbed
over me—more like fell over me—and then toddled
away. Next thing I knew, we were taking off. At some
point he'd bolted, right off the plane, leaving me there
like a stooge."

"L-leaving? He left?" Cassie pushed down her
panic, unwilling to get hysterical until she had to.

"By the time I figured out the old coot was gone,"
Dylan said darkly, "it was too late for me to get off
and go after him."

"So he didn't come at all? Not at all?" But how
was she supposed to pick him up and take him to his
appointments if he wasn't here?

"It's not that surprising. He likes to pull stunts like
this to keep me on my toes."

"You don't understand." She felt like grabbing Dylan Wright by the front of his T-shirt and shaking him. But she couldn't do it while she was holding one of the liquor bottles. So she had to settle for hanging onto the thing for dear life, hugging it like a life preserver. *The Wild Man is my one and only client during my very short stint as Polly, and I can't mess this up!*

"Yes, I do understand." With a muttered oath, he reached over and removed the scotch from her grasp. "Your job is to get him to all these signings and appearances and his hobby is to screw with your mind and make it impossible. I thought you knew that." He gave her an odd look. "You did know who you were dealing with, didn't you?"

"Yes, of course. Hiram 'Wild Man' Wright. But where is he?" she asked impatiently.

Dylan shook his head. "Aren't you paying attention? He didn't take the flight. The old bugger actually called me on the plane when I was somewhere over Pennsylvania. He said he got off because he hates to fly. He always hates to fly, but then again, he may just be playing that card now to keep things interesting. You never can tell with him."

"I don't care about any of that." Her mind was whirling as she tried to figure out what she should be doing to handle this. But none of her instructions said anything about a missing Wild Man. "Do you think he'll be on the next flight? Should we wait here?"

"Hell, no. I just told you, he's refusing to fly."

"He won't fly at all? Then what do we do?" Polly had said the golden rule was "If in doubt, call the office," but then she'd also said, *Don't do it unless you absolutely have to because they might know you're not me and then we'll be in the deepest of doo-doo because Lenora will kill me for just running out of town and handing over one of my clients to my sister, who doesn't really know anything about PR.* And then Polly had wailed that Lenora Bridge was really sharp and really mean and not to mess with her unless it was an all-out emergency, like someone died. This wasn't *that,* was it?

Even if they didn't immediately see through the masquerade, Cassie had visions of everyone at Lenora Bridge and Associates pointing fingers and yelling, *You lost the client? What kind of imbecile are you?*

"No, I can't do that," she said out loud. "On the other hand, I can't just cancel the whole list of appearances, either." But what was her choice when Mr. Wright was totally not there?

"Okay, okay. Don't panic." Dylan's gaze narrowed. "I have to tell you, if you're going to lose it the first time my uncle throws you a curve, you're never going to make it in this line of work."

That wasn't very nice of him to point out, was it? Okay, so she was a fake and the likelihood of her ever making it in this line of work was minuscule. He had no way of knowing that. Especially not yet. She had barely gotten started!

Cassie took a deep breath, holding her head high. Every single person in Pleasant Falls knew that Cassie Tompkins was calm, cool and collected no matter what happened. She might not be the smartest girl in any given room, but she knew how to keep a smile on her face, no matter what the disaster. Not that she'd ever faced that big a disaster. But she had had her share of challenges.

*I was a cheerleader,* she told herself. *I was homecoming queen* and *prom queen and I arranged the country club garden luncheon. I can do this!*

"I can handle whatever your uncle comes up with," she declared.

"Uh-huh. Well, Little Miss Muffet, you're not doing that well with me so far," he muttered, raking her up and down with that devastating gaze, "and compared to my uncle, I'm a piece of cake."

He was a piece of cake? A piece of... Oh, dear. She couldn't believe her brain was feeding her images of what it would be like to have that brand of cake and eat it, too. She could feel a hot flush coloring her cheeks, and she tried to think cool, collected thoughts. Cassie reminded herself that even though he was unbelievably handsome, it didn't change the fact that he was also rude and grouchy. *Handsome is as handsome does,* after all.

With a sense of determination, she met his beautiful eyes and said carefully, "Let's get back to Mr. Wright. If he isn't coming on the next flight and he doesn't want to fly, how is he getting here?"

"He isn't." Dylan's lips curved into a grim smile. "When he called, he told me he'd decided that Chicago had bad karma and he didn't want to come. He said he was taking a bus to Cleveland instead. And if I wanted to meet him, I could show up at the bus station in Cleveland tomorrow afternoon."

Cassie swallowed. "C-Cleveland? Tomorrow afternoon? But he can't do that. He's supposed to be at a radio station and two bookstores tomorrow, plus he has lunch with the winner of the Survival of the Fittest contest, you know, where they had to write an essay about how to survive something really dire, like if you got caught in an avalanche or your car fell off a bridge or—"

"I know about the contest," he interrupted. "I judged the essays for him."

"You did?" Her mouth fell open. "Is that fair? Didn't it say that the Wild Man himself would be the judge?"

"What are you, the contest police?"

"No, no, it's just that, well..." Cassie didn't know what to say.

Apparently when you were a Wild Man, you just broke all the rules and let the chips fall where they may. Which was very inconvenient for everyone else, wasn't it?

"But even if he didn't really read the essays," she argued, "he can't just stand up the contest winner. Why, there would be heck to pay for sure."

Dylan raised one golden brown eyebrow. "Did you say *heck* to pay?"

"Yes. Why do you ask?" She realized too late that he was making fun of her. But she had no time for him and his snarky jokes. "Okay, listen. You said you were going to pick him up tomorrow, right? And tomorrow's schedule was light on purpose, to kind of ease him into things. So maybe I can squash tomorrow's appointments into the next day and it should still be okay, right?''

Dylan shrugged. ``If we can find him and bring him here and get him to go to any of this stuff.''

``We can. We have to.'' She was already planning ahead. She had her sister's cell phone. And Polly had left a master list of appearances with contacts and phone numbers, just for an emergency like this.

Reaching for the cell phone, Cassie halted. But what about Cleveland? She glanced at Dylan. Was she supposed to go, too?

She had no idea whether PR people routinely dropped everything and ran off to strange cities with strange men in search of their clients. Or should she wait here in Chicago, trusting Dylan to round up his uncle by himself?

She chewed on the end of her nail. She was not a nail-biter by habit, but it was the best she could come up with while she considered.

Run off to Cleveland? Or stay here and wait?

Well, sitting around stewing by the phone didn't sound like a great idea. So far, Dylan had been annoying and uncooperative and not the least trustworthy. She could see herself, biting her poor, scraggly manicure down to the nub, wondering what in the world was going on with Hiram Wright and his infuriating nephew. They'd be partying hearty halfway across the country and never show up. And then she'd be stuck explaining the Wild Man's absence to all those people, including the very scary Lenora Bridge.

But could she go to Cleveland with him? With *him?*

She looked him over on the sly, noting again how well he filled his khaki pants, how tall and intimidating he was, how insufferable he was with his raised eyebrows and smug glances.

There was also the problem of not being sure where Cleveland was or how long it would take to get there, geography not exactly being her strong suit.

*Stop being a baby,* she told herself. So things weren't turning out the way they were supposed to. This was exactly what she wanted. Freedom, spontaneity, excitement! And with a great-looking guy. Even if he wasn't the world's nicest great-looking guy.

She would be spontaneous and take a quick road trip in search of the Wild Man.

"Should we get plane tickets?" she asked, pulling out her sister's corporate credit card, trying to act as if it were perfectly normal to just pop off to any-old-where on the spur of the moment.

"No planes. I'll drive. There's plenty of time, and that way I can tie him up and throw him in the trunk if I have to," he said with a real spark of anticipation.

"You wouldn't really do that, would you?" Lock the famous Wild Man in the trunk of a car? How would he breathe?

"Listen, if you want to come with me, that's fine. But don't think you get to run this little mission." He broke off, simmering with resentment, making her think that including her was not fine at all. More like the last thing on earth he wanted.

"I'm not trying to run anything," she returned.

``But if you're going to be all surly before we even get started—''

``I'm not surly. I'm just...'' He broke off, running a hasty hand through his hair. He had very nice hair, now standing up in attractive little spikes that just itched to be smoothed and soothed and stroked.... Cassie caught herself, tuning into his words again and ignoring his cute little hair spikes. ``Listen, I know it's unfortunate for both of us,'' he continued, ``but I need you along on this.''

She tried to arch an eyebrow like he had. She hoped it looked arrogant and smug. ``You need me?''

``The thing is,'' he admitted ruefully, ``I'm a little strapped at the moment. It's another one of my uncle's favorite tricks. He stole my money and ID when he climbed over me on his way off the plane. Picked my pockets clean.''

``You're kidding.''

``I don't kid about things like this.'' If possible, his expression grew even more pained. ``He thinks it's funny. You know, all part of this `life on the edge' stuff. As in, without credit cards or cash or even a driver's license.''

Her eyes widened. No credit cards? No cash? ``But how did he expect you to get to Cleveland? How did he expect you to live for even five minutes without any money? I mean, you can't even go to Mc-Donald's.''

That got him to crack a smile, even though she wasn't trying to be funny. ``I'm supposed to be living by my wits instead of on my credit cards. And that's where you come in.''

``I'm supposed to provide the wits?'' she asked, incredulous.

``No. But maybe a car. You've got a car, right?''

``Um, yes.'' She had a car. Her sister's car. And her sister's license. Was it fraud to drive across state lines with fake ID?

``Fine. All I need is your car and your cash card and we're good to go first thing in the morning.'' Dylan hefted his shoulder bag onto one arm, and then bent down to commandeer the other bottle of whiskey, as if he didn't trust her to carry the precious scotch without dropping it. ``Let's get out of here, shall we?''

Before she could respond, he took off down the concourse, his long legs eating up the distance.

She juggled the shopping bag and the book and her purse, struggling to catch him. ``If we're not leaving till morning, where are we going now?''

Stopping abruptly, he turned back. With a frown, he took the shopping bag, too, and then fastened her with that sultry, blue-green gaze. ``Your place. Where else?''

``M-my place?''

He smiled again, full and wide and mischievous, and his eyes crinkled in the corners. And she could feel herself melting into a puddle of warm goo.

``It'll be fine,'' he said encouragingly. ``Come on.'' And then he took off again.

Cassie stumbled after him, trying to figure out what was happening. One thing she knew for sure—Dylan's full-out smile had the effect of an oven set at about four hundred and fifty degrees. She could feel herself getting all wimpy and compliant, ready to follow him anywhere, even though it was the silliest thing in the world to let happen.

And while she was in the midst of this melting business, she had to contend with the frightening fact that Dylan Wright, the hottest, best-looking, most annoying man she had ever met, wanted to spend the night at her house. Except it wasn't her house, it was her sister's.

And there was only one bedroom.

DYLAN WAS beginning to think there was something really strange about this Polly woman.

First she'd acted more like a fifth grader than a polished publicist, showing up late and flustered, hauling around all that crazy stuff like she didn't realize the whiskey should be waiting at the hotel and she wouldn't need M&M's or pens until tomorrow's autographings. Shouldn't that have been obvious?

Then she'd been so slow on the uptake he could swear she didn't recognize her own name. And now she had forgotten where her car was parked, plus she seemed totally thrown for a loop by the whole Cleveland idea.

Okay, so it *was* out of the ordinary. But she ought to know what his uncle was like by now—the two had been trading faxes and phone calls for weeks, and Hiram never bothered to keep his eccentricities a secret. Hell, he reveled in them. Just a few days ago,

Dylan had caught the old guy cackling as he composed a particularly pithy missive to send off to try to get a rise out of Polly Tompkins.

So why was all this suddenly a surprise to Sweet Polly Purebread?

``Didn't you say it was a red convertible?'' he asked kindly. ``There's one over there.''

``Well, that looks like the right one.'' She examined it for a minute, as he considered asking why she didn't know her license plate number. But she sighed with relief and unlocked his door. ``Yes, this is it.''

Thank goodness. He was tired of toting scotch and whatever else she had in these bags. He certainly hoped she knew how to get home better than she knew how to find her car.

But she fooled him. She had directions.

``Are you new at this?'' he inquired, noting the way she was squinting at the piece of paper.

``At what?'' she asked absently. ``Driving?''

``The PR biz.''

``PR? New?'' She nearly missed a cement pillar as she whipped around a corner and headed for the exit booth. In a strange, fractured tone, she announced, ``No, not… I mean, gee whiz. I've been in PR… I've been with Lenora Bridge…since I left college—which was Northwestern.''

``Watch out for the—'' But the blare of a horn and the squeal of brakes drowned him out. Whew. That was close. Not that Polly seemed to notice she'd almost rear-ended a van.

``I'm twenty-five now and I was twenty-two then.

So, uh, three years in PR. Yessiree, Bob. Three years.''

''Uh-huh.'' At the moment, he was more concerned about her driving than her résumé, especially since she came very close to clipping the gate off the booth as she handed over a company credit card to pay for parking.

But he couldn't help wondering who said ''gee whiz'' and ''yessiree, Bob'' outside of *Petticoat Junction*. She also looked as if she were straining to think of something to say, biting her cheek and kind of scrunching her nose. A publicist with nothing to say was a first in his experience.

''I, uh, majored in English in college,'' she volunteered suddenly, ''at Northwestern University.''

''Yes, you mentioned that you went to Northwestern.'' Twice. ''Go, Bruins,'' he said cheerfully, although he knew very well Northwestern's mascot was a Wildcat. But she didn't rise to the bait or bother to correct him. Uh-huh.

''And then I came to Lenora Bridge and Associates.'' She smiled nervously, sending her gaze over his way. ''Right out of college. Into PR.''

Definitely not a conversationalist. ''Well, you just concentrate on the road, okay?''

''Right.''

It didn't take incredibly long to make it to her house, thank goodness, because he was getting worried about his safety. Polly Tompkins might be cute as a button, with her sincere blue eyes, that strange whip of blond hair and an extremely short red dress that revealed a great pair of legs. He even liked the overgrown bloom perched precariously over her breast, although it seemed like a strange spot for a flower. But no matter how cute she was, she was one lousy driver.

He winced as she screeched on the brakes and slammed to a stop in front of a small house that he assumed was hers. Cool house, he mused, following her inside.

His own brownstone had been mostly empty since he'd bought it. He traveled a lot with his uncle, so there wasn't much time to put down roots or invest in furniture. But Polly's postmodern cottage had loads of personality, with a shocking blue front door, purple velvet couches perched on bare wood floors, skylights in strange places, and tall, spindly sculptures made out of twisted bronze and bits of tin that drifted in the breeze. It was very hip and now. And it didn't fit Polly "Gee Whiz" Tompkins at all. She'd go better with lace curtains and Home Sweet Home samplers.

He sent her a suspicious glance. "Lived here long?"

"No."

He waited for more of an answer, half-expecting to hear her mantra that she'd been here for three years, ever since she left college, which would be North-western. But she didn't offer a peep.

"It's very nice," he said finally.

She smiled nervously, teetering where she stood, almost falling off one sexy red stiletto heel. "Thank you."

"Are you going to show me where I'm sleeping?"

"Okay." But she didn't move. "I'm considering," she told him after a minute. Her eyes seemed to get rounder and bluer. "You see, there's just the one bedroom. I wasn't exactly, um, expecting you."

"I don't need anything fancy," he assured her.

"But there's a suite already reserved for your uncle at the most fabulous hotel on the Magnificent Mile. It wouldn't be any trouble to drive you there," she said hopefully.

After the rough trip to the house, Dylan didn't plan on letting her drive him anywhere again as long as he lived, especially if he wanted to keep on living. Besides, he had his reasons for bunking here in the first place, one of which was a deep desire to figure out who this crazy woman was. Not that getting a look at her home turf was helping. Yet.

He voiced other, saner reasons for her benefit. "If we're leaving at the crack of dawn, it's easier to start from the same place," he noted. "And we won't have to buck morning traffic in the Loop. Besides, this way we can set up some plans to deal with my uncle."

She seemed to struggle for a counterargument, but didn't come up with anything. "I guess that does make sense," she said softly.

"Good. Then we're all set."

After a long pause, she backed up a step. "So I'll just, um, straighten up the bedroom for you."

He glanced around, taking in the plush purple sofas. He'd slept in a lot worse places, and he hated kicking someone as cute as Polly Tompkins out of her own bed. "Actually, I'm fine in here."

"Are you sure? I don't mind sleeping on the couch. Really. I mean, I'm smaller, so I'd fit better," she offered.

"No need. After some of the places I've been with my uncle, a regular old sofa is a luxury." He smiled, but it didn't seem to ease her anxiety. "Really. I'll be fine."

"Right. Okay, so I'll go get you some, um, sheets. And a pillow. And towels, soap, that kind of thing." She took a step or two in the direction of the hallway, stopped, turned back, and waved one hand at him. "It'll take just a minute. Make yourself comfortable."

"Sure." As she vanished into the rest of the house, he found the kitchen on his own, prepared to drop off the scotch and other parcels he'd been toting. Hmmm... The place was overflowing with little yellow notes, stuck to the counters and the cabinets, even the sink. *Don't forget to read* Life on the Edge *before you go to the airport,* he read. *Special whiskey at Mickey's Rare Spirits and Wine, 555-BOOZ. Will deliver if you push them. Take no excuses!!*

There were even detailed instructions on how to sift out blue M&M's.

As he got himself a bottle of water from the fridge, he pondered the reason for all the memos. Either Polly had the world's most anal retentive boss who came over and littered her apartment with reminders, or Polly didn't trust her own memory and posted the yellow messages herself. But who needed instructions on how to sort M&M's?

It was all very strange, and it only contributed to his growing curiosity about just who Polly Tompkins was. No short-term memory? Loved list-making? Fond of ordering herself around?

Whatever the answers, he was very intrigued.

Dylan ambled back into the living room, noting the eccentric artwork that spoke more of a stage set than a real person's house. Polly still hadn't returned, and it seemed to be taking her a long time to find a couple of sheets and some towels. Plus there was a whole lot of bashing and crashing going on in other parts of the house, as if she were rifling through cupboards and closets.

Just another clue to the mystery that was Polly Tompkins. He felt sure he could figure out the whole puzzle if given a chance to scope out her place and poke around her drawers.

He shook his head, trying to clear away some cobwebs. It had been a very long day. And right now, he was in dire need of a few hours sleep. Analyzing Polly would have to wait until his brain was clearer.

Dumping his backpack next to one of the couches, he settled in. Pretty comfy, he decided, bouncing a little, testing the springs. Wouldn't make a bad bed for one night. Except...

It felt suspiciously like a sofa bed. He pulled away the cushions, exposing a loop of fabric and the unmistakable frame of a pull-out mattress, complete with sheets and a blanket folded up with it. "Yessiree, Bob," he said out loud.

Did Polly not know she had a sofa bed in her living room, or had she just forgotten to mention it?

"Oh." She stood there near the hallway, now bare-foot in her teeny red dress, that big, fluffy flower drooping over the round mound of her breast, with a toothbrush clutched in one fist and a pile of sheets and towels draped over the other arm. "I guess I forgot about that."

"I guess you did."

"Well, I have linens for you. And a matching set of towels," she added in a triumphant tone. "I had a little trouble finding things because this place is really not very well organized, if you ask me. But, anyway, all is well now."

"Glad to hear it."

As she marched over, obviously intent on making his bed, he backed up, letting her see that there were already sheets tucked neatly into it.

"Oh."

"Tell me, Polly, did you rent this house already furnished?"

"I don't know," she murmured, gingerly touching the top sheet as if she expected it to sit up and bite her. And then she seemed to catch herself, as if she were straining her memory. "The, uh, office put me here."

"The office put you here?"

"You know, they leased it for me, or rented it or whatever. I can't remember exactly." With a sudden burst of inspiration, she added, "I'm house-sitting for this guy who went to Europe or something."

"Ah, that explains it." But it didn't really. There was still the matter of the world's most innocent city girl who didn't act like any PR person he knew, didn't know exactly how she got her house, didn't recognize her college mascot and had phrases like "gee whiz" in her vocabulary.

What was it about Polly Tompkins? And why did he find her and her abnormalities so fascinating?

Pulling open the bed, Dylan plunked down on the end of it, looking at her expectantly, indicating she could join him if she wanted to. But she backed out of the living room on the double, as he'd known she would.

"Good night, then," she called out as she retreated, with a nervous tremor in her voice that amused him.

"Good night, Polly."

But as he settled into the sofa bed, Dylan grinned. He hadn't expected this at all. But he was actually looking forward to this road trip to Cleveland.

Not the part after they got there, when he would have to round up his infuriating uncle and somehow retrieve his credit cards and his wallet, hogtie the old reprobate and drag him back to Chicago kicking and screaming.

But before they got the Cleveland, before he had to contend with Uncle Hiram...

Well, it promised to be a long ride, with plenty of time to interrogate Polly Tompkins. Before they crossed the Ohio state line, he would know all of her secrets.

That was a promise.

# 3

May 23: *Nine days before the wedding*

"TIME TO GET UP!" announced a disgustingly cheerful voice that was way too close to his ear. And then she started *singing*.

It wasn't really all-out singing, more like humming. But it was jolly and teeth-achingly sweet, some kind of "what a lovely day" nonsense that reminded him of his grandma—the one who sang in a senior citizens' "all-girl" choir.

"What the...?" Dylan lifted his head. He was, as a rule, easy to wake and fast on his feet. But this was early, even for him. He cracked open an eye, finding Polly near the bed. There she was—up, dressed, pretty as a picture and rarin' to get going. She was positively *perky*.

"Good morning!" she chirped.

"Good God," he mumbled, shifting around in the sofa bed. "What time is it?"

"Five."

Her gaze seemed to linger somewhere in the area of his bare chest, and Dylan was oddly pleased that she couldn't seem to tear her eyes away. He consid-

ered pushing the sheet away altogether and letting her
see whatever she wanted to see. But then he took in
what she'd just said.

He sat up straighter, forgetting about the sheet.
"Five o'clock in the morning? Are you insane?"

"You said the crack of dawn. I'm not exactly sure
when that would be, but I didn't want us to be late,"
she said helpfully.

Dylan was not amused. Last night, he would've bet
money she was a late sleeper, and he would be dragging her away from her mirror at ten o'clock while
she begged for more time to get her makeup just right.
Wrong.

She had it all together, that was for sure. She was
wearing a tight black suit that looked like it had cost
plenty of bucks, and when she bent over to talk to
him, he saw the most enticing curves peeking out from
the wide open collar of her white blouse. Her hair was
much different from last night, all shiny and sleek,
turned under gently in a perfect line just beneath her
chin. She wore chunky hoop earrings that dipped below her hair, making her look even more like the polished PR woman she was supposed to be. Stylish
makeup, classy gold jewelry, a pair of slinky red high
heels that wouldn't quit… Yowza.

"Okay, well, you get up while I put breakfast together," she told him, backing away and taking the
view with her. Damn it, anyway. "Don't be long."

It took him a second to realize that she had just said
she was making breakfast. And from the smells coming from the kitchen, it wasn't Cheerios or leftover

chocolate cake, either. He'd never met a woman who jumped out of bed and started cooking. Both his grandmothers and his mother felt strongly that if you wanted to eat, you could pour your own granola in the morning. And the women he dated in New York would much rather die than pick up a pan.

But this...this smelled like eggs and...sausage? She was making sausage? As in pork and grease and all the good politically incorrect stuff that women of his acquaintance wouldn't go near?

No doubt about it—in his universe, Polly Tompkins was one weird chick.

But she emerged from the kitchen, still way too perky, but somewhat more unsure. "I just had this thought." She stopped abruptly. "About my outfit. Do you think it's all right? I wanted to wear the Prada suit, but then I thought, maybe the Gucci dress with the cool buckles. But if I go with that, then the shoes aren't right and I love these shoes. So what do you think?"

Dylan had no idea. He stared at her, noting the way the tiny black skirt stretched to accommodate her hips and the crisp white blouse gaped, revealing just enough to make him want more. Meanwhile, the red shoes were kind of scary. High heels, skimpy leather, showing off the tiniest hint of her toes, making her legs look long and sleek and... There was something very dangerous about those shoes.

"So, what do you think?" she prompted, tugging at the skirt to make it lie just right, tormenting him even further.

What did he think? He thought he would like to peel her out of those clothes right this second. But he could hardly say that. So he stalled. ``Why do you ask?''

``I'm just not sure.'' She frowned down at her outfit. ``I've never done this before, you know, run off to Cleveland to pick up a client. I don't want to wear the wrong thing for the first time I meet your uncle. I mean, he's famous and important and everything. And I have to look right while I'm representing Lenora Bridge and Associates.''

If meeting Uncle Hiram was what she was worried about, she should probably be wearing a flak jacket and carrying a whip. Plus, he couldn't think of many outfits less practical for a long car trip than that skin-tight black suit. Not that he was going to tell her to modify even a thread on that body.

``Don't change,'' he said in a voice that came out a lot gruffer than he expected.

``Okay.'' Shrugging, she went sauntering back into the kitchen, totally unconcerned, while he sat there on the couch, feeling like he'd just been mugged.

``Am I paranoid, or is she messing with my head?'' he asked out loud. Up at five, singing, cooking, modeling snazzy little outfits... He was definitely keeping an eye on this one.

But as he showered and shaved and tossed a black T-shirt over his khakis, he decided he had no clue as to what made Polly tick. After an elaborate breakfast where she made the food, served the food and then hummed a tune as she cleaned it all up, he was even more mystified. She told him this thing he was eating was a "breakfast scramble" of eggs and sausage and that it was her mother's recipe and how she was especially proud of the crust. She knew how to make *crust?* As in pie crust? He stared balefully at the thing she'd called a breakfast scramble. He'd never met anyone who made anything remotely like this.

Was she right out of *The Brady Bunch?* Some weird leftover from the 50s?

"Where are you from, anyway?"

"A town," she said, blushing as she cleaned away the remains of his toast and refilled his coffee, "that I'm sure you've never heard of."

He knew it had to be a small town. But what he wondered about was why she'd ever left when she seemed so wedded to the place.

Looked like it was going to take some more time to figure this out. Well, they were going to be sharing plenty of that stuck in a small car together all the way to Cleveland.

As she tripped out to the car, toting a red purse that matched her high heels *and* the convertible, Dylan lagged behind. He had one matter to resolve right away.

"I'll need the keys," he said flatly.

"What do you mean?"

"I'm driving."

"But it's my car!" she protested. "And I'm the one buying the gas and footing the bills and—"

"Not negotiable," he interrupted. "I drove with

you last night, and I'm not doing it again. I'd like to get to Cleveland in one piece, thank you.''

``So, so,'' she sputtered, ``you think I'm a bad driver?''

``Honey, you are a terrible driver.''

She opened her mouth, and he knew she wanted to argue with him but couldn't think of anything to say.

``Give me the keys,'' he ordered, holding out his hand.

She chewed her lip and pouted a little, but in the end, she turned them over. Still, she wasn't happy about it, and he could tell she was stewing.

``Come on,'' he said finally. ``It shouldn't be that big a surprise that you're a lousy driver. You must've been in a million accidents.''

``I have not! I've never had an accident at all.'' She paused for a long moment, and he waited for the payoff as he opened her car door. ``Well, there was that one time on my second driver's test when I hit the parking meter and kind of crunched the front of the car. But that's it.''

He didn't say anything, just gave her an amused look as he settled into the driver's seat.

``That's the only one,'' she protested. ``And it wasn't my fault.''

Calmly adjusting the mirrors and then flipping the switch to send the top down on the car, Dylan shook his head. ``How can hitting a parking meter not be your fault? What'd it do, throw itself in your path?''

``Okay, so technically it was my fault.''

``Right.'' He pulled out onto the street, enjoying

that it was pretty much deserted at this time of the morning.

``It was just one little accident ages and ages ago and no one was hurt.'' Her voice seemed to falter. ``Well, the driver's examiner guy had a slight concussion, but it was very slight. And really I don't drive that much. I mean, I walk to work and—''

``How do you walk to work?'' He took his eyes off the road long enough to send her a probing glance. ``Isn't your office in the Loop? And you live in what? Wicker Park? Not exactly walkable.''

``Oh.'' She hesitated. ``I didn't mean here. I meant that I used to walk to work, when I was younger, before I left Pleasant Falls.''

He had the name of the place, anyway. Pleasant Falls. And didn't it just sound like the sort of burg where Andy and Aunt Bea raised little girls like Polly Tompkins?

``Now, of course,'' she went on, ``I don't drive because I, uh, take the El.''

``Of course.''

He felt relatively sure at this point that Polly was lying through her teeth most of the time. Not about Pleasant Falls. That sounded like the first true thing she'd said since he met her. No, it was the rest of it. He didn't think she'd ever attended Northwestern University or ridden the El, he didn't believe she had any experience in public relations, and he was confident that she had not lived in the city more than a few weeks, if that.

So who was she? Why was she lying?

And when had finding out the answers become so much fun?

CASSIE WAS NOT enjoying this masquerade. Yes, the clothes were excellent, the convertible was fun—especially since she'd remembered a scarf this time to keep her hair under wraps—and, yes, Dylan could be amusing when he tried. He was the first adventurer sort of person she had ever met, and he was fascinating, telling her about skiing in Chile and kayaking around Tahiti, searching for lost tribes in Alaska and the proper way to eat Norwegian fermented herring.

How lucky he was to have seen so many things and been so many places. How lucky he was to have an uncle like the Wild Man, who took him on all these adventures.

But the car was much too small for comfort, with his hand on the gear shift so very close to her thigh, his wide shoulders encroaching on her half of the front seat, his arm brushing hers every time one of them shifted even slightly.

Besides, he kept looking at her. Not necessarily saying anything, just *looking* at her, all speculative and mysterious. It was flattering to have a great-looking guy all transfixed and hypnotized by little old Cassie, but kind of spooky, too. What was he looking at?

Plus, he was way too interested in her route to work and her first client and her favorite restaurant and her best subject in third grade. *Just passing the time,* he told her.

Well, pooh! If she kept making up tales to answer

his questions, very soon she'd rival the Wild Man in storytelling ability.

She hoped her fairy tales were okay, but Polly was the creative one, not her. *I'm doing the best I can,* she thought indignantly. It was giving her a headache trying to keep track of her own lies and steer the conversation away from his probing questions all the time.

Meanwhile, with all the phone calls to bookstores and radio stations out of the way, she was supposed to be navigating this little mission, and she wasn't doing very well.

``Did you figure out where we are yet?'' he asked, as she turned the map a different way to get a better view.

It didn't help. Who knew how to read a map? She already knew where everything was in Pleasant Falls, and she hardly ever went anywhere else.

``I think we may be here,'' she tried, poking a finger at a point on a squiggly blue line.

``That's the middle of a river.''

``No, it isn't.'' Yes, it was. ``You know, I wouldn't even have to look at the map if you had taken the tollway, like a normal person. One road, all the way to Cleveland. But noooo. That was too easy.''

There was that darn eyebrow again. ``Aw, come on. What fun is a tollway? It's just one slab of concrete that never ends. But this…'' He waved an arm out the window, indicating the rolling green landscape. ``This is up close and personal with the real America.''

``This is boring small towns and farms like everywhere else I've ever been.'' She slumped in her seat, trying to find a comfortable way to sit in a bucket seat in a too-short skirt that kept riding up and exposing way more skin than she'd intended. It felt like they had been in this car forever, with no end in sight. She exhaled a long, aggravated breath. "Okay, so it's vaguely less flat than where I come from, but it's the same basic idea. Bo-ring."

"How can you say that? The heartbeat of America is pounding all around us."

Was he actually this excited by a couple of diners and some vegetable stands? Or was he putting her on?

"I was thinking this trip was going to be all bright lights, big city," she grumbled, "not the blue plate special at Mom's Café in… Where was that? Harding-ville?"

"Something like that. And it was a great lunch," Dylan protested.

"I thought we would be there by now." She was starting to feel antsy after such a long trip, a little too hemmed in by the monotonous scenery and the small car and…Dylan. "Why aren't we there by now?"

"If you could read the map, we'd know how much farther it is," he reminded her with an annoying dis-play of good spirits. "You want me to pull over so I can look at the map?"

"No, I don't want you to pull over. I just want to know when we'll get to Cleveland."

"Traveling with you," he said dryly, "reminds me of family vacations when I was about ten. My parents had this nasty old van, and my brother and I would fight about who should get the last piece of candy, and who'd left the crayons by the window and melted them, and—''

"Just like me and my sister," she said with a laugh. "Only it wasn't a van, it was a station wagon, and our battles were over where we drew the line down the middle of the back seat."

"So you have a sister?" he asked quickly.

Uh-oh. Cassie stopped and thought about this for a minute. Admitting she had a sister wouldn't necessarily give anything away, would it? Darn it, anyway. She had been so careful so far. But surely there was no harm in him knowing she had a sister.

"Yes. Two, actually." Quickly, she hit the ball back into his court. "And your brother—younger or older? What's his name?"

"His name is James and he's three years younger. He's an accountant and a major disappointment to my hippie parents." He grinned. "And what about your sisters?"

Okay, this was complicated. Her little sister Ashley was easy. But aside from Ashley, should she describe the real Polly, or talk about herself? After all, she was Polly's sister and the person Polly would describe if she were here. So should she say something about herself? Go with smart, sassy city girl Polly, or small-town nobody Cassie?

"My youngest sister is fourteen, and the other one… She's closer to my age, but a very dull girl," she said, hedging her bets. "There isn't much to say."

"Uh-huh."

"Oh, look!" Cassie sat up and pointed to the sign,

relieved for the distraction. "Cleveland—sixteen miles. Whew. I was beginning to think we'd never get there."

"The sign said the Greyhound station was that way," she argued. "You missed the turn."

"We're not going to the Greyhound station. My uncle always travels by the Red Dog line."

"I never heard of Red Dog," she said doubtfully. "What kind of bus is that?"

"It's a little bit lower down the food chain. Uncle Hiram likes them because they'll let him hang out the windows and smoke cigars and dance in the aisles." Dylan winced with the memory of previous road trips. "You haven't lived till you've ridden Red Dog with Wild Man Wright."

"Oh, dear" was all Polly said next to him.

Yeah, well, she was in for a baptism by fire once they met up with his uncle. She'd better get out her oven mitts while she still had time.

"Th-this way?" she inquired delicately. He could tell she was trying not to stare at the grimy street or make eye contact with any of its grimy denizens.

"Just a few blocks from here." He'd actually been to the Red Dog station in Cleveland before, since Cleveland was one of his uncle's favorite destinations. Uncle Hiram had friends everywhere, but a big bunch of them seemed to hang out in and around Cleveland.

After entering and exiting the town on Red Dog buses a few times, he remembered exactly where the station was. However, he now wished that he'd thought to put up the convertible top before they reached the bad side of town. He was used to life on the wild side, but somehow he doubted Polly was ready to embrace it.

Still, they made it to the dilapidated bus station without any trouble, even though she got very quiet when she saw the Red Dog sign outside the door. He didn't tell her that, yes, it *was* riddled with bullet holes. But as they walked inside, she sidled up close and stayed there, and he didn't push her away.

"Do you see him?" Polly whispered.

He wasn't sure why she was keeping her voice down—the place was full of people shouting at each other and blaring boom boxes and the general clatter of bottles and cans, even a harmonica, so no one would've heard her if Polly had jumped up on the counter and belted out "Yankee Doodle Dandy." She did stand out in this place, however, with her dressy little black suit and round blue eyes, getting rounder by the minute as she took in their seedy surroundings.

Dylan peered into the murky confines of the small station, looking for any sign of his uncle. It wasn't usually tough to find him, since Uncle Hiram managed to create a major disturbance wherever he went. But not this time.

"I don't see him," he said tersely. Damn it. The old man had better not stand him up. Not after he'd driven all the way to Cleveland to find him, after Polly had dutifully rescheduled all of the first day appointments in Chicago just to cover the old goat's butt. "Maybe his bus isn't here yet. We'd better check."

As they found their way around the crowded waiting room at the Red Dog station, Polly clung to his arm, edging her hot little body right next to his. "No, I definitely don't see him," she murmured, although he didn't know how she could see anything plastered up against him that way. Not that he was complaining.

As he asked the clerk whether the bus from New Jersey was in yet, Polly dropped his arm.

"Was that him?" she whispered in a conspiratorial tone. And she edged away.

"You should probably stay with me," he began, but she was already gone, cutting a quick path over luggage and around legs to get to the battered vending machines that passed for food service at Red Dog.

"The Newark bus came in early," the man behind the window told him, pulling Dylan's attention back that way. "It's been in for a good two hours."

"Okay, thanks." Two hours? That was way too much time to expect the Wild Man to stay out of trouble. But Dylan was distracted, back to watching Polly's progress. As she neared the vending area, a scuzzy guy in army fatigues stepped into her path. That didn't look good. Dylan moved closer, trying to keep a low profile.

"What are you doing here, Jeanine?" the man in the fatigues shouted, grabbing her elbow. "I told you to stay away from me. They're watching all the exits, you know!"

"Excuse me, but I'm not Jeanine," she tried, but the man in the fatigues only picked up his volume, refusing to let her pass.

"Jeanine, I'm warning you—we'll both get busted!"

"Aw, jeez." The last thing Dylan needed was a fight with some whacked-out slimeball in the Red Dog waiting room. But Polly wrested her arm away from the crazy man, desperately looking for Dylan, making a face that told him to get over there pronto.

So he got over there pronto.

"Polly, honey," Dylan interrupted, sliding in between her and the wacko. "Thank you, mister, for looking out for my little Polly," he said, clapping the guy on the arm, trying not to notice the big honker of a knife that clattered to the floor. "Come on, sweetie, let's get out of this nice man's hair, all right?"

And he twisted her around in front of him, shepherding her along as he got the hell away from the nutball with the knife.

"What were you thinking?" he demanded. "Why would you run off in a place like this, where you are clearly not safe?"

"You brought me here," she returned swiftly. "This horrible, filthy place. What were *you* thinking?"

"Oh, so now it's my fault?"

"No, it's your uncle's…" She broke off. "I forgot. I saw him. Over by the vending machines. I'm sure it was him, peeking out around the coffee machine." She craned her neck, frowning as she scanned the area. "He's gone."

He scanned the vending area, finding no sign of his uncle. "I doubt it was him. His bus was way early and he's probably hanging from a chandelier some-where by now.''

But Polly gasped beside him, squeezing his arm and positively humming with excitement, nudging him around the other direction. *"Psst,"* she hissed. "There he is. By the water fountain. See him?''

Big as life. Ol' Hiram was engaged in an intense conversation with a tall redheaded woman in a tube top. That explained why he wasn't looking for them. The tall redhead was way more entertaining than any nephew.

"Let's take him." Grim with determination, Dylan pulled Polly along behind him as he went after his wayward uncle. The redhead was still there when they got to the small hallway near the restrooms, but Uncle Hiram had apparently slipped into the men's room. There didn't seem to be anywhere else he could've gone.

"Stay here," Dylan ordered, dropping Polly next to the drinking fountain. "Do not move. And if the guy in the army surplus wardrobe comes back, scream.''

"Scream? Are you kidding?''

But Dylan wanted to trap his uncle before he slith-ered away again. "I'll be back in five seconds." And he turned away, slamming open the door into the rest-room, feeling like Gary Cooper in *High Noon.*

He made eye contact with his uncle for all of one heartbeat before all hell broke loose.

"Get your hand off my butt!" someone yelled, and everyone else started hopping around and shouting, too, trying to either mix into the fracas or make tracks.

Among other choice comments, Dylan heard, "Pickpockets! Thieves!" and "There he is! Somebody stop that guy!"

A large man smashed into Dylan, knocking him aside and barreling out of there, followed by about three other people hot on his trail. Squashed between the crush of men trying to get in and out at the same time, Dylan was carried along by the crowd. Punched in the gut, smacked in the head, pushed into a wall, he was no closer to nabbing his damn fool of an uncle than he'd been since he left New York.

By the time things quieted down, he was alone in the hallway except for Polly. She stood there, her hands on her hips, staring at him. "He got away, didn't he?"

"Yep." He brushed off his pants, disengaging himself from the wall. "I don't know how much you heard, but as soon as he caught sight of me, everybody started yelling about pickpockets and thieves and things got crazy. I'm betting he squeezed past me in the general melee. I don't suppose you saw where he went."

"Not one hair on his chinny chin chin."

"Huh?"

"Never mind." She considered for a moment. "Do you think he staged the whole thing as a way to escape?"

"Oh, you bet he did." Dylan set his jaw into a hard line. "This little escapade had my uncle written all over it."

# 4

―――――

"SO WHAT DO WE DO NEXT?" she asked, hoping he would say *Get the heck out of this hideous place.*

No such luck. "We reconnoiter," Dylan told her, although she had no idea what that meant.

"Come again?"

"We look around," he said impatiently. "We look for clues. We see if we can figure out where he went or where he is now."

"Okay, well—"

But she was interrupted by an ear-splitting squeal coming from somewhere near the ceiling. It sounded like it was trying to shriek at them in Greek. Or maybe Martian.

She did the smart thing. She covered her ears.

Dylan waved his hands in front of her face. "Polly? Polly? You're being paged."

"Me?" She hadn't heard anything remotely like her name. Either one of them. "You're sure about this?"

"Yes, I'm sure. Come on." He was practically pushing her up to the glassed-in counter. "It's got to be some kind of message from Uncle Hiram."

"Hello, um, sir," she said politely, bending enough to speak into the small hole in the window. She still felt funny saying it, but she barged right ahead. "My name is Polly Tompkins. Did you call me?"

"That make you Sweet Polly Purebread?"

"Well, maybe." After Dylan glared at her, she allowed, "Yes, that's me."

Without even looking up, he tossed a folded note out the window.

"Okay. Well, then..." Gingerly, she unfolded the crumpled piece of paper.

"What does it say?" Dylan demanded, trying to get in closer for a better view.

Cassie scowled at him, holding the paper behind her back. "Did he leave a note for you? No. He left a note for me. So stop being so pushy."

"Will you read it already?"

"Sheesh. Grumpy, grumpy." It took her a second, even though there were only a few words written there. "He says we should meet him at his hotel at midnight. Room 302. But it doesn't say what hotel."

Apparently unable to wait any longer, Dylan snatched the message out of her hand. "Let's look at the paper it's written on." He swore under his breath, flapping the small note with its cheesy gold crest. "Oh, man. Not the Château Paulette."

"It sounds nice," she tried. "Is there something wrong with it?"

"If you didn't like the Red Dog bus station, you are really going to hate the Château Paulette," he said darkly.

Cassie's heart dropped, but she tried to be optimistic. After all, how could anything be worse than the Red Dog bus station?

She found out when they got to the Château Paulette. Why anything that nasty should bother to call itself a château was beyond her. But, heck, at the station she'd stepped over three winos and a bag lady, and then exchanged words with that horrid man wearing army clothes and carrying a big knife. And there was the person hanging out by the water fountain who was dressed as a woman, but didn't seem much like a real one, even with that outrageous tube top stretched over her plastic curves and enough red curls to shame Annie. ``Should've called the fashion police on that one,'' she muttered.

``What did you say?''

``Nothing.''

He gave her another one of those searching glances. ``Are you sure you wouldn't rather wait in the car?''

``Are you kidding? All by myself? I'll get carjacked before you're gone for two minutes,'' she protested, feeling very smart and savvy that she'd thought to be wary of carjackers.

``All right. If you're sure.''

``But the front door is over there,'' she noted, gazing dubiously at the blinking ``château'' light over the entrance as Dylan made a beeline for the alley.

``I know. We're not going in that way. I've been here before.'' He took her hand and pulled her along with him. ``They have really beefy guys working the front desk and they don't like trouble. I know my uncle well enough to suspect he'll have warned them we're coming and set up some kind of showdown.''

''So how are we getting in?'' she asked, although she already had an idea. And she didn't like it one bit.

First Dylan pushed her up onto a fire escape that didn't make it all the way to the ground, planting his hands on her bottom and hoisting her as if she were a sack of potatoes. The narrow metal steps were hard to navigate in her high heels, too, and they took two flights before Dylan stopped on a landing.

And then he pried open a window, as if he were very familiar with this place and how best to burglarize it. He offered a hand, helping her wiggle over the sill first.

It was fairly dim in there, but she could tell they were touching down in a hallway. ''Good gracious. This carpet is horrible,'' she whispered, planting her feet.

''Yeah, well, we can critique the décor later.'' He took her hand again, but crept ahead of her down the hall, stopping before a room with only two metal numbers on the door. There was a 3 and a 2 with an empty space between them, but Dylan seemed sure this was the place.

''Hiram?'' he called out, knocking quietly. ''It's me, Dylan. Are you there?''

''He may not be here yet. It isn't even close to midnight,'' Cassie pointed out helpfully.

''Yeah, well, I'm not coming back at midnight.'' Dylan jammed a hand into his pocket and came out with a Swiss Army knife. ``Don't worry. I'm good at picking locks.''

``Oh, my goodness. We're breaking in?'' She glanced around the hallway, hoping no one would see them acting like criminals.

``Honey, we already broke in. Fire escape? Window? Ring any bells?'' As he jiggled the lock with the corkscrew on his knife, he leaned into the door, finally easing it open.

Cassie was both appalled and excited. They had broken into a hotel room! They were practically felons!

Although she closed the door neatly behind her, she hovered near the doorway, not really ready to go barreling in and acting like she owned the place. Besides, the room looked filthy, and she didn't want to touch anything unless she had to. But Dylan wasn't so shy.

He was already poking around, picking up a glass here, examining a box of cigars on the bedside table and the stub in the ashtray, going through the pockets of the safari-style jacket hanging over the chair, even lifting the mattress.

``Are you sure this is your uncle's room?'' she asked tentatively. God forbid they should spend one minute in this fleabag place if it wasn't the right room.

He grinned, crinkling his eyes again and making her feel weak in the knees. ``Yessiree, Bob.''

Why did that sound so strange—and kind of endearing—coming from him? She edged over closer, feeling skittish in the strange room, especially after breaking in. ``How do you know this is his room?''

she persisted. "I mean, I would hate for you to be rifling someone else's possessions and then in comes Billy Bob, carrying a club or something."

He looked up momentarily. "Are there people named Billy Bob where you come from? Because I don't think the Billy Bobs of the world are lurking around this particular hotel."

"What?" She shook her head, confused as usual. "So why are you so sure this is your uncle's room?"

"I recognize the jacket. The cigars are his brand. That's his handwriting scribbled on the memo pad, which matches the sheet you got at the bus station, by the way. And I know my uncle." He squinted. "This room has him written all over it."

"So what exactly are you looking for?"

But he didn't answer. After scrounging around under the bed, he said something that sounded like "Aha" and stood up. He wheeled around, looking triumphant as he brandished a square, thick envelope with tape still stuck to it. "He had it taped to the bottom of the bed," he declared as he pulled out a wallet. After a brief check of its contents, he stuffed it into his pocket.

"I'm assuming that's your wallet and you're not stealing anything," she said slowly, but he didn't bother to fill her in. She gave him the benefit of the doubt. They'd been traveling together all day, and she knew him well enough by now to know he wouldn't steal. Right? "Okay, so you got your ID and credit cards back. That's good. Now what? How do we find your uncle and get him back to Chicago in time for tomorrow's appointments?"

Dylan spun the chair around and straddled it. "I guess we wait."

"Till midnight?"

"He could come back earlier," he said with a shrug. "Or he could know we're waiting and not come at all tonight. But his stuff is here, so he'll have to show up sooner or later. This is our best shot, right here."

"Oh, dear." Cassie stepped back. "So we're waiting here, then." She dithered there for a second, not thrilled by the idea that she was going to have to sit on something if she was going to be there for any length of time. "I guess...the chair. I'll wipe it off and then I'll sit on the chair. So you're going to have to move to the bed or something. Because the only place I can sit is the chair."

Dylan abandoned his seat without a protest, and she found a towel, wetted it, moved the safari jacket onto the bed next to him, and gave the whole chair a good scrub. She stopped in midswipe. "I just want you to know that I'm not cleaning the chair because you sat on it. It's because the place is icky."

"Icky?"

"Okay, enough with the eyebrows. I don't know what's wrong with the things I say that you are always arching your darn eyebrows at me. Icky is a perfectly good word." Finished with her cleaning job, she perched her bottom on the very edge of the chair, delicately balancing as little as possible on its surface.

"You don't look very comfortable," he said sardonically. "Sure you want to sit like that for hours and hours?"

"I'm fine," she returned, but she jumped up and shrieked, "Eeew!" as a big, fat bug crawled over her foot. It wasn't so bad just feeling the thing, but then she saw it. "Eeew!" she cried again. That was one gross and disgusting bug. It turned around, waving a tiny tentacle at her, and that was all it took. She launched out of the chair, lost one shoe and vaulted into Dylan's lap, where she hung on for dear life.

"Let me guess," he said kindly, patting her arm, "your first roach?"

"That was a roach? A *cockroach?* Oh my God! A cockroach touched me!" She felt sure she was going to barf, and she leapt up again, unwilling to sit, unsteady in only one high heel. "A cockroach!"

"Hey, you can sit on me if you want to. I'll protect you from the big, bad roach." He sort of leered at her, but she ignored him. She had other fish to fry at the moment.

"Okay, we are not waiting here," she decided.

"Relax. You scared it more than it scared you."

"I don't think so," she contended. "The bottom line is that a cockroach touched my foot, and I am not staying here one more second because—who knows?—it could come back, and bring back all its friends." She shuddered. "So? What do we do?"

"I have a plan," Dylan said in a very charming voice that made her suspicious. This was a new mood for him. He was smiling, with this funny crocodile grin that made her want to check and make sure she had all her clothes on.

No, she didn't trust him or his plan. But what choice did she have? She wanted out of here!

"Okay," she said warily. "What's your plan?

"You have a company credit card, right?"

"Um, yes."

"And a cell phone?"

"Yes." She narrowed her gaze. "Why?"

"So I'll call and get us a suite at the Hotel Verdi."

He held out her shoe, but she didn't really want it back, not after the roach had touched it. Awkwardly, she found the handy towel and took her shoe back inside the safe folds of cotton. After a careful rub, she finally slid her foot back into the high heel. Meanwhile, Dylan was still standing there with his hand out, as if he expected her to put something in it.

"The cell phone," he reminded her. "If you were on top of your game, you would've already taken care of this, by the way, but I know all this running around looking for my uncle has thrown you off, so I'm willing to pinch hit."

"Do you always talk in riddles?"

"Hotel Verdi," he repeated slowly, as if she had an IQ hovering around three. "PR people make hotel reservations at nice places for visiting celebs. Which includes my uncle, right? Except you didn't. So I'm going to do it now." He smiled again, another shifty smile. "You'll like the Hotel Verdi. It's hip, it's happening. Everything in the place is green, if you can imagine. Oh, and it's not here."

"That part I like. But how does this get us any closer to your uncle?" she inquired, trying to work her way through this tangle. "We check into a suite at a fancy hotel… And where is he?"

"I'll get to that. But first, the cell phone," he said, holding out his hand. "And the company credit card, too."

Against her better judgment, she gave him what he wanted, listening as he got the number, called the place and arranged for the presidential suite.

"Are you sure I'm supposed to be doing this on the company card?" she asked uneasily, envisioning Lenora Bridge scanning her expense report and pitching a fit. "The presidential suite?"

"I'm sure." He handed back the card and the phone. "What's that card for if not to take care of your clients? I'm surprised you don't know that, experienced PR professional that you are."

She kept her mouth shut.

"Now for the rest of the plan," he mused. "We'll need a glass—there's one over there—and the pad of paper. Do you have a pen?"

She found one in the bottom of her purse.

"Good. And we'll also need one of those bottles of scotch. You brought the scotch, right?"

"Not up here," she countered. "It's down in the trunk, locked away."

"Okay. So I'll go get it and you wait here."

"Wait? Here?"

"You'll be fine. It will only take me two minutes." And before she could argue further, he was backing out the door, one finger to his lips as if to tell her to keep silent.

"Wait!" she tried, but it was too late. Stuck. In this horrible place. All by herself.

Well, she'd wanted an adventure, hadn't she? Adventure didn't come in neat, clean packages. She reminded herself of that fact as she paced away the minutes, cursing Dylan's name as well as his uncle's, keeping an eye peeled for any disgusting bugs.

It was a major relief when he finally got back, and she felt like throwing her arms around his neck and hugging the stuffing out of him. She didn't.

"Okay, then." He held up the special bottle of peat bog scotch, hauled all the way from Chicago. "So we give him just a taste..." He poured an inch into the bottom of the glass. "And we write, 'There's more where this came from if you meet us at the Hotel Verdi.'"

"You really think that will work?"

Picking up the pen, scrawling his message onto a small sheet of paper, Dylan grinned. "He may be a Wild Man but, trust me, my uncle will not be able to resist the lure of his favorite whiskey and a suite at a fancy hotel."

Cassie fervently hoped he was right. As nearly as she could figure, they had to collect his uncle soon, or they'd never make it back to Chicago in time for tomorrow's appearances.

"Please let this work," she pleaded, "or my sister will kill me."

"What did you say?"

"Nothing," she said brightly. "Are you finished yet? I am so ready to blow this pop stand."

"Blow this…?" He laughed out loud. "The things you say."

What was wrong with *that?* Cassie was getting very tired of Dylan Wright and his vocabulary lessons.

HE LOVED the Hotel Verdi. Not stuffy, just classy and fun, the Verdi mixed every shade from emerald to evergreen, and that was just the lobby. The green-on-green artworks were splashy and fun, and the cool marble and mirrors in the lobby reflected it all back at you, wherever you stood.

Dylan walked right up to the VIP counter to check them in. It only took a minute, which was no surprise considering how much it was going to cost Lenora Bridge and Associates for this one night of luxury. Oh, yeah. A suite in a posh hotel, a beautiful woman to share it with…and somebody else to pick up the bill.

Did life get any better than this?

All right, all right, so he probably shouldn't have conned Polly into turning over her credit card. He wasn't all that sure she actually worked for Lenora Bridge and Associates in the first place, and if she was a fake employee she could hardly get fired over this. Besides, it was fun pulling Polly along by her pert little nose, leading her down the garden path.

"Shouldn't we leave a note for your uncle?" she asked, reluctant to leave the front desk even after he had the key.

"If I have to," he muttered under his breath. Turning back to the desk, he wrote out a quick message with the room number, just in case the old snake showed up. But Dylan harbored a strong hope that he wouldn't.

He hadn't lied to Polly—it really was a good lure to leave a little whiskey and a cryptic note where Hiram would find them—but he also knew it would be a hell of a lot more fun sharing a nice hotel room with just Polly than with his exasperating uncle, too.

"Dylan, when do you think we can lasso him and get out of here?" she inquired once they were safely in the elevator. "If we're driving, we'll need to leave by 1:00 a.m. at the latest if we have any hope of making our schedule tomorrow. That will give us just enough time to maybe wash our faces and change our clothes before we have to leave for the first appointment. Do you think we can make it by one? Will you be able to drive that late?"

He shrugged. "If we make it, we make it. If not, blame it on my uncle. It's his fault."

"Yes, I know, but my job is to get him to these places on time and make sure he's, you know, friendly and responsible—"

"You might as well forget about that stuff. No way the Wild Man is ever responsible," he told her.

"Well, we can try—"

"No point. It won't get you anywhere." He frowned as he put the lime-colored key card in the matching door and let them both into their suite. Why did he keep trying to warn Sweet Polly about what a rascal his uncle was? If she hadn't figured it out from all these weeks of exchanging faxes, she never would. Of course, if she wasn't the real Polly and had avoided the obnoxious faxes, then she was a total fake and deserved what she got, anyway.

But somehow, in some strange depth of his soul, he still felt responsible for naïve, innocent Polly. Or whoever she was. Go figure.

"This place is beautiful," she said in awe. "It even has a piano."

A baby grand—green, of course. The piano stood over by the windows, which showcased a spectacular view of the Cleveland skyline. There was also a spacious parlor area with two overstuffed couches in a soft sea-foam shade of leather, a stark modern dining room table with a bunch of eccentric, curvy pine chairs, and two bedrooms that opened into the main room. He and Cassie wandered around, opening doors, checking out the facilities.

Very nice. From the pale jade bathroom with the whirlpool tub to the wide, expansive balcony, it was a very nice suite.

"Are you hungry?" he asked, once they had seen pretty much everything. "We don't really have anything to do while we're waiting, so we may as well order some dinner and chill out, enjoy the suite."

"I guess so. Um, go ahead if you want to."

Looking a little uncomfortable, she removed her suit jacket and hung it neatly in the closet. She even deigned to roll up the sleeves of her crisp white blouse, which was a little wilted after the day they'd had.

"You look great," he assured her, just in case she was worried.

But Polly didn't say anything. She chewed her lip, she chewed her fingernails and she took a seat on one of the leather sofas, clasping and unclasping her hands.

"Do you think we're going to be waiting long?" she asked finally, craning her neck to get a better view of the door.

If he'd had a seduction scene in mind—and he wasn't really sure whether he had or not—it wasn't going well. He was actually relieved when the room service waiter showed up with their dinner.

Polly perked up immediately at the sight and smell of food. "Oh, how pretty," she whispered, lifting covers and looking at the dishes as the waiter laid them out on the table. Her round blue eyes sparkled with anticipation. "Look at this fruit display. With the cheese! I love fruit and cheese. And what's this? Pasta, but... Something with lobster? I love lobster. And, oh! Did you see these tiny salt and pepper shakers? They're adorable."

*She* was adorable. He'd had a lot of room service in his time, so the tiny salt shaker no longer thrilled him. But he was enjoying it through her eyes just the same.

"Champagne!" she said with a gasp as the waiter set up the bucket. "Two bottles! You ordered champagne?"

"Sure. Why not?" He winked at her. "Beautiful women need champagne."

Okay, that was way too obvious. He had overplayed

his hand and Polly would be running for the door. But she didn't. She just drained the champagne flute he'd poured for her and held it out to be refilled.

Now that was encouraging.

And then she dug in. He couldn't tear his eyes away as she nibbled on a big, beautiful strawberry, as she sucked a piece of fettuccini into those pouty lips, as she daintily licked away a dribble of champagne, flicking her pretty pink tongue against the rim of the flute.

And he kept refilling her glass, saying little, just watching. They were almost at the end of the first bottle now, and he'd only had a few sips. Surely Polly's tongue would start to get loose any minute.

She must've noticed the way he was staring, or maybe it was just the bubbles going to her head, because she got more flushed as the meal wore on. Her cheeks were positively rosy by the time they finished the dessert. She ate the last bite of cheesecake and then drained her glass one more time.

"I really do love champagne," she confided in an apologetic tone. "It's so...you know, fun."

He was starting to feel guilty about plying her with wine. But, come on, she was much too uptight. She really needed to relax. He was only helping her out. "Fun," he repeated, refilling her flute with the dead end of the bottle. "Uh-huh."

She made a tiny hiccup, very politely, and then she scooted away from the table, splashing champagne but keeping a firm hold on her glass. "Oooh, let's go out on the balcony. It's dark now and the lights are so pretty."

He did his best to keep up, but she was pretty quick on her feet for a girl with too much wine under her belt. She had the sliding door pushed open and her frisky little body hustled out on to the balcony before he caught up.

"Isn't it…pretty?" she whispered.

"Very."

Dylan came up behind her, slipping a secure arm around her before she had a chance to fall over. He also removed the empty champagne flute from her fingers, easing it to the balcony floor.

"Mmmm," she murmured, turning around into his embrace, draping her hands behind his neck. "That feels nice."

It certainly did.

Her voice dipped even lower as she pressed herself nearer. "You know, Dylan, at first when I met you, which was only yesterday, but seems like forever, I thought, wow, is he cute, but, wow, is he a butthead."

"Thanks. I think."

She closed her eyes, swaying slightly, brushing her legs and hips against him. Her smile was dreamy, her arms fast around his neck, and he knew she was poised and ready, waiting for his kiss. How could he disappoint her?

So he bent down, gathered her closer, and slanted his lips across hers. Delving into her mouth, he was shocked to feel a major pull of electricity and connection. Whoa.

He dragged himself away, looked down at her heavy-lidded eyes and bruised, soft mouth, and promptly kissed her again. Oh, man. This was bad. This was way too much.

He hadn't really expected this amazing jolt, but even if he had, it was too late now to pull back. She tasted sweet and eager, warm and responsive, like cheesecake and champagne and some strange, sexy innocence that was all her own. It was a heady mix, and he felt toasted down to his toes.

Polly Tompkins, or whoever she was, was a damn good kisser. What she lacked in experience she definitely made up for in enthusiasm.

He whispered, "You are really very tempting, Polly."

But she let out a long sigh. "Could you please not call me Polly?" she pleaded. "Not now, okay?"

That took him back. "Why not?"

"Oh, I don't know." But she shook her head, as if trying to clear away the cobwebs. "When I'm kissing someone, I'd just like to *not* be called Polly. It makes me feel weird. I just... I don't like that name, okay?"

"I don't really care if you want me to call you Snoopy as long as you don't walk away," he murmured. "We'll talk about your name later, okay?"

"Mmm-hmm." She smiled again, leaning up into him, taking the initiative and kissing *him* this time, dipping her tongue under his, knocking him back with the sheer force of her ardor.

Wow. Sweet, shy Polly had turned into a hot number somewhere along the line. Bless her naughty little heart.

"Should we move this inside?" she asked drowsily, nuzzling his neck, nudging him toward the door.

"Should we?"

It was a strange time to get a conscience, but he couldn't help it. He knew she'd had too much champagne, but she was an adult, she was there under her own free will, she'd admitted she was attracted the first time she saw him...

What was he waiting for?

He slid open the balcony door, her hand in his, prepared to take this as far as she was willing, when the door to the suite burst open. Dylan stopped where he was, with Polly tucked behind him.

Even half on the balcony, he could hardly miss the noise, the commotion and—no, he wasn't imagining it—the mariachi band coming in the front door. First in was his Uncle Hiram, wearing a bandana tied around his head, carrying a large piñata, followed by a flock of guys in ruffled white shirts—one with a guitar, another shaking maracas, a third blasting away on a trumpet, and three or four others with no instruments at all. Snaking into the suite in a demented conga line, they were all singing at the top of their lungs, while several exuberant young ladies brought up the rear, carrying tall pitchers of what appeared to be margaritas.

How you sang, danced and drank margaritas all at the same time was yet to be explained. Not that it would matter to the Wild Man. This was par for the course for him.

"Goodbye romance, hello riot," Dylan muttered.

# 5

"THE WILD MAN!" Polly exclaimed, squeezing past Dylan to get to the party. "He's here!"

He tried to catch her, really he did. But it was too late.

"I have been dying to meet you," she announced, trying to shake both of his uncle's hands around the piñata cradled in his arms. "I would have recognized you anywhere."

Uncle Hiram handed the thing—was it a horse or a dog?—over to one of the guys in the band, pitching his voice louder to make it heard above the music. "If it isn't Pretty Polly P!" he announced, giving her a massive bear hug and lifting her off the ground.

Dylan rolled his eyes.

"You look just like your picture," the old coot told her.

From her perch suspended in the air, she asked, "I do?"

"She does?" Dylan echoed. But he had been so sure she wasn't really Polly. "You're sure she looks like her picture?"

"Spittin' image," Hiram growled, releasing her abruptly. She teetered a little on her heels and Dylan offered a steadying hand. "That Lenora dame keeps sending me company brochures to convince me I signed on with the right folks, and damned if our little Polly's face isn't on all of them.'' He laughed out loud, clapping his nephew on the arm. ''Guess she must be the best-looking broad in the bunch. What do you say, Polly? You headin' up the looks department at Lenora's?''

''Well, I don't know,'' she faltered, but Hiram was already bored with the conversation, which he indicated by glowering at them and looking around for something else to amuse him. Dylan recognized the profile. Bumming a cigar and a match off one of his buddies, his uncle lit up, inhaling with exaggerated contentment.

''This is a no-smoking hotel,'' Polly said suddenly. She blinked, narrowing her eyes, and Dylan knew she was trying to sober up and act like a professional. An ill-timed hiccup pretty much ruined the effect, however. ''I saw No Smoking signs all over.''

His uncle just guffawed. ''Lighten up, Sweet Polly P. Lighten up! Life is to be lived, not stifled. Life is to be *enjoyed*. You have to suck the marrow right out of it!''

''Hiram, cool your jets, will you?'' Dylan tried.

''Don't be a downer, Dylan,'' the old man chided.

''When have I ever?''

The Wild Man scowled. ''Always. You're always bringing me down.''

''This is a nice hotel. Let's not get kicked out, okay?''

"I've been kicked out of better joints than this one."

Dylan sighed. "While that's probably true, it isn't very helpful."

But the old man was ignoring him, exhorting the musicians to pick up the tempo and the volume. "Come on, kids! Live a little! Dance while you got the chance!"

With that, he stuck the cigar in his mouth, grabbed Polly away from Dylan, and with his meaty paws on her hips, pushed her out in front of him.

"Dance," he ordered.

"Oh! I don't know—" she squealed, but the conga line and the insistent music swallowed up her protests. Dylan tried to reel her back in, but Hiram wouldn't let go. And she seemed to be enjoying herself, too, the little traitor. He actually heard her giggle as the line of hopping, gesticulating weirdos snaked around the room, moving to their own bizarre beat.

*Oh, man.* He stood there, waiting for her to dance past again, wondering if steam was coming out his ears. He was used to this kind of behavior—too used to it—from his impossible uncle. But now Polly was ensnared, too. Just when he was finally getting somewhere with her, Hiram had to charge in and wreck everything. With cigars, trumpets, a piñata, the conga, margaritas sloshing out of the pitcher... Could it get any more obnoxious in here?

Meanwhile, Dylan felt responsible for the fact that Polly was pretty much loaded, which meant he also felt a certain duty to keep her safe, on her feet and out of the Wild Man's clutches. He was so focused on where she was and what she was doing that he yelped and jumped a foot in the air when his own bottom got pinched.

"Excuse me?" He spun around, frowning at the inebriated young lady—one of the margarita girls, although she smelled like straight tequila—who stood there, grinning at him.

"You want salt with your margarita?" she asked in a sultry tone, pulling up her shirt far enough to reveal a salty circle on her flat, tanned stomach. And then she started giggling so hard she couldn't hold up the fabric.

They were all giggling, weren't they? Dylan blamed his reprobate of an uncle for turning them all into a bunch of dopes. It was certainly no fun being the only sober person in the room.

"Yeah, sure, some other time," he returned. "But at the moment, I'm not interested."

"You didn't even give me a try," the woman pouted, dragging on his hand to get him alone in the front hallway. "Come on, we can have a drink, we can have a dance...."

"I can't." He winced as the noise level shot up dramatically on the far side of the room. Someone sat down and started plunking out a solo on the piano, but it didn't match the rest of the music. So the other guys tried to drown out the piano by singing and playing even louder. People started pushing and shoving and laughing, all as noisily as possible. "I'd better warn everyone to be quiet."

"Quiet? Who wants to be quiet? That is so not fun!"

Miss Margarita tossed her arms around his neck and wiggled her hips suggestively.

"Not interested," he said again, trying to disentangle her hands and get away from her before she transferred any salt to his body.

What with the blaring music and fending off unwanted advances and trying to keep an eye on Polly all at the same time, Dylan barely heard the persistent knocking and stern voices outside the door. But there was a fraction of a second when the wall of sound in the suite died down, and he caught the words, "Open up. Hotel security."

It wasn't like it was a surprise. For better or worse, he was very experienced with this sort of thing. So after some shushing and a few threats, Dylan went to answer the door, all ready to use his most soothing tones and apologetic manner. He also reached for his wallet.

"Sorry, guys," he offered, trying to keep the door closed behind him while he spoke to the authorities. God forbid they should get a gander at what was actually going on in there. "I realize the noise level is a little out of control, but it's just my uncle—"

"It's more than a little out of control." The leader of the pack of hotel cops stared him down, looking very sour. "And you can smell cigars all over the rest of the floor. This is a non-smoking hotel, you know."

"You're absolutely right. And I'll get him to calm down, quiet down and put out the cigars. Promise."

"You'd better promise."

"I do. I swear. That's Hiram Wright causing all the fuss. Ever heard of him? They call him the Wild Man." He paused, letting his uncle's celebrity status sink in. "This crazy stuff is kind of his trademark, y'know? So if you'll just give me a few minutes—"

"Nope." The head guy set his square jaw into a firm line. "I don't care if he's Santy Claus. Either the music and all the stomping and smoking stops now or you're all out of here. How does your Wild Man feel about a jail cell for the rest of the night?"

"No, no. No need to go there," Dylan insisted. "I'll take care of it right now. No smoking. No music. No stomping." As a matter of fact, it sounded quieter behind him already. "Listen, you tell me your names, and I'll have the Wild Man sign some books for you, okay? Free autographed books for everyone, on the Wild Man."

They grumbled a little, but they seemed mollified, whether by the book offer or the relative calm now coming from the suite, he couldn't say. As they trundled back toward the elevator, Dylan slipped back inside, firmly closing the door behind him.

Huh. He didn't know how it had happened, but the mariachi guys were much calmer now, sitting on the sofas and lying on the floor, generally chilling out. One was actually sleeping on the piano bench, his guitar still strapped over his stomach as he snored away.

But where was Uncle Hiram? And, more importantly, where was Polly?

Thank goodness it only took a few minutes to find

them. As soon as someone opened the door to the balcony, he heard raised voices. He recognized his uncle's patented roar followed by a snarl of disagreement that sounded a lot like Polly, and he knew they were out there, arguing at the top of their lungs.

"You guys are going to have to keep it down," Dylan commanded as he joined them. He also made a grab for his uncle's cigar and stubbed it out on the floor of the balcony without further ado. At least he'd gotten rid of that problem. "We've already gotten the first warning from hotel security. Next time they'll mean business."

If they heard him, they gave no sign. Except for a dirty look from Hiram when his cigar disappeared, they just continued their argument as if Dylan weren't even there.

"No!" Polly declared, going nose to nose with the Wild Man. "It is not acceptable to wash your hair in a rain puddle. Eeew! It's just not!"

"Rain water is excellent for hair," her opponent rumbled. "Almost as good as beer."

"Eeew!" she said again, sounding even more appalled. "And don't even get me started on the doughnut thing. Once they hit the Dumpster, bucko, they are off-limits."

"What a waste of perfectly good doughnuts."

With a flourish of disgust, Hiram took a step backward, peering at the smashed cigar stub as if he were considering giving it another go. That gave Dylan enough of an opening to slide between them. "Come on, you two, break it up."

"No Dumpster-diving for doughnuts," Polly said angrily, standing on tiptoe to yell over Dylan's shoulder.

"What about if they're still in their original boxes? Huh? Did you think of that?" Hiram shot back.

"Well, no, and that might be okay, if nothing else from the trash has touched them or, you know, soaked through." She shuddered. "And even if I give you that one, which I don't think I should, I still will not agree to going on a week's trip with only one outfit. Wearing the same clothes every day? I don't think so!"

"Polly, does this really matter?" Dylan asked helplessly. What could he do? Pick her up and carry her off? Gag her? It was beginning to sound like the best idea.

"What's wrong with packing light?" Uncle Hiram argued. "There's no need for all that vanity and excess. Consumerism, charlatanism, vanity, vanity, vanity."

"Hrmph," she countered. "No one in Pleasant Falls would ever speak to you again or invite you to any social event if you wore the same clothes all the time, not to mention if they caught you washing your hair in a puddle. You would be a laughingstock. An outcast!"

"Don't call him that," Dylan warned, but it was too late. His uncle was already wound up.

"You call me an outcast and I say poppycock! I tell you that I epitomize the value of the individual and the glory of the man who thinks for himself. You, my dear,'' the Wild Man proclaimed, stubbing a finger at her, ''are in desperate need of some life lessons. You need to learn how to get rid of excess baggage and live by your wits. You need to stop following the herd.''

Dylan tried a lighter tone to get his uncle away from this familiar song. ''Yeah, yeah, Hiram, we've heard it before, but you know, some people prefer to live with cash and bathtubs and hair dryers.''

For the first time, they both seemed to notice that Dylan was standing between them.

''Shut up!'' they said in unison.

Coming from his uncle, rudeness was expected. But from Polly? He turned around to face her. ''I can't believe you just told me to shut up.''

She glanced up, attempting to focus. And then she smiled at him, and he caught a glimmer of the soft, sweet, seductive woman he'd had in his arms on this very balcony such a short time ago. Damn it.

''Oh, Dylan. Dylan, Dylan, Dylan,'' she said mistily, tipping her chin into his chest. ''You are so cute, you know that? How did you get so cute?''

But behind them, his uncle ranted, ''Herd mentality! Moo moo moo. You have to stop riding with the herd, Pretty Polly!''

He tromped back inside, and Dylan hoped he stayed there. Permanently.

He caught Polly in his arms as she sort of fell into him. All he knew was that she felt wonderful there, all curvy and melty and warm, with her cheek on his shoulder and her hand tangled in his hair.

She maneuvered her head around so that she could see him. "I love it when you crinkle," she said dreamily, tracing the corner of his eye with one finger. "Did I ever tell you that I love it when you crinkle?"

"Polly, what am I going to do with you?" he whispered. He could think of a few things, none of them G-rated.

But Uncle Hiram, the spoiler, came slamming back onto the balcony, waving the handbag Polly had been carrying earlier as if it were a red flag instead of a red purse. "Is this yours?" he demanded.

She lifted her chin, giving him a dismissive glance. Very carefully, enunciating each word, she asked, "What if it is?"

"This purse, this *thing*, is exactly what I mean," Hiram continued, picking up speed and energy. "Ha! It's fancy and silly and serves no useful purpose."

Polly stiffened in Dylan's embrace. "How dare you?"

Dylan was starting to get really annoyed. Every time he made a move, Hiram screwed it up. One minute Polly was pliant and soft and ripe for the plucking, and the next she was rigid and cranky and ready to spit nails. Just because of his uncle and his rotten timing.

Her mouth was a round *O* of outrage. "That purse has all my stuff in it," she yelled. "My organizer and my phone and, and, *everything*. How much more useful can you get?"

"You need to simplify," Hiram lectured in his most annoying know-it-all voice. "You need to learn to enjoy what life and fate want to give you and not depend upon the false idols of consumerism and vanity.''

And with that, he flipped open the flap on her purse, grabbed her Palm Pilot organizer and her cell phone, and pitched them both off the balcony into the deep distance of the Cleveland skyline.

''Now you'll learn to simplify, won't you? Ha ha!'' And with that, the Wild Man stomped back into the suite, crashing the sliding door closed behind him to punctuate his exit.

Dylan just stood there, looking at Polly. Girls were, as a rule, very attached to their stuff. And Polly was very girly. She undoubtedly loved her tiny flip-phone. And he'd seen how organized she liked to be, with her hundreds of posted messages, and now her organizer was somewhere on the pavement in downtown Cleveland, thirty floors below them, smashed to smithereens. ''Aw, man.''

Polly made some sort of choked ''but-but-but'' noises. After a moment, she managed to speak in sentences.

''But I need that phone!'' she cried, hanging on to the railing and staring down into the black night. ''I have to have that phone. It's how my sister and I agreed to stay in contact. How else is she going to find me? What if there's an emergency in Pleasant Falls?''

Well, okay, that wasn't the reaction he was expecting. ''Are you expecting an emergency in Pleasant Falls?''

She seemed to consider that for a second. ''Ssssh,'' she whispered. ''It's a secret.''

"What's a secret?"

"Me and my sister and Pleasant Falls. Jeez Louise. Polly, Polly, Polly. And Skipper. Oh, God, Skipper." She rubbed the heel of her hand on her forehead. "I am really making a mess of things, aren't I? I didn't know how bad I would be at this. And now the cell phone.... I'm so sorry."

Dylan felt sure there were important clues hiding in there somewhere, if only he had a translator.

"What is that racket?" she asked out of the blue, lifting her head and squinting in through the glass door. "Is it music?"

Not hardly. Dylan shook his head. Hiram was standing on top of the green grand piano, howling something or other. His performance was slightly muffled by the balcony door, but not enough. And now Dylan was going to have to go in there and put a stop to it before the hotel security team made a return visit.

"It sounds like..." Polly squeezed her eyes shut and then popped them open. "Like the theme from *Mission: Impossible*. With words. Dirty words."

Swearing bitterly, Dylan pulled her along behind him as he ventured back inside. "Uncle Hiram, could you please stop the music? Like, ten minutes ago?"

But it was too late. As the Wild Man launched into another verse of his improvised bawdy lyrics to the theme from *Mission: Impossible*, shouting out, "Sing along, everyone!" there was a booming knock on the front door.

This time the security guys charged right in, not even waiting for someone to open the door.

"Busted," Dylan muttered, keeping Polly safely behind him where she couldn't get into any trouble.

"Okay, everyone," the square-jawed man who was in charge of this detail announced. The other men began fanning out, rousing and rounding up the mariachi band, while the main man tried to get Hiram off the piano. "Party's over. You'll all have to leave the hotel now."

Quickly, Dylan backed up, pushing Polly toward the nearest bedroom. "Stay here," he whispered, shutting the door on her before she could argue.

When he returned to the main room of the suite, he began to help get rid of the musicians and their girlfriends, making sure the hotel men knew he was on their side. Uncle Hiram was losing steam, but he had enough moxie left to poke a finger in the security man's face, arguing that everyone was just having fun, no harm, and why were they all such killjoys? Dylan headed him off the pass, extricating him from the discussion before he did any real damage, shoving him headfirst into the other bedroom and locking the door. Phew. He should've tried that hours ago.

His uncle beat on the door a few times, demanding to be let out, but then he either passed out or found something else to do, as the last of the mariachi men were ushered down the hall and onto the freight elevator.

"Thanks so much," Dylan said heartily, pressing money into the hands of the hotel guards. "As soon as you guys take off, I'll just put my uncle to bed and everything should be copacetic."

"I don't know." The head guy frowned. "We're supposed to kick out the whole lot of you."

"Nah, you don't want to do that." Dylan grinned, peeling off a few more bills. "With no booze and no playmates, the Wild Man will be tapped out pretty quick. Don't worry. I know my uncle. He'll be out for the night."

The guard's face was stern. "Well, all right. But if we hear even a peep from up here, we're not fooling with you people, it's jail this time."

Reluctantly, with several suspicious glances directed at the door to Hiram's bedroom, they consented to march off.

The place was a mess, but at least it was quiet. For now. Dylan took care of his uncle first, letting himself into the bedroom, dragging Hiram off the carpet where he was taking a nap and rolling him toward the bed.

As he tucked in ol' Hiram the Horrible, he envisioned Polly waiting for him in the other bedroom, all warm and cozy, ready to start up again where they'd left off.

Maybe she would have stripped out of her clothes and slid between the sheets by now, and she'd offer a come-hither look and turn back a corner, inviting him in. Oh, yeah. He sped up, trundling his uncle into the bed with one big whump, ignoring that Hiram still had his clothes on and more of him was off the bed than on. Too bad. The old man had been through worse.

Dylan checked the window to make sure it wouldn't open, and then backed out in record time, locking the door behind him. Hiram couldn't get into any more trouble tonight. He hoped.

"Okay, Polly," Dylan murmured, putting himself in a better frame of mind as he made a beeline across the suite, ready for whatever she was willing to offer.

But when he opened the door, he knew he was in trouble. Not only was she not naked and nubile and waiting for him to join her, she wasn't even awake.

Polly was asleep, lying mostly facedown as she sprawled across the bed, wearing everything but one shoe. "What is it with this shoe?" he asked, tossing it into the corner. For good measure, he removed the other shoe, too, sending it back with its mate. She didn't wake up, just hiked her knee up, revealing even more of her bare, silky leg.

Oh, yeah. He stood there, watching the steady, even flow of air in and out of her pretty mouth, wondering if he should leave her like that, or if he should at least undress her and put her into bed properly.

He edged a bit closer, hovering over the bed. "What do you think, Polly? You want me to be the good guy and go sleep on the couch again?" He smiled. "Or should I unwrap you like a birthday present, join you in that big ol' bed, and see if maybe a few hours from now you're up for something more interesting?"

He'd never pretended to be an angel. So he got to work stripping off her clothes, one sexy bit at a time, slipping open the hard little buttons on the white blouse, unzipping and unpeeling the tight miniskirt, unhooking the delicate white bra and maneuvering the straps down her arms. He couldn't believe she didn't stir once, not even when he edged off, ever so carefully, her teeny, tiny panties.

But the joke was on him. If he'd thought it would be fun to strip her, he was sadly mistaken. Instead, it was torture.

He held his breath, he counted to one hundred and he repeated the Yankees starting lineup a few times, but it didn't help. His hands were shaking. He was sweating.

And Polly was as naked as the day she was born.

Pure torture. He should've just left her in there fully dressed and gone to sleep on the couch. Yeah, well, hindsight was 20-20, wasn't it?

As he considered his folly, she finally opened her eyes, scaring him, but all she did was smile at him and say, "Kiss me, Dylan" in a sleepy, husky voice that slid down his spine like molasses.

He obliged, leaning in over the bed and softly brushing his lips against hers, acting like an emasculated Prince Charming or some other stooge. She fell asleep again while his mouth was still on hers.

"She's messing with my head," he whispered for the second time that day, backing away from Sleeping Beauty before this got any worse.

But he tucked the sheet around her as gently as you please, shed his own clothes and crept in beside her. He felt certain he now qualified for sainthood. He'd kept his hands off Polly Tompkins, and that ought to get him right in heaven's door, no waiting, no reservation necessary, when the time came.

As he laid his head on the pillow and tried not to

think about the naked lady breathing in his ear, Dylan's mind filled with very disturbing thoughts.

He was supposed to be having a great time, taking chances, seducing beautiful women, living life on the edge. What a joke. Turning down everyone's covers and practically singing them lullabies, he'd turned into a freaking nanny.

Dylan Wright, adventurer, man about town... nursemaid. It was depressing.

"There are gonna be some changes made," he said under his breath. "Tomorrow."

# 6

*May 24: Eight days before the wedding*

CASSIE AWOKE slowly, finding it difficult to pry her eyes open and swallow around the cotton in her mouth.

"What in the world...?" She tried to sit up, but her head was pounding and she was oddly dizzy. So the best thing to do seemed to be to give in and sink back into her pillow.

Even lying on feathers, she felt awful, as if her head were too big and heavy for the rest of her. And there was something going on down in her stomach area, too. Some sort of cartwheels and loop-de-loops. Did she have the flu?

She tried to lift her head, but didn't get very far. Where was she, anyway?

"It's very bright," she mumbled, wincing at the sunlight streaming in the window. "What time is it?"

If she squinted with her left eye, she could just make out the red, glowing numbers on the bedside clock. That was weird; she didn't remember ever having a clock with red, glowing numbers—but the numbers said 9:45 nonetheless.

"It's after nine? It can't be!" That got her out of bed, shooting up so fast that she got woozy and weird from the effort. She planted her feet on the floor, determined to be out of there. "I have never in my life slept past seven, let alone nine."

As she perched on the side of the bed, she felt a chilly breeze of air-conditioning waft across her skin, and she happened to look down at herself. "I'm naked?"

"Mmmm," someone said from the bed behind her.

She sat ramrod stiff, carefully hanging on to enough of the sheet to cover her breasts. Naked. Disoriented. In a strange bed. With a strange clock. And a strange man!

Now she was in trouble.

If only there weren't a series of hammers clonking around in her head. If only she could remember where she was or how she got there. *Think, think,* she commanded herself. But trying to put thoughts together actually hurt.

She ventured a tiny glance over her shoulder. Dylan. Of course. His golden brown hair was tousled against his pale green pillow case in the cutest possible way, and his moody, elegant features were softened by sleep. He looked adorable, his lashes thick and lush against his cheek, his narrow, tempting lips parted slightly.

Dylan. Of course. She wasn't in bed with a stranger; she was in bed with Dylan. Beautiful, maddening, amazing Dylan. Cassie sagged with relief that lasted all of two seconds.

Dylan? Dylan with *her?* Naked in the same bed?

"How did I get here? How did he get here?" she whispered, staring at him as she racked her brain for clues. "I remember...I remember..."

What did she remember?

Cleveland. The bus station. How long ago was that?

"Yesterday. And then last night," she murmured, trying to fast-forward her brain. Okay, wait, a few images were emerging from the murky depths. She remembered arriving at the Hotel Verdi, all green, which must be where she still was, judging from the pale jade-colored linens splashed with ferns, and the carpet the color of a pine forest.

She remembered waiting for the Wild Man, eating dinner, having a glass or two of champagne, and then...

And then not a whole heck of a lot.

"Dylan and I were on the balcony," she mused. "Weren't we? I remember... Did he kiss me? Oh, God." She clapped a hand over her mouth. Her lips didn't feel any different, but she definitely thought he'd kissed her. Or maybe she'd kissed him.

"I didn't. I couldn't." But she felt almost certain she had. She had this bizarre recollection of her arms wound around Dylan's neck as she tipped herself up to slide her tongue into his mouth. Her tongue. His mouth. Oh, dear.

Even now, she could feel the tingles and shivers racing down her body, in her arms and her legs, her breasts, her... Oh, dear. Her *everywhere*. She'd wanted that kiss to go on forever.

Memory? Or fantasy?

She swallowed. She traced her own lips with one finger.

If that wasn't a real kiss, she was Mary Poppins. But what about after?

"The balcony," she said again, trying to put her mind back there. "There was the kiss, and then we were going inside to…" Cassie gulped. "Oh, boy. I wanted him to make love to me. I told him I wanted him to make love to me."

What had she been thinking? How could she suddenly lose a lifetime of good manners and start throwing caution to the wind and acting like…like a hussy!

She half rose from the bed, sliding back down again when she realized she had no clothes on. Yanking the sheet out from under Dylan would surely wake him. That was the last thing she needed at the moment, to look him in the eye and see her own shameless, wanton nature reflected back.

"Wait, wait. We didn't." Again, relief coursed through her. "Because suddenly the Wild Man was there. When we came in off the balcony, the Wild Man was there." Concentrating, she narrowed her eyes. "And everyone was dancing the conga and we started arguing. About…about Dumpster diving."

But after that, as hard as she tried, she drew a blank. A total blank.

So what was she doing in Dylan's bed, wearing nothing but a pair of hoop earrings, with her whole body still humming and vibrating to beat the band?

The only thing she could come up with was that

something more had happened after the conga and the arguing, that she and Dylan had somehow connected up later in the evening, when she was full of champagne and music and general wildness, so full that she had no memory of any of it.

But her nakedness and proximity to Dylan were pretty good hints.

Oh, *God*. "We didn't *do it*, did we?" She stood up, letting the sheet drop, pacing near the edge of the bed. "Why isn't my brain working? Why can't I remember?"

While she was hyperventilating, trying desperately to remember anything that transpired after the argument on the balcony, she could hear him starting to stir behind her. Quickly, quietly, she slipped back in between the sheets, careful to stay as close to the edge as possible, as far from Dylan as she could manage, firmly turned away, pointing herself toward the window.

Over on his side of the king-size bed, Dylan made a garbled "mmmph" sound and sat up, clumsily knocking away his bedcovers. Now she was stuck not looking at him while she was dying to know what he was doing over there. Trying to be discreet, Cassie delicately, carefully, rolled over, her eyes pressed shut as if she were still asleep. When there was no new sound, no "Good morning," no sign that he knew she was faking, she peeked through her lashes, opening up enough of a slit to see him.

Paying no attention to her spy games, he stood up and stretched, seemingly oblivious to the fact that he wasn't wearing a stitch. She watched every move, getting an eyeful and then some. Whoa, boy. He had a fabulous body, sculpted and honed in all the right places, with tight muscles and sleek skin and… Lots and lots of skin. She started tingling all over again, feeling way overheated and undersatisfied. Did she sleep with *that?*

He padded off to the shower, giving her a good view of his hot little derriere, and all she could do was lie there, melting and itching and dying inside. When she heard the water kick on, she stuffed her head into the pillow facedown, screamed silently, and pounded her fists for a good minute and a half.

Which was worse? That she had acted like a wild, wanton slutpuppy and slept with Dylan Wright last night? Or that she had had a chance to make love to *that* and missed out?

Okay, much worse to have done it. Much, much worse.

"He wouldn't have," she whispered, hoping she was telling the truth to herself. Surely he wouldn't have taken advantage of her like that when she was not herself and under the influence of too much champagne.

But who was she kidding? He was Mr. Life on the Edge, Jr. His motto was to take what you wanted and worry about the consequences later.

Besides, he was the one who'd kept refilling her champagne glass. He'd probably done it on purpose, part of some master plan to get her into bed.

But still… Wouldn't she remember?

"I'm ruined," she said out loud. She didn't know why her mind had chosen this exact minute to remind her what day it was, but it did. Friday. As in, one week and one day before she was supposed to marry Skipper Kennigan. "I'm getting married a week from tomorrow, to a man who tells me every day that what he loves most about me is my purity."

She felt like screaming again, really loud this time, but she didn't want to risk Dylan hearing her in the shower. "Purity," she choked.

And that wasn't the worst of it.

"I'm supposed to be back in Pleasant Falls in two days. *Two* days! Taking up my old life with Skipper, who is a card-carrying member of the Moral Imperative, for goodness sake!" She slumped back down into the bedclothes, covering her face with the tail end of the sheet. Not sure whether she was talking to herself or speaking out loud, she added, "And now I may have slept with another man just before our wedding. Skipper is never going to forgive me—"

"What are you mumbling about?"

She dropped the sheet away from her face. It was Dylan, standing next to the bed, wearing nothing but a towel knotted casually at the waist, revealing long, strong, tanned legs. Since she was lying down, his thighs were at her eye level, and she was staring right into his crotch.

Oh. My. Goodness.

As she gasped for breath, he leaned down and planted a sweet, lingering kiss on her lips. "Good morning, sunshine," he said cheerfully.

"I haven't even brushed my teeth!" she wailed, smacking him away. Her own voice reverberated in her head, making the headache worse. "Owwww. It's ten o'clock in the morning and I'm still in bed and I haven't brushed my teeth, and... This is terrible."

"Guess you're not as perky today," he noted, backing away. "Can I help?"

"Can you tell me where my clothes are so I can get dressed enough to get from here to the bathroom to brush my teeth and comb my hair?" she begged.

He retreated far enough to retrieve her bra from a chair and her blouse off the floor, tossing them both on the bed. Frowning, he began puttering around the room, checking under the desk and the bed skirt. "Hmmm...I know your skirt and your underpants are around here somewhere."

"This is a disaster," she muttered, pulling her bra and blouse under the covers where she tried to wiggle into them and get them fastened without losing her sheet. When she had them on, sort of in the right place, she reemerged. "No man has ever seen me without my teeth brushed and my hair combed, well, except you, when I showed up at the airport after driving the convertible—"

"You can toddle into the potty without your clothes, you know." He smiled lazily. "You don't need to put them back on on my account."

She could feel hot color flood her cheeks immediately. "I—I—"

"Sweetie, it's nothing I haven't already seen," he

murmured, sending his steamy, sensuous gaze licking all the way up and down her.

Her temperature just kept rising. Her thoughts were a jumble of weird images, of Dylan's bare, beautiful chest and hard abdomen, displayed so nicely by the towel, of her own lack of clothing and pulsating nerve endings, of her whacked-out hair and scuzzy teeth and... "Oh, no."

"What?"

"I just realized." Now it was definitely time to panic. "I don't have a toothbrush!"

"You can borrow mine," he offered kindly, and she felt like leaping off the bed, paying no attention to the fact that she was still naked from the waist down, just so she could kick him.

"I'm not borrowing your toothbrush. Eeew!"

"Did you hear something?" Dylan asked suddenly. He paced away, very quietly, cracking open their door. "I thought so."

"What?"

"There's someone at the front door. Whaling the hell out of it, as a matter of fact." He winked at her. He actually had the nerve to *wink* at her. There she was, falling apart, and he was playing flirty games. "Did you order breakfast?"

"Heavens, no! When would I have done that?"

But he was off to answer the door, and Cassie heard a very loud female voice telling him to get out of her way. "Where is Polly Tompkins?" the woman demanded.

Cassie vaulted out of the bed so fast it made her

head spin. Who was out there? It wasn't a voice she recognized, but this woman knew Polly's name. Thank goodness she spied her skirt, crumpled into a little ball under the bedside table, and she jumped into it and zipped it up—without benefit of underwear, which made her feel like a total sleazebag—just as Dylan came wandering back into the bedroom.

"Your boss is here," he said in a charming, unconcerned tone. "She's kind of anxious to see you."

"My boss?" *Her* boss was back in Pleasant Falls, probably taking inventory or propping up mannequins in Ladies' Better Dresses. "You mean…?"

"Lenora Bridge," he supplied helpfully.

"Lenora… Here?"

It was a nightmare. Without another word to Dylan, Cassie whirled and ran to the bathroom on the double. With the door securely locked, she gaped at herself in the mirror. What should she do? She didn't know Lenora Bridge from Adam. She wouldn't know what to say or how to act or…

"Oh, God! Polly is going to kill me." But that gave her an idea. "Polly!"

She could call Polly and ask her what to do. She had the cell phone, and all she had to do was hit the button that had their family's preprogrammed number back in Pleasant Falls attached to it, and she could talk to Polly, who was, of course, safe in Pleasant Falls pretending to be Cassie.

"Now where is the phone?" she asked herself. "In my purse, which is…"

Not only did she have no idea where her purse was,

but she had this distinct memory of her Palm Pilot and her cell phone sailing off the balcony last night. She sat down on top of the toilet with a thump, holding a weak hand to her forehead. That idiotic Wild Man had been yelling something about how she needed to stop following the herd, and then—and this part seemed very clear—then he'd thrown her cell phone off the balcony.

"I could kill him right now," she whispered, making a fist.

But there was no point in whining about it, especially since there was a phone sitting right there, attached to the wall of the bathroom. Why there should be a phone in the bathroom she had no idea, but she had no compunctions about using it. What were a few long-distance charges added on to the bill they'd already racked up at the Hotel Verdi?

Quickly, she punched in her home number. It rang twice, three times, and she jumped each time. Finally, on the fourth ring, someone picked up.

"Hello?" he said.

Good heavens. She suddenly saw stars in her periphery. She'd never even considered she might get *him*. "Skipper? Is that you?"

"Yes. Cassie?"

She panicked. It was Skipper and he recognized her voice! "No, no," she said quickly. "This is Polly. Identical twins, you know. We sound just alike."

"I'll say. So, Polly, what do you need?" His voice sounded stiff and unpleasant. He never had liked

Polly, who he considered to be a bad influence on her sister. If he only knew!

She squeezed her eyes shut, trying desperately to think of what she could say to Skipper when she had probably just betrayed him and she didn't have any underpants and her entire life was a sham. Faking a cheerful voice, she asked, "Well, Skipper, how are you? Everything going okay?"

"I'm fine," he said slowly. "Thank you for asking."

Oh, God. It occurred to her that she hadn't really thought about Skipper at all, that she didn't miss him or his company, and she didn't really care if he was fine or not. How awful was that?

"So, Skipper, is, uh, Cassie there? Can I speak to her, please?"

"I'm afraid she's not. But I can certainly give her a message."

"Right." She had to tell Polly something to explain where she was and why she hadn't been in contact. "Could you please tell my sister that everything is fine, but I'm really, um, tied up at the moment—with work, I mean. I may not be in touch. Oh, and don't try to get me on the cell phone because the Wild Man threw it off a hotel balcony in Cleveland." She paused. "I know that sounds crazy but she'll understand. I think."

"A wild man threw your phone off a hotel balcony in Cleveland?" he repeated doubtfully. "Are you sure?"

"Quite."

"Okay, I think I can remember all that."

And she hung up with a sinking feeling. Calling home had only made things worse. And now she was on her own, and she was going to have to face Lenora Bridge...with dirty teeth.

Cassie got herself together as best she could. She washed her face, she combed her hair with her fingers, and she smeared some toothpaste over her teeth, smushing it around in there and spitting it out. She still felt like someone had put rocks in her head, but she straightened out her clothing and tried to make herself presentable. Too bad her underpants were still lost in the bedroom somewhere.

She tried not to think about how they had gotten lost.

*Not going there,* she told herself firmly. She took a few deep breaths, reminding herself that she was a former cheerleader and a homecoming queen and that she had faced down Skipper's mother on the issue of the wedding invitations before Mrs. Kennigan had had her sherry, and still lived to tell the tale.

"I can do this," she gritted between her semi-dirty teeth.

And she went to meet Lenora Bridge.

Lenora was every bit as intimidating as Cassie had expected. At least there was only one person there, so she didn't have to worry about who was who. Nope, there was just one candidate and she could only be Lenora.

Tall, whip-thin, with flame-red hair that was clearly not a natural shade, Lenora stalked back and forth in front of the piano in a killer purple suit. The jacket had a stand-up collar that framed her face and was curiously reminiscent of the Evil Queen who gave Sleeping Beauty the poisoned apple.

Meanwhile, as she turned and swept Cassie with her gaze, her expression was severe enough to zap bugs at a backyard barbecue. Cassie had the presence of mind to wish she had an Evil Queen suit and spiky purple pumps like those. Maybe then she would be intimidating, too. Not likely, but you never knew.

Dylan, who had changed out of the towel into his usual khakis and T-shirt, was attempting to talk to Lenora in his most charming voice. But Cassie could already see that it wasn't working. Lenora was not a happy Evil Queen.

"What did you think you were doing, coming here?" she demanded, directing her interrogation Cassie's way.

"Here?"

"Here. To this hotel. You're all supposed to be in Chicago." Lenora's eyes got smaller as she glared daggers at Cassie. "You live in Chicago, remember? You work in Chicago. Cleveland is outside your jurisdiction, yes?"

"My jurisdiction?"

"Will you stop repeating everything I say!" Lenora snapped. "I want to know why neither you nor the client showed up for yesterday's scheduled appearances." She checked the slim Rolex watch strapped to her wrist. "Not to mention the second round of appointments which began half an hour ago. Back in Chicago!''

"It's tricky." Cassie considered the best way to approach this. She didn't have an explanation for today's screwups, because she wasn't sure herself what had happened last night. But as for the previous day... "I got to the airport, as scheduled, on Wednesday evening, but the Wild Man wasn't there. I mean, Mr. Wright, Mr. Hiram Wright, was not there. Mr. Dylan Wright was, however.''

He smiled, crinkling his eyes. Lenora appeared perfectly able to resist his charm and his crinkles, and Cassie wished she knew the trick.

"Anyway," she went on, "Dylan, er, Mr. Wright the younger, explained that his uncle did not want to fly and that our new instructions were to drive to Cleveland to pick him up. Today. I mean, yesterday. At the bus station. So once it became clear that we were not going to make the first day of appointments because Mr. Wright the older was not going to be in Chicago but in Cleveland, I called everyone on that agenda to reschedule—''

"And I can vouch for that, since she was in the car with me at the time and I heard her make those calls,'' Dylan interjected.

Lenora looked down her patrician nose at him. "Thank you. I'm sure that Ms. Tompkins appreciates your support.''

"Actually, yes, I do," Cassie tried, but that only seemed to make Polly's boss crankier.

"Be quiet," she said coldly.

"I'll just, uh, excuse myself to see what's happening with my uncle," he said, backing away from the cloud of disapproval emanating from Lenora. "I'll just make sure he didn't rappel down the side of the hotel and escape in the wee hours of the morning or something."

"You do that." Turning to Cassie, Lenora dropped her voice, but not the attitude. "Why didn't you check in to let someone at Lenora Bridge and Associates know what was happening? You have an assistant who should've made those calls to rearrange things and you should've kept us notified so we could have done damage control. Do you realize how far away from office policy you've strayed?"

"Well, actually, no." She tried to look contrite. It didn't seem to help.

"I got calls all day about the Wild Man not being where he was supposed to, and I had no idea what to tell them. 'I don't know' is the worst possible thing a publicist can say."

"I'm really very sorry—"

"I'm sure you are." As she worked herself into a lather, Lenora's voice kept getting lower and harder to hear. Her words seemed to shoot out, one at a time, and Cassie had to really concentrate to understand. "At midnight last night, I got dragged out of a reception by the manager of the bank that holds our corporate credit cards. Do you know why?"

Oops. "Because of the hotel?"

"Bingo." The other woman rolled her eyes dramatically. "They thought someone had stolen one of our cards and was running up a huge tab in a hotel in Cleveland, including all sorts of damages for a wild party. It was your card so I tried to call you on the company cell phone, but it's out of service. Out of service!''

"Mr. Wright, the older Mr. Wright, that would be the Wild Man, threw it off the balcony last night,'' Cassie explained.

"A likely story. So here I am, flying to Cleveland, of all places, just to pick up the pieces of the disastrous trip you never should've taken in the first place. And what do I find?'' She waited a lot longer than was actually necessary, until Cassie wondered whether she was supposed to provide an answer. But no, Lenora did finally deign to finish her thought. "I find you in a love nest with the client's nephew! It's a disgrace.''

"Oh, no. No, no, no,'' Cassie hastened to assure her. "It's not a love nest. Not at all.''

"Yes, I see. And that's why he answered the door in a towel and you weren't up yet, and he went to fetch you in the same bedroom he changed his clothes in.'' Her thin smile was so chilly it looked as if ice were forming in the corners of her mouth. "All very cozy.''

So how was she going to get around the fact that she and Dylan had shared a bedroom? Polly was the one with the gift of gab. Cassie had no clue how to talk her way out of anything. "It isn't what it seems,'' she said finally. That was the best she could come up with. "You see, we were waiting here for Mr. Wright, the older one, because he kept trying to elude us. So we tempted him with his favorite scotch, just to, you know, trap him. But when he got here, he launched a sort of impromptu party, bringing all the guests with him, and it was a little over the top and we're still sort of stamping out the fires.'' Awkwardly, she added, ''Mr. Hiram Wright is very hard to control.''

''Forget the love nest. It's tacky, but I really don't care what you do to keep the clients happy. And I'm aware that Hiram is a problem child. But controlling him is supposed to be your job, Polly,'' Lenora said acidly. ''If you can't handle the most basic aspects of that job, then maybe you ought to look for a different line of work, or at least pursue it at some other agency which does not have my name on it.''

If Cassie weren't in such bad shape, what with the exploding head and the fluttery stomach and the fluky memory, that speech would've pushed her over the edge. But she simply didn't have the energy. Still, her heart sank.

She was perilously close to getting fired—to getting her poor, innocent sister Polly fired—and she knew it. After a long, torturous pause, she whispered, ''I can handle Mr. Wright.''

''And why should I believe that after the mess you've made so far?''

She cleared her throat and attempted to sound more positive. ''I swear! I can handle it. I will do better. If I have to, I will bind and gag the Wild Man to get him back to Chicago.''

''Bind and gag?'' Lenora purred, rubbing her hands together. ''That sounds more like it.''

IN THE BEDROOM, Dylan laid down the law for his uncle. "You need to stop screwing up my life."

"When have I ever done that?" his uncle asked, all innocence as he gulped down his sixth or seventh glass of water. Fluids and more fluids were his remedy for just about everything. Too bad it actually seemed to work. It would've served the old goat right if he'd had to contend with a hangover from hell like everyone else who partied with him.

"Listen," Dylan said more sternly, "I've been willing to go along with you since we both knew you needed me, but not anymore. Are you listening? I refuse to write the books for you if you don't straighten up and fly right."

"Ssssh." Uncle Hiram sent him a black look. "They could hear you, you know."

"They're occupied. Lenora is busy reading Polly the riot act because of all the ways you've misbehaved."

"Aaaaah, I don't believe you, anyway. You always threaten to pull the plug and you never do. You're just a pantywaist." Uncle Hiram made a pooh-poohing noise before he gargled with his water, tilting back his head and spewing it up like a whale.

Dylan ignored the floor show. "I don't know what a pantywaist is, but it doesn't matter. This time I mean it. Read my lips—no more books."

"Hey, writing my books is a pretty good deal for you, too, you know." Wiping his face with a towel, he trudged closer to his nephew. It seemed Dylan had finally caught his attention, and he had to switch to a more accommodating mode. "I do the PR, you write the books, we trade off my reputation to sell the damn things, and we share the dividends." He locked an arm around the shoulder of his taller nephew, cuffing him affectionately, dragging him down far enough to rub Dylan's hair. "It's an awful lot of money to throw away, boyo. I'd think twice before cashing in."

"If you behave yourself, no one needs to cash in," Dylan said quietly, detaching himself from the head massage.

"But if I behave myself, I'm not the Wild Man," Hiram protested. "No one will want to buy the books."

That was, unfortunately, partially true. Hiram walked a fine line between maintaining his quintessential bad boy image and alienating the people around him completely. Including his nephew.

"I understand that there are some theatrics involved. But how about if you restrict the over-the-top behavior to public appearances? And maybe tone it down?"

"Tone it down?" his uncle returned in a horrified voice.

"No more picking my pockets and ditching me on

airplanes. No more games at the bus station." Implacable, Dylan crossed his arms over his chest. "And no more busting up my love life."

"I have never busted up your love life!"

"You did last night," he countered. "You see, Polly and I were just getting close. I like her. I might like her a lot. And if I have to deal with you and your mariachi pals every time I'm going in for a move, I'm never going to get anywhere with her. It's..." He paused, searching for the right word. "Frustrating."

The Wild Man laughed out loud. "So now the truth comes out. All of this, over a girl! So you have a thing for Sweet Polly Purebread. She's a cute one. But kind of uptight, don't you think?"

"Well, she's definitely a little strange, I'll give you that. But I like her." Dylan's lips curved into an agreeable smile. "She's been a real trouper, trying to keep her balance while we keep pulling the rug out from under her."

"She may be strange. She is also not who she says she is," Hiram declared, waggling his eyebrows.

"Not an experienced publicist, you mean? Yeah, I figured that out, too. So she lied about her résumé. Who cares?"

But his uncle shook his head from side to side. "No, I mean she's not Polly Tompkins. I've corresponded with the real Polly for some time now. And this isn't her."

"Isn't her?" He would've dismissed Hiram's suspicions as the usual nutball delusions, except that Dylan himself had had his doubts ever since he met Polly.

And then there was the fact that she had asked him not to call her Polly when he kissed her. Now *that* was weird.

"I don't get it," he said slowly. "Yesterday you told me she looked exactly like her picture. And if she's not Polly, why is her boss, who would presumably know her own employee, sitting in the living room with her right now, not noticing she's the wrong person?"

But Hiram just offered a wily grin.

"Well?" Dylan prompted. "Are you going to tell me why you think she's not Polly?"

"I got suspicious last night. Like I said, Polly and I had been corresponding by fax and e-mail, so I felt like I knew her pretty well. But this one..." He paused. "This one wasn't what I expected. Oh, she looks the same. But the Polly I had been talking to is a real firebrand. She gets very fussy and calls you a sexist pig all the time. She's into issues, you know, anti-fur, anti-meat, anti-everything interesting."

"Really?" Dylan flashed back to breakfast the day before, home-cooked by a woman who could've subbed for Donna Reed. Hard-core feminist? Hardly. And she'd put sausage in with the eggs and then had meat loaf for lunch. So how could she be anti-meat?

"Yep. And it's very easy to get a rise out of her by pushing any one of those buttons." Hiram's eyes focused on some point off in the distance. "But last night, when I tried to flip her switches, she didn't react. I even made a crack about hooters and she didn't say a word. And then, *then* she got all hot and bothered because my book suggested washing your hair in puddles and eating old doughnuts. She got on her high horse, remember? She said anyone who did those things would be an outcast in Pleasant Valley.''

"Pleasant Falls.''

"Whatever. But the Polly I knew wouldn't have cared if she were an outcast. In fact, she would've thought that sounded like a great idea. But this one... It was like she was straight off the boat from Smallville. Nope.'' He shook his head with conviction. "Not the same Polly.''

"Oh, come on. That's it? So she made herself out to be some image of what she thought she should be, Miss Urban Anti-Fur, because she thought the small-town white gloves thing wouldn't play in the big city.'' Dylan was unconvinced. "So she lied to make herself sound sophisticated. That doesn't mean that's not the same Polly?''

"I have proof.'' His eyes sparkling, Uncle Hiram sauntered over to the battered canvas shoulder bag that accompanied him everywhere. After rummaging around for a few minutes, he stood up. "Voilà!'' he said, producing a rolled-up magazine.

Dylan raised one brow. "You think she's not who she says she is because of a magazine? Don't tell me, it's a UFO magazine, and it's got a ten-minute quiz to see if your publicist has been replaced by an alien clone.''

"No, 'fraid not. It's some new Chicago magazine. It came express from Lenora Bridge and Associates, with a note from Lenora herself attached to let me know that Polly was in it.''

He opened it up, flashing a full-page picture of the girl herself. There she was, the Polly Tompkins that Dylan recognized, smiling into the camera. Except for the fact that her hair had been longer and less neatly styled when she had the picture taken, it was definitely the same Polly. Saucy blue eyes, sunny smile, short skirt, great legs.

"So? She's got her picture in a magazine. Good for her."

"Polly is profiled in this thing as one of Chicago's hottest singles." The old man was so excited about whatever it was he was planning to reveal, he was hopping up and down. "They asked her a bunch of stupid questions and she answered them. Like three words to describe herself. Guess what Polly's three words are. Just guess."

"I don't know." Dylan was starting to get aggravated. "Spit it out."

"Guess."

Shaking his head, well aware that his uncle was impossible to push when he didn't want to move, Dylan played along. "Naïve, polite, and, I don't know, terrible driver. Satisfied?"

"Wrong on all counts, and that's four words, by the way. No, our Polly said the three best words to describe her were..." Stalling, Hiram pretended to have lost his place. After a long pause, he said, "Ah, yes, here it is. Smart. Up-tempo. And..."

He wouldn't have picked either smart or up-tempo

for Polly, but that could just mean she wasn't particularly self-aware. "And?"

Hiram grinned like a possum. He tapped a particular line in the magazine with his index finger. "Twin. *Twin* is her third word. No alien clone necessary if you have an identical twin."

"Polly is a twin?" Dylan reached for the magazine.

"Yes, Yes, I believe you," Lenora said, raising a hand to forestall any more pleas. "But just to be sure, I'll fly back with you."

That sounded like a recipe for disaster. All the way back to Cleveland, with Lenora breathing down her neck, looking for slipups. "Well, that would be fine, except that Mr. Wright refuses to get on an airplane."

"Oh, no, no, no!" Hiram came stomping into the room in time to interrupt. "I've changed my mind."

"You changed your mind?" Cassie echoed. "Now?" *Now that you dragged me off to freaking Cleveland you're ready to fly.* She wondered if she could personally tie him to a rocket and send him into orbit. She'd show him how to fly. She lowered her eyelids, trying to keep out excess light and stop the hammering in her head.

"A couple quarts of water would take the edge off that hangover," the Wild Man put in helpfully.

"I don't have a hangover."

"Of course you do." But he turned his attention to Lenora, taking her hand in his, bending down and planting a kiss on the back of it. "I'm ready to fly only if the lovely Ms. Bridge will consent to sit beside me and hold my hand on the trip back.''

''Absolutely,'' she replied with her usual air of superiority. ''As I just told Polly, the best idea is for all of us to fly back together.''

''Why don't we make it just us two?'' he asked in a low, rumbly voice. ''Let the kids bring up the rear in the car. We can get a head start on those signings I'm supposed to do before they get there.''

Cassie couldn't quite believe how meek and accommodating the Wild Man was acting. She sent a suspicious glance at Dylan, wondering what in the world he had done to his uncle since she last saw the older man. But he turned up his palms, all innocence.

''See?'' Lenora said in a silky voice Cassie hadn't heard her use before. She linked her arm through Hiram's, whispering to Cassie, ''You just didn't know how to handle him.''

''I COULD cheerfully kill your uncle,'' she said, shifting restlessly in her seat. She had to sit very still, since her skirt was every bit as short as it had been coming the other direction, only this time she didn't have any underwear.

For the trip back, Dylan had chosen to take the expressway, and they were moving more quickly. He was right, though—except for the occasional toll, it was a very boring trip. ''I am so glad we didn't end up being trapped in this car with the Wild Man for seven hours. Let Lenora have him if she wants him.''

Groaning, she dropped back onto the headrest, closing her eyes.

"Oh, he's not so bad."

"Yes, he is." She could hear Dylan reach into the back seat, into the small cooler he'd bought before they left Cleveland. She opened her eyes. Without comment, he handed her another bottle of water. Apparently he, too, thought she had a hangover, and he and his uncle were both pushing water as the best cure. All she knew was that her head was still throbbing and she'd had to make him stop five or six times to go to the bathroom.

"If you think Hiram is a wacko, you should meet the rest of my family," he said with a laugh.

After taking a long swig, she murmured, "I think I might like that."

"It could be arranged."

Although he made his words sound casual, the meaning wasn't casual at all. Cassie sat up, purposely looking down into the clear, cold liquid and not at him. Dylan had become a problem, one she should just eliminate from her life. On the double. If only she didn't like him quite so well.

It was upsetting and complicated, but she really *did* like him. And it wasn't just his looks, although those were spectacular. No, it was the way he handled things with a minimum of fuss, the way he went straight to the heart of the matter, whether it was picking a lock or reserving a suite or making sure she drank enough water. Sure, he could be grumpy. But more often, he was sweet and sensitive and...

Oh, lord, she sounded like a gooey teenager. Next she'd be writing "Mrs. Dylan Wright" on her notebooks.

And there was also the tiny problem of whatever had happened between them last night, which she had so far not had the courage to ask. She chewed her lip, wondering how to broach the subject.

"Speaking of families," he ventured, and Cassie glanced over at him, "you haven't told me much about yours."

"There isn't much to tell. Pleasant Falls, Mom is a teacher, Pop runs a hardware store, two sisters, blah, blah, blah." She needed to change the subject, quickly.

"And you and your sister, are you a lot alike?"

"No, not really." She leaned over to turn on the radio, but Dylan's hand covered hers, holding her still.

"Either of you into politics, issues, that kind of thing?" he probed.

What was this all about? She wished she had enough brain cells working to try to figure it out. "My sister may be." She lifted her shoulders in a careless shrug. "She doesn't eat beef and she's always demonstrating about something. Is that what you mean?"

"Yeah. Like that."

"In fact," she said, warming to the subject, "she was the valedictorian of our high school class and she used her speech to yell at the Kennigans, the most powerful family in town, for being... What did she say? Robber barons, I think." Quickly, she added,

"They're not really. They're fine, fine people. A top-notch family."

And she was supposed to marry one of them a week from tomorrow. Poor Skipper. Poor, clueless Skipper. For the first time, she glanced down at her hand, feeling odd without her heavy engagement ring.

"Polly?"

"What?" As Dylan interrupted her thoughts, she congratulated herself for responding to the name so quickly.

"If I asked you to pick three words to describe yourself, what would they be?"

"Huh?" Where did that come from?

"Three words," he repeated. "Whatever pops into your head."

"Three words? To describe me?" She mulled it over for a second or two. There was no harm in playing word games, was there? "I suppose…well, nice. That's one. And polite. I'm very polite. And…" She frowned. "I could go with quiet or calm, because that's what everyone says about me. But I think well-dressed would be my next choice. You know, like, *together?* Everyone always says I'm very together."

"Right."

What was up with that? Why did he seem so disappointed in her answers?

Uneasily, she asked, "Did I pick the wrong words?" Maybe he was expecting *easy* or *slutty* or something else that referred to her horrifying behavior last night—*if* her behavior had been all that horrible.

"Dylan, as long as we're asking questions…" She

hesitated, still not sure how to get at it. *Did we make love last night?*

"What?" He glanced over, taking his eyes off the road momentarily. "What?"

But she couldn't come right out and ask. "I just wanted to say," she dithered, "you know, if I did anything last night that you think I shouldn't have, well, I want to apologize right now."

"Not that I know of." His eyes darkened to a murky shade of teal. "What do you think you might've done that you should apologize for?"

"Nothing. Nothing at all."

She whipped her head around, away from his gaze.

"Polly?" he prompted. "Is there something you want to tell me?"

"Dylan, can we pull over? I need a restroom."

"Again?"

"If I keep drinking water, I will keep needing restrooms."

It was one way to get away from him and his penetrating gaze.

"YES, I AM SO driving the rest of the way," she insisted. "It's my car and we're almost back to the city and I want to drive. Besides, I need you to navigate and watch for the right signs because it gets harder here. And we both know I can't read a map. So give me the keys."

Dylan must have been feeling magnanimous, because he set the key ring in her hand with only a token protest.

Smiling, Cassie got behind the wheel. "I really do love to drive," she declared, "especially this car."

"Yeah, well, just be careful," he said gingerly.

"I'm always careful. Wasn't that one of the three words I gave you?" she joked.

"No. I believe you said smart and up-tempo and—"

"I did not! I said nice, polite and well-dressed." She rolled her eyes at him, which made her drift to the right and nearly clip a trailer. But she corrected her direction before any damage was done. "I know what I said. Smart and up-tempo? Why would I say that?"

"Watch it!"

"I am, I am."

"Our exit is coming up. You have to change lanes. Are you ready?" he asked swiftly.

"For someone who's had so many adventures, you sure are a nervous Nellie," she complained. "Look, we made our exit just fine, and now we're on the Dan Ryan, and then it turns into the Kennedy, and then we turn off on Milwaukee. See? I know where I'm going."

She could tell how relieved he was when they finally took the turn onto Polly's street. Home free! Except she didn't see the car pull out of an alley and try to squeeze in front of her until it was too late. Swerving to the side to avoid a crash, she plowed up over the curb, rolling into a skinny maple planted on the tree bank.

It was only a small tree, and she had been driving very slowly, but the air bag still deployed. Sitting there with the hissing, sagging air bag in front of her, she was very still for a second, taking stock.

"Are you okay?" Dylan asked, leaping out his side to come around.

"Yes, I'm fine." Humiliated, but fine. She got out, wobbling around the side of the car. As she surveyed the extent of the damage, where a tree was now imbedded in the front of Polly's convertible and smoke poured out from under the hood, what she had done began to sink in.

She had lost Polly's phone and Palm Pilot, put her sister's job in jeopardy and wrecked her company car. What next?

"The good news is that we can walk home from here," Dylan tried. He pointed to her house, only a hundred feet away. And then he put his arm around Cassie and held her close, which was a lot more than she deserved.

"Thank you for not saying I told you so."

He smiled sardonically. "You're welcome."

"You are all right, aren't you? If anything happened to you because I insisted on driving, I would never forgive myself." She felt like weeping. What a terrible day! And now *this*. She'd almost killed Dylan! Or at least maimed him. That beautiful face could've been scarred for life. "Your modeling career could've been over," she cried.

"What? Are you in shock? I don't have a modeling career," he said dubiously.

"Yes, I know, but you could," she argued. "You look exactly like the men in my favorite catalogs. I noticed that the first moment I saw you.'' She raised a hand to stroke his perfect cheek. ''And it could've been over!''

Looking confused, he patted her on the top of the head. ''Okay, well, that doesn't make any sense, but that's all right. You're just shaken up. I appreciate your concern and you just don't worry about it, okay?''

Tipping forward into his chest, she held on tight. ''Just hold me.''

''That I can do.''

He really shouldn't have been so nice. It only made her feel worse.

She sat on the grass as he moved their junk—his backpack, the cooler, her shopping bag full of M&M's and copies of the book—into her house. She didn't even ask where he was staying. After what they'd been through, she wanted him with her—24-7. And she didn't care if it was stupid.

The air bag had deployed! She'd wrecked the car!

Life was a mess, and only burrowing closer to Dylan seemed to make it bearable.

He was back by her side by the time the police and the tow truck arrived, which was when Cassie realized she had to turn over *Polly's* driver's license and insurance information. She tried to close her mind to the implications of fraud and deception.

Meanwhile, why was Dylan so interested in the driver's license?

He looked at it and he looked at her, and he did the whole process over again when he took her to get a rental car, using the company credit card, of course. She swore Dylan to secrecy, making him promise he would not breathe a word to Lenora about the crash or the rental car. She hoped she'd get a few days lee-way before the statement came back and Lenora found out about the rental. It was just one more cheap lie of omission to lay at her door, one step closer to getting Polly fired.

As soon as they were back from the rental car com-pany, Cassie mumbled that she was dying to clean up and change her clothes, and practically ran down the hallway. She was so ready to be out of the grimy clothes left over from Cleveland.

First she dumped the black suit and white blouse into the hamper. If they were her clothes, she would've pitched them completely, but they were Polly's, and maybe a good cleaner could help. The bra was her own, and that she did throw in the garbage.

Then she pulled on a robe and brushed her teeth for about fifteen minutes.

Running herself a bubble bath, she soaked for a good, long time, pondering her own ethics or lack thereof. Liar, liar, pants on fire.

The funny thing was that she had always prided herself on her honesty. And now she was a barefaced liar who probably belonged in the *Guinness Book of World Records.*

Since Wednesday, she had lied about who and what she was, broken and entered, stolen from Lenora Bridge and Associates by using their credit card and maybe, just maybe, cheated on her fiancé under a false identity.

She was scum.

When she finally forced herself to get out of the bathtub, tossing the robe back on and brushing her teeth one more time for good measure, she stumbled into the living room. When she saw Dylan, she would put on a cheerful face, she would be nonchalant, she would say, *"Hey, let's order some dinner,"* and act like this kind of thing happened to her every day.

But he wasn't there.

Cassie blinked. "Dylan? Are you in the kitchen?"

No answer. There were several Post-It notes stuck to the couch, however, and she picked them up, one after the other, following the trail of Dylan's slashing handwriting.

> I think you need some rest, and I need to check on my uncle. I'll see you tomorrow at the signings. I took the car.
>
> Love, D.

Love, D.

Cassie sank to the couch, clutching the messages. What had she done? And what were they both going to do tomorrow?

# 8

*May 25: One week before the wedding*

SHE WAS, AFTER ALL, a morning person, so it shouldn't have come as any surprise that she felt much better in the morning.

First, Cassie put the mishap with the car out of her mind as much as she could. Chin high, she called a cab to take her to the first appearance, a bustling bookstore at Navy Pier where the Wild Man was supposed to sign his autograph for a couple of hours.

All the way down there, she told herself that she had gotten herself—and her sister, by proxy—into this mess and she was just going to have to get them out. Maybe she wasn't the brainiest person within a three-block radius, but surely she could think of something. And in the meantime, there was Dylan to consider.

Ah, yes. Dylan.

Her body hummed to life at the mere thought of his name.

Bad idea. She slapped herself on the cheek, trying to force herself to wake up and behave like a human being. The last thing she wanted to think about was Dylan, because then she would start worrying all over again about what the two of them might have being doing in that hotel in Cleveland.

"He and his uncle are leaving tomorrow," she whispered. "One last appearance at the zoo in the morning, and then they are out of here. I can handle him until then. I can get through today and tomorrow morning like a pro, say goodbye to both of them, and take the train back to Pleasant Falls in the afternoon."

Back to Pleasant Falls where she belonged. With Skipper and the rest of the Kennigans, with a country club membership and a brand-new house and the world's most perfect wedding.

But a nasty little voice inside her wouldn't be quiet. It inquired coyly, *If you slept with another man a week before your wedding, can you still go through with it? What would Skipper say if he knew about the Hotel Verdi and the missing underwear and you and Dylan, tangled up together in the same bed? What would his parents say?*

Would what *her* parents say? Not to mention her sister Polly, who'd never wanted her to marry Skipper in the first place.

Oh, God. She was scum.

"I will think about that later," she said tersely, throwing some money at the cab driver and scooting out into the main Navy Pier entrance.

It was odd to consider that this signing was the sort of thing she'd thought she'd be doing on the road with the Wild Man. What had actually transpired up until now was so far away from that it wasn't even funny. Not that she was going to think about that...

Thank goodness Hiram was on his best behavior. Cassie actually began to relax a tiny bit. With a smile pasted on her face, she hovered behind the table where he was signing, refilling his M&M's bowl, offering a new pen, replenishing the stack of books. And he just kept signing away, offering a big, toothy grin like a grizzly bear, without making any waves.

"Polly," he kept saying, emphasizing her name, popping his *Ps.* "Polly, will you get me a glass of water? Polly, this lady needs another copy of the book. P-P-Polly…"

Even though he was all sweetness and light, she still wanted to kill him.

Dylan was there somewhere—she could feel his presence on her radar—but she pretended she was too busy to notice. Lenora was also lurking, but she departed after the first hour of the Navy Pier autographing since things were going so well.

*My work here is done* seemed to be her attitude. Good riddance, Cassie thought. She didn't need the added pressure of Polly's boss there, looking over her shoulder.

When they piled into a limo to go to their next stop, Cassie ended up with Hiram on one side and Dylan opposite, his knees brushing hers. She had no choice— she had to look at him.

"Are you doing okay?" he asked, in this solicitous voice that slid down her nerve endings, soothing and ruffling them at the same time.

"Yes, I'm fine." But she wasn't fine. She felt like she wanted to throw up. *You're leaving tomorrow and*

*I don't want you to leave tomorrow,* and *I'm getting married next Saturday and I don't want to get married next Saturday* kept rocketing to the forefront of her mind.

"You don't look fine," he said with evident concern.

She made it through the next two appearances with a minimum of fuss, although Dylan kept a watchful eye on both of them. Very watchful. Some might say obsessive.

"Could you give me a little more room?" she muttered, really starting to get itchy. He'd been hovering around her near the signing table.

"I'm worried about you," he said darkly. There was this light in his eyes that seemed to shine just for her, as he bent nearer, gazing at her, not even touching, just…tantalizing her.

"I'm fine," she said again, wishing she could remember to breathe when he was around. But they both knew she wasn't fine. Somehow she found the strength to back away, scurrying off to contact the limo driver to tell him when to pick them up.

Things got progressively worse as the day wore on. "Maybe I'm just tired," she said under her breath. Another lie. Her rapid pulse and Jell-O knees had far more to do with Dylan's nearness than they did with her lack of sleep.

As they wound up the Wild Man's last appearance, Dylan appeared at her elbow. "We need to talk," he announced.

"Okay, well… When? Like, now?" *Here it comes,*

she thought. But which would it be? *Gee, it was fun exploring new erotic boundaries with you and maybe we'll run into each other someday?*

Or maybe, *I have whiplash from that accident you caused and you owe me big time, sister?*

"I think we should get rid of my uncle and have dinner together." Dylan drew his brows together, looking very solemn and uncomfortable. "I think there are some things we need to say to each other, don't you?"

Oh, no. Nothing in her unremarkable life had prepared her for this kind of conversation. She didn't even know what he planned to say, but it didn't matter. It scared the pants off her.

No, she'd already lost her pants once. This was going to have to scare off some other piece of clothing.

"Okay," she whispered, trying very hard not to think about the missing underpants. "But not dinner. I'm not very hungry." And she couldn't imagine airing the private details of her life at a restaurant, where any old body could overhear. "Can we have this talk somewhere else?"

He nodded, jamming his hands into his pockets. "Your place," he said after a long moment.

Her voice dropped so low she could barely hear herself. She cleared her throat. "Okay," she managed. "Do you want to meet me or...?"

"I've got the rental car back at my hotel. I'll drive you," he told her, brooking no objections.

Dylan could certainly be pushy and arrogant when he wanted to. On him though, it was kind of sexy.

Neither said a word in the limo on the way to the hotel, although Hiram was in high spirits, chatting on about this and that, not really noticing that he was the only one talking. They left him by a phone, calling some old friends in Chicago, as Dylan escorted Cassie to the rental car.

She tried to get a hint of what it was he wanted to discuss, but he wasn't offering any. So she allowed them to lapse into an awkward silence for the rest of the trip to Wicker Park.

But the moment they were in the door, she wheeled around to face him, determined to know what she was up against. They both began speaking at the exact same moment, and their words toppled over each other.

"Can I know what this is about?" she opened with, as he said, "Maybe I shouldn't be here."

And then he started again with, "Let's just sit down," and she moved on to, "Should we really be doing this?"

They both stopped abruptly, staring at each other for a long, intense pause. And then Cassie swore out loud, a really bad word, which was very unlike her. Dylan reached for her, she took two steps closer, and she fell into his arms with a hunger she had never known.

"Bad idea?" he mumbled, shoving away her jacket and fumbling for the buttons on her dress.

"Terrible idea," she agreed, sliding her hands under the edge of his T-shirt.

His skin was so sleek and hot, she almost expired

just touching that much of him. But then his mouth crashed into hers, harsh and unyielding, dangerous, unbelievably sexy. She wanted him. She wanted him bad.

"No, no, wait." He broke off, bracketing her face with his hands, balancing his forehead against hers. "We should talk first."

"No, we shouldn't."

"Yes, we should," he persisted. "I need to know who you are and what's happening here."

She met his hot, flickering gaze with all the honesty she could muster. "We're just two people who are amazingly attracted to each other. I know this is probably old hat to you, but I've never felt like this before. I want to be with you. And I want to remember it this time!"

"You're so sweet," he murmured, pressing his mouth into hers for a softer, slower kiss.

It was so luscious she could barely stand up. "So are we okay? Are we going to, um, continue?"

"Yes," he murmured, leaving a trail of kisses across her cheeks and down her neck. "I can't turn away after that little speech. You convinced me."

She sighed with relief, melting into him. "No, no. No, wait." If they were going to do this, she wanted to do it right. She pushed back a few inches. "Let me go, you know, get things ready. We don't want to do it here in the front hallway."

"All right." He backed up, too, holding up his hands. "You're driving me crazy, but...whatever you want."

Up on her tiptoes, she kissed him quick, before she changed her mind. "It will only take a second."

Cassie raced down the hall to the master bedroom, sliding inside and slamming the door shut behind her. She leaned back into the hard wood, her eyes wide, her thoughts spinning around on top of each other.

"What are you doing?" she asked herself. "Are you insane?"

It only took a second before she answered her own question. "No, I am not insane. I may be exhausted, and my nerves are a little frayed, but I know what I'm doing."

She checked the sheets—okay—cleaned off the top of the dresser in a rush, and began to look in the drawers for candles. Lighting two near the bed, she stepped back to enjoy the glow. "The thing is, I really believe that I deserve this one moment of happiness."

She thought about it and changed her mind. "Of total and complete *bliss.*"

Mindless, head-over-heels, guilt-free bliss. Shouldn't everyone experience that at least once in a lifetime?

As she searched through Polly's lingerie for something exciting to wear, she found not a single white nightgown. "Forget the white nightgowns. This will do," she decided, holding up a satin, tiger-print crop top and pajama pants. The newer, hotter Cassie could wear this stuff and not look back.

She began to slip off her dress. "Besides, what difference does it make if we make love ten times to-

night? At least this way I won't have to torture myself
wondering whether we did or didn't.''

She'd know for sure they did. And she would remember every single second.

DYLAN WAITED in the living room, growing increas-
ingly impatient. What was taking so long? And why
was it so hard to figure her out?

One minute she was lying about her identity, and
the next she was stroking his cheek and acting like he
was precious to her. An hour later she was avoiding
eye contact. And then she was jumping his bones and
pushing him to make love to her, right then, right
there.

''Maybe she's a mental patient.'' No, she was just
a confused, mixed-up woman who, for whatever reason, was masquerading as her sister.

He knew by now that she was not Polly Tompkins
and he didn't even care. He still wanted to sleep with
her, to imprint himself on her body and soul until she
would never be able to forget him.

''Who are you?'' he whispered. ''And what do you
want from me?''

How about enjoying this one hot night of passion
and worrying about tomorrow later? It worked for him.

As he cooled his heels in the living room, he
couldn't help but notice that a red light was flashing
incessantly on her answering machine. He held himself back for the first five minutes she was gone, but
then he just couldn't take it anymore.

"Call me nosy, call me a jerk, but I want to know who's calling her," he growled.

So he seized the moment and hit the play button. "It's me," whispered a voice that sounded very much like the woman in the bedroom. "You have to call me right away. Right away. I'm not kidding." And she hung up.

Message #2 started with, "Damn it, anyway, where are you? I have to find out who Gigi and Harvey are and where they live. This whole thing is going down the toilet! Call me!"

And that's when he knew for sure. Polly was leaving messages for her twin sister, Cassie, and *Cassie* was the woman he was about to sleep with.

He tried it on his tongue. Cassie. It suited her.

The next message was more frantic. "Cassie, where are you? I don't like your life!" There was a pause. "Michael is here. It's a mess. Everyone thinks I'm having a fling with Michael when I'm supposed to be engaged to Skipper and *where are you?*"

The next six or seven were also from Polly, who seemed to be losing her mind. "Get your buns back here!" she said angrily in the last message, which was dated earlier that day. "It's time for you to take back your stupid life!"

If Dylan didn't know for sure before, he did now. Some of the details were fuzzy, like why the two had traded lives in the first place, but the basic idea was clear. Cassie Tompkins, small-town girl, and Polly Tompkins, her big-city twin sister, had switched places days ago.

Dylan stared down at the silent answering machine. He might appear to be a perfectly nice guy, but he wasn't. Anyone who knew him well knew that he was more than capable of living by his wits and doing whatever he had to in order to get what he wanted.

And what he wanted was Cassie.

Quickly, he erased the messages and unplugged the phone. Okay, so it was a deceitful thing to do. But Cassie had written the book on deceitful. Why should he be held to a higher standard?

Right now, he was unwilling to let the strings of her former life tangle up his plans for the two of them. Whoever Skipper and Michael were, he had no intention of letting them get in his way. And if this meant he and Cassie had only one night of incredible lust before they went their separate ways, so be it.

He was leaving tomorrow. And if he plugged her phone back in, it sounded as if Cassie would soon get the summons again and be headed home to Pleasant Falls.

"Dylan?"

He glanced up, wondering if she'd watched him erase the messages. But no.

Her face was a study in trust as she gazed at him. He stared right back, drinking in the sight of her silhouetted in the hallway, wearing an exotic jungle-print outfit with a tiny top and soft, flowing pants. It accentuated everything he loved about her—vulnerability, innocence and overwhelming desire.

Polly—no, Cassie—was about the most tempting

thing he'd ever seen. He wanted her so much his whole body ached with it.

Without a word, he strode over, swept her up into his arms and carried her back to the bedroom. He briefly noticed the candles burning on the bedside table, the lacy sheets turned down invitingly—Cassie's idea of a seduction scene.

But he had more important things on his mind. Like taking his time.

He laid her carefully on the bed. Then he stood back, meeting her eyes, sending promises with his own about what they would do and how long it was going to take. Forever.

Dylan smiled, leaned over and blew out the candles. "Fire safety," he whispered. "We wouldn't want to set off the sprinklers."

"We may, anyway." She extended her small hand, inviting him in.

Taking her hand, Dylan slid into bed beside her and pulled her near. Then he slipped one strap over her sweet, soft shoulder, and bent down to brush her skin with his greedy mouth. "The two of us together," he said with a crooked grin. "We may just set this bed on fire."

"Count on it."

And then they set about trying to do just that.

*May 26: Six days before the wedding*

THIS TIME, when she woke up in the same bed with Dylan, she was expecting it.

She stretched, as lazy and content as a cat in a sunbeam. Who knew you could feel this good after such a long night? Oh, my, what a night!

If anyone ever tried to tell her that she wasn't taking risks or living life to the fullest or sucking the marrow out of it or whatever else that old coot had said, she could truthfully say, "Oh, yes, I did! I had this one night where I went the distance, bucko!"

Talk about over the top. And she was feeling pretty proud of herself, too.

"Good morning, Dylan," she murmured, poking at his ribs with one finger, propping herself up on her elbow where she could get a better view, hoping he might be ready for another round.

He lifted his head. His beautiful blue-green eyes were unfocused, as if he weren't quite awake, but then he smiled, and she knew he was remembering, too. As he reached for her, dropping a kiss on her bare shoulder, she saw those crinkles in the corner of his eyes. Her heart seemed to turn over in her chest.

"Good morning, Cassie," he said in a husky, sexy voice.

She almost didn't notice. Definitely a delayed reaction. "What did you say?"

"I said, good morning, *Cassie*. Remember, you didn't want me calling you Polly when I kissed you." His smile looked smug all of a sudden. "So I thought, after what we've been doing, I should probably never call you Polly again."

She felt as if the wind had been knocked out of her. She was sucking in air, but not getting any oxygen. "How long have you known?"

"Ah, pretty much from the beginning." He yawned, raising his arms over his head. "You were a mess at the airport, you thought Northwestern was the Bruins instead of the Wildcats, and you kept throwing 'gee whillikers' and 'yessiree, Bob' and all these other hokey things into the conversation. Let's just say you didn't ring true as Polly Tompkins, experienced PR exec from the city."

Cassie's jaw dropped so far she had a hard time pulling it back up. "So, so, you were just having fun, stringing along the stupid country girl, when you knew all along?"

"Well, I didn't *know* exactly. I just suspected." He leaned over closer, tickling her ear with his hot breath. "It wasn't until I saw this magazine article about the real Polly, where she said she was smart, up-tempo and a twin. A twin. And suddenly everything made sense."

As if nothing had changed between them, he started nuzzling her neck and slipping his hands under the sheets, showing every indication of picking up where they'd left off last night.

"Excuse me," she cut in, edging away from his lips and pushing away his hands, "but all that's okay with you? You don't even care if I'm not who I kept telling you I was?"

"Not really." But he pulled back, his gaze unreadable.

Cassie didn't know what to think. Her mind didn't work quickly enough to process this new information. Dylan knew who she was. And he didn't mind? She shook her head. "But what about my name? You called me Cassie. How did you know my name?"

"Oh, yeah. I listened to your messages while you were lighting candles and turning down the sheets."

"There were messages?" Good grief. She hadn't thought to look at the machine. What did he hear? And how much did he know? She sent him a quick glance. Did he know about Skipper or the wedding? Did he know about Skipper and sleep with her, anyway?

Well, after all, *she* knew about Skipper and it hadn't stopped her. She buried her head in her hands. Guilt, guilt and more guilt overwhelmed her.

She shoved away the covers. "I have to go listen to my messages."

"The phone's not working. I was going to make a call last night, and I noticed it was dead," he said, and his words seemed clipped and funny somehow. "There was only the one message, anyway. It was from Polly. She said she's doing great, everything in Pleasant Falls is fine, and don't rush back on her account."

"She said not to come back? Why would she say that?" This made no sense to her, and she began to think out loud, which was always dangerous. She blurted, "I'm supposed to go back. I have to go back. I mean, there is the small matter of my wedding!"

"Your *what?*" That got a charge out of him.

"So you didn't know about the wedding?" she asked in a very small voice.

"No, I didn't know about your wedding. Do you really think…?" He broke off, suddenly jumping out the other side of the bed. And then he just stood there, all naked and gorgeous and furious. Cassie tried not to look. "So when is it? Today?"

"Heavens, no! It's next Saturday."

"Like that makes it any better? Instead of sleeping with some other guy the night before your wedding, you do the honorable thing and make it a whole week ahead?" Dylan grabbed for his pants. "So who are you marrying? And what the hell were you doing here with me?"

As he glared at her, he hopped into his clothes, hastily slamming them onto his body. Apparently massive surprise and betrayal made him want his pants on. She couldn't blame him.

"Cassie, are you going to answer me? What were you doing, trading places with your sister?"

"I was…" She swallowed. There was no good way to put it. "I wanted some excitement, and Polly was annoyed with the Wild Man and sick of her job, so I talked her into switching. I don't know. It seemed like a good idea at the time, just for a few days, to be this sophisticated city girl, you know? I had no idea it would turn into Cleveland and you and…" Cassie waved a hand in the air. "All of this."

Dylan's face was a study in shock and outrage. "Who is he?" he asked again. "The guy you're supposed to marry. Who is he?"

"His name is Skipper," she said reluctantly. "He's very nice and his family is very rich, but…"

"But?"

"He's boring!" she shouted. "Okay? He's boring

and predictable and Polly thinks he isn't very smart, and she's probably right.''

She wanted to add more, about how the very thought of marrying Skipper was enough to send her to a loony bin. How in the world, after what she and Dylan had shared, was she ever going to make herself go back to *that?*

Cassie wanted to scream.

"This is obscene," Dylan said angrily. Fully dressed now, he was pacing back and forth at the end of the bed. "How can you even consider going through with this wedding? You can't marry someone else, Cassie, because it's very obvious that you're in love with *me*."

Cassie blinked. "I am?"

# 9

SHE RECOVERED QUICKLY. "No, I'm not. I can't be."

"Yeah, right," he sneered.

"Well, I'm not. So get over yourself. And even if I were, I wouldn't be, because I have certain obligations and responsibilities," she argued. She couldn't help but notice that Dylan had claimed she was in love with him, but hadn't said a word about vice versa. "I come from a small town where you do what you're told and follow a certain path and that's just how it is."

"Oh, please." Dylan gave her a look that would've scorched her where she sat if she hadn't already been toasted from the inside out. "Even you can't really believe that crap."

"You don't understand." She lifted her chin and tried to maintain a little dignity, which wasn't easy considering that she was only partially covered by a sheet and she'd been performing erotic gymnastics with this man all night. It made her words sound even more ridiculous, but she kept on, determined to have her say. "I have always been the mature, reliable one, the one that people could count on. Polly was the crazy one, not me."

"I think you're giving her a run for her money," he returned sarcastically.

"You don't seriously expect me to forget my own wedding, do you? And leave everyone back home in the lurch?" she cried. "I can't do that."

He tossed her a chenille robe from a chair near the bed. "Put something on, will you? It's..." His jaw clenched into a grim line. "It's distracting."

"Sorry." She tied herself into the bulky thing as quickly as she could, rising from the bed but steering clear of Dylan.

"So you dump Skippy and he's ticked for a few months and you stay out of Pleasant Falls till things cool down." He shrugged. "Works for me."

"Oh, no. My parents live there. My sister, the little one, is still in high school. And Skipper..." She swallowed. "The Kennigans are the most prominent family in Pleasant Falls—they own half the town, maybe more than half—and if I crossed them by leaving Skipper at the altar, why, I don't know what they'd do. Probably ostracize and shun my entire family." She shook her head firmly. "I can't do that."

"Yes, you can," Dylan muttered. His tone changed as he crossed to her, taking her hands, fixing that stunning blue-green gaze on her. "You can run away with me and forget about Pleasant Falls and Skippy and the whole lot of them."

Her eyes widened. "Run away with you? Are you kidding?"

"No, I'm not." He seemed to pick up enthusiasm on the fly, squeezing her hands, improvising new details. "I'm supposed to go back to New York today. My flight leaves at, I don't know, two o'clock. So you come with me. It's no big deal."

"No big deal?" She fell back. "Would we be together just for tonight? A few days?" Softly, she asked, "Or forever?"

"I don't know about forever," he admitted, "but I do know we can make mad, passionate love and live life on the edge, the way it was meant to be." Dylan's eyes sparkled as he carried on. "We can jump a freighter to Pago Pago tomorrow and hitchhike to Katmandu the day after. Whatever you want."

"Oh, no," she said quickly, backing away into the hall. "That isn't me. That's your stupid uncle talking. Yes, I wanted some excitement, but just a little, just for a few days before I settled down. But for real, forever, I need to be with someone with ties and commitments, a job, a real life, and not this watered down Wild Man baloney."

"I do have a job," he protested, following her.

"Yeah, playing nursemaid to your stupid uncle," she shot back.

He circled around in front of her, blocking her path. "Quit calling him stupid. At least he lives his life by his own rules, not some dopey small-town conventions, where everyone agrees to turn off their minds as long as they stay in the city limits."

"That is so unfair I don't even believe it." She laughed, making a curt, unpleasant sound. "Way to convince me to run off with you, smart guy. Yeah, sure, belittle my whole life."

"Cassie, listen to me—"

"No, I won't." She lifted a hand in front of her face to fend him off. "Forget it."

She didn't hear what his next volley was, because the doorbell rang loudly, and she stomped away from him to answer it. Swinging it open, she was surprised to see Lenora Bridge on the doorstep. "Lenora? What are you doing here?"

Polly's boss pushed past her. "Change of plans. I tried to call but your phone's not working. Anyway, the zoo's getting picketed because somebody thinks it's wrong to have the grand opening of the new great ape house on a Sunday. Anti-Darwinists or something. So the big reception for Mr. Wright..." She caught sight of Dylan lounging in the living room, all rumpled and hot, and she spun back around to Cassie. "Charming."

"Lenora, nothing is going on—"

She waved her perfectly manicured hand. "I don't care what you do with that one. It's the other one that counts. So, listen up. Hiram and his reception are postponed till tomorrow. That means the two Mr. Wrights are going to have to stay an extra day."

She gaped. "An extra day?"

"And you'll have custody. I already talked to Hiram at his hotel and he's fine with the new plan. It doesn't look like it should be a problem for you, either, considering how well you're handling this Mr. Wright."

Cassie blushed. Handling? "Excuse me, but how can we just postpone the zoo thing? Don't they have to go back to New York today?"

"So they'll stay over till tomorrow. One of the girls at the office is making new flight arrangements." Lenora lifted her narrow shoulders in an impatient shrug. "The Wild Man got here a day and a half late. The least he can do is add an extra day to make up for it."

"That's fine for them, but what about me? I was also supposed to leave soon, to go home to Pleasant Falls," she tried.

"Well, dear, if you want to continue as an employed person, you'll put off your trip, too, won't you? Why are you so anxious to get out of town, anyway, and break up your love nest?" Lenora's curious gaze flicked back and forth between the two of them, as if she wanted to know more. But she seemed to forego the temptation to ask. "No matter. I only came over to tell you that the zoo reception was postponed, and it's your job to make sure the Wild Man is there tomorrow."

"I don't know if I can—"

"You can. You have to," Lenora snapped. "It may be the last, but it's also the most important stop on the tour. We'll have even more press there than we expected because of all the brouhaha and the picketing of the great ape house. Plus, I've tried to get everyone who got shut out the first day to come and give us a second chance. Don't screw it up." She narrowed her eyes. "You've screwed up far too many things this week. If you don't manage this one small assignment, you can clean out your desk at Lenora Bridge and Associates."

Cassie held her breath. She'd already wrecked Polly's phone and her car. All she needed to do was lose her sister's job as well.

Straightening, shoulders back, Cassie stiffened her resolve. It looked as if Polly and Pleasant Falls were just going to have to wait one more day, until Cassie got through this latest crisis. She couldn't lose Polly's job. She just couldn't.

"I won't screw it up," Cassie vowed, as Dylan made a choking sound.

"All rightee then." Lenora swept out the front door, offering one last coy smile. "You two stay out of trouble, you hear?"

"Wait, Lenora, you didn't say what I was supposed to do with them today," Cassie called out, but it was too late to catch her. She glared at Dylan. "Weren't you just leaving?"

"No, I wasn't."

"Yes, you were."

"I can't. I have the car. Or maybe I should tell Lenora that you cracked up the company car and that she'll have to wait and give us all a ride to wherever it is you're taking us today. And I was so looking forward to the great ape house." His smile was so mean she almost hit him.

"Fine." Cassie crossed her arms over her chest. "I'll need half an hour to take a shower and brush my teeth. And then we'll go pick up your stupid uncle and figure out something to do with him today. Although if you ask me, the great ape house is exactly where the two of you belong."

CASSIE FELT as if she were in the middle of some kind of topsy-turvy dream. Here. Not here. Zoo today. Zoo tomorrow. What difference did it make?

She did manage to do something useful—she found a pay phone at the Wild Man's hotel, so she could call Pleasant Falls and let Polly know she wouldn't be coming until later on.

Unfortunately, the phone was right outside the atrium where they were serving brunch, with clattering dishes and a piano playing show tunes and a whole lot of other commotion, so it was very hard to hear. Par for the course, Polly wasn't there. No Skipper at least. Thank goodness. But this time she got her little sister, Ashley.

In a strangely guarded tone, Ashley told her that they were all "really hot" for her to get there on the double, which was exactly opposite to what Polly's message had conveyed, according to Dylan.

"Is anything wrong?" Cassie asked. "Is everything okay there?"

"Not really," Ashley responded in the same funny voice. "We're all *dying* to see you."

"Okay," Cassie said slowly. "I'm sorry I'm not there yet. Could you tell Po...I mean, could you tell Cassie that things are not going very well here? I'm going to have to clear up one little problem before I can leave. But hang on, I'll be there as soon as I can."

"What did you say? Is that a piano? I can hardly hear you."

"Okay, well, I have to go. I'll be there as soon as I can," she repeated loudly.

And she hung up on her last connection to Pleasant Falls.

Dylan was waiting for her, leaning against the wall, his hands in his pockets. "I called him," he said. "He's coming down in the elevator." He arched one of those infuriating golden eyebrows. "Everything okay back at the ranch?"

"It's not a ranch, not even a farm, just a regular old small town," she bit out, continuing to walk away from the atrium and all its noise as she talked. "And, no, everything is not fine. I still haven't talked to Polly, but my other sister, the fourteen-year-old, says they're all very anxious for me to get back there."

"After all, you're getting married in less than a week," he noted dryly.

"Exactly." She kept her head held high, turning back long enough to give Dylan a dismissive glance. "There's no real reason for you to stick around, is there? You could get on your plane as scheduled and let the Wild Man go it alone for once."

"Oh, yeah, that's a great idea," he said, deadpan. "He can hang from the rafters by himself with no one but you to drag him down."

That stung. "You really think I am so lame I can't handle anything by myself, without you to pull my fat out of the fire?"

"What does that mean?"

"It doesn't mean anything, except that..." She could feel her lips trembling, and she didn't want to show that kind of weakness. "I had hoped you would think better of me than that. I mean, you asked me to run away with you, for goodness sake. Why would you do that if you think I'm this brainless dweeb who can't even handle one day with the Wild Man?''

"No," he murmured, "what I think is that you are a mess, babe. The job, the wedding, this insane sister switch... You're just a sweet, naïve girl who doesn't know what's good for her and is in a whole pack of trouble."

"I'm twenty-five," she said flatly. "I'm not a girl."

His gaze was kinder as he reached out one finger and gently traced the line of her upper lip. "Hon, you are the most girly girl I ever met."

"That is so unfair!"

But the brass elevator doors opened and the Wild Man blasted out. "So, kiddies, what are we up to today?" he asked gleefully, rubbing his hands together. He focused on the two of them, looking from one sullen face to the other. "Uh-oh. Trouble in paradise? Is P-P-Polly holding out on you, Dylan?"

Why was he always playing games with her name? Or her sister's name? This P-P-Polly stuff was getting old. And then she realized why he did it. "He knows, doesn't he?" she asked Dylan. "You told him?"

"No, actually, I told *him*," Hiram corrected. He let out a big guffaw. "I'm always ten steps ahead of that boy."

Frowning, Dylan told her, "He had the magazine. He's the one who figured out the twin thing."

"Are you going to tell Lenora?" Dizzy with disaster overload, Cassie pleaded with him, "You're not going to tell Lenora, are you?"

"Why would I do that? I applaud your moxie, Sweet Polly P., or whoever you are." He put a beefy arm around her, shepherding her out of the lobby into the spring sun. "This little escapade is dangerous and exciting, everything a life on the edge should be." He waggled his thick brows. "Deception, trickery and playing Lenora Bridge for a fool. What's not to like?"

It sounded so terrible when he put it that way.

"My name is Cassie, by the way," she told him quietly. "Except around Lenora, you might as well call me by my real name."

"Hmmm... Sassy Cassie. Cassie the Sassy Lassie..."

She was already sorry she'd told him.

Clasping her to his massive chest with one arm, the Wild Man added, "I think this is the beginning of a beautiful friendship."

Peering around Hiram, she tried to see enough of Dylan to gauge his reaction, but he was just strolling along back there, bringing up the rear.

Cassie took a deep breath. One more day with the Wild Man. One more day with his insufferable nephew.

One more day? She wasn't sure she could take one more minute.

*May 27: Five days before the wedding*

SOMEHOW, SHE'D MANAGED to stumble through that terrible Sunday. Actually, the Wild Man made it easy, chattering nonstop, spinning tall tales, and dragging both of them along for the ride. A ride on the Ferris wheel at Navy Pier, high-wire lessons at the Midnight Circus, a high-tech video arcade, hours and hours looking at mummies at the Oriental Institute…Hiram had a zest for life, that was for sure.

And as for Dylan—it was as if the two of them had an armed truce. No arguments, no discussion, no nothing. They were polite and distant and that was that.

After wolfing down some pizza, Hiram and Dylan dropped her off at home while they retired to the hotel. Not so bad, was it? Except for all the issues lying between them, unresolved.

Now here she was, dressed in Polly's uptown clothes for the last time, peeking out the window as she watched for Dylan's car. He was due any minute for their trip to the zoo.

"Who are you kidding?" she said out loud. "There's nothing unresolved. He went temporarily crazy and asked you to run away with him, but it's over. You had your ten minutes of fun, and it's over."

For one last time, she reminded herself that he would be gone soon. She had to get through the zoo reception, and then Dylan and his uncle would fly away, out of her life. "And I'll be on the train to Pleasant Falls." Brother, did that sound grim.

With her eye pressed to the window, she saw the car pulling up. She also noticed that the infamous tree was casting to one side, with a wide crack where her car had smashed it. Thinking about the accident, just one more in a series of calamities that were all her fault, she felt awful all over again.

"I am never going to live down this week," she

muttered, slashing the curtains closed. She hurried to let herself out before Dylan had a chance to come up to the door.

She slid into the back seat, lying low as Dylan played chauffeur and Hiram wound up and let a few more stories loose. The armed truce was still on. Awkward, but not too tough to carry off.

She'd never been to this zoo, and she thought it was really quite pretty, with its garden-like setting profuse with flowers. Big red and gold banners everywhere proclaimed the opening of the new great ape habitat, with posters pasted on the low brick walls advertising the Wild Man's appearance.

"That was a natural tie-in," she murmured.

"Did you say something?" Dylan inquired.

"Who, me? Not a thing."

The reception, set out in front of the new ape house, was lovely. There were lavish displays of food and drink, including a champagne fountain and large ice sculptures of gorillas and orangutans. Around the corner, another table held stacks of copies of *Life On the Edge*, where Hiram could sign books until his hand wore out.

The place was swimming with VIPs and big donors—including Lenora Bridge—who wanted to be first to tour the new facility, as well as reporters and TV crews covering some aspect of the event or other. Cassie was quite happy to let the zoo's PR people swarm around taking care of all the details, while all she had to do was keep an eye on Hiram.

So far all he was doing was monopolizing the

shrimp dip. He had spoken to a few reporters, but as Cassie hovered nearby, she heard only low-key, friendly chitchat, as the Wild Man related what he thought of the *Survivor* TV show and what kind of bugs and worms you really should stay away from on your dinner plate.

Cassie glanced at her watch, ready to go nab him when it was time for his presentation. He was supposed to give a few prepared remarks to promote the book, the same spiel he'd done at the bookstores and on the radio for the past few days. It was the usual junk about grabbing life by the throat and sucking the marrow out of it, yadda yadda yadda. Not much of a stretch.

Dylan showed up at her elbow, carrying a plastic glass of champagne. "Would you like some?"

"You've got to be kidding. I'll never go near that stuff again." She shuddered at the memories.

But he smiled, the dog. "It wasn't so bad."

She cast a baleful eye at the bubbly. "I don't see you drinking any."

"I'm not much of a drinker."

"What?" she mocked. His carefree I'm-perfectly-okay-with-this-and-it-meant-nothing-to-me attitude was starting to get on her nerves. "What's the matter? Life on the edge as a sloppy drunk not all it's cracked up to be? Or do you only ply unsuspecting women with booze so you can take advantage?"

"Who took advantage of whom?" he countered.

"Excuse me?" She inched closer. She was just mad enough to finally ask him what she'd been dying to know ever since Cleveland. Nose-to-nose, she demanded, "So, tell me, once and for all, did we or did we not have sex at the Hotel Verdi?"

"When?"

"*When?* Is that the best you can do? You know very well when," she snapped.

"Cassie, please don't start this. If you were too drunk to remember, it's not my fault," he said wearily.

She clenched her teeth. "So can I find out before you fly off to New York? Or are you planning to keep this a big secret for the rest of my life?"

"What do you think? After all, you're the expert on secrets."

"Sssh," she hissed. "Lenora is around here somewhere. If she hears you, Polly could get fired for my mistakes."

"Of which you make plenty," he shot back. "Like letting my uncle talk to reporters with no one to run interference."

"He's fine."

"He *was* fine, honey," he pointed out in an acid tone. "But he's beginning to look bored. And you know what that means. Imminent meltdown."

"He's fine," she said again. But she couldn't actually see him anywhere. She spared a glance at her watch, realizing that her latest tiff with Dylan had made her late getting Hiram's talk started. "I have to go."

"Uh-oh." Dylan's tone caught her attention. "Too late."

The Wild Man was definitely visible now. He was

standing on the food table, trying to pick up the ice gorilla. It was, of course, a little slippery. "Attention, everyone!" he shouted. "I think you know who I am. I write books about adventure and survival, about existing and embracing the urban and the primeval jungle, testing ourselves, going beyond the limit."

Okay, so he shouldn't be up on the table. She sent Lenora a nervous smile. But the speech was all right, with echoes of the normal material. Now he just needed to hold up the book and tell everyone that he would be signing copies for the next hour, and proceeds would benefit the great ape habitat.

"I'm supposed to tell you," he went on, "to buy copies of my book and help fund this great ape habitat."

So far, so good.

"But I refuse!" he roared, as curious onlookers collected around his table.

When he began to beat on his chest, howling like a banshee, even more people gathered. Reporters were taking notes frantically, as the TV cameras rolled.

"This is a travesty!" he proclaimed. "The great apes are our brothers, not our prisoners. And I call on the true adventurers among you to join me! Let's take up arms and release our brothers!"

As in, spring the apes? "Dylan, come on." Cassie scrambled to get nearer to Hiram, pushing through the crowd. They seemed to be much more interested now, blocking her way in their enthusiasm, some shouting back at him in support and some in horror.

"Who's with me?" he blustered. As he was counting heads to see if he had enough fellow ape liberators, the table collapsed underneath him, scattering strawberries and grapes and sending the melting gorilla and orangutan sliding into the wreckage.

As Hiram toppled, Dylan managed to catch him. "Fun's over, folks," he called out. "Mr. Wright is going to get out of the sun and calm down now."

Cassie clapped her hands over her cheeks. Sure, blame it on the cool May sun.

She couldn't seem to focus, but there was a buzzing sound in her ears. She could only stand there, helpless, as Dylan forcefully escorted his uncle off to somewhere more private.

And that was the end of the Wild Man's Chicago tour. But not the end of Cassie's troubles, she knew.

Lenora slid up behind her. "I'm sure I don't have to tell you." She twisted her lips into a ghoulish smile. "You're fired!"

"Lenora, it wasn't my fault. I just looked away for a second and—"

"I don't really care. My agency is now a joke, and you're out, Polly. *O-U-T*." Lenora wheeled away, whipping her flame-red hair back at the last moment. "Oh, and I'll need the company car returned to the lot today, and the keys to the company house back by the end of the month, which is, as it happens, Friday."

"The house, too?" She couldn't even take this in. House, car and job—was there anything else it was humanly possible to destroy in her sister's life?

# 10

___

CASSIE GOT OUT of there on the double. It didn't occur to her until she hit the street that she had no way to get back to Polly's house.

She ended up flagging down a cab and hanging on for dear life while he screeched into a U-turn and almost got hit by two cars and a bus. Maybe there was a future for her as a Chicago cabbie.

Gallows humor, she told herself. She slunk back to the house, totally and completely devastated over the shambles she had made of her sister's life. Not to mention her own.

"I was unfaithful to Skipper," she admitted. "I blamed Dylan, but it wasn't his fault. I knowingly and willingly enticed him into bed while I was still planning to marry Skipper and live a big, fat lie."

She couldn't even look at herself in the mirror. Instead, she got a pint of chocolate ice cream out of the freezer and lay on the floor in the living room, a puddle of misery.

"A fat puddle of misery," she whispered, going back for a larger spoon. "The heck with it." She started eating huge spoonfuls directly from the scoop.

But when she said "heck" it reminded her of Dylan making fun of her vocabulary. "The hell with it!" she swore instead. That felt good for about three seconds, until her thoughts returned to where she was and what she had done.

Oh, sure, she tried to rouse herself. She knew very well that she should be packing and getting ready to catch her train. Talk about facing the music. She was going to have to explain what had happened the minute she arrived if there was any hope for Polly to come back and clean out her belongings from the house before Lenora threw them on the street.

All those adorable outfits and killer shoes. The fabulous jewelry. The snazzy convertible.

"I lost it all!" she wailed.

Worse yet, she was going to have to face Skipper and tell him the truth, too. He was so into her supposed purity. Surely he deserved to know he was engaged to a woman who slept with any convenient stranger who came down the pike.

"I'm a sleaze!" she cried even louder.

She could see the clock from where was lying, and she knew the hour was approaching when Dylan and the Wild Man would be airborne. "He won't go," she said out loud, not sure if she really believed it or was grasping at straws.

But she couldn't forget the way they had parted— all cranky and unpleasant, sniping at each other over who seduced whom. And then he'd marched off with his uncle, not even giving her a backward glance.

"Maybe I should've waited." She pondered that momentarily. "Naaah," she decided. "It wouldn't have solved anything. We just would've gotten in another fight. He doesn't love me.''

But some small flicker of hope stayed alive inside her. She couldn't voice it, but she could hear her thoughts.

*If he loves me, he will fight for me. He won't get on that plane, but he'll be here, at my door, and he'll tell me that he won't let me go to Pleasant Falls, that I should marry him instead.*

In her heart of hearts, that's what she wanted. She wanted Dylan to swoop in and fix everything.

It was pathetic.

So, as she lay on the floor with the melting carton of ice cream, the time for his plane to leave came and went. The time for her train to leave came and went. No rescue. Not even one sign of his crinkly eyes.

As it began to grow dark inside the trendy little house, casting shadows among the brass sculptures, Cassie was right where she started, lying there in a puddle of misery. And that was when realization struck her.

"Oh, my God." She sat up. "He's right. I am in love with him."

*May 29: Three days before the wedding*

TWO DAYS LATER, without so much as a peep from Dylan, Cassie decided it was time to stand up and be a person again.

Even if she was at the end of her rope, even if she had lost her sister's job and smashed her car, even if she had been acting like a scared baby by hiding out for the past two days, even if she was nursing a broken heart and a lot of anger, she still had to take responsibility.

Oddly enough, she discovered that the phone was not out of order but just unplugged. She considered calling Skipper or Polly or even her mom first, but she chickened out. For one thing, she wasn't sure yet what she was going to say. *I'm sorry, I met someone else who doesn't care about me anyway, but the wedding is off?*

Even Skipper deserved to hear that kind of news in person. Was it really any better to hear it three days before the wedding than two days before? Not hardly.

And maybe it would be best to try to rectify what she could before she trekked back there. First up— Polly's job.

So her first call went to Lenora Bridge and Associates. Her heart was racing when she asked, "Is Lenora in?"

"Hmph. Did you just call and ask for Polly Tompkins?" the receptionist huffed.

"Um, no." She could honestly say, "I've never called this office before."

"Well, you sure sound exactly like the person I spoke to a few minutes ago."

Polly. Polly had called and asked for herself, hoping to get Cassie. That didn't sound good. "Just curious, but what did you say to the person who asked for Polly?"

"I told her the truth, that Polly was terminated and no longer worked here."

*She knows. She knows I lost her job.* "Okay, thank you," she said weakly.

"Anything else?"

"Oh." She remembered why she had called in the first place. "I was wondering if it would be possible to speak to Lenora." To beg and plead and offer bribes to get Polly's job back. Whatever it took.

"May I ask who's calling, please?" the woman asked politely.

Well, that was a problem, wasn't it? "Just tell her it's about Hiram Wright's book tour."

There was a long pause. "I don't know who you are, but I know this is about Polly Tompkins, and you *are* the same person who called a minute ago." There was an edge of irritation when she continued, "Ms. Bridge does not wish to speak about Hiram Wright or Polly Tompkins except to say that Mr. Wright is called the Wild Man for a reason, that this company, Lenora Bridge and Associates, does not condone or condemn any behavior of Mr. Wright's, and that Polly Tompkins is no longer an employee of this firm."

And with that, she hung up. Okay, so it was going to take more than a phone call.

Cassie set out for her sister's closet, determined to find the most striking, dynamic outfit in there. She was also going to need a large tote bag of some kind to hold her weapons when she bearded the lion in her den. "Look out, Lenora, I'm coming to get you."

*May 30: Two days before the wedding*

TWO DAYS BEFORE the wedding. Polly must be going crazy.

Just a few more hours, Cassie pleaded. *If I can convince Lenora to take you back, then the house and the car are fixable, and I don't have to come back a total failure.*

Wheeling into the office, Cassie bypassed the receptionist. "Wait, you can't go in there," she shrieked. "You're not supposed to even be in this office. You're fired!"

"I don't think we've met," Cassie said sweetly. "I'm Cassandra Tompkins. My sister used to work here."

"Oh my God. There are two of you?"

She ignored the question. "Which one is Ms. Bridge's office?"

The young woman pointed the way with a shaky finger. As Cassie waltzed in, she could hear the receptionist pick up her phone and say, "Rita, did you know Polly Tompkins has an identical twin?"

Lenora sat behind a massive desk in a large leather chair that made her appear small. Without any preamble, Cassie leaned in over the desk. "I haven't got much time, so I'm going to make this fast."

"What are you doing here? You're fired!"

"Yes, I know. But you couldn't actually fire me, since I never worked for you. Technically." She smiled, pleased with herself for thinking of that. "You see, I'm not Polly. I'm her sister, Cassandra."

"You are not!"

"Yes, I am. I'm the one who screwed everything

up, so it's my fault, not Polly's," she explained. She could tell from the sky-high eyebrows and open mouth that Lenora hadn't quite grasped that yet. "Don't worry about it, okay? The bottom line is that Hiram Wright is an impossible old man determined to throw monkey wrenches into the works and no one else could've done any better."

"Now, just a—"

"I'm not finished. I convinced Polly that I should take her job with the Wild Man because I..." Here she found a handy fib to plug the hole in her story. "I was a major Wild Man fan. Just fanatical. Polly did me a favor and I did her one, too, since she couldn't stand the man. Except the Wild Man messed everything up from beginning to end and you blamed me."

"It was your fault!"

"Yes, but it got tons of publicity, didn't it?" She reached into her tote bag, pulling out a pile of newspaper and online clippings from the past few days, as well as a couple of videotapes. "He and his primate liberation front made the *New York Times,* for goodness sake! Not to mention *E! News Daily* and the 'Top Ten' list on Letterman. What better publicity could you want?"

"Well, there is that, but—"

"No buts. That book is rocketing up the bestseller lists, and wasn't that the whole point?"

"Well, maybe, but—"

Resolute, Cassie shook her head. "You need to hire Polly back. She did a great job for you and she deserves it."

"And where is Polly?" the woman asked slyly. "If you're really not her, which I'm not sure I believe."

"She'll be back on Monday. And unless you want some really bad publicity, all about how mean old Lenora Bridge made me the scapegoat for an eccentric client—and they've already asked me to go on *Nightline*—then you'll welcome her back with open arms." Cassie stood back, folding her arms over her chest.

"You've got moxie, I'll give you that."

"You know, I do, don't I?" With a smile, she pondered that for a second. "I never used to, but I do now. And I think that's a good thing."

"All right, all right. Just get out of here, will you?" Lenora grumbled. "You're giving me a headache. But tell Polly I want to see both of you in the same room sometime, will you?"

"Done." Feeling very cocky, Cassie wheeled and prepared to leave, victorious. Then she thought of one more thing. "Polly will need to be able to keep her house. And get a new car. The client smashed up the old one," she lied.

And then she skedaddled before Lenora changed her mind. *My work here is done,* she thought. Time to get back to Pleasant Falls.

SHOULD SHE CALL AHEAD? As she stuffed her things in a suitcase, she decided it was better just to get down there right away and let Skipper down as gently as possible. In person.

When the doorbell rang, Cassie grabbed her bag,

assuming it was her cab to the train station. But when she opened the door, she found... "Dylan?"

Two days ago, she would've thrown herself in his arms and said, *Yes, yes, let's go. I don't care if it's five minutes or fifty years. Let's go.* Now, emboldened by her own moxie, she wasn't sure she wanted to be swept away.

"We have to talk," he said softly. His face looked even moodier and more drawn than usual, and she wanted to reach out and soothe away the dark shadows.

Instead, she held her ground in the doorway. "The last time you said we needed to talk, we ended up in bed in about two minutes."

A half smile lifted one side of his mouth. "Well, since I missed an opportunity at the Hotel Verdi, I wouldn't object to that."

Her eyes shot to his face. "So we didn't..." She thought about that for a moment, then firmly shook her head. "And we won't now either. My brain hasn't been the same since we did." *And neither has my body. Or my soul.* "Listen, Dylan, I would let you in, really I would. But I was just on my way to, um, Pleasant Falls. I don't want to miss my train. It's the last one tonight."

"Oh, man." His eyes searched hers. "You're still going to marry that guy?"

"I don't think so." Actually, she was quite sure. There was no way she could marry Skipper now. "I haven't told him yet, though. I just feel like he deserves to find out in person, you know, instead of on the phone or in a letter or something. No more running away. I'm trying to take the bull by the horns."

She offered an apologetic smile, maneuvering past him on her way out the door into the cool evening air.

"Cassie, wait."

He was too close and the pain was too fresh. Now that he was within inches, her knees threatened to buckle. She commanded herself to be strong. "What?"

"I want you to marry me."

She blinked. "That is not what I expected you to say."

"Well?"

Had she just been hit with a brickbat? Or did it just feel that way? Cassie blew out a long breath. And then she backed up, opening the door. "I guess you'd better come inside."

Quietly, she took a seat on the couch, tucking her suitcase next to her feet. Dylan paced back and forth in front of her, offering a final argument as if she were the jury.

"I've had some time to think, and I hope you have, too." He sent her a quick glance, as if checking out her reaction so far. "The fact that you're still here, that you didn't run right home, tells me I'm right. And what I decided, Cassie... No, let me start this again. What I really believe in my heart is that we belong together."

"Really?" Now *that* had not occurred to her. They were from such different worlds, such different families, such different people. Did she and Dylan belong together?

All she knew was that when she saw him, she wanted to be with him. She wanted to hang on for dear life and go along for the ride. Was that belonging? Maybe it was.

"You know me," he went on, edging closer, leaning down to make eye contact. Good grief. He wasn't going on bended knee, was he? Not exactly, but pretty close. Sitting on the floor with his back to her sofa, he declared, "You know I don't fool around with this stuff—I'm very direct, I make up my mind and I go after what I want."

"Okay, that I definitely agree with."

"Good. And I know that we belong together, living life to the fullest, loving each other to the fullest." His eyes were so earnest, and his words were so sweet, she was beginning to feel all warm and runny inside. "Cassie, I love you. And I think you love me, too. That's why we should be together. Here, New York, Pleasant Falls, wherever."

"Dylan, I—"

"Wait." He held up a hand. "Before you say that I'm irresponsible or unreliable or you need someone with roots, I just want you to know that I do have a job, a good job, and a brownstone in a very nice area, and my prospects are very good."

"Your prospects?" she asked, incredulous. "You sound more old-fashioned than I do. So what is this good job with prospects?"

"You already know." He shrugged, looking sheepish. "I write Wild Man's books."

"You?" Cassie leapt to her feet, almost clonking him in the head with her knee. "You wrote *Life On the Edge* and all that stuff about Dumpster diving for doughnuts and washing your hair in rain puddles?"

"Well, yeah, I did," he confessed. "The two books before that, too, since Uncle Hiram hasn't been disciplined enough to sit at the typewriter for years."

"You're just as much of a deceiver as I am," she breathed, her eyes round.

"It would be pretty hypocritical for you to hold it against me after all the lies you've told," he pointed out.

Cassie nodded. "The deception I can handle. But your advice in that book was really terrible."

"One of the things I like best about you is your weird ability to lie through your teeth and be brutally honest, all at the same time." And then he smiled, the full-out, barn-burner of a smile that got her every time. "You know, if you marry me, you can do your best to convince me to change the advice. Goodbye Dumpster diving."

"Uh-oh," she whispered. "Your eyes are crinkling again. I just can't resist a man with eye crinkles."

"So don't." He reclined back into the couch, offering a hand, pulling her down into his lap. As her arms encircled his shoulders, he began to brush kisses against her neck. "I've missed you. It's only been a few days and it feels like forever."

Cassie closed her eyes, leaning into his sensual assault. "Me, too," she murmured lazily. "Oh, yeah. Me, too."

He tipped her over into the couch cushions, reaching for her buttons, making his intent clear, but the one iota of sanity she had left found a way to poke through.

"Dylan, wait." She sighed. "I have to go to Pleasant Falls. Now."

"You're sure? Right this minute?" he asked, still playing with her buttons.

She set her lips in a firm line. "Right this minute."

"It's going to be very late when you get there. No one will be up, anyway," he said hopefully. "Maybe you should wait till morning."

But Cassie was immovable. "I've waited too long already."

Dylan caved, removing his hands from her clothes. "Okay, but I'm coming with you. And I'm driving." He reached into his pocket for a set of keys, tinkling them in his hands. "I got the cutest little convertible for a rental car."

"You sure you don't want me to drive?"

Dylan laughed out loud.

PLEASANT FALLS was a bit more than three hours from Chicago by car, and it wasn't a bad drive. Just an uncomfortable, weird experience.

"You didn't answer my question," he reminded her. "Will you marry me or not?"

"Keep your eyes on the road."

"That's not an answer."

Cassie tipped back her head, staring up into the stars overhead. "Don't you think maybe I'd better get rid of the first fiancé before I pick up another one?"

"I think I'd like an answer," he persisted.

"I'm not ready to give one yet." Cassie took his free hand in hers, linking her fingers through his. "Dylan, you said it yourself—my life is a mess. I want to clean it up a little before I jump into any more messes. And, you know, I think I might be on my way."

His glance was searching. "In some ways, you've really changed since I met you."

"I know." She grinned then, bringing their entwined hands up to her lips and kissing his. "I went on this journey to find fun and excitement, and I did. And it sounds stupid, but I think I found myself, too."

"So you won't marry me?"

"I told you, I don't know yet. Besides, you have to meet my twin sister." She winked at him. "Who knows? You might decide you like her better."

"Not a chance, Cassie. Not a chance."

It ended up taking a lot longer than three hours. He was hungry, she had to go to the restroom, he found a shortcut that turned into a long detour, and they ran into a nasty thunderstorm that only seemed to get worse the closer they got. Dylan pulled off by the side of the road to put up the top on the car when the first drops hit them, and they actually stayed there, tucked inside, waiting for the worst of the thunder and lightning to abate. Cassie fell asleep leaned over the gear shift into his lap, and she stayed there for a good hour.

She couldn't believe how right it felt to be with him this way. Was that belonging? Maybe it was.

It was quite late, or early, depending upon your point of view, when they finally got to Pleasant Falls.

Dylan looked around in awe. Even in the dark and in the rain, Cassie knew what he was seeing—good or bad, the quintessential small town. He cracked, "It's like Mayberry or something."

"Everyone always says that. Look, there's the department store where I work. And that's the old movie theater, the Bijou, where they do community theater now." The streetlights reflected on the wet pavement, making it look even more charming.

But her tour of town only took a few minutes, and then she finally, reluctantly directed him to her parents' house. "I know they'll all be asleep. Maybe we should wake them up. Maybe not."

But the Tompkins' home was ablaze with lights.

"They can't already be up," she said in surprise. Dragging Dylan by the hand, she charged in the front door.

"Cassie?" Ashley, her younger sister, came flying down the stairs wearing her pajamas. "Thank goodness you're here. Everyone is frantic! Polly—well, they all think she's you. But, duh, I know the difference. Anyway, she's been gone with Michael, I think, for absolute ever. Overnight!"

"Polly went off with Michael? I was worried about her and she was running away with her old boyfriend?"

"Things have been horrible here, Cassie! We tried

to get a hold of you a million times, but your phone didn't work and Polly did her best, which really wasn't all that great because, my goodness, she was kissing Michael in the country club gazebo about ten seconds after she got here—''

"Hi," Dylan said, offering his hand as he cut in. "Maybe you should breathe every once in awhile."

"Okay." Ashley looked him up and down with evident curiosity. "Awesome."

Dylan looked pleased with her assessment. "Thank you."

"Okay, so now I know where you were," her little sister announced, whipping around to focus on Cassie. "With the hottie. Good work, Cass."

"Ashley, what's going on?" Cassie interrupted, eager to get her back on course. "Polly went off with Michael, and then what?"

"No one knows where they are! Skipper is having a cow, because he still thinks she's you, so he got, like, a rescue party together. Mom and Dad went, too," she added, quivering with excitement, "in separate cars, so they could cover more area looking. They all took off hours ago, but no one has heard anything yet."

As if on cue, the phone began to ring.

"Should I answer it?" Cassie asked, feeling like a stranger in her own home. "Probably not."

"I will." Ashley was gone for a few minutes, but then she came running right back. "Oh," she rushed to say, waving her hands in the air, "they found her all right—in a car, canoodling with Michael! Dad said all hell broke loose.''

"He didn't say that.''

"Yes, he did. Well, close.'' Ashley scampered away, turning on more lights. "He said they're all coming back here. Should we make, like, coffee or something? Mom would want us to be ready.''

"At least it gives us something to do.'' Cassie tiptoed into the kitchen, looking around. And it seemed strange and foreign to her, as if she'd been gone a very long time.

After she put the coffeepot on, Cassie and Dylan took chairs at the kitchen table, just sitting there, not saying much. They knew the quiet wouldn't last long. And, sure enough, the coffee was barely percolating before members of the posse came streaming back to the Tompkins's house, including, of course, Skipper Kennigan.

"Cassie?'' He gaped at her. He looked tired and worn out, and she realized that she had almost no feelings for him at all, not even pity. How had that happened?

It didn't take him long to recover his voice. "Where have you been?'' he demanded. "Who is that man with you? And what did you think you were doing, running away and leaving Polly in your place?''

"I guess I can forget the plan to quietly call off the wedding and not humiliate Skipper,'' Cassie noted.

"Call off the wedding?'' Skipper was livid, standing there all puffed up and red in the face, squeezing his hands into small fists. "You should be down on your knees, begging my forgiveness. You should be begging me to marry you. After what you did? Ha!''

"Skipper, we shouldn't be getting married," she said quietly. "We don't belong together."

"And what changed, Cassie? What changed? We had it all planned!'' he tried, so upset he squeaked. He advanced on her, his face getting redder and redder by the moment. "You tell me what changed!"

Rising from the table, Dylan stepped in between Cassie and her ex-fiancé, blocking Skipper's path in case he tried to get to her. Coldly, he announced, "I think we can all understand why she did what she did rather than marry a stiff like you."

Skipper looked like he was going to burst a blood vessel as he twitched his fists at Dylan. "Get away from my fiancée."

But Cassie couldn't take any more of this. She pushed herself away from the protection of her mother's kitchen table and she waved a hand to get their attention. "Listen," she declared, "both of you. This isn't about either of you."

"He," Skipper bristled, sticking a finger in Dylan's face, "has ruined you. He's hypnotized you or something. The Cassie I know would never have done this."

"It isn't Dylan's fault," she contended. "It's mine. All mine. I did it. I ran away because something inside me wouldn't let me marry you, Skipper. Because it wasn't right."

He folded his arms. "I don't believe you."

"It doesn't really matter if you believe me or not,

because it's over." Calm, self-possessed Cassie Tompkins had come back to stay. "Dylan," she whispered, taking his arm. "I have to tell you something."

And he crinkled his eyes again, just for her, and she knew she was totally and completely right.

"Dylan, I love you," she said with conviction. "I'm going with you. If that freighter to Katmandu is still available, I'm on it."

But more people spilled in the back door, including her parents, and they were all asking way too many questions. "Cassie? Where have you been? What is this all about?"

"Be quiet!" Cassie ordered. "You'll just have to wait. I have some important things going on right now."

"Oh, my," her mother said, blinking her eyes. "I think Cassie has changed."

"Well?" she asked Dylan. "Are we on for Katmandu?"

"New York, Katmandu and anything in between," he vowed, tugging her up against him. His smile was bright enough to light up the room. "Forever. You and me."

Cassie threw her arms around him, right there in her mother's kitchen. "I will risk whatever I have to risk. I will live by my wits, and take no prisoners."

It was at that moment that the kitchen door opened again, admitting her identical twin sister, arm in arm with Michael, the man of Polly's dreams since she was ten.

"Well, now I know there really are two of you," Dylan muttered, casting an eye over Cassie's double.

"We have an announcement to make," Polly proclaimed happily. She beamed up at Michael. "We've decided to stay in Pleasant Falls and raise a huge family, just to annoy all of you. Like, ten kids? What do you say, Michael?"

"Whatever you want," he returned with a twinkle in his eye.

"You're staying?" Cassie couldn't hold back a giggle. "And we're going out into the big, wide world. Whoever would have guessed that this is the way things would turn out?"

"Meanwhile," Polly said darkly, "isn't there something you need to tell me? About losing my job? And my car? And my house?"

Cassie took a small breath. "I was going to get to that, Polly. But the good news is, I fixed it. All of it. With Lenora Bridge."

"You did *what?*" It was Polly's turn to look surprised.

But her twin just shrugged. "I marched in and demanded that Lenora give back your job and all the rest of the stuff. She caved."

Polly laughed out loud. "Okay, Cass, now I believe you really have become someone new. You're telling me you faced down the Evil Queen and won?" She shook her head. "Way to go, Cassie!"

"Okay, Polly, but you aren't thinking about going back for that job, are you?" Michael asked with quiet determination. "I thought we were staying here so we could start a campaign to stop Pleasant Valley Estates.''

"You're *what*?" Skipper shrieked.

"Be quiet," the twins ordered in unison.

Polly continued, explaining quickly, "Don't worry, Michael. I'm planning to stick around for a good, long time. I never was crazy about that job, anyway. But that Cassie went head to head with Lenora Bridge on my behalf... It's *monumental*."

Cassie was pretty pleased with herself, too. She might've messed up here and there, but she had found herself in the process. With her hand securely clasped in Dylan's, she realized that her world was a pretty cool place to be.

But how funny that Polly had chosen to stay in Pleasant Falls, while Cassie was ready for the adventure of a lifetime.

The Tompkins twins really had changed places. And it had worked out perfectly for both of them!

*These New York Times bestselling authors
have created stories to capture the hearts and minds
of women everywhere.
Here are three classic tales about the power of love—
and the wonder of discovering the place
where you belong....*

# FINDING HOME

## DUNCAN'S BRIDE
by
# LINDA HOWARD

## CHAIN LIGHTNING
by
# ELIZABETH LOWELL

## POPCORN AND KISSES
by
# KASEY MICHAELS

*Available only from Silhouette
at your favorite retail outlet.*

**Silhouette®**
™
*Where love comes alive™*

Visit Silhouette at www.eHarlequin.com          PSFH

If you enjoyed what you just read,
then we've got an offer you can't resist!

# Take 2 bestselling
# love stories FREE!
# Plus get a FREE surprise gift!

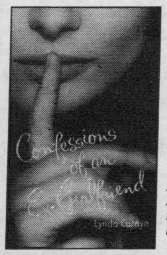

# MONTANA
## *Bred*

From the bestselling series

## MONTANA MAVERICKS

### *Wed in Whitehorn*

Two more tales that capture living and loving
beneath the Big Sky.

**JUST PRETENDING by Myrna Mackenzie**

FBI Agent David Hannon's plans for a quiet vacation
were overturned by a murder investigation—and by
officer Gretchen Neal!

**STORMING WHITEHORN by Christine Scott**

Native American Storm Hunter's return to Whitehorn
sent tremors through the town—and shock waves of
desire through Jasmine Kincaid Monroe....

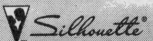

*Silhouette*®

*Where love comes alive*™